CHELSEA,

THE FINAL CHAPTER

A FICTIONAL NOVEL OF MURDER, PASSION AND SHADOWS OF
CHELSEA'S PAST UNTRADITIONAL RELATIONSHIPS.
THIS IS A NOVEL OF A WOMAN WHO OVERCAME HARDSHIPS AND
EARNED SUCCESS, A WOMAN IN A MAN'S WORLD.

by author
AL TARVIN

Published by
C. J. H. ENTERPRISES
Gulf Breeze, Florida

Printed in the United States of America

Library of Congress Cataloging-in-Publication Data,

Tarvin, Albert L. 1929 —

1. Fiction Novel. Sequel to Chelsea, Chelsea. A story of murder, passion, and shadows of Chelsea's past untraditional relationships. A woman who overcame hardships and earned success.

ISBN 0-9643250-2-0

Final copy prepared by WORDSMITHS UNLIMITED, Pensacola, Florida

Printed by PACE PRINTERS, Pensacola, Florida

Published by CJH ENTERPRISES, Gulf Breeze, Florida

FROM THE AUTHOR

Men have not truly accepted the successful businesswoman as an equal partner. Gains have been made by women in sharing the upper echelons of business organizations, but acceptability of the woman in some positions of authority remains elusive. The suspicion that women use their "womanly attributes" to gain management positions is evident even though sexual harassment laws are now in place.

The girl and woman "Chelsea" proved men wrong in the first episodes in her professional life.

Chelsea, The Final Chapter, continues the same characters found in *Chelsea, Chelsea.* The first book dealt with Chelsea's very tragic life from young girlhood to womanhood to the top position in a major corporation. Her love and caring for her adopted family caused her to accept what was described as God's calling in bearing a child for them. Circumstances created by one man forced her to manage a legal husband, a bigamous husband/lover, and two families. She became successful in spite of her emotional entanglements.

One may ask, "Is it necessary to read the first book, *Chelsea, Chelsea,* before reading *Chelsea, The Final Chapter?"* Not really! But the fullness of Chelsea's life can be better realized by also reading the first book.

This is a fictional story! Much of the material in the book is based upon real-life situations and in-depth research of specific areas. Readers have related very strongly to characters in the novel. The reader must decide what is fact and what is fiction!

As the Author, I take full responsibility for any errors, omissions, and mistakes in the Queen's English. I thank my wife, Christle Jean Holzman, for her "Labor of Love" in reading and editing the manuscript. A special thanks also to my daughter, Valerie Tarvin-Kibler, and sisters Marguerite Clayton and Ann Austin. I also thank the many other readers who helped to make the novel more readable and enjoyable. Thanks to Shirley Bone for assistance in editing the manuscript. And finally, a very special thanks to Mimi Meredith of Wordsmiths Unlimited, who formatted and finalized the manuscript for publishing.

DEDICATION

This book is dedicated to my wife, Christle Jean Holzman, whose life philosophy was instilled by her father:

"What does liking or not liking an event have do with it? If there is something that must be done, then do it!"

TABLE OF CONTENTS

CHAPTER ONE
CHELSEA'S CONFESSION

1 Business was hectic in the Thorndike Corporation. After I was selected to succeed the president and chief executive officer, Mr. Thomas Thorndike, the old gentleman of 93 became bedridden with the ills of old age. In spite of his poor health, he and I met two or three times a week for several months. Finally, the demands of teaching me to become the type of CEO he felt I could be became too much for him. When I noticed the strain in his eyes I stopped the business discussions. Instead, I visited with him and we talked about our lives. He often spoke of his granddaughter who was killed at eighteen. I felt that I had replaced a part of her in his heart. I knew I reminded him of her. He continued to discuss the "homespun family philosophy" he wanted continued in the corporation. I absorbed his wisdom and everything he said like a sponge in water. It was apparent, with each visit, that the old warrior was slowly losing his grip on life. He said he still had one score to settle before he died. I felt I knew what he meant, but I didn't question him. Soon I would know what score he was talking about.

Jason, Mr. Thorndike's butler, came to my office late one afternoon. He was visibly disturbed. He said, "Miss Chelsea, I believe my master is deceased. At this time I am not totally certain, but I feel it in my soul." I screamed.

"*Mr. Thorndike dead!* Oh, God, please don't let it be true! My dear, dear, loving friend." I began to cry, and the tears burned my cheeks as they flowed down my face.

"*Oh, Jason, tell me what happened!*"

My heart felt so heavy and my mind could not accept that he was dead. I knew he was very weak and I really expected him to die. *But now it has happened!* I have lost a part of me! His concern for everyone as a person was his mark. I prayed silently, God, you have one of your finest, please look after him. We all loved him so very much and he made such magnificent contributions in life. Have mercy on his soul. Amen. My pain was reflected on the face of Linda, my executive assistant, as tears streamed down her cheeks. Jason, Linda, and I embraced and stood very still. The sounds of our sobbing broke the silence of the office.

Jason said Luther Quigly had made an appointment to see Mr. Thorndike at his home. Quigly had arrived at his appointed time. Jason had escorted Quigly to Mr. Thorndike's bedroom, then gone to the pantry to prepare the afternoon tea. Jason said he had been readying the tea service when he heard loud bangs. At first he thought he'd heard only one, but later realized there had been two loud bangs. When the tea was prepared, he had taken it to Mr. Thorndike's bedroom and was shocked at what he saw: Mr. Thorndike was lying under Quigly's body, at the foot of the bed.

I could not think — I was so upset. The thought of Mr. Thorndike dying shattered me. What really happened? Did he kill Quigly and then himself? There were two sounds, one bullet for Quigly and one for himself? Quigly was apparently dead and we were not sure about Mr. Thorndike. When Linda called the hospital to check, she was told Mr. Thorndike died shortly after his arrival at the hospital. Jason said the sheriff had not arrived when he left. I realize many of the questions will never be answered. If Mr. Thorndike killed Quigly, I know his love for me and Thorndike Industries were the driving forces which led him to do it.

I wondered, what else can happen to me? Chelsea Carodine, you're the chief executive officer of Thorndike Industries. You are faced with the death of the owner and founder of the corporation and one of its executives under very mysterious circumstances. Where do you go from here? I knew in my heart what Mr. Thorndike's motive was, but I couldn't tell anyone about it.

Mr. Thorndike knew Quigly was blackmailing me and could have destroyed me as the chief executive officer and would have ripped apart my marriage to Morgan. Mr. Thorndike knew about my past and he had accepted it as he accepted me, totally and unconditionally.

Jason, Mr. Thorndike's butler, and Linda, my executive assistant, remained in the office with me as we reconstructed the events of the evening. Mr. Thorndike had recorded the last conversation between himself and Quigly, and Jason brought that tape recording to my office. Mr. Thorndike had instructed Jason to permit me to hear the tape and then to destroy it. Quigly's threats to expose me were clear. Mr. Thorndike questioned him several times as to what he intended to do. When Quigly demanded $500,000 to keep his silence, it was apparent that Mr.

2

Thorndike had been pushed too far. The sound of two loud bangs and crashing noises were heard and the tape ended.

We played the tape a second time to cement the events in our minds. The voices on the tape were easily identified as Mr. Thorndike's and Quigly's. Mr. Thorndike's voice was heard first. We gathered around the desk to hear every word again.

"Mr. Quigly, do you remember the conversation we had when you were hired as an executive with the corporation?"

"Of course, sir. You said the corporation was somewhat like a family, each member respecting the rights of the others, or words to that effect."

"I must commend you on your memory, Mr. Quigly. My purpose in explaining the corporation's dynamics in such a fashion was to impress new members with our operation. As family members we would hold each other in high esteem and if we experienced any differences, of any type, we would settle them within our corporate family."

"Sir, may I ask, what does my memory of our first conversation have to do with our present discussion? I was given the impression that I was being considered for a promotion to a director's position."

"Mr. Quigly, you were hired because you had promise as an executive. Your recent actions are very disturbing to me. I have been informed you are applying pressure to a senior executive in order to gain a promotion. Is that true?"

"So that's why I'm here. You didn't intend to offer me a promotion, you just want to protect your Chelsea Carodine from public exposure because of her personal escapades. Her personal life is a laugh, it's so screwed up."

"Mr. Quigly, my purpose in meeting with you was to have you think about what you are attempting to do and to offer you a solution."

"Well, Mr. Thorndike, what are you willing to offer to keep me quiet?"

"Mr. Quigly, I advise you to leave Thorndike Industries. I suggest you tender your resignation immediately."

"Thorndike, you can't be serious. Chelsea Carodine is the top officer in your corporation. Neither you nor the board can afford to have her private life exposed. Think about it."

"Mr. Quigly, I had hoped you still had a bit of decency in you. I see now that you must be dealt with more harshly."

3

"Thorndike, I have my own solution to the problem. I will just disappear from the scene for, say, $500,000 and a recommendation from you."

"That is absurd, Mr. Quigly. I don't intend to pay a blackmailer nor do I give letters of reference to someone like you."

"In that case, Mr. Thorndike, you leave me no alternative. I will … put that … down, old man, you can't … "

Two bangs that sounded like pistol shots rang out — bang, bang — and then loud harsh noises, sounds that ended the tape. As soon as the tape finished playing this second time, Jason took it from the machine. I tried to stop him.

"Jason, please don't destroy it, at least not until we are sure what happened." Jason ignored me and with the tape in hand he did as his employer had instructed him. He took the scissors from the desk and cut the tape into small pieces. He had now completed his promise to his master. "I don't know just when the master died, but to destroy the tape was his last request to me and I assured him I would abide by his wishes."

2

Before these tragic events had taken place I was going to meet Morgan, my husband. I couldn't live with what was on my conscience! I owed it to Morgan to tell him about my past life, about secrets I kept from him for the last three years. Secrets that would be with me forever. *My terrible secrets!* I was a very naive and stupid 18-year-old girl who was talked into having a baby by Pastor Abel Clayborne. His wife Kersi masterminded that event in my life with love, kindness, and what I thought God wanted me to do. The Claybornes took my baby and I didn't see her until she was twelve years old. Caesar, Matthew's son, was the result of a premeditated act by Matthew Glyndon. He duped me into a "phony" marriage in Mexico. I feared exposure of our sexual indiscretion, so *I allowed myself to be held in bondage!* Morgan was my legal husband and the father of my son, Raynor. I could not let Matthew tear my marriage apart if he went public with our *"bigamous"* marriage. When I became pregnant by Morgan, Matthew thought the baby was his, so when Raynor was born, I led Matthew to believe the baby had died at birth.

Later, Matthew's great desire to be a father enticed him to change my birth control pills to harmless "placebos." He knew I would become

4

pregnant with his child. Matthew wouldn't release me from the illegal marriage. And now I am faced with telling Morgan the truth about my past. Morgan doesn't know that Abel Clayborne is Chelsea Lyn's father nor that Matthew is Caesar's father. These are the terrible secrets I must now confess.

I was too emotional to meet Morgan. I had been crying most of the evening. My face and eyes were a mess. I had to have time to mourn Mr. Thorndike's death before I could talk with Morgan about my past relationships. No, I had to wait to talk with Morgan. I asked Linda, my executive assistant, to call Morgan at the restaurant and tell him I would see him at home.

Linda, Jason, and I left the office in silence. Mr. Thorndike's death affected each of us in a different way. Jason had served Mr. Thorndike for twenty-five years as his butler, loyal friend, and manager of the estate. His loyalty and love for the old man was immeasurable. Jason took Mr. Thorndike's death very sadly. He was shaken to the depths of his soul. His stiff British upper lip quivered and tears formed in his eyes several times while we listened to the tape a second time. The British stiffness and letter-perfect politeness he always maintained was now but a faint veil, hardly covering a face filled with the sadness of Mr. Thorndike's death. He was trying very hard to maintain his composure. He assured me that he would be "just fine." But twenty-five years of love and service to the old man had ended and I wondered what would happen to Jason.

Linda's relationship with Mr. Thorndike was as a distant employee. She talked with him many times when he called to talk with me. She had a fondness for him and I knew she would miss the cheerful telephone calls.

Mr. Thorndike always referred to himself as my surrogate grandfather, but I learned to love him as a true grandfather. He guided my business life almost daily. He placed challenges before me that would have caused many people to break mentally and to quit. Now I can only show my love for him by being the kind of CEO he wanted me to be. I knew I would be challenged, mostly because of my gender. I decided when I earned my law degree that I would succeed in whatever I chose to do. I never realized I would have someone of Mr. Thorndike's stature personally challenge me over and over again. Somehow I had succeeded even beyond Mr. Thorndike's expectations. When he recommended that the corporate board appoint me chief executive officer of the Thorndike

Corporation, I felt he had proved to himself that I would measure up to his expectations. I loved the old man very dearly. He will never be replaced in my heart. I shared my life with him. I had confided in him about everything that had ever happened to me. His response was that, "No one is perfect and your problems have only made you a better woman." Now that Mr. Thorndike is dead, I wonder what my status will be?

Chelsea Carodine, you are at a new beginning in your life, I thought. Exposure of my past life with the Claybornes and the involvement with Matthew would have prevented me from advancing in industry as a woman. A man could have done the same or more than I did and his personal life would never stop his advancement. If he were judged by his male peers, his "conquests" probably would have boosted his stature in their minds. In today's world, a man succeeds quicker with a stigma of sexual relationships. A woman accused would never advance in management.

When I arrived home, Morgan, my dear husband, was anxiously waiting to question me. I could tell by his manner he was worried about me. He asked, "Chelsea, sweetheart, what happened? I heard that Mr. Thorndike died. I'm so sorry. Please tell me, darling, how are you holding up?" My mind was emotionally drained. I thought, God help me. What am I going to say if he asks me why Quigly was at Mr. Thorndike's home? I can't lie to him any more. I had to talk about the situation, but I had to be careful. I was still crying, and between my sobs and gasping for breath I tried to explain what happened.

"Morgan, Luther Quigly was found shot in Mr. Thorndike's bedroom. We know only that Mr. Thorndike died after he was taken to the hospital. I really don't know what happened. Jason called Mr. Thorndike's doctor, who took him to his hospital. It seems that Mr. Thorndike had made arrangements with Doctor Benoni to be buried immediately after his death. We think Mr. Thorndike was placed in his tomb earlier this evening. And Morgan, that is really all I know ... and most of it is speculation."

"But how could the old man be entombed so quickly? Isn't there normally a police investigation any time a violent death occurs?"

"I really don't know the facts, Morgan. I am so exhausted I can't think." I continued to sob hysterically. Morgan held me gently and said

6

we could talk later. His warm hands caressed me and he repeatedly told me how much he loved me and how sorry he was for me.

"My dear Chelsea, I feel so sad for you." I could feel his tears as they ran down his cheeks and onto mine. "I know you loved Mr. Thorndike very much. We'll miss him. Honey, try to relax. I'll take care of the boys and Chelsea Lyn. Take your bath and I'll give you a rubdown. And Chelsea, remember I love you very much."

"Oh, thank you, Morgan. I do love you very much, you're so sweet and kind to me. And Morgan, thank you for *just being my friend!*"

After a very restless night, morning came and my eyes were red from crying. I couldn't believe Mr. Thorndike was dead. I felt cheated. His entombment last evening deprived me of saying good-bye to him. The district attorney will conduct an investigation. I pray the findings don't involve Mr. Thorndike in Quigly's death. His doctor would have listed the cause of his death. If he did die of natural causes, he would not be the subject of a police investigation. I prayed his name would not be tarnished by a despicable man like Luther Quigly.

Morgan had taken the children to school and left me in bed to rest. They hadn't disturbed me. I'd slept through their preparations for school, breakfast and departure. I was alone. My mind wandered back to last evening. I was still very saddened that I did not see Mr. Thorndike. Some people would say I never had my closure with Mr. Thorndike's death. I began to cry hysterically; I couldn't control my emotions. I asked God why Mr. Thorndike had to die as he had. *I felt so alone!* I needed someone to talk with. I wondered if I could call my father and talk with him. I dialed his office number. His telephone rang and he answered on the first ring.

"Dad, this is Chelsea. Do you have time to talk with me?"

"Yes, of course, Chelsea dear. Are you all right? You don't sound like yourself. Has something happened?"

"Yes, Dad, Mr. Thorndike died last evening."

"Chelsea, my poor little girl. I know you loved the old man very much. I will get the first plane I can and come to be with you."

"No, Dad, please don't. I mean, not now. I'm all right. Morgan is here and he is helping me cope. I will call you if I need you to come. Will you come to the memorial service?"

"Yes, of course I shall come. Is there anything I can do for you, dear?"

"Dad, how did you feel when Mother died and you couldn't talk with me?"

"Sweetheart, do you really want to talk about your mother's death now?"

"Yes, Father, I must know how you felt when you first discovered Mother was dead."

"Chelsea, we have talked about the terrible guilt I carry over losing your mother. I felt that guilt so deeply when she died and I didn't have you there with me, I could have ended my life. That's how distraught I was."

"Dad, you remember I didn't know Mother had died until I received the letter Pastor Abel read to me, that was three weeks after she was gone. I feel so ashamed of my feelings now." My tears continued to flow. I couldn't stop crying. "Dad ... , I feel the loss of ... Mr. Thorndike more than I felt for my mother ... when I learned of her suicide. *Dad, this isn't normal, is it?* I mean for me to feel the way I do about Mr. Thorndike?"

"Oh, my dear Chelsea. Don't ever think like that! I don't know what to say to ease your pain! But I can say your feelings are really very normal. You have lost part of who you are. You may feel a little unsure about the future. Just remember, dear, I will always be with you. Have your cry and when you want me with you, just call. *I love you, dear!*"

"Oh, Dad, I just needed someone I could talk with for a few minutes. I'll be OK now. I just feel so sad. Several good crying sessions will help me, I am sure. And Dad, thanks for listening. I love you very much."

"My dear daughter. Please go to church, Chelsea, and talk to God about how you feel. You will find comfort when you pray for Mr. Thorndike and yourself. Good-bye, my dear."

"Good-bye, Dad, and thank you. I will talk with you later. And Dad, do you remember saying Mr. Thorndike wouldn't remember being on your college campus? Mr. Thorndike did remember meeting you when he visited your college several years ago."

My heart ached for Mr. Thorndike, but I still had to tell Morgan about the secrets I have kept from him about Chelsea Lyn and Caesar. God, how am I going to tell him? Mr. Thorndike and my Russian friend, Doctor Olga Doubreski, were the only two people to know about my terrible past sins. *Why didn't I think of Olga before!* She will help get me through this terrible time of losing Mr. Thorndike. And I know she will help me explain things to Morgan so that I won't hurt him so much. Yes, I must call Olga. I immediately dialed Olga's number and her secretary answered.

"Doctor Doubreski's office, may I help you?"

"Yes, this is Chelsea Carodine. I need to speak with Doctor Doubreski."

"Do you need an appointment with Doctor Doubreski?"

"No, but I must speak with her. Is she available?"

"The doctor is with a patient. I will ring you when she is free. May I confirm your telephone number?"

"Yes, the number is correct. Please have the doctor call me at my home as soon as she is free."

I sat at the kitchen window overlooking the lake. Morgan and I had sat here so many times. The trance I was in prevented me from enjoying the beauty of the trees and the lake. The beautiful breathtaking view was the reason we built the house. Our house is located on a hill in the middle of a two-acre plot. Morgan was proud of the white farm fence he built around the lot. The pretty white slats of the fence reflect the light from the sun and the lake's water. Somehow, the view didn't console me this morning. I was not comforted by the beautiful, swaying weeping willow trees with their long fingerlike branches waving in the wind as if they were dancing. Nor the crystal-clear water of the lake as it glistened in the morning sun. I looked into the water and felt drawn into the depths of the lake. The shades of blue and green water seemed to take me down and up again with the changes of color. Suddenly I was awakened from my trance by the fish jumping out of the water!

Mr. Thorndike had Sunday brunch with us here not too long ago. He was a very happy old man. He never married. When I shared my past with him he told me about a son he had with his one and only girlfriend years ago. He was in college when his girlfriend became pregnant. She left town and had a baby boy. She would not marry Mr. Thorndike because she felt he would have to leave college. His sweetheart protected him to the end. His name was not used as the father on the child's birth certificate. She died during his senior year in college. He said he never felt he could marry because of his love for the one woman who loved him so much. The son was raised by his aunt, and Mr. Thorndike paid his support through law school. The son never knew where the money came from. Mr. Thorndike paid through a trust fund and the source of the funds was never to be revealed to the son.

9

Mr. Thorndike loved children. He enjoyed my daughter, Chelsea Lyn, and my sons, Raynor Saul and Caesar. He knew about my past. I felt his strength of living happily every day as if it were to be his last day. And now he was gone. Again, I couldn't stop crying. Mr. Thorndike was so much more than a surrogate grandfather. He was my counselor, my confidant, and my true friend I could turn to when I was troubled. I will miss him so much.

3 The sound of the telephone ringing brought me back to reality. It was Olga.

"Chelsea, this is Olga. You need to talk with me, da?"

"Olga, thank you for calling. Olga, Mr. Thorndike died last evening ... did you hear about his death?"

"Yes, I heard on radio when I drive to my office. I called your office and Linda told me you would be in later in the morning. Tell me how are you holding up, Chelsea?"

"I guess I'm OK. I just feel so terribly depressed. I can't seem to talk with people. Olga, you're so dear to me, I need you. Can you come to Lewisburg?"

"Yes, my dear one, I will come to you, but please, what did happen to Mr. Thorndike?"

"No one is sure at this time, although we suspect he died naturally ... "

"The radio man said one other man, Luther Quigly, was found dead in Mr. Thorndike's bedroom. What is the story with this situation?"

"I don't know, Olga. The police are conducting an investigation and I have not talked with them yet. I will let you know when I know what happened. Olga, can you come today? Please stay overnight with us. I'll meet you at the airport and we can have lunch together. I must talk with you."

"Da, where do you want me to come, there to Lewisburg?"

"Yes, would you please? Our corporate airplane is there in Boggsville. I will have them wait for you."

"Da, I have no more patients for today. We had a medical lunch planned for today, but there is nothing new at these meetings. I will come to you."

10

Olga was my doctor when my two sons were born. She knows about my past life. She is really the only person I can talk with. Olga has such a beautiful philosophy of life. She is direct, truthful, but ever so gentle and compassionate. She must help me find a way to tell Morgan. I checked the time of arrival of the corporate jet and drove to the airport to meet her. Soon the airplane settled onto the runway. Olga was straining to look through the window as it taxied toward the company hangars. She was waving frantically as if we had not seen each other in months. I was waiting at the foot of the ramp as she made her way to me. We embraced and I began to cry. Olga had a way of making logic out of tragic life situations. Her life in Russia and subsequent escape taught her survival skills the normal person could never imagine. And now I needed her to help me survive. We left the airport and drove to a small restaurant. As soon as we were in the car Olga asked, "Chelsea, my dear one, are you well? Tell me what is your problem?"

"Olga, I am so happy to see you. I am so upset about Mr. Thorndike's death that I can't think straight. The evening Mr. Thorndike died I was to meet Morgan and tell him about Matthew and my Chelsea Lyn and the Claybornes. I couldn't talk with him because I was so upset over Mr. Thorndike's death. I needed to talk with you. Can you please help me sort out my terrible past?"

"Chelsea my dear, you may think you are the only one in the world with bad things in your life. You Americans have a saying 'old bones in the closet' or something like that. Child, everyone who has ever lived has events in their lives they wished would not have happened. I believe anyone can overcome tragic things that happened to them if they have faith in themselves and some kind of help from one up in the heavens."

"Oh, Olga, I seem to have more things happen to me than anyone I know."

Olga patted me and said, "Let me explain one thing in my life where good came from a very bad event. When I was twelve years old an owner of a food store asked me to have sex with him in exchange for food for my family. Chelsea, my family was hungry. I did not hesitate. I had sex with him and took the food for my family. Only me and the store owner knew what had happened. I lived with the thought for a short time, then put it out of my mind. And Chelsea, I became a doctor. *My point to you is not to feel sorry for yourself! Just get on with your life! Overcome your past and forget it.*"

11

"Olga, you make everything so simple. I feel I am hurting Morgan by not telling him about my past."

"But, my dear Chelsea, if what happened will destroy lives of people who you love by confessing, then I would advise you to think twice."

"Olga, I'm so sorry for what happened to you. I know I am not the only one with a problem. But Olga, my conscience is troubling me. I feel I am cheating Morgan by not telling him. And yet I realize if I tell him, he may want to end our marriage. Oh, Olga, I'm so confused."

"You think maybe Olga can make a scheme so Morgan will stay married to you."

"No, Olga. I will accept whatever the outcome is, I have made up my mind. I need help. I don't know where to start nor what to say to him. Will you let me talk with you as if I were talking with Morgan so you can give me a little feedback? Maybe what you think his reaction would be. Do you understand what I mean?"

"Da, I know what you want to do. 'Bounce your story on me,' as you Americans would say. Is that right, Chelsea, my dear one?" she said as she looked at me with her eyes sparkling. Sometimes I think of Olga as my real mother.

"Olga, you're just a wonderful one, my dear friend. You could always read my mind, couldn't you?"

"Chelsea, I love you like my daughter. I know you never did discuss all situations with your father. But did you ever tell him about Chelsea Lyn and Caesar?"

"No, Olga, *I could never bring myself to confess the things I have done to my father!*"

"You don't think your father has any faith in you? Maybe you think he would not love you any more if you told him about what you have done in your life."

"Olga, I could never stand to lose my father again. You remember we didn't speak for about three years when I left home at 17. *I can't let anything like that happen to us again!* I am really not sure how he would accept what happened in my life."

"Chelsea, I advise you first to reconcile the loss of Mr. Thorndike before you take on another emotional crisis."

"Yes, I know, Olga. But I must think about what I am going to say to Morgan. I am so confused over what happened to Mr. Thorndike. Yes, I know I must wait for awhile before I talk with Morgan, but I have to plan what I am going to say."

"Chelsea, I think it is too soon! But, if you want to talk, I will listen to you."

"Oh, Olga, I just don't know. I must talk with Morgan soon. Please let me try with you … that is, try to decide how I would approach Morgan."

"Very well, you try to think I am Morgan. Where do you want to talk with him?"

"I thought I wanted to meet him at our special restaurant, you know, at Hoffman's. You remember the place he took me the first time we dated?"

"Chelsea, I don't think the happy place is where you should talk with Morgan about your past. I think a place where you and he have never been before would be a good place to talk with him. Go to the woods, get outside some place."

"Oh, Olga, you're right. Hoffman's is our special place. It would not be kind to talk about what I have done to him there."

"Then think you and Morgan are some place and you are going to talk with him. What would you say? How would you start?"

"I think I would say, 'Morgan, I want you to know that I love you very dearly. What I am about to tell you may destroy your love for me. I only hope you can forgive me after you have heard what I have to say.' Then I would tell him about Abel and Kersi and how I had Chelsea Lyn with Abel … "

"*Chelsea, wait!* Don't tell me you are just going to say, 'Morgan, I had a baby by a pastor'? No! No! I think you should tell him how you and your father had the fight when he told you to leave his home. I remember when you explained what happened to you when you went to work in the home of Abel and Kersi. You told me that Kersi, the pastor's wife, used God and talked you into having a baby for them because she couldn't have a child. Do I remember correctly, da? I think you said something about brainwashing you with religion."

"Yes, Olga, that is what happened, but I was never brainwashed. I was loved by the Claybornes. I was stupid, but Kersi did keep pressuring me, saying it was God's directions to have a baby for her and Abel. You know the rest of the story."

13

"Then my dear, tell Morgan how it happened to you. You were very young and had never had sex. You thought you were doing the right thing with the Claybornes."

"Olga, I'm scared. How am I going to explain Matthew and Caesar?"

"Chelsea, I would do straightforward story and tell him what happened in Mexico with the 'phony' marriage certificate. I do not believe in making excuses, but maybe you could tell him how upset you were about his affair with the secretary. I leave that to you to decide."

"I just know he will not believe me when I tell him how scared I was that Matthew would expose what happened between him and me in Mexico. And, Olga, just tell me how I am going to explain having Caesar by Matthew."

"Chelsea, I think you don't know Morgan. You may be very surprised how he will react to what happened in your life. I think if he really loves you, he will, what you say, 'give you the benefit of the doubt' before he does anything."

"Olga, I am so ashamed. I love Morgan with all my heart. I always loved him even when I was with Matthew. But, I just couldn't keep control of my emotions when I was with Matthew. Even if Morgan forgives me for what happened to me with the Claybornes, I don't think he will accept me having a baby by Matthew while I was married to him."

4 "Chelsea, after Morgan told you about his affair, how did you feel?"

"I felt betrayed, like he didn't love me! I recall you told me I shouldn't have made too much of the fact that he had sex with another woman … "

"I ask you, *did you forgive him after he confessed his sin to you?"*

"Well, not right away. I think of what he did now and then. But then I put it out of my mind."

"Tell me, Chelsea, when did you forgive Morgan and want to save your marriage with him?"

"I guess it was my guilt feeling after Matthew and I had the affair in Mexico. Olga, my conscience bothered me. I thought if Morgan knew what happened between Matthew and me in Mexico he would have left me."

"Chelsea, you worry too much. I think Morgan to be a fair person. He will listen to you and I think he will show you compassion. I tell you not to expose everything about your past at one time. Test him by telling him a little. Maybe you should ask him what he would think of a 'friend of yours who has a problem' and test his reaction before you confess everything to him."

"No, Olga, I'm going to be totally honest with him. I will always love Morgan. I owe it to him to tell him everything. I only hope he will understand how sorry I am for doing anything that offended him. I never meant to hurt him. I know in my heart that I shall always love him even if he divorces me."

"Chelsea dear, you say you hurt Morgan. How do you know you hurt him? Does he walk around crying?"

"Olga, I cheated on him with Matthew!"

"Chelsea, my dear, do you think Morgan gets pain every day because you had sex with Matthew?"

"No, of course not! But, it's only because he doesn't know about Matthew ...." She raised her hand and stopped me.

"Then my conclusion is that you are going to give Morgan pain by telling him about your past life. Is that right, Chelsea dear?"

"Olga, you don't understand ... *my conscience* ... "

"Let me disturb you. Do I understand you want to clear your conscience? Is it for *your peace of mind* or for Morgan's?"

"Olga, how can I go through life with Morgan and keep the secrets of what happened to me?"

"My dear Chelsea, do you believe all people who marry bare their souls to each other? I think only more problems come from, what you say, 'confessing' all to your partner."

"I know what you are saying, Olga. But this is my decision and at this moment, I feel I must tell Morgan."

"Chelsea, you must do what you must do. But I ask you to think of other people and not only that you must clear your conscience."

"Are you going to help me, Olga? I appreciate what you have said, but it is still my decision to do what I feel I must do."

"I do not think you use your head, Chelsea. You have big job and you boss many people, but don't be too stupid with Morgan, da? Do you feel Morgan loves you and the children?" I thought, *what a simple picture she paints!*

15

"Yes, there is no question, he is totally wrapped up with me, Chelsea Lyn, and the boys."

She continued to probe my mind with her questions.

"What was his reaction when you brought Chelsea Lyn home with you and told him she was to be adopted by you two?"

"He was elated. He fell in love with Chelsea Lyn at first sight. And he has always loved the boys. Do you remember when I took Caesar to visit Raynor Saul how badly Morgan wanted to adopt him?"

"Yes, I do remember. Chelsea, I think you have good standing with Morgan and he will understand what has happened in your life. Be gentle with him, I think he is a good man." I wondered if Olga could see things in Morgan that I couldn't see.

"Thank you, Olga, for listening to me and helping me to decide how I should tell Morgan about my past. You are going to stay the night with us, aren't you?"

"Yes, of course, my dear. I would love to have dinner with Morgan and your family. But please remember, people love you more than you think they do."

"Yes, Olga, I feel the love of Morgan and my children. Maybe you could help me to show Morgan how much I love him before I must confess to him."

5 Olga and I drove to my home. Morgan had taken off early and driven the children home from school. They all greeted me as if I had been gone for a month. I think Morgan talked with them about Mr. Thorndike and how upset I was. The children were very happy to see Olga, and Morgan was elated to see her again.

"Olga, thank you very much for coming to see Chelsea. She needs her loved ones around her at this time. She has taken the death of Mr. Thorndike very hard."

"Yes, Morgan, I understand her. She is very loving with everyone. She loves her family with all her heart. I want you to remember this, Morgan, da?"

"Yes, or da. And Olga, I want you to know that I love Chelsea with all of my heart. I couldn't live if anything happened to her or any member of our family. She is all the family I have, my entire family is dead. I lost

16

my only brother two years ago. You may remember, he owned Hoffman's restaurant."

"Yes, that is the special place Chelsea talks about. Morgan, you must remember she has been under great strain. Her position as the number one boss in the corporation is very demanding on her. Now with the death of Mr. Thorndike, her emotions are near the breaking point. She needs you more than any other time in her life. And Morgan, I ask as one who loves Chelsea and her family for you to be kind to her. She is a wonderful woman and mother."

"Yes, Olga, as we say in America, 'you are singing to the choir.' I don't think anything could happen to disrupt our love for each other and our family."

"I hope you are right, Morgan. Please remember our conversation."

We had a wonderful visit with Olga. Chelsea Lyn adopted her as her aunt and the boys remembered her from past visits. She is a real part of our family. I don't know what she and Morgan discussed, but I hoped she helped my cause when I have to talk with him about my past. I am not a procrastinator, but the fear of what may happen between Morgan and me has been a strong deterrent to my talking with him. I can't imagine life without Morgan.

6 Although the meeting with Olga didn't solve my problems with Morgan, she helped me to formulate how I should tell him about my past. In my own heart I know that I must confess to ease my own guilt and pain. When I look at my three children together, my heart swells and I cry out to God with overwhelming gratitude for the gift of their lives. I pray Morgan's attachment to the children will guide him in his decision, whatever it may be. If he is hurt beyond repair and wants a divorce I shall abide by his desires. If he does leave me I will still have the children and I shall continue to live for them. My life will go on with or without Morgan. I only hope he loves me as much as I love him; maybe he will stay with me.

Mr. Thorndike's memorial service was scheduled for Saturday at 2:00 P.M. Dad arrived Friday afternoon late and we all had dinner together. They remained with us overnight. Dad and Olga seemed to have an instantaneous friendship. I thought, wouldn't it be something if Dad and

Olga became serious about each other? I dismissed the thought as quickly as it had entered my mind.

When we arrived at the Thorndike convention center, the size of the crowd overwhelmed us. There were as many Thorndike competitors as employees and friends. I was greeted by the members of the board of directors and each expressed condolence for the loss of Mr. Thorndike. The memorial service reflected the way he lived his life: strong and yet gentle; wise and yet close to the common man and without fanfare. At the conclusion of the service, Mr. Putman, the senior member of the board, suggested we hold a board meeting as quickly as possible after the probate of Mr. Thorndike's will. None of us knew how Mr. Thorndike would dispose of his 65% ownership of the corporation.

Mr. Thorndike's executive assistant had received written instructions from him as to how the service was to be held. The old man left nothing to chance. He planned everything, even the epitaph for the vault where he was entombed. I ordered the corporation to cease operation for the afternoon of the memorial service. It seemed every employee and every retiree and anyone who had ever worked for Thorndike Industries attended the memorial service. The service was very meaningful to me.

I thought, good-bye, my dear friend, as I cried silently. As I sat through the service, I remembered when Abel read me the letter about my mother's suicide three weeks after she had died. I had my own private memorial service in a local church. I sat in the church for several hours praying that my father and I could become a family again. I prayed that he and I would learn to love each again. I never really felt the love he had for me because of our concern for my mother. But now, I thought, we're the only family either of us has and my prayers were answered. My father and I are closer than we have ever been.

My prayers at Mr. Thorndike's memorial service were very special. I thanked God for the wonderful relationship we shared. I thanked God for giving me the friendship and love that he had shown me for the past several years. He was 93 years old and I knew for a long time that he could die any day. It is tragic that he died in the company of a scoundrel like Luther Quigly. Morgan and the children were with me at the service. Chelsea Lyn had experienced death when Kersi died. Kersi's last act was to return my daughter Chelsea Lyn to me and — then she quietly died. Mr. Thorndike had tried to protect me and Thorndike Industries with

18

"Good-bye, my dear friend," I cried silently.

his actions against Quigly. Soon after the memorial service was over, I knew I would face the next crisis in my life. *My confession to Morgan!*

7 I was given another brief reprieve when Morgan had to make a sudden trip to one of the plants in the southern part of the state. He would be gone for a few days. I had to go back to work. I couldn't think about my personal life.

The Thorndike board of directors was convened to review the corporation's position since the death of its founder. I was surprised at the support I received from the senior members of the board as we began to review the status of the corporation's charter and the actions required following the death of Mr. Thorndike. After we reviewed the corporate actions necessitated by the death of its owner, we decided to delay all other items until after the probate of Mr. Thorndike's will. The feeling ran high that the old man might have left his share of the corporation to a charitable institution. It seemed strange that Mr. Thorndike had not left instructions with me concerning the disposition of his share of the corporation.

Mr. Thorndike did not have any known living relatives. He told me about his illegitimate son Stan Jones, a lawyer who worked for Thorndike Industries at one time. In fact I was the one who fired Stan for insubordination and failure to follow instructions during the Parker buy-out program. I did not know if anyone else knew Stan Jones was Mr. Thorndike's son.

After a few days, Morgan returned from his trip and I made up my mind to confess my transgressions and let the chips fall where they may. I had thought about talking with him; it was on my mind all the time.

I asked Morgan to take me to the park for a walk so we could talk. Chelsea Lyn and Sylvia, our housekeeper, remained with the boys, and Morgan and I were free to take whatever time we needed.

The park was beautiful! It was the fall of the year and the leaves had begun to change colors. The reds and greens and various shades of yellow all cascaded into a picture only nature could paint. The wind was blowing lightly. There was a chill in the air. Morgan and I wore light winter jackets. I hoped the weather would not spoil the time I planned to have alone with him. We left the car at the parking lot and walked along the nature trails. I noticed not many people were in the park because it was the middle of the week and most people were working. Morgan took my hand and we walked along in silence for a long time. My mind was racing; I had to get started somehow. We stopped at the edge of the forest and as we sat on the huge rock overlooking the beautiful fall scenery, I decided it was time.

"Morgan, are you happy with me?"

"Of course I am, honey. We have everything anyone could ever dream of wanting. Our beautiful children are healthy, we both have very satisfying positions and I love you very much." I thought, how can I tell him about my past when he shows so much love for me and the children?

"Morgan, if you could have more of anything, what would it be?"

He responded with a smile. "My greatest desire is for us to have more time together as a family. I think it's important we give our children more guidance, especially Chelsea Lyn."

"Morgan, have you ever wondered who Chelsea Lyn's parents were?"

"Not really. She apparently came from very intelligent and beautiful parents. One parent was probably a very determined person. Chelsea Lyn will succeed in whatever she chooses to do. She is growing into a beautiful woman, and she is bright and is about the happiest young girl I have ever seen."

"But, aren't you concerned that I completed the adoption just with your signature on the court papers? You really didn't even meet the parents."

"Chelsea, I trusted your judgment totally. If you had adopted a crippled little person from some faraway country I would have supported you because I knew you had a good reason for doing it."

"Morgan, *I'm trying to tell you something ...* "

"Chelsea, do you think the sun will rise tomorrow?"

"Morgan, what does the sun rising tomorrow have to do with what I am trying to say to you?"

"I am trying to be gentle with you, CEO! Our lives will go on, like the sun rising every day. Let me say something about our life. We have the most beautiful life anyone could have. Our three lovely children need both their parents to be able to develop into their own beings. *I would never, ... and I mean never*, accept anything that would disrupt our lives. Enough preaching, now what are you trying to tell me?"

"Morgan, *I'm trying to tell you something* … "

"Oh, Morgan, you disrupt me so. I have terrible guilty feelings about things that have happened to me that you don't know about."

"Chelsea, some people say knowledge is power. *But it can be a very destructive power!* Do you remember when I confessed to you about the sexual encounter with the Parker secretary?"

"Yes, Morgan, I remember, but what does that have to do with me talking to you about something very important to our lives?"

"Tell me, Chelsea, when you remember about that situation, do you become angry and upset?"

"Morgan, what are you trying to say to me? Of course, I remember what happened and maybe I do get a little upset. I also realize that event is buried very deep in my mind and I don't think I will ever let it affect our relationship, *I mean, not consciously.*"

"But Chelsea, it did affect our relationship and every time I think about it I feel guilty all over again."

"Oh, Morgan dear, you really don't have to feel guilty." I took his hand and kissed it very gently and tucked it into mine.

He held my chin and looked into my eyes and replied, "That is precisely my point, I don't have to, *but I do feel guilty,* and I always will feel that way because I hurt you."

"Morgan, are you trying to say I shouldn't talk to you about my problems ... ?"

"Chelsea, you must do what you feel you must do. But consider my views. What would I do with the information you are going to give me? Would it enhance my life? Or will it just place a guilt trip on both of us?"

"Morgan, are you saying nothing in my past is important to you?"

He hugged me gently and placed his hands on each side of my face, kissed me lightly, and said, "Sweetheart, everything about you is important to me. I love you with all of my heart, but Chelsea, I will not listen to anything that will destroy what we mean to each other. I suspect you are trying to tell me about an indiscretion ...." I was very shocked! He's guessing, *but he really doesn't want to know!*

"Morgan, what I have to say may affect our lives. You must listen to me."

"Honey, you and I have come a long way together. When we met I knew you were a mature woman who had other lovers. Was I concerned that you were not a virgin when we first made love ... and later when we were married?" I thought, Morgan, please stop being so logical and let me tell you about my emotions and what I have done to you.

"Well no, but we agreed that whatever happened to us before we met shouldn't affect our love for each other."

"That is what I am trying to say to you now! Chelsea, I love you. *No! I do not want to talk about anything that will affect our marriage and children!* I love you and my family and that is all that matters to me."

"Morgan, are you very sure you don't want to know what happened to me before we married, and some things ... "

"Chelsea, do you love me?"

"Morgan, how can you ask such a question? I love you and my children more than life itself."

"Then if you really do love me, please drop what you are trying to confess to me. Honey, don't you get the drift? I really don't want you to tell me what happened to you along the way. What is truly important to me is that our family remain as it is. We are happy, honey, so let's keep it that way."

"But, Morgan ... ," I began to cry. I didn't know if I was frustrated ... that he wouldn't listen ... or relieved that he would not let me bare my soul to him.

"Honey, if you must confess something that is heavy on your mind, I suggest you go to church. The Guy upstairs is very forgiving. Please don't use me to help solve problems that will cause dissension between us. OK?" I felt he would never listen to me about my past. I am so thankful for him.

8 "Morgan, I do love you with all my heart and I promise to be a loving and loyal wife to you as long as I live."

"Hey, that's heavy. Maybe we should have confession days more often if I can get promises like that."

Morgan took me in his arms and held me for a long time. He stroked my hair gently and told me how much he loved me and how proud he was to have a wife with so much honesty and integrity. I thought I must be the luckiest woman in the world. I really believed Morgan knew some things about me and Matthew, but he never questioned me nor would he listen to anything I wanted to say. *I really wanted him to know! Then again, I didn't want him to know!* I thought, what

24

good would come from him knowing it all? Olga was right again. What a strange paradox. He told me how happy he was and he didn't intend to have anything or anyone interfere with his love for me and our family. I think Olga had more confidence in what Morgan's reaction would be than I did. We walked back along the nature trail and suddenly the beautiful fall colors glistened and waved in the wind as if they were sharing my happiness. The beautifully colored leaves took on even brighter colors and the sounds of the birds and ducks in the pond seemed to harmonize with my love for Morgan.

The next day I called Olga to tell her what happened and express my relief that the ordeal of my past life was now really over. Olga was extremely happy and told me to hang on to Morgan because he is one in a million. Olga said, "Chelsea, I ask you to go to church and pray to God for his forgiveness and once you have done that you will be complete again."

"Yes, Olga, I will thank the Lord for what I have in life. And Olga, thank you for listening to me. You will always be my dear friend."

My life began to take on more meaning now that I was not worried about confessing to Morgan and expecting him to leave me.

Morgan insisted we go to the mountains for the weekend. We packed up the children and away we went. Chelsea Lyn was just wonderful with her little brothers. She kept them occupied during the motor trip, playing cards and other games. I could see the kindness and gentleness of Abel in her ways. We had a wonderfully relaxing and fun time with our children. We walked the nature trials and listened to the boys as they described the leaves and plants. We went fishing in the lake. Chelsea Lyn didn't want to bait her hook with the "squiggly worm." Morgan showed her how to bait the hook with a lure. When I saw how happy Morgan was with the children, I wondered how I ever could have considered confessing to him and spoiling the lives of so many people. The past is dead. I know God has forgiven me. *Hopefully, it will remain that way, in the past!* Since Morgan refused to listen, only Olga and I will ever know what happened to me.

Morgan was right. He still carries the guilt from cheating on me the one time. If he had listened to my sins against him and the Lord, he'd know I have ten times his guilt to carry in my heart. Before we left for the mountains I had to go to church. Sitting in the church pew was very

25

comforting. Olga, thank you! I thought, what a wonderful person she is.

9 We returned from the mountains Monday afternoon and checked the answering machine. A message from John Capps, Mr. Thorndike's lawyer, scheduled the probate of the will and requested that Jason and all members of the Thorndike corporate board be present to hear the reading Tuesday morning at 9:00 A.M.

The board members and Jason were at the law office when I arrived. It was nice to see Jason again. He remained at the Thorndike residence and was waiting for the reading of the will so he could pack up Mr. Thorndike's personal items.

"Jason, how are you? Are you getting along OK?"

He replied, "Good day, Miss Chelsea. Yes, thank you. I do have bad times during the day, but I am sure my disposition and my outlook will improve as time goes on. There is one thing I must say. When I returned from your office, the police asked me a number of questions about the happenings in the master's bedroom. It's a very strange thing, Miss Chelsea. My fingerprints were taken and my fingernails were scraped while I was at the mansion."

"Jason, did the police tell you why they took your prints and scraped your nails?"

"No, Miss Chelsea, except to say it was standard police procedure."

"Jason, don't worry. It was probably just as they said, routine police crime scene work."

The lawyer, John Capps, a prominent attorney in Lewisburg, handled many of the large estates in the city. I had not been aware that he would be handling Mr. Thorndike's will. I sometimes wondered why Mr. Thorndike had not named me as the executrix of his will. I would soon learn the reason for his decision. Mr. Capps began the reading of the will.

"I shall dispense with the formalities of the will; suffice it to say that Mr. Thorndike expressed his appreciation to the board of directors and to many individual managers and employees of the corporation. His appreciation also ensures those named will receive specific amounts of money and several personal items. The total of the several bequests amounts to a little over one million dollars to each board member. Mr.

26

Thorndike's will deals with each item in individual paragraphs. I shall read the pertinent parts of the will." He began.

"First, I request that Thorndike Industries remain a private corporation. With this stipulation, those named in this, my last will and testament, and upon acceptance of my bequest, must agree with the terms and conditions of the bequest. I ask this of all parties named in the will. Do you agree with these specific terms and conditions?"

Mr. Capps canvassed the board members one at a time, and asked each person if he or she agreed to maintain the corporation as directed by Mr. Thorndike. I was the last he asked, and he said, "Ms. Carodine, Mr. Thorndike specifically listed you as one to question separately on this issue."

I said, "Yes, I certainly agree with Mr. Thorndike's wishes and if I have the power to see that it is done, he has his wish!" Mr. Capps continued.

"Second, I vote my share of Thorndike Corporation voting stock for the support of Chelsea Carodine to continue as the chief executive officer as long as she desires.

"Third, I decree and bequest 60% of my personal stock to Chelsea Carodine to ensure that she shall remain in control of the corporation as the chief executive officer.

"Fourth, I bequeath and bequest $5 million dollars, my presently owned automobile, and my summer home to Jonathan Elmer Jason, my loyal and trusted friend and employee for the past twenty-five years.

"Fifth, I bequeath $5 million dollars to a person known only to Chelsea Carodine and myself. My attorney may now become privy to the existence of this unnamed person through Chelsea Carodine. Chelsea Carodine shall be the trustee for this bequest until such time as she determines the person (unnamed) shall receive the funds or they are transferred to another trust for administration.

"Sixth, the remaining 5% of my Thorndike Corporation stock is hereby bequeathed to the city of Lewisburg, yearly earnings of which shall be used for the construction and maintenance of a sports complex for youth in the north four sections of the Thorndike Corporation property.

"Seventh, my personal physician, Doctor Benjamin Benoni, previously was given my instructions for the preparation of my remains

27

for entombment. A copy of this will, authorizing his actions, was also in his possession."

The reading was concluded and almost every member of the board of directors sat in silence as others began to file out of the office. I approached Jason and told him how happy I was that Mr. Thorndike had provided for his welfare. He was very appreciative. I told him if he ever needed me, to call and I would be there for him.

The board members passed by and congratulated me. The board secretary and senior member, Alex Putman, suggested a meeting of the board at the earliest time to review any directions that I may have concerning the operations of the corporation. At first, I had no idea how much money was involved in the 60% block of shares Mr. Thorndike had left me. When I realized I was now the owner and in control of more than $950 million dollars of the corporation, I almost fainted. Now it was time to get on with running this magnificent monster of a corporation of *which I now own 60%!*

Immediately after the reading of the will, I called Morgan and asked him to meet me at our special place. I was waiting for him as he came through the door. How I remember the first time he came through the door to meet me here at our special place. His golden wavy hair was disarranged, but he had that "baby boomer" look in his fitted jacket and sport pants. He hurried to our table and greeted me with a kiss.

"Hello, pretty woman. My, you look like you are about to burst. Has something happened?"

"Morgan, you won't believe what has happened to me, I mean us. It's unbelievable, I'm still in shock..."

"Well, is this to be a lifelong secret locked in the pretty head of one Chelsea Carodine-Gage, or do I get to share whatever it is?"

"Morgan, order us a bottle of the most expensive champagne in the Hoffman house."

Morgan called the manager and ordered the champagne. The manager sensed the excitement in the air and said he was buying the champagne for whatever the special occasion was. Morgan opened the bottle and filled our glasses to the brim.

"Well, Chelsea, here's to whatever ... "

"*Morgan,*" I screamed, "*Mr. Thorndike left the corporation to me! I mean to us!*"

"*He what?* Chelsea, you've got to be joking with me. Say that again very slowly. Mr. Thorndike left you what?"

"I can't believe it either. It's true. Mr. Capps, his lawyer, just read his will and the corporation — well, really *only 60% of it* — *was left to me!*"

"*Only 60%!* Well, tell me, Miss Millionaire, what are you worth in real money?"

"Morgan, I really don't know, but the figure tossed about is something like 950 or so, *millions of dollars!*"

"What you are saying is that I am married to a very rich lady. I raise my glass to you wonderful, beautiful, and *rich* lady, and incidentally, my wife!"

"Morgan, it is wonderful, isn't it?"

"Yes, it is Chelsea, and mind-boggling. Lady, we have a lot of financial planning to do — and soon."

"I know, Morgan, but right now just pour me another glass of champagne and just enjoy this wonderful feeling of being lost in the heavens with all that wealth."

"It scares me, sweetheart. We have always had enough money to do whatever we wanted to do, but this much money gives me the willies."

"It does me, too, but relax with me tonight. Give me another drink. How about sleeping on a million dollars one day next week?"

The shock, excitement, and wonderful feelings that came with our new wealth will stay with us for several days. I need to take a few days away from the office and sort through the will and just try and understand what Mr. Thorndike meant in leaving the corporation in my control. My thoughts were of him but all I could say — even though he would not hear me — was "*Thank you, my dear grandfather,* for this wonderful gift you have given to me and my family."

Morgan and I will meet with Mr. Capps and try to understand the real impact of the 60% bequest of Thorndike stock. Much of it is tied up in the assets of the corporation and several real estate investments Mr. Thorndike had made. Mr. Thorndike was an excellent manager of his wealth.

10 I left Morgan at Hoffman's and returned to the office. Linda had a message for me from Jason — from the local jail. Since he couldn't speak with me directly, he left a very frantic message: *"Miss Chelsea, I am in prison!* Will you please help me?"

I had Linda call the sheriff's office immediately.

"Sheriff Johnson. What can I do for you?"

"Do you have a Mr. Jonathan E. Jason in your facility?"

He responded gruffly, "Who wants to know?"

He made my blood boil, I was so angry! I responded very angrily. "Listen, Sheriff Johnson, I am Chelsea Carodine and I am Mr. Jason's lawyer. Now I suggest you kindly tell me if you are holding him."

I could imagine the sheriff sitting up very straight and saying in a more satisfactory manner, "Yes, Ms. Carodine. We are holding Mr. Jason ... "

"May I ask why you are holding him? Has he committed a crime, or don't you like Englishmen?"

He cleared his throat and said, "Madam, I'm holding him for the district attorney. And no, madam, he has not been charged with anything as of this time."

I told Sheriff Johnson I would be coming to the jail to speak with Mr. Jason. He said I had to clear the visit with the district attorney. By now, it was seven o'clock on Tuesday evening. Linda tried to contact the district attorney, but was informed he would be out of town overnight. I asked the sheriff to have Mr. Jason come to the telephone; he complied.

In a moment Jason's very shaky voice said, "Hello, this is Jonathan Jason ... "

I almost screamed into the telephone, "Jason, it's me, Chelsea. *What are you doing in jail?"*

"Miss Chelsea, I am not quite sure. I have been informed I was only being held because of suspicion and something about my citizenship." I told him we couldn't get in touch with the district attorney.

"Jason, it seems we can't see you or get you out until tomorrow. Will you be all right until then?"

He responded very wearily. "Yes, Miss Chelsea. If I must remain in this Godforsaken place until then, I will be all right. Thank you for your call, Miss Chelsea."

I hung up the telephone and called J.C., the chief of Thorndike Industries' law division. I hoped Jason would be all right until I can find out what is going on and why he's in jail. *And someone had better be able to explain why a person can be held in jail when the one with the authority to approve a visit or a release has left town!* I'll be sitting on the district attorney's doorstep when he returns.

CHAPTER TWO
JASON ACCUSED

1 Jason's telephone call left me terribly disturbed. I wondered why the police were holding him. He said they told him it was because of his citizenship. But that's a weak excuse. No! There is some other reason and I'm going to find out why he's been arrested. Jason said he had not heard what was on the tape before he listened to it the two times in my office. Therefore, he couldn't have been near Mr. Thorndike's room when Quigly was there nor when the loud bangs sounded. Jason didn't go into the room when he heard the loud noises because he didn't know the noises were from a gun. He took the tea to the bedroom and that's when he saw Quigly's body lying over Mr. Thorndike at the foot of the bed. The time of Quigly's death has not been established, but it had to have been within several minutes of the time Jason entered the room. Mr. Thorndike was not dead when Jason went to the bedroom. Jason said he pulled "that awful man" off the master and placed Mr. Thorndike at the head of the bed. That is when Jason was told to take the tape from the recorder and bring it to my office. What a mess! It was late Friday when I decided plans had to be made.

I don't know what happened nor whether Jason is in real trouble, but I'm going to be prepared for the worst possible case. I need to get something going to defend Jason for whatever the district attorney is planning. I thought, we have criminal lawyers here in Thorndike!

"Linda, try to get J.C. from the law division on the telephone before he leaves. Tell him I need to speak with him immediately."

Linda rang my intercom to tell me J.C. was on the telephone.

"J.C., who do we have in the law division who recently practiced criminal law before coming to us?"

"Well, Chelsea, we have three lawyers trained in criminal law. You can almost take your pick."

"That's what I want to do, J.C. Did they take the state bar when we hired them and can they practice here in the state?"

"Yes, Chelsea. Our policy has always been to have our lawyers legally licensed in the state where Thorndike interests are located. And yes, our lawyers are all legal in this state." Since it was late Tuesday I assumed the lawyers would already be gone for the day, but I asked J.C. if they were still in the office. He said they were.

"Will you please send them to me, one at a time, so I can talk to them about a possible criminal action … ?"

"Chelsea, *what criminal case*? I haven't heard anything about a criminal action against Thorndike."

"You're right, J.C. This case is not against Thorndike Industries. Jason, Mr. Thorndike's butler, has been picked up by the police. I am worried. The district attorney may be trumping up charges against Jason. J.C., since no one knows what happened to Quigly, the district attorney may be preparing to charge Jason, *possibly with Quigly's death!*"

"Chelsea, that is terrible. What do you think, could he have possibly killed Quigly?"

"I really don't know, J.C. You know Mr. Thorndike's body was entombed the same evening, don't you?"

"No, I didn't know that. Why was he entombed so quickly? Who had the authority to do such a thing?"

"I really don't know what happened. Jason said Mr. Thorndike had given his doctor directions to entomb him the day he died. Why, I don't know.

"J.C., after I interview your lawyers I intend to use one or two of them with me as a co-counsel to defend Jason. I will let you know who I choose and you can cut them loose from any corporate business."

"Sure, anything you say, Chelsea. Can I be of any personal assistance to you?"

"I don't know, J.C. I'll keep in touch with you. You can sign on as an additional co-counsel and keep up with whatever may happen."

"Thanks, Chelsea, I will be pleased to help with the defense. When you have a few minutes, I think you and I need to talk about the case, from a personal viewpoint."

"OK, J.C., we'll talk after I select the attorneys. I want them placed on a temporary leave of absence without pay from the corporation. Jason has funds and what he can't pay, I'll pay. If necessary we can establish a defense fund for Jason and all expenses will come from the fund, not the corporation."

"Chelsea, are you aware that Jason is still an official employee of the corporation?"

"No, J.C., I didn't know that. How long has he been an employee?"

"Not too many people are aware that he works for us. But he's been with us about twenty years. He works through the food service department. He prepares their menus, selects and orders the foodstuffs, and personally selects the chefs for the dining hall and the executive dining room. Since he is still an employee, the corporation could pay for his defense."

"No, J.C., I don't want to involve the corporation financially. Jason has money. And we can set up the defense fund I mentioned, which means we all can make contributions for his legal expenses. I want it done this way. I don't want even the hint of improper actions on the part of anyone in the corporation in helping to defend Jason."

"Any way you want to handle it, Chelsea. I'll stand by to help any way I can."

"Thanks, J.C., we will probably need your experience in criminal law."

The first attorney J.C. sent was a young woman, 31 years old. Jessica Roberts graduated at the top of her class and practiced as a public defender for three years. She then joined a medium-sized law firm and served as a defense counsel in the criminal department of the firm. Her record was not impressive, but she had won a number of rather important criminal cases — and she had won acquittal in three capital murder cases. Linda had talked with the law firm and was told Jessica was a strong courtroom and investigative lawyer. She would be one of the attorneys I would use in Jason's defense. She was nervous when I interviewed her. I tried to put her at ease so we could talk frankly about Jason's case.

"Miss Roberts, have you heard that Mr. Luther Quigly was found murdered in Mr. Thorndike's bedroom?" I asked as I watched her eyes.

She looked directly at me and answered in a very straightforward manner.

"Yes, I have heard the news about Mr. Quigly and Mr. Thorndike's death."

"Are you aware that Jason, Mr. Thorndike's butler, has been arrested and may be charged with Luther Quigly's death?"

"No, Ms. Carodine, I am not aware of his arrest."

"I am forming a team to defend Jason. Would you be interested in joining the team?" She sat up straight in her chair and her eyes glistened as she responded excitedly.

"Oh, yes, Ms. Carodine … *I would love to help!*"

"Good, Miss Roberts. Please complete any projects you have or transfer them to another attorney. We will use the vacant offices and

35

conference room across the hall from my office as our defense team's working room. Pick a desk and move your personal items into it."

The second attorney J.C. sent for an interview was Kelly Filbright, a 30-year-old, very confident young man with an outstanding record of convictions as an assistant district attorney for Wayne County, Pennsylvania. He'd completed law school at 25 and went into the district attorney's office following graduation. His attitude of "I just work here" turned me off completely. I didn't think I could work closely with him, given his outlook. When he said he "worked for the corporation," I thanked him for coming.

"Thank you, Mr. Filbright, I'll be in touch with you." I thought he would be an asset to the team, but didn't like his attitude toward joining the team.

John Keats Harrison graduated from Florida State University Law School and went to work for the state attorney general's office. His record indicated his strong points were court procedures and excellent knowledge of criminal law. He had worked as a defense attorney for two years, defended nine cases during those two years and won eight of them. The one he'd lost was later won on appeal. I liked what I saw in his record.

"Mr. Harrison, have you heard of the murder of Mr. Luther Quigly, who worked for the Thorndike Corporation?"

"Yes, Ms. Carodine, Quigly's murder and Mr. Thorndike's death are being discussed all through the corporation."

"Have you formed any opinions about any part of the case?"

"No! I really don't have any of the facts, only what I've heard through the rumor mill and on the news."

"Would you be interested in serving on a team to defend Jason, Mr. Thorndike's butler? He is being held and could possibly be charged with Luther Quigly's murder."

"Ms. Carodine, *that would be great!* I love to practice criminal law."

"Very good. Complete any projects you have. I shall expect you across the hall in the team's office tomorrow."

2 When I talked with Jason I told him not to talk with anyone unless one of his attorneys was there. I told him he would have attorneys with him Wednesday morning. I didn't believe we had much to worry about since Jason had not been officially charged with the murder of Luther Quigly. I was concerned about the preliminary investigation. I informed the sheriff that Jason's lawyers were to be present in the event of any questioning.

I arrived at my office early Wednesday morning to find Jessica Roberts and John Harrison setting up their desks in the defense office. They seemed very excited about being selected for the defense team. The corporation's personnel department had hired Jason for Mr. Thorndike, which meant he was paid through the accounting department. I sent for his records. The three of us reviewed everything the corporation had on Jason. I filled the others in on Jason as a person. We realized that Jason was capable of murder and certainly would protect Mr. Thorndike at all costs. We didn't know what really had happened. Our first task was to lay out areas that Jessica and John could begin to investigate.

"John and I will go to the police station and review everything they have in their preliminary investigation. We will try to get Jason released on bail.

"Jessica, review everything you can on Jason. Don't leave a stone unturned.

"We must know our client from head to toe. If necessary take a trip to England. Check his bank account, citizenship, family and friends. Know him through and through. We must know before anyone else if Jason had a motive, other than protecting Mr. Thorndike. I know Jason, but then again, I really don't know anything about him. I was told he had been with Mr. Thorndike for about 25 years. I don't know how he became a part of the Thorndike household. We must know if anything, and I mean anything, existed in Jason's and Mr. Thorndike's relationship that might have a bearing on the case. Don't overlook anything.

"After John and I have looked at any evidence the district attorney has, he and I will see Jason. If the district attorney doesn't charge him, he must be released."

Jessica took Jason's records and began studying them. She talked with people in the corporation who knew Jason, and she visited the neighborhood around Mr. Thorndike's home, talking to neighbors. She couldn't find out whether Jason had a bank account or any investments in the States. All of the people she interviewed thought Jason was a "fine English gentleman." I suggested she take a trip to England and dig up facts about Jason's early life. Jessica already had her passport and Linda purchased airline tickets for her. She left for England.

"Boss lady, J.C. called. He said he needs to talk with you about Jason's case." Linda's announcement made me wonder why J.C. was so insistent about talking with me about Jason. He must realize I don't know any more than what we both have heard and read in the media.

I said to Linda, "Call J.C. and tell him I will talk with him as soon as possible."

Linda set appointments with District Attorney Elton Hightower for John and me. Our first meeting with him was to review any evidence against Jason. The district attorney, Elton Hightower, was very cooperative but very firm that he was going to "hang" someone for one or both of the deaths in Mr. Thorndike's bedroom.

"Mr. Hightower, I am Chelsea Carodine and this is John Harrison. We also have another attorney, Miss Jessica Roberts, who is part of the defense team as co-counsel for Mr. Jonathan Elmer Jason. Mr. J.C. Kippins will serve as a standby counsel."

"I am pleased to meet you, Ms. Carodine, and you, John."

"Will you please tell me what you intend to do with Jason?"

"Well, for the present he is being held for suspicion of murder and clarification of his citizenship status. We know he has been in the United States for about 25 years, but we don't think he is a citizen. He is being held until we can decide his status. If he is not a U.S. citizen, he may leave the country … "

"*Pardon me, Mr. Hightower!* I assure you Jason will not leave until whatever you intend to do is over. Do you plan to charge Jason, Mr. Hightower?"

"I can't answer that at the present time, Ms. Carodine. Rest assured you will know if I do charge him."

"Mr. Hightower, is it standard procedure in your office to lock up a person and leave town without delegating any authority?"

He could see and hear my anger. He seemed shocked and responded, "Ms. Carodine, I don't know what you are talking about!" I thought, that does it! He's apparently not aware of his responsibilities as a district attorney. Then again, some of these little towns have elected sheriffs who last only one term because they're so corrupt. I repeated my encounter with the sheriff for him to think about.

"I called the sheriff last evening, asking to see my client, and he informed me I had to clear my visit with you. Were those your instructions, Mr. Hightower?"

"I'm very sorry you were not able to see Mr. Jason. I think the sheriff just didn't understand my instructions."

"Mr. Hightower, release Jason in my custody. I will guarantee he will be available when you decide what you are going to do."

"I can't do that, Ms. Carodine ... "

"You can't, or you won't, Mr. Hightower? I'll file a writ of habeas corpus for release and you can answer the judge about charging or releasing Jason."

"Wait, Ms. Carodine. Give me 24 hours and I will either release Jason to you or I will charge him, agreed?"

"OK, Hightower, but I want to see my client immediately."

John and I waited in the prisoner holding area while Jason was escorted in. He was handcuffed. I demanded that he not be handcuffed again. The deputy simply said it was standard procedure and the district attorney would have to authorize him to leave the cuffs off. I told him I would speak with the district attorney.

Jason looked pale and a little frightened. I could see his English pride had been injured almost beyond repair. In spite of his treatment, Jason maintained his dignity, even though he was among common criminals who tried to intimidate him with snide remarks about the great Englishman being in an American jail. The Lewisburg County Jail must be one of the oldest jails in the country. The structure is over 100 years old, and it shows. The county attempted to install modern cells and locks, but it was apparent from the ill-fitting doors that the update did not succeed. The old jail has the same "jail smell" that all jails seem to have. If I were blindfolded I could tell I was in a jail. It has a scent of wood that's been soaked in pine oil and then burned in a building with the windows and doors closed. I could never live in a place with that horrible smell. The scent was in every inch of the jail. The smell and closeness was stifling to me, and it was obvious the conditions bothered Jason. His first words to me were to please remove him from the horrible confinement.

When Jason brought the cassette tape for me to hear, I never dreamed I would be defending him against the state for something that happened in the last hour of Mr. Thorndike's life. I took his arm and gently asked him, "Jason, how are you?"

He stood up straight and replied, "My health is fine, Miss Chelsea. This horrible place and these people have upset my disposition terribly. I do hope you are able to arrange my release."

"Jason, the district attorney said he would either charge you or release you within twenty-four hours. Can you stand it a little longer?"

He looked wearily at me and said, "Yes, Miss Chelsea. If I must remain here, I shall survive."

"Jason, did the police question you?"

"Yes, Miss Chelsea, they had a long go at me about the findings in Mr. Thorndike's bedroom." I asked if he were advised of his rights.

"Jason, did any of the police advise you that you didn't have to answer their questions without an attorney?"

His expression changed and he said, "Miss Chelsea, someone asked if I understood my Miranda rights. I didn't know what Miranda rights were, but they continued with probing questions."

"What kind of questions, Jason?"

"They asked if I had done anything to that awful man Quigly."

John asked, "Jason, what about Quigly? Was he dead when you came into the room?"

"I am afraid I don't know, Mr. John. He was lying across the master, and I pulled him off and he fell to the floor. I did not inflict him with injury."

John continued his questioning. "What else did the police do, Jason? Did they fingerprint you?" Jason lifted his hands to show the ink and scrape marks around his fingernails.

"Yes, Mr. John, I had my fingerprints taken once again. The police also very rudely scraped my fingernails and fingers, a second time, I may say. The clothing I wore on that fateful day of the master's demise was also taken by the police. I did not know what they were looking for nor did they tell me."

I continued the questioning. "Jason, what did the police find when they entered Mr. Thorndike's bedroom?"

"Miss Chelsea, I must assume they found that Quigly person lying on the floor."

"Where was Mr. Thorndike when they arrived?"

Jason looked at his watch and responded. "Well, Miss Chelsea, when I placed the master back on his bed he instructed me to call his doctor and then the police. I called from his telephone. After the calls were

"Miss Chelsea, I must assume they found that Quigly person
lying on the floor."

completed he directed me to take the tape to your office for you to hear. I departed as the doctor and the carriage crew arrived."

I said to him, "Then, when you left the mansion, Mr. Thorndike was alive?"

He responded, "Yes, Miss Chelsea. Were you aware the master gave instructions to his doctor to prepare him for burial before the sun set on the day of his death? The master did this in anticipation of his impending demise." That surprised me; I didn't quite know what to say.

"No, Jason, I was not aware of Mr. Thorndike's directions to his doctor."

"Jason," John said, "who moved Mr. Thorndike to Doctor Benoni's hospital?"

"When the doctor arrived he brought an ambulance carriage. Four attendants came to Mr. Thorndike's bedroom and prepared him for movement ... "

"But, Jason, wasn't Quigly's body there in the bedroom?"

"Yes, Miss Chelsea. He was lying there on the floor at the end of the bed when I departed." John kept trying to have Jason surmise what had taken place.

"Well, Mr. John, the master apparently fell forward toward Mr. Quigly and he was at the end of the bed lying half on and half off."

"Jason, were you in the bedroom when the attendants removed Mr. Thorndike?"

"No, Miss Chelsea, I was departing as they entered. The master gave me very specific instructions to quickly go to your office with the cassette tape. I immediately departed."

"Jason, were you the first to find Quigly's body? Were you in the bedroom before the doctor and the attendants arrived?"

"Why yes, Miss Chelsea! When I heard the loud noises, very much similar to an auto engine mis-sparking, I was not sure from where they came. It was when I took the master's afternoon tea to his bedroom that I discovered the horrible scene."

"Jason, didn't you see that Quigly was lying there bleeding? Did you check to see if he might have been alive?"

"No, Miss Chelsea, the master directed me to go to you. I obeyed his command and left for your office."

"Jason, did you do anything else before you left Mr. Thorndike's home?"

"Yes, Miss Chelsea. As I said, I called the doctor and then the police as Mr. Thorndike directed. He said he would be, 'just fine' were his words, I believe."

"Did you go directly back to Mr. Thorndike's when you left my office?"

"Yes, Miss Chelsea, I proceeded directly to the mansion."

"What was happening when you arrived?"

"Well, as I reached the mansion the doctor and attendants were ferrying Mr. Thorndike to the ambulance carriage for departure to the hospital."

"Was Mr. Thorndike alive, or do you know?"

"Miss Chelsea, I am rather confused about the whole mess. I really don't know if the master was alive or dead when I returned. I seem to remember the doctor rushing the attendants to get Mr. Thorndike to the hospital."

"Jason, had the police arrived by the time you returned?"

"Yes, Miss Chelsea. I believe three or four police automobiles were at the front of the mansion when I returned. I was stopped from entering right away until I explained who I was."

"Jason," John raised his eyes as he asked, "did the police ask you any questions at the mansion?"

"Mr. John, I was rather frightened when I returned. I mean with that man Quigly lying on the master's bedroom floor. One of the officers took a statement from me about what I knew and as I previously said, they made impressions of my fingers and extracted debris from my fingernails."

"Jason, did you touch anything, or move anything in the room before the police arrived?" I realized Jason's confusion, but we had to have answers.

"Miss Chelsea, Mr. Quigly was on top of the master on his bed. I removed him from the bed to release the master from his grip before I left the bedroom."

"Jason, did you see a gun?"

"Why, no, now that you have given me time to think. No, Miss Chelsea, I did not see a pistol."

"Jason, at this point in time, we don't know what the police have. Is there anything else you can remember about the scene in the bedroom that may help us to get a clearer picture?" John was relentless with his questions.

"I am still rather confused, Mr. John. I shall put my mind to the task and attempt to remember every detail I observed. I am rather exhausted and my mind is not totally at my command."

I cautioned Jason about the police. "I understand, Jason. Remember, do not talk with the police unless one of your lawyers is present. If they attempt to question you, inform them you will not answer any questions without your attorney present. Do you understand me, Jason?"

"Yes, Miss Chelsea. But it is rather strange. I have done nothing to make the police suspicious of me. However, I shall abide by your request."

I hoped I didn't intimidate John because I asked most of the questions. I was so anxious about Jason's safety. We left the jail and drove back to the Thorndike building. As we drove we had time to review what had happened.

"Well, John, what do you think? What do you think the police have?"

"Ms. Carodine … "

"John, call me Chelsea. We can drop formalities. We're co-counsels, OK?"

"Yes, fine. I am not comfortable with the details Jason gave us. We already know Quigly was shot. What happened to the gun? Why didn't Jason see it when he rushed into the bedroom?"

"Yes, that is a question we must resolve. I am disturbed that Jason moved Quigly's body, although I can understand he had to free Mr. Thorndike."

"What charges do you think Hightower will file, if any?"

"John, right now that is the sixty-four thousand dollar question. We don't know what Hightower has or what he is looking for. Let's try and build a scenario."

"OK, Chelsea, but, let me ask: Jason said he brought a cassette tape to your office for you to hear. What was on the tape?"

"John, I don't want to be rude, but I don't think the tape has a bearing on the case at this time. If the contents of the tape are germane to the case I will prepare a memo of what I remember. Is that OK?"

"Sure, whatever you say. You're the boss."

"So what about the scenario of events that took place in Mr. Thorndike's bedroom?"

44

"Chelsea, why was Quigly in Mr. Thorndike's bedroom in the first place?"

"Mr. Thorndike's executive assistant probably made an appointment for Quigly to see Mr. Thorndike at his home because of his illness."

"Chelsea, did Mr. Thorndike see his executives at his home frequently?"

"Yes, he did, especially during the past year. I met with him on many occasions to discuss corporate business. I am sure others did also."

"Do you think Jason's statement to the police may incriminate him?"

"Oh, no, John. I wouldn't think so, anyway. His answers to their questions should have been about only what he observed. I hope he did not elaborate on moving Quigly's body," I said as I looked over at John.

"Well, we won't know until we get a copy of his statement," John said. "Then the district attorney is within the law holding Jason for an additional twenty-four hours?"

"Well, John, if I had demanded Jason's release we probably would have a very uncooperative district attorney on our hands. I want to try and work with him and his people until we see what he intends to do."

"Then, do you think he will charge Jason?"

"At this point I don't know, John. We must get everything we can before Hightower makes his move."

"Do you think Jason will be all right for another day in jail?"

"Of course. He's English. You know how tough they are."

"Chelsea, I think I should review Luther Quigly's personnel file when we get back to the office."

"Yes, that would be a good place to start."

As soon as the words were out of my mouth I began to wonder if anything in Quigly's file could be damaging to me. I knew it would show my recommendations for his hire from Parker Industries. I needed to know what else might be in his file before John examined it. I told John I would expedite getting the file by calling Linda on the car telephone.

"Linda, have personnel send Luther Quigly's file to my office and hold it for me, please." I hoped she picked up my concern over the telephone and would not offer the file to John before I could review it. I hated to begin Jason's defense with a cover-up with my co-counsels. I thought, I have to protect the corporation and myself from any adverse publicity. If we need to use the tape to clear Jason I will reconstruct it

45

and provide it to them. In the meantime I have to protect what is dear to me.

3 When I returned to my office, J.C. had called again and said he needed to speak to me as soon as possible. I had Linda call him and tell him to come to my office. He seemed rather upset when he arrived.

"Chelsea, your involvement in Jason's case is rather disturbing to me."

"Oh, in what way, J.C.?"

"Chelsea, let me be brutally frank. You are not a criminal attorney. The only involvement in any criminal cases you have had were the Casey event and two other minor ones. Chelsea, I don't think you are qualified to lead Jason's defense!"

"J.C., you're correct, but I am a lawyer and I know constitutional and criminal law. I also have experience in the courtroom. And I have selected two very competent attorneys who have extensive criminal caseload backgrounds. What else do you expect of me?"

"Chelsea, remember, you're the CEO of Thorndike Corporation. Your involvement, whatever it is, will reflect directly on the corporation. I recommend you remove yourself from the defense team and become an interested onlooker."

"J.C., I owe it to Mr. Thorndike to make sure Jason gets a fair trial and is vindicated of any charges the district attorney will make."

"Yes, I share your concern, but your loyalty to Mr. Thorndike may be overshadowing your good judgment. Jason's defense can best be handled by an outside criminal lawyer, or even a team of lawyers. Then win or lose, the corporation remains outside of the publicity spotlight."

"I'll consider your recommendations, J.C., but for now I feel I must make sure all the bases are covered to protect Jason."

"Chelsea, if you insist in keeping the corporation in the picture then let me handle the defense team. I will keep you informed of any developments so you can sit in the courtroom any time you desire."

J.C. seemed very worried about my involvement in Jason's defense. I could understand his concern for the corporation's CEO and legal department becoming involved in a criminal case, but this was not any criminal case, it was the corporation founder's personal servant and friend. Defending Jason is like defending the honor of Mr. Thorndike. I don't think a total stranger, even a qualified criminal attorney, could feel the anguish and hurt I feel for Mr. Thorndike and Jason. No, I must remain on the case until I am sure what is going to happen to Mr. Thorndike's name and Jason's safety.

After John left my office, Linda brought Quigly's file in for my review.

Quigly's file contained my original recommendation for his employment with Thorndike as Matthew Glyndon's special assistant. Quigly's personal history statement indicated he had been arrested, but not charged, for extortion two years before he was hired by Thorndike. This background item was not stated in his executive application to Thorndike. His executive ratings were not up to the level normally required for progression in Thorndike. My recommendation for promotion could seem political if Quigly's background became an issue. I passed the file on to John so he could build a profile on Quigly in the event we needed it.

Jessica completed her investigation on Jason's background. Jessica did an excellent job of digging up information about his early years — the FBI could not have done a better job. Jason was abandoned by his mother at birth, left on the steps of a hospital with a note stating she couldn't take care of the baby. He was adopted by a young couple who gave him their last name and raised him as an only child. Until he was twelve, his childhood was like that of most English children, school, family, and his township. When he was twelve, he watched helplessly as a farm hand killed his father. The killer then tied Jason to a bedpost and forced him to watch as his mother was raped, then murdered. The farm hand attempted to kill Jason, but Jason survived. At the tender age of twelve he had witnessed the complete destruction of his family. When the police captured the killer, Jason identified him and then was forced to relive the ordeal by testifying against him.

Jason's teenage years, to the age of seventeen, were spent shuffling from one foster home to another. Mr. Thorndike was in England at the time and somehow met Jason. He apparently was so moved by Jason's disruptive life that he sent him to butler school with the stipulation that Jason come to the United States and work for the corporation and Mr. Thorndike. Employment records indicated Jason was hired by the Thorndike Corporation in September almost twenty-six years ago. He had been employed with the corporation since that date. Nothing damaging could be found about Jason: he was still an English citizen, his employment with Mr. Thorndike was with a work permit on a green card, he never applied for U.S. citizenship. I hoped we were ahead of District Attorney Hightower's efforts by collecting the background information on Jason and Quigly. The one area that concerned me was that Jason's background check did not indicate he ever received counseling or an examination by a psychiatrist after the trial of his parents' killer.

Jessica suggested we also review Mr. Thorndike's personnel records to close the loop on the three principals involved. I didn't want Mr. Thorndike's life exposed to everyone. I informed Jessica I would take care of reviewing his records. Linda laid Mr. Thorndike's large personnel file on my desk. I sat and stared at his records for a long time, frozen with my memory of him. I remembered the first time I met Mr. Thorndike. He came to the law school with his college recruiters to interview prospective lawyers for Thorndike's law division. I was one of the few he interviewed. When I was informed that the chief executive officer and board chairman of Thorndike Industries was to interview me, I became very nervous. As soon as I met the dear old man I knew I had no reason to be anxious. To be in his presence was very calming. His friendly mannerisms and happy body language seemed to engulf all who were near him. His questions were firm and direct.

"Miss Carodine, what prompted you to go to law school?"

"Well, sir, I really wanted to contribute to society. I felt being a lawyer would provide me with that opportunity."

"Does the field of law still hold the enchantment it had for you when you started school?"

"Yes, sir, it does. I look forward to fighting issues and finding answers."

"Tell me, what do you expect now that you are a lawyer?"

"Well, I still have the same altruistic view toward the law that I had when I began my studies. Now that I have completed school I hope I can make a difference. I believe in our justice system."

"Miss Carodine, I am very pleased you think you can make a difference in people's lives now that you are a lawyer."

"Thank you, sir."

"I presume you are interested in corporate law since you asked for a Thorndike interview?"

48

"Yes, sir. I hoped a corporation would provide me with court experience in both civil and criminal law."

His voice still rings clearly in my ears. My loyalty to the old man is probably not as great as Jason's, but I will not have his name dragged through the mud. His personnel file did not reveal anything I thought would be useful in Jason's defense if we went to trial.

"Jessica, visit Mr. Thorndike's doctor. What's his name? Oh, here it is: Dr. Benjamin Benoni. Get everything you can get that will help Jason. Get a copy of anything Mr. Thorndike gave the doctor as authority to have him entombed."

"Chelsea, do I use kid gloves with the doctor, or is he fair game?"

"Go easy until we know what Jason is being charged with. If Jason is charged, go to the hilt — don't overlook anything. Question his staff, anyone who knows anything about the events of the day Quigly was killed.

"John, find the ambulance company who transported Mr. Thorndike to the hospital. Question any employees who were on the scene. The police said only one shot was fired from Mr. Thorndike's gun and it was in Quigly's chest. There were two shots, there has to be a second gun. John, find that weapon!"

"I'm on my way, Chelsea. Did you ask Jason about the weapon?"

"Not since we talked with him about the overall scene. He said he didn't see a weapon. Remember, he was in the room before the ambulance attendants arrived and again after they arrived. Someone removed the second weapon — and we must find it."

4 On Thursday, September 25th, District Attorney Hightower called to say he was going to charge Jason and wanted his lawyers present when the charges were read. Linda had taken the message and said the caller from the district attorney's office would not reveal what charges were to be filed. I called for John.

We dashed for the district attorney's office. When we arrived Jason was already in Hightower's office. I greeted him and immediately asked if he had been questioned.

"Jason, has anyone attempted to question you?"

"No, Miss Chelsea. I was informed I was to be charged with a crime. My fingerprints were taken again and the authorities took my photograph. I respected your directions. I have not spoken with anyone about the events that took place at the master's home."

About that time District Attorney Hightower entered the room.

"Ms. Carodine, I am sorry I could not reach you sooner. I wanted to confer with you and your attorneys prior to Mr. Jonathan Jason's charge. However, now that you are here we can all hear the charges. The charges will be read after we review the preliminary investigation with Judge Joseph Tinnus. I thought, Judge Tinnus is a good friend of J.C.'s. If he presides and J.C. is an official part of the defense counsel and the judge does not disqualify himself, this little item may be used on an appeal if we lose.

We entered the courtroom and in a few minutes Judge Joseph Tinnus entered. The bailiff called for the room's occupants to stand. The judge slammed his gravel onto his elevated pedestal and the proceedings began. The judge reviewed the preliminary investigation and began reading the charges against Jason.

"As a result of an investigation by the sheriff's department the evidence clearly indicates involvement of Mr. Jonathan Jason. This court finds sufficient evidence to charge Mr. Jason." The bailiff went to Jason and asked him to stand. "It is my duty to charge you, Mr. Jonathan Elmer Jason, with murder in the second degree for the murder of one Luther Quigly on September 10 at the home of Mr. Thomas Thorndike, 1660 Rue Hill Lewisburg, Pennsylvania. Secondary charges to this writ of murder include tampering with evidence, movement of the murder victim's body to obscure the motive for murder, and the removal of evidence of the crime from the scene of the crime. How does the defendant plead?"

"Your Honor," John and Jason stood up and faced the judge. Jason said, "I plead not guilty to all charges."

"The court remands the prisoner to the custody of the sheriff of this county, pending trial."

I raised my hand to signal the judge and pleaded. "Your Honor, may we have a date for a bail hearing?"

"Very well, counsel, the first open date is late September. I shall set the bail hearing for 9:00 A.M. September 30th in this courtroom." The judge slammed his gavel down and ended the preliminary hearing.

"Ms. Carodine, I will fight against bail for Jonathan Jason. He is not a United States citizen and I think he may try and leave the country if he has an opportunity."

"That is nonsense, Mr. Hightower. Jason has interests in the United States and I assure you, he will not leave the country until his personal matters are settled."

"Then I will demand at least a million dollar bail."

"Mr. Hightower, *why don't you let the judge make that decision!* I'll see you in court. I also want to meet with my client before he is taken back to your smelly jail."

"Very well, Ms. Carodine. It appears our lines have been drawn. Good luck with your defense."

"Thanks, Hightower. I want disclosure of evidence, a copy of the police investigation, and a list of witnesses you intend to question — before the bail hearing."

Jason was visibly upset. The stiff British upper lip had begun to quiver.

"Miss Chelsea, what does all this mean? I cannot understand what has happened. How can the authorities charge me with a crime I did not commit?"

"Jason, we have a great deal of work to do. Have you thought out what happened on September 10th?"

"Yes, Miss Chelsea. I have reconstructed every detail within my mind. I am ready to discuss that day with you now."

"John, get your tape recorder ready. I want every word on tape. OK, Jason, proceed. And don't leave out anything, no matter how insignificant you may think it to be."

Jason very carefully reconstructed every detail of the day. He began at 2:00 P.M. the day preceding the event. Mr. Thorndike asked Jason to contact the corporate office and request Mr. Quigly meet with him at 3:00 P.M. the following day. Jason placed the call to Quigly's secretary, Karen King, and arranged the meeting.

"Jason, did you know if a gun was in the house?"

"Of course, Miss Chelsea. Both the master and I maintained pistols in our bedrooms. It was simply a matter of security to have the pistols in the mansion."

"What happened to the gun you kept in your bedroom, Jason?"

"Why, Miss Chelsea, I presume the pistol is still in my lockup."

"Where would that be, Jason?"

51

"Miss Chelsea, I have a painting of Buckingham Palace hanging to the left of my bed. The painting opens to the right and inside is a holder for the pistol."

"John, after we finish here, call for a sheriff's deputy to meet you at the mansion. Check for the gun, but don't disturb anything. Wait until the deputy arrives and show him where Jason said he kept the gun. Take your camera and use it before the painting is moved. Take a couple of pictures when the deputy opens it and finds the gun."

"Chelsea, there is still the question of the second gun that was supposedly in Mr. Thorndike's bedroom. Do you have any clues as to how we find that one?"

"One thing is sure, the police apparently don't have it. I don't have any ideas as to how it disappeared, but it must be found. It may be the key to proving Jason didn't fire a weapon."

John asked, "Jason, did the police take paraffin tests of your hands?"

"Mr. John, I don't know. My hands were scraped and a very gooey waxlike liquid was applied. Would that be a paraffin test?"

I answered him. "I don't know, Jason. But if that was a paraffin test, the findings will be in the report of investigation."

John was to continue reviewing the police reports and looking for any witnesses who could substantiate Jason's whereabouts just before the shots sounded. I reminded him.

"John, don't forget to question the ambulance attendants about the gun. I'm sure the police have already asked their questions, but don't be influenced by anything the police may have already completed."

"Mr. Jason," Jessica questioned, "try to remember and define exactly what you did when you first came into the room — and Mr. Jason, did you hear the gunshots?"

"Miss Jessica, I am not quite sure if the sounds I heard could be described clearly as that of a pistol firing. I was downstairs in the pantry area preparing Mr. Thorndike's afternoon tea when I heard two loud noises."

"What did the noises sound like, Jason?" Jessica asked.

"Rather loud, as if an automobile 'fired back' as you Americans would say."

"But Jason," John said, "the police stated there was only one shot accounted for. Since they don't have the gun or spent shell casings they are guessing as to the exact number."

"Mr. John, the noises I heard seemed to be two very loud noises. I did not sense any noises that I could without question classify as pistol shots." Jason continued with the description of the scene.

"I shrugged off the loud noises since I could not identify them. I prepared the tea and took it to the master's bedroom. As I opened the door I saw this Mr. Quigly person lying across the master at the foot end of the bed."

"Now Jason," I said, "tell us exactly what you did."

"Miss Chelsea, I was in total shock. I stood frozen, not able to move myself until I heard the master call out for help. I must have instinctively lifted Mr. Quigly's body to the floor to free the master."

The penetrating questions caused Jason to stop and wonder about his actions. John asked him to try and remember exactly where he had touched Quigly, then continued questioning Jason about the gun.

"Jason, did you see a gun at that point in time?"

"Mr. John, I was only concerned with the master, I didn't look for a pistol. I was not completely sure what had taken place. I do remember there was a very strong smell, a smell I experienced once before in my life, yes, it smelled like expended gunpowder."

Jason said he had placed Mr. Thorndike on his pillows at the head of the bed. Mr. Thorndike then told Jason to call his doctor and the police, and take the tape recorder and tape to me at the corporation's offices. After he made the telephone calls, Jason said he immediately departed the mansion and came directly to my office. He did not know whether Quigly was dead or alive when he left. I tried to assure Jason we would be doing everything possible to have him released and freed of the charges. He said he had faith in our courage to defend him, but he could not trust an institution such as the American justice system that he knew nothing about. I sent Jessica and John on to continue the investigation.

5 Shortly after Jason had been charged, Morgan had left messages with Linda for me to meet him at our special restaurant for lunch. Our special place! I wondered if Morgan had something grand to tell me. We always shared the good things in our lives at our place. Morgan was waiting for me at the entrance. He greeted me with a peck-like kiss to the lips and told me he loved me. What a wonderful relief in my hectic life: to have a husband who loves me and trusts me and, more importantly, is not jealous of my position as head of the corporation. I thought, how lucky can one woman be!

Morgan always greeted me with the same expression.

"Hi, beautiful. How's my wonderful wife and mother of my children?"

"Just wonderful, Morgan. Morgan, do you know how much I really love you?"

"Well, I do have a short memory. Do you care to repeat it?"

"Morgan, stop playing with me. You know I love you with all my heart."

"Well, that's nice. How about a nice meal? And let's start with a nice bottle of wine."

"Morgan, is there something special you have to say to me — are we just having a dinner together because we love each other?"

"No, sweetheart, I don't have anything earth-shattering, but we just don't seem to have much time together. And I know the kids miss time with us."

"You're right, Morgan. We have to readjust our schedules and make time for us and the kids. Jason's trial and what is happening in the corporation both are very much on my mind these days."

"Yes, I know, sweets. You're carrying a big load."

"Morgan, let's just pack up, get Sylvia and the kids, and go to the mountains this afternoon. Jason's bail hearing is not until September 30. J.C., John, and Jessica can continue work on the case. Honey, I really need a break."

"Chelsea dear, that's a grand idea. OK, babe, let's do it this afternoon! When we finish our meal, I'll go home and pack. If you need to talk with Linda about any pressing problems, do it and come on home. I'll have us ready to go and we will leave tonight, OK?"

"Oh, Morgan, yes, yes. Give me a couple of hours and I'll be home and we will take off to the high country."

I called Linda from the restaurant and she met with me at the office. I also called John and Jessica to discuss what was next in Jason's trial. I really felt I shouldn't leave with the trial going on. But, what if I were sick? Could the case and the corporation really go on without me? I thought, Chelsea, get real. You're trying to be everything to everyone. Be a real chief executive officer — delegate to your second in command and give the two young lawyers an opportunity to show what they are

54

made of in Jason's defense. Linda lined up the signature items and I delegated the rest of the work to the directorates and divisions. I talked with John and Jessica and they felt comfortable handling Jason's defense with J.C.'s support. In less than the two hours Morgan had given me, I was on my way home to join my family for a trip to the mountains.

The children were elated about the trip and fun in the mountains with the family. Sylvia, our housekeeper, is such a wonderful person with Chelsea Lyn and the boys. Sometimes I feel a little jealous of her because she seems more like the mother than I do. I have to accept what time I can be with the children and keep my job from robbing me of all their growing-up time. We sang songs for the three hours it took to reach the cabin, a complete mountain home that we use in the summer and the winter months. The weather was clear but cold. We built a fire and all sat about as Sylvia prepared our dinner. The time with Chelsea Lyn, Raynor and Caesar, and Morgan seemed to refresh my soul and let me know how wonderful our life is and how happy our children are.

The next day Chelsea Lyn and I went for a walk along the trail by the lake. I had so much time to make up as a mother to her. As we walked along she told me about school and the silly things a 15-year-old thinks about. We had often talked about boy-girl relationships and her goals in life. She said she wants to be a doctor, but she's not sure of the specialty.

As we walked along she shocked me with questions I had not anticipated.

"Mother, one day shall we talk about my early life with Mother Kersi and Father Abel?"

"Chelsea, my dear, dear girl. Is something troubling you?"

"Well, you know how involved we were in the church … "

"Yes, dear, and you aren't going to church very regularly now, are you?"

"Well, no, Mother. I would feel so good if we all could go as a family, I mean going regularly to a church."

"Yes, dear, I understand, and we will. Your father and I have discussed our work schedules and we have decided to spend more time with you and the boys — and Chelsea Lyn, my dear, we shall go to church together as a family."

"Oh, Mother, that is grand. I do miss going to church and praying like I did with Father Abel and Mother Kersi. Oh, thank you, Mother."

We held hands and continued our walk. The mountain air was so clear and clean I could almost taste heaven. The leaves had fallen from the trees and the branches and trunks appeared to be stretching their arms out to us, calling us to come to them. It was almost frightening to us as the sun sank and the night became dusk and then dark. I thought of Abel's sermons, one in particular: "and a child shall lead …." And now my child will lead her family to church.

After the wonderful dinner Sylvia had prepared we sat around the fire and told ghost stories. The boys cuddled up with me and Chelsea Lyn insisted her father keep her safe and hold her. I can see the love and loyalty between Morgan and Chelsea Lyn. She now has a real father who loves her and wants everything for his little girl.

When the children had gone to bed Morgan and I put our jackets on and sat on the cabin porch. I told him about my conversation with Chelsea Lyn. He said she had the same conversation with him. He told her we could talk about going back to church when we were in the mountains. Morgan had set her up to talk with me. I wondered why he had not talked with me about their conversation. I asked, "Morgan, why didn't you tell Chelsea Lyn we would go to church? You didn't really have to wait for me to decide."

"Chelsea, our little daughter has said her prayers with me every night since she has been with us. She is a very devout little Christian. You had to hear her talk about church … "

"Morgan, honey, you don't have to wait for me to decide what we are going to do."

"Honey, I know how busy you are. I mean, now with Jason's trial, you don't have a minute you can call your own. Really, Chelsea Lyn and I planned this trip very secretly."

"Morgan, you are so wonderful. Do you think I can repay you tonight?"

"Well, my lady, do I understand you are trying to make out with me?" He pulled me to him and began kissing me very hard. His hands went slowly down my body until he had me pushed close into him. He kissed my neck and ears and caressed my hair as he held my head in his hands. His mouth was very hot. He began to breathe very deeply and excitedly. I thought, we had better go to our bedroom before one of the children or Sylvia needs a drink of water. I didn't want this magical moment to end. Morgan picked me up and carried me into the bedroom. He always likes to undress me. I only make the movements required to remove my clothes. In a few moments we were cuddled up under the covers. He continued his hot, passionate kisses. Our bodies were interlocked as if we were one. Morgan has such a deep penetrating love. I felt his love to the depths of my soul.

Our lovemaking set my mood for the few days we had together here in the mountains. We had a wonderful adventure with the children. We became acquainted as a family again. And yes, Chelsea Lyn, my darling daughter, *we shall go to church!*

6 The corporate directors' meeting, the first since the reading of Mr. Thorndike's will, was scheduled for September 30 at 9:00 A.M. I didn't have time to review the agenda until I arrived at the board meeting. One item on the agenda struck me as being very political: "The board to consider a leave of absence of the CEO pending the completion of Mr. Jason's trial." The composition of the board had remained the same. I was very suspicious why someone on the board wanted me away from the corporation until Jason's trial was over. As the board members entered the room each one greeted me with extreme courtesy. I thought, Chelsea, stop mistrusting the board's motives until you know what is happening.

The meeting was called to order, the last minutes read and approved, and then we moved on to unfinished business. Alex Putman had served as the secretary and now was the senior member of the board; he had conducted previous board meetings for Mr. Thorndike. He began, "Chelsea, the board is aware you have undertaken the defense of Jason, Mr. Thorndike's butler. We understand he has been charged with the murder of Mr. Quigly, a former executive of Thorndike Corporation."

"Yes, that is true, Mr. Putman."

"Chelsea, the board would entertain a motion to grant you a leave of absence from corporate management until the trial is completed."

"Mr. Putman, I am quite capable of continuing my duties as the CEO and directing Jason's defense as well."

"Chelsea, we as board members are very concerned about the adverse publicity the corporation may receive while you are acting as leader of Jason's defense team." I didn't know what Putman's intentions were, but I was not going to step down for anyone.

"Mr. Putman, I assure the board that the corporation will not escape the adverse publicity of the trial whether I take the leave of absence or not. And may I thank the members of the board for your concern. However, I shall remain active as the CEO of Thorndike as well as head the defense team for Jason."

"Chelsea, are you aware of our charter's guidelines with respect to a deceased member who held stock in the corporation?" Putman asked.

"May I ask what specifically you are referring to?"

"The corporate stock willed to you by Mr. Thorndike must remain within the control of the board for a period of thirty days following his death. Additionally, the five million dollars in stock Mr. Thorndike willed to the City of Lewisburg is open public stock for the same thirty-day period. This stock may be purchased by the corporate board or by individual board members."

"Mr. Putman, just what is your point?"

"My point, Chelsea, is that you are not yet in control of your stock and the board controls 35% of the resident stock. The five million in stock left to Lewisburg has been purchased by two other board members. Therefore, Chelsea, control of the corporation during the waiting period rests with the majority stockholders on the board."

"So, gentlemen — if I understand you all — as a board, you want me to step down as the CEO for the next couple of weeks."

"Please don't put it so harshly, Chelsea. We are only thinking of the corporation." Putman smirked as he finished his statement.

"Gentlemen, I ask that you delay any vote on the matter until I have had time to consider your proposal to remove me from my position."

"Of course, Chelsea, but I suggest we set another board meeting for two days from now to complete this action."

"Thank you, gentlemen, that is just fine with me. Can we move on to other business now?"

The board secretary detailed each item of new business. I directed actions be taken on the location of new production plants in the southern part of the state; the hiring of a lobbyist to represent Thorndike Corporation with the federal government's health plan; the realignment of the manufacturing division from eight to fourteen new product lines; and several other new items. I was surprised not to be opposed on any of the items. I thought, maybe the board is simply trying to appease me for the next two days and then reject my directions.

The board meeting ended and as the members filed out, several of them pledged the same loyalty to me as they had given Mr. Thorndike. I knew I now had a number of powerful enemies on the board. I must stay a step ahead of them and maintain control of the corporation.

I went directly to the law division to see J.C., my old chief and still a loyal supporter. As I explained what happened he became very excited and said, "Chelsea, I shall get an injunction against Putman and the board to cease and desist their actions until the waiting period passes. I can keep them tied up in court, with you still in as CEO, until the stock is released from the corporate charter's hold."

"How soon can you get the injunction, J.C.?"

"I will file by tomorrow. Judge Joseph Tinnus is an old classmate of mine. He's also the night duty judge for the next few days. And, I may add, he is also presiding over Jason's trial. He will sign the injunction. Shall I have it served on Putman?" I thought, so Judge Tinnus is J.C.'s very real buddy!

"No, J.C., I'll serve it personally at the next board meeting. And J.C., check out Putman's holdings and strength with the other board members. I want to know my opposition when I walk into the board meeting on Thursday."

I wondered again if my gender had prompted Putman and company to oppose me. What do they have to gain to remove me from the CEO position? For a moment, I felt the same pressures from males that I'd had to overcome as I was trying to climb the corporate ladder. I hoped this power play by Putman and his cronies would reveal itself along gender lines. I could really fry them if they were trying to silence me because I am female. No, I thought, they can't be that naive. They want control of the corporation for some other reason. I must know what they are trying to do.

Early on Thursday J.C. came to my office with the injunction, signed by his former classmate and filed in the superior court. He also had a report on Putman.

"Chelsea, Putman was the person who convinced Mr. Thorndike to go public with the corporation back in '75. As soon as the stock was listed on the New York Stock Exchange, Putman and his partners purchased 35% of the stock at its first offering."

"Did Mr. Thorndike know what Putman and company had done?"

59

"Only after the deal had been consummated, and from all reports the old man was furious with Putman. Shortly after that incident, Putman and his partners offered Mr. Thorndike twice the New York Stock Exchange price for an additional 22% of his stock."

"What did Mr. Thorndike do?"

"He traded with other holders and bought up all but the 35% still controlled by Putman and his partners, and this put the corporation back in the hands of private stockholders."

"J.C., Putman said that two members of the board had purchased the 5% stock left to the City of Lewisburg ... "

"Not possible, Chelsea. The hold on your stock is the same on the 5% left to Lewisburg — no one can touch it until the 30-day controlled period is over."

"Then why would Putman deliberately mislead me?"

"Chelsea, I think Putman is gearing for a possible buy-out. He may have funds from another company. *Watch him!*"

"J.C., draft the papers for me to purchase the 5% stock left to Lewisburg. The city would rather have the cash than stock anyway. I can't let Putman and his group buy that stock."

"The only thing we can do at this point is to make an offer to buy the stock."

"J.C., do you have any other 'former classmates' in high places in Lewisburg?"

"Well, now that you ask, yes: the city budget director was once a lawyer with us here in the law division. I have sent quite a bit of business his way."

"J.C., at this point I will accept all the help I can muster. Please get an offer-to-buy option over to him. Let me give you a check. What would you suggest? Would $1,000,000 let him know I mean business?"

"Let me find out what Putman and group offered. I'll let you know what we need to do."

I could now better understand J.C.'s concern that I not take part in Jason's defense. I must talk with J.C. again and be ready to withdraw if things get too sticky in the boardroom. I questioned J.C. about the apparent conflict of my involvement.

"J.C., thanks for your concern about me leading the defense team. I can better understand where you are coming from."

"Chelsea, you're not only the CEO, but you are my very special friend. I watched you grow up, along with Mr. Thorndike. He often spoke of you to me. I do know how you feel about handling the defense team. But Chelsea, please be careful. Don't give Putman and his cronies any fuel for their fire."

"Thanks again, J.C. I appreciate your help and concern. I will be careful. If things get too tough for me, I'll call you immediately. We'll go whatever way you think is best at that time."

7 When I returned to my office, Linda had messages about the bail hearing which had been set for September 30 at 2 P.M. I called the district attorney and assured him I would be personally putting up the bail money for Jason and asked him to reduce his demand for the high bail. Surprisingly, he agreed his first demands were high and said he would settle for a $100,000 bail.

I had Linda call for Jessica and John to accompany me to the bail hearing. John had not returned from questioning the hospital and ambulance attendants. Jessica came to my office and the two of us appeared before the judge with Jason for the bail hearing. The district attorney did not object to my request to lower bail to $100,000. Jason was extremely happy to be free of his ordeal of incarceration with the criminal elements.

Jason returned to the Thorndike mansion to await his fate. We held long talks with him about every detail he had remembered as well as what he couldn't recall. Jason remembered Mr. Thorndike instructing him to ensure the tape was destroyed.

It was apparent Mr. Thorndike did not want the tape to fall into the wrong hands.

"Miss Chelsea, I knew if anyone else had heard the tape they would suspect that Mr. Thorndike may have caused Mr. Quigly to expire. I could never let the master's reputation be ruined by any suspicion that he would commit a crime such as murder."

"Jason, do you understand how serious this matter is? You are under indictment for the murder of Quigly. You could be convicted and sentenced to life in prison."

"Miss Chelsea, I am prepared to accept my fate, whatever it may be, in order to protect my dear departed master."

"Jason, is there anything else you may have remembered that we need to know?"

"Miss Chelsea, I believe I have covered everything I remember. I have faith in you. I know you will perform your very best for me and I shall be satisfied with whatever the outcome may be."

"Jason, please remain at the mansion. Please call and let Linda know any time you are going out. We must stay in constant contact with each other."

"I shall comply with your wishes, Miss Chelsea."

The trial date was set for October 15 in the superior court in Lewisburg. John, Jessica, and I still had a great deal to do to get ready to defend Jason.

"Boss, John is here to see you."

"Thanks, Linda. Tell him to come in."

"John, did you find Jason's gun where he said it would be?"

"Yes, and the sheriff's deputy was hot under the collar about us knowing where to find Jason's gun."

"Did you get pictures of the painting and gun, before and after?"

"Sure did. The gun was a .38 caliber revolver. It didn't look like it had been fired in years. In fact, I don't think it would fire. I asked the deputy to have the gun examined for any defects that would prevent its firing."

"Did you learn anything about the gun supposedly used to kill Quigly?"

"Yes, it also was a .38 caliber revolver which was found lodged between the bed and the wall. And it was not found *until the morning after Quigly was killed*! Since Jason's gun had not been fired, I don't think the district attorney has any information on any other gun."

"Did you get any information from the hospital staff or ambulance attendants?"

"The hospital staff was very cooperative. They answered all my questions. But frankly, all they knew was what happened after Mr. Thorndike was taken to the hospital."

"Was Mr. Thorndike still alive when he arrived at the hospital?"

"Yes, that is, barely alive — he was close to death. He was taken into the emergency room and lifesaving procedures begun. His vital functions apparently began to fail in the ambulance."

"Did you talk with Mr. Thorndike's doctor?"

"Yes, but I had a feeling that he was not being completely honest with me."

"How do you mean, John?"

"I don't know, Chelsea, just a feeling I had as he answered my questions."

"Did you find out why Mr. Thorndike was buried so quickly?"

"Chelsea, did you know that Mr. Thorndike was Jewish?"

"Why, no, John. That's a complete surprise to me. Then his burial was because he was Jewish! He had to be buried the day of his death and before sunset. I don't know much about the Jewish religion. But I think that is how the older Jewish people follow their religious rituals."

"John, did Mr. Thorndike's doctor know what had happened at the mansion?"

"Chelsea, that's part of what is bothering me. He said he didn't know anything about the circumstances of Quigly's death until later in the evening — after Mr. Thorndike had been entombed."

"Did you get the impression that Doctor Benoni was trying to hide something?"

"I really don't know. Maybe it's the prosecutor in me, suspicious of everything that I can't get a handle on."

"What about the ambulance attendants? Were you able to talk with them?"

"I talked to two of the four who responded to the call. Neither could add anything to what the doctor said."

"Did you ask about the missing gun?"

"Yes, and the two attendants I spoke with did not see a gun. But the first two attendants who arrived on the scene were out on a call and I didn't get to talk to them yet."

"Follow up on that point, John. Maybe one of them did see the gun or maybe know what happened to it."

8 I arrived at the boardroom early. The two board members who Putman had said purchased the 5% stock from the City of Lewisburg were there ahead of me. As I entered they asked to speak with me in private. About that time Putman and the other board members assembled for the meeting. I suggested they meet in my office later. I called the meeting to order and asked for a review and approval of the previous board meeting's minutes.

I shocked Putman and his partners because the minutes contained the board's recommendation, in old business, that I be placed on a temporary leave of absence from the CEO position until after Jason's trial. The minutes were approved and I called for new business. Putman was the first to stand and raise the question of my leave of absence.

"Mr. Putman, I do not accept the board's recommendation that I be placed on a temporary leave of absence. I am the CEO of the corporation and I shall remain CEO."

"Ms. Carodine, you don't seem to understand the situation. You are not in control of the stock left to you by Mr. Thorndike. Until such time as you are, the board is well within its authority to request you to step down until you have completed your assignment as defense counsel for Jason."

"Mr. Putman, may I present you and your supporters with this document?"

He took the document and looked at me with a shocked expression and said, "Why, Ms. Carodine, this is a restraining order directed toward me and three members of the board of directors. What is the meaning of this?"

"Mr. Putman, please don't insult the other members of the board and my intelligence. I am sure you can understand the restraining order enjoins you, and your associates who are named in the order, to cease and decease any action you have initiated against placing the CEO on a leave of absence. Now, may we continue with the business of running this corporation?"

After the board meeting the two directors, Jeb Keats and Harry Hawkins, who had asked to speak with me earlier accompanied me to my office. I asked Linda to serve refreshments as we sat down to talk. Keats was the first to speak.

"Chelsea, I want you to know I had no intention of joining with Putman and his associates in voting my stock against you. Putman put up the offer money and asked Harry and me to place the Lewisburg stock in our names. At the time I didn't see anything wrong with his suggestion."

"Now, Jeb, I suggested that Putman was not being honest with us. I suspected he was going to try a power move on Chelsea."

"You're correct, Harry. I should have suspected him of some underhanded tactic, but I have known him for a long time. He's always been honest in the past."

"Thank you, gentlemen, for being honest with me. I welcome your support. I have an offer out to buy the Lewisburg stock. If Putman asked you two to make the offer, I would appreciate you withdrawing your present offer. I have a few more days of the control time and I intend to make recommendations for the restructuring of the board of directors."

"Chelsea, we want you to know we are with you. Jeb and I each hold 7% of the stock, and with our 14% added to your 65% I think you can do just about what you want to do."

"I intend to proceed with the realignment of the southern plant and the restructuring of the corporation as indicated in the minutes of the board meeting prior to this last meeting."

I thought to myself, over another hurdle. I still wonder if Putman was going after me because I am a woman. I guess it doesn't matter now. Thanks to J.C., I won this battle.

9 We talked with Jason again and he continued to remember a little more than before. The police report stated Quigly was killed with a .38 caliber revolver. That explains the missing shell casings: a revolver does not expel shell casings. They are still in the revolver, wherever it is. Jason couldn't remember the type of gun Mr. Thorndike owned. A tracing of the registration revealed he had purchased a .38 caliber revolver. The police report of the shooting indicated powder and nitrate residue were found on Quigly's hands and gunpowder was found on his clothing.

As we reviewed the evidence the three of us wondered how the district attorney was going to present his case against Jason. The police did blot Jason's hands for powder and nitrate and only a small amount of either substance was found. We became more puzzled with each review of the evidence. We sat in the office and built scenario after scenario to try and outguess what the district attorney was going to present.

"Chelsea, powder and nitrate residue are only detectable for a few hours after a person fires a weapon, and the time can be shortened if any cleaning compound is used to remove the residue."

"John, new techniques will reveal traces of these substances long after a person fires a weapon. We just don't know if Jason fired a gun or was so close to one being fired that he collected the residue on himself."

"Chelsea," Jessica said, "Mr. Thorndike's doctor was a coroner in Florida before he went into private practice here in Lewisburg. I am sure he is still up-to-date on police procedure when a homicide is suspected. His reluctance to talk with John may be because he knows something he doesn't want to reveal."

"You could be right, Jessica. Go back to the hospital and go over the evening with him again. Be sure and tell him you are working with me on Jason's defense. He may remember a few more things that took place that he didn't discuss with John. Be specific with him about his preparing Mr. Thorndike for burial."

The date of the trial arrived and we were very anxious about doing battle with the district attorney. We reviewed the reports, talked with the same people the police had talked with, and still couldn't come up with anything that really incriminated Jason except possibly his impulsive move of Quigly's body.

The first two days were consumed selecting a jury to hear the case. The Thorndike Corporation is one of the major manufacturing industries in Lewisburg and many of the townspeople crowded the courtroom to witness the events of the trial.

John and I were at the defense table with Jason. J.C. sat immediately behind us so he could offer counsel if needed. Hightower had two assistants with him at the prosecutor's table. The clerk called the court up as the judge came into the courtroom. As the gavel fell, we knew we were in for a battle; we hoped we were ready for it.

The judge said, "Is the prosecution ready to proceed with the state's case against defendant Jonathan Jason?"

"We are, Your Honor," replied District Attorney Hightower.

"Is the defense ready to proceed with the case?"

John replied, "We are, Your Honor."

"Does the prosecution have an opening statement?"

"Yes, we do, Your Honor." Hightower turned to the jury and began his presentation of what the state hoped to prove, that Jason had committed the murder of Quigly.

"Ladies and gentlemen of the jury, the state will prove motive, opportunity, and capability, and that the accused murdered Luther

66

Quigly. The state may concede that the motive that drove the defendant to kill was to protect his longtime employer, Mr. Thomas Thorndike. In addition, the state will introduce another aspect of a motive, which we believe was to protect the reputation of the corporation and unnamed individuals in the corporation. Anyone can see by the defendant's size that he possesses the strength to have committed murder.

"The state's witnesses will further prove the defendant attempted to cover up his crime by altering evidence and disposing of the murder weapon. Ladies and gentlemen, I am sure you will find the evidence sufficient to prove beyond any reasonable doubt that the defendant, Jonathan Elmer Jason, is guilty of murder in the second degree. Thank you."

"Does the defense wish to make an opening statement?"

"We do, Your Honor." John proceeded toward the jury to begin our opening statement. We had talked about the points to cover, but we also would counter any claims the prosecution would make. We did not discuss our plan of attack before John began his opening statement.

"Ladies and gentlemen of the jury, this is a murder trial. The state has accused an honorable gentleman of a crime that he could not have committed.

"The defendant was a loyal employee of the Thorndike Corporation and its founder, Mr. Thomas Thorndike, for a period of 25 years. We do not doubt the prosecution's statement that the defendant may have acted out of loyalty to his employer; however, the state must prove, and I emphasize *must prove*, beyond a *reasonable doubt*, that the defendant, Jonathan Elmer Jason, did in fact commit a crime. The evidence the prosecution will present is entirely circumstantial. There were no witnesses to the crime the district attorney claims was committed. The investigative procedures used to collect any physical evidence they may have were flawed and very untimely.

"Testimony will show that several persons contaminated the crime scene before the arrival of the police. The weapon used to kill Luther Quigly is claimed to be a .38 caliber revolver owned by the deceased Mr. Thorndike. You will hear witnesses claim they heard two loud sounds, possibly from two different pistols. Only one of those weapons was found. A second weapon has not been found. I am sure, ladies and gentlemen, you will find for the defendant not guilty once you have heard and evaluated the evidence. Thank you for your kind attention."

"The prosecution may call your first witness," the judge directed.

"The prosecution calls Detective Sergeant James Smith." The witness was sworn by the clerk.

"Sergeant Smith, you are employed by the Lewisburg County Sheriff's Department, are you not?"

"Yes, sir."

"Please tell the court what you discovered when you arrived at Mr. Thorndike's home on the afternoon of September 10."

"Well, sir, a Mr. Luther Quigly was found shot to death in the upper bedroom of Mr. Thorndike's home."

"Where specifically did you find the body? And were there any marks on it?"

"The body was lying at the left of the foot of the bed. The victim had one bullet in his chest. We also found deep bruises and scratch marks on the neck of the victim."

"Sergeant Smith, did you identify how or who shot the victim?"

"Yes, sir, we believe Jonathan Jason shot the victim." He looked at Jason with an accusing stare.

"*Objection*, the witness is not competent to testify that the defendant shot anyone. The witness has no personal knowledge of any evidence linking Mr. Jason to the shooting."

"Sustained. The district attorney is cautioned to lay a proper foundation for his questions," the judge responded. Hightower nodded his head.

"Sergeant Smith, do you have any evidence as to who or what caused the bruise marks on Mr. Quigly's body?" Again, that same hard stare.

"We believe Mr. Jason did. We found skin and hair of the deceased under the nails of the defendant."

"And is that the reason you say the defendant killed Quigly?"

"Yes, sir."

"Objection, Your Honor, calls for speculation on the part of the witness."

"Objection sustained. The prosecution will rephrase the question."

"Sergeant Smith, does your evidence tie into anyone in this courtroom?"

"Yes, sir, Mr. Jason, the defendant." He pointed to Jason.

"That will be all, Sergeant. Your witness."

"Sergeant Smith," John began as he questioned him, "did the police find the weapon used to kill Mr. Quigly?"

"Yes, sir."

"Can you please tell the court where the weapon was found?"

"The .38 caliber revolver was found between the headboard and the wall."

"When did the police find the weapon, Sergeant Smith?"

"The day after the victim and Mr. Thorndike were taken from the bedroom, a search was made and the gun was found."

"And Sergeant, again, how long after the deceased was taken was the gun found?" Sergeant Smith shifted from side to side in the witness stand.

"It was found the next morning."

"Did your department check the fingerprints?"

"Yes, sir."

"And what did the police find?"

"There were no identifiable fingerprints except the one thumb print of the deceased Mr. Thorndike."

"Would you please tell the court how you made the comparisons of a deceased person's fingerprints to the weapon?"

"Yes, sir. Mr. Thorndike possessed a government security clearance and his fingerprints were in the FBI's central fingerprint files."

"Sergeant, you are accusing Mr. Jason of murder. But are you saying you did not find the defendant's prints on the revolver?"

"No, sir, I mean ... we did not find the defendant's prints on the weapon."

"Then how can you say that Jonathan Jason fired a weapon and caused the bruises and scratches on the deceased's neck?"

"The laboratory found traces of powder and nitrate on Mr. Jason's person. In addition, the victim's neck had skin abrasions, and traces of his skin were found under the defendant's fingernails."

"And from that mere amount of evidence you concluded that Mr. Jason had committed the crime?"

"No, sir, not only from what we have presented. Mr. Jason made statements to the gardener that he was very angry with that 'Quigly person' and could extinguish the victim."

"Were there any witnesses to the shooting and the so-called mutilation of the body?"

"No, sir, no direct witnesses."

"Nothing further, Your Honor."

About the time John completed his questioning of the sergeant, Jessica came to the defense table and asked that we seek a delay. John asked to approach the bench, and Hightower joined him.

"Your Honor, some additional evidence has come to the defense's attention that must be verified. Your Honor, we feel this evidence is essential to the defense's case." The judge asked the prosecution's agreement.

"This court is adjourned. Court shall reconvene at 9:00 A.M. Monday morning. The defense is cautioned to be prepared to continue this case."

Jessica had been at Doctor Benoni's hospital. The doctor had been in a serious automobile accident and was seriously injured. When the doctor reached the emergency room he asked to speak with someone from Ms. Carodine's defense team. Jessica had been summoned to the hospital. The doctor wanted to make an official statement concerning the events in Mr. Thorndike's home when Quigly was murdered. Jessica was taken into the emergency room in the presence of two doctors and a nurse. The doctor knew he was in very critical condition. He wanted to talk to someone about what had happened at the Thorndike home.

"Doctor Benoni, I'm Jessica Roberts. I am working with Chelsea defending Jason against a murder charge. Do you have any information about the events at Mr. Thorndike's home?"

"Yes," the doctor whispered. "I took paraffin tests and nitrate samples from Mr. Thorndike and Quigly's hands while I was at the mansion. I didn't think they would be needed, but I was a medical coroner and I just did what came naturally to me at the time."

"Yes, Doctor, and what did you find, sir?"

"The tests showed that before they died, both Quigly and Mr. Thorndike had either just recently fired a weapon or had been in close contact with one as it was fired."

"Doctor, where are the results of the tests?"

"They are in my personal file, locked in my office safe."

"Doctor Benoni, how can I get a copy of the test results?"

"Let me write you an authorization to enter my safe. Give the authorization to my head nurse — she will get the test results for you."

"Ms. Roberts," the emergency room doctor said, "the doctor is failing. You must leave the room."

"Doctor Benoni, how can I get a copy of the test results?"

"Doctor, get the authorization for me, please." The staff escorted Jessica from the emergency room area. She immediately came to the courthouse to inform me and John about her discovery. She didn't get the authorization from the injured doctor.

"John, get a court order to enter Doctor Benoni's safe to get a copy of the test results of Mr. Thorndike's and Quigly's hands."

"Chelsea, that's going to take time. We must be back in court by 9:00 A.M. Monday."

I turned to J.C. who was sitting behind the defense table. If anyone can get the court order he can. I pleaded!

"J.C., I need your help again. Get the details of Doctor Benoni's paraffin tests of Quigly's and the boss's hands from Jessica. We need copies of the tests as quickly as possible. Make sure what you get is admissible in court and get it to me before court reconvenes." J.C. left the courtroom immediately.

Court reconvened promptly at 9:00 A.M. Where were J.C. and the results of the paraffin tests? The prosecutor continued with his witnesses. The gardener and two neighbors tried to discredit Jason as much as possible. The district attorney's questions were not damaging to our case and we dispensed with most responses to his charges.

The judge called the court to order and directed the prosecutor to proceed with his next witness.

"The state calls Ms. Karen King." The clerk administered the oath and the prosecutor began.

"Ms. King, where are you employed?"

"I work in the Operations Division of Thorndike Industries. Mr. Luther Quigly was my immediate supervisor."

"Ms. King, do you recall the defendant making an appointment for your boss, Luther Quigly, with Mr. Thorndike?"

"Yes, sir. Mr. Jason called Mr. Quigly's office on the 9th of September to schedule an appointment the following afternoon at 3:00 P.M. at Mr. Thorndike's home."

"Did Mr. Quigly relate to you what he said about that meeting?"

"Objection, Your Honor. The prosecution is attempting to elicit testimony from a deceased person. This is the height of hearsay evidence."

"Objection overruled, for the moment. Mr. Hightower, I will allow you to complete your questioning of this witness. But if you do not

72

"Sergeant, you are accusing Mr. Jason of murder. But are you saying you did not find the defendant's prints on the revolver?"

establish a clear direct line of questioning, I shall have this witness's testimony stricken from the record." The district attorney nodded his head in agreement to the judge.

"Ms. King," the prosecutor continued, "the question concerned Mr. Quigly's state of mind and what he said to you after you made the appointment with Mr. Thorndike. Please state in your own words what happened after the telephone call was received from the defendant."

"Well sir, Mr. Quigly was extremely jubilant. The part I remember was something like, 'I've got Chelsea Carodine just where I want her.'"

"Objection, irrelevant and hearsay." John was furious at the line of questioning. "Your Honor, the state has yet to show the relevance of bringing other people's statements into this court. The hearsay testimony, supposedly uttered by a deceased person, has no place in this trial ... "

"Sustained. Mr. Hightower, I warn you this court will not tolerate much more of your hearsay evidence."

"Your Honor, the state has another exhibit to introduce at this time which will substantiate this witness's testimony." Hightower took a cassette tape to the clerk for marking.

"The state would like this cassette tape marked as Exhibit Number 10."

"Objection, Your Honor. The state has failed to offer a foundation or to show the relevance of whatever is on the cassette tape being introduced as an exhibit in this trial."

"Before I rule," the judge stated, "Mr. Hightower, will you please explain what the tape contains and what relevance it has to this trial, and be prepared to prove its authenticity?"

"Your Honor, this tape contains the comments of Mr. Quigly immediately after the appointment was made with Mr. Thorndike on September the 9th. The state requests permission to play the tape for the jury."

"Objection, the state has not laid a proper foundation for the contents of the tape to be heard by the jury."

"Sustained. However, I shall permit the tape to be heard. I warn the prosecution once again, if the tape is not specifically relevant and does not have a direct bearing on this trial I shall disallow it and have it removed from the record. What is the source of this tape?"

"Your Honor, we have learned that it is common practice in Thorndike Industries for the executive secretaries to record conversations on their dictaphones pertaining to appointments and meetings. Ms. King's machine was left on the day of the conversation between the defendant and herself, but she failed to turn it off and subsequently recorded the voice of Mr. Luther Quigly. The prosecution discovered this evidence after the trial had begun."

"You may proceed, Mr. Hightower."

The tape was played, beginning before the appointment was made between Ms. King and Jason, and then Quigly's voice was loud and clear: "I finally have the great CEO Chelsea Carodine just where I want her and she's going to …." The tape stopped before Quigly's comments were concluded.

"Your Honor, objection! Irrelevant and immaterial. The defense strongly objects to the contents of this tape becoming a part of the record of this trial. It has no bearing, whatsoever, of the charges before this court."

"Sustained. Mr. Hightower, either you explain to this court what relevance the tape has or I shall have the entire testimony stricken from the record."

"Your Honor, the defendant's motive for the murder of Luther Quigly has been established by this tape. The state contends the defendant committed this crime out of loyalty — to protect Thomas Thorndike, Chelsea Carodine, and the Thorndike Corporation."

The judge looked toward the witness box and excused Ms. King. He called the defense and prosecution to the bench.

"Gentlemen, I will meet with you in my chambers to discuss this last witness's testimony and the admissibility of the contents of the tape."

Once in the chambers, their discussion began. The judge spoke first.

"Mr. Hightower, your foundation for the evidence presented through your witness, Ms. King, is very questionable. Your motive theory lacks opportunity and capability of the defendant. In order for this evidence to be accepted by the court you must prove the 'loyalty' aspect, which you have failed to do."

"Your Honor, the defense has listed the defendant as a witness to testify on his own behalf. The state would then prove the 'loyalty' theory through cross-examination of the defendant."

"Your Honor, the defense has not decided, as of now, to call the defendant to testify. Therefore, we request that the tape recording and the testimony of the witness, Ms. Karen King, be stricken from the record."

"Mr. Hightower, you leave me no alternative but to disallow the tape and the testimony since you failed to lay a proper foundation for the evidence."

"But Your Honor, these are the facts! The state still contends the defendant acted out of loyalty when he killed Luther Quigly. We will admit he was attempting to protect his employer. But the fact remains, the defendant did commit the crime."

"Your Honor, the state has not proven its case. Neither the tape nor the testimony of the last witness has any relevance to the trial before this court."

"Counselors, the hour is late. Shall we return to the courtroom so that I may adjourn the court for the day?" The court was adjourned.

The prosecution completed its case the following day. The most damaging evidence was the gunpowder residue and Quigly's flesh found under Jason's fingernails.

One of the scenarios we had worked out pictured Mr. Thorndike and Quigly struggling over the gun that killed Quigly. We couldn't get the pieces to fit. Quigly was a much bigger man than Mr. Thorndike, and the boss had been ill. We could not imagine Mr. Thorndike taking a gun from Quigly.

Another of our scenarios had Quigly drawing Mr. Thorndike's gun to threaten Mr. Thorndike. As he neared Mr. Thorndike, the old man grabbed the gun, it turned into Quigly and went off. The one bullet that had been accounted for was lodged in Quigly's chest, critically wounding him. If Mr. Thorndike had grabbed the gun, he and Quigly would have had the gunpowder residue on their hands and clothes. This theory now had some substance. Once we have the test results we may be able to build a case around the theory.

Court was reconvened and we now had our opportunity to present our defense of Jason. John called the county medical coroner as our first witness.

"Doctor Pickins, did you examine the body of Luther Quigly after his death?"

"Yes. Any person whose death results from a violent act, that is, by gunshot or other means must be medically examined by my office."

76

"Doctor, please tell the court what your findings were in the examination of Luther Quigly's body."

"The deceased had been shot in the chest with a .38 caliber pistol. In addition, bruise marks and several scratches were about the deceased's neck."

"Doctor, could the bruises and scratches have been inflicted accidentally after the victim's death?"

"Yes, that is possible. The coagulation of the blood did indicate they could have been inflicted after the victim was clinically dead."

"Thank you, Doctor. Your witness."

The prosecutor asked, "Doctor, how sure are you of your findings that the debris found under Mr. Jason's fingernails actually came from a deceased person?"

"I would say about 95% confidence factor that the skin was from a deceased person."

"Thank you. No further questions."

"Will the defense and prosecution approach the bench?" came directions from the judge.

"Gentlemen, the hour is late. I suspect the questioning of the next witness will consume a great deal of time. I prefer we begin this questioning at the opening of the court tomorrow at 9:00 A.M. Do you gentlemen agree?"

"The prosecution has no objections, Your Honor."

"The defense agrees, Your Honor."

"This court stands in recess until 9:00 A.M. tomorrow."

We were relieved. Another day gives us more time to get the results of the tests on Quigly's and Mr. Thorndike's hands and to construct a firm defense case. Jason was also relieved. We still had not abandoned the possibility that Jason would testify. We had not informed him that we did not intend for him to testify.

We had to rework our theory. John, Jessica, and I agreed to replay the fatal day at Mr. Thorndike's mansion. We had to know exactly how Jason had pushed Quigly's body from Mr. Thorndike after he had been shot. The matter of the missing gun was another area we had to pin down. John was assigned to find the two ambulance attendants who had been first on the scene and question them. We agreed to meet at Mr. Thorndike's at four to develop our final scenario.

CHAPTER THREE
THE TRIAL

1 John and Jessica met me at the Thorndike mansion promptly at four o'clock. We rang the bell and waited for Jason to answer the door. After what seemed like a long time, Jason opened the door and said, "Miss Chelsea, I am sorry to have kept you waiting. You must see what the police have cordoned off as the 'crime scene' and you will understand my delay in responding to your ring."

"Not to worry, Jason. You remember John and Jessica, your defense team?"

"Why, yes, of course, Miss Chelsea. I am very grateful for your assistance on my behalf against these awful charges. My sincere appreciation for your kindness."

"Jason, I realize we have been over what happened here at the mansion several times, but the three of us still have unanswered questions as to what could have taken place. We want to examine every inch of Mr. Thorndike's bedroom. The police could have missed something very essential to our case."

"Miss Chelsea, I shall assist in any manner you choose. But should we enter the crime scene without police permission?"

"Don't worry, Jason, we have permission to be here."

"Very well, Miss Chelsea, this way please." We followed Jason into the mansion.

"Jessica, review everything in the entire mansion. Make note of the different paths to the bedroom from the front entrance. John and I'll go on with Jason to the bedroom. Meet us there when you finish here.

"Jason, before we go to the bedroom, take us to where you were when you heard the loud noises you thought might have been an automobile backfire."

"Miss Chelsea, as I have stated, there were two such noises, one immediately after the other."

"Jason, the police found only one bullet, and that one was in Quigly's chest."

"I beg your pardon, Miss Chelsea. I distinctly heard two such noises."

"Did you tell the police about the two noises?"

"Yes, Miss Chelsea, but I sincerely believe they doubted my word."

We followed Jason to the pantry, as he labeled it, really the kitchen. He said he was standing at the window overlooking the garden and polishing one of the silver services when he heard the noises. He was waiting for the water to boil for the tea he was to serve to Mr. Thorndike and Quigly. We retraced his path to Mr. Thorndike's bedroom on the second floor. Jason estimated he didn't leave the pantry until five minutes or so after he heard the noises. He then went to Mr. Thorndike's bedroom.

"Jason, which way did you take to the bedroom?"

"I took the south corridor. I remember the Richardson's maid waving good-bye as I passed the windows." I wonder if Jessica has spoken to the Richardson's maid?

"Jason, when Jessica comes to the bedroom, we want you to slowly go over your movements and anything you might have said. I realize this is probably the tenth time you have recited what happened. But we do need you to do it one more time."

"Miss Chelsea, every time I recount that horrible day I seem to think of another item, or change some item that I remembered. I beg you to forgive me for any inconsistency in what I may remember."

"I understand, Jason. But try very hard to remember everything very accurately for us, will you please?"

"I shall do whatever you wish, Miss Chelsea."

We returned to the pantry and Jason walked, very deliberately, along the route he traveled to Mr. Thorndike's bedroom. He said he rapped loudly and immediately opened the door. He explained what he found. His expression changed from the very formal one, with which he had greeted us, to one of sadness. Tears formed and ran down his kingly British cheeks. He reached for his handkerchief and said, "You must forgive me, Miss Chelsea, I have been weakened by one of these awful American colds and I must wipe my eyes periodically."

"I understand, Jason. We all have contracted colds since Mr. Thorndike passed away."

Jessica met us at the entrance of the bedroom. I told Jason to tell us exactly what he had seen.

"As I entered the bedroom I saw this man Quigly lying on top of the master."

"Jessica, you act the part of Quigly and I will be Mr. Thorndike. Now, Jason, show us exactly how Quigly was lying on Mr. Thorndike."

"Well, Miss Chelsea, the master was lying with his face toward the south window, in this direction. Mr. Quigly was lying face down on top of him, facing north. The positions seemed to indicate one of the two pulled the other one forward when the loud noises sounded. They were here. Lie there, Miss Chelsea. Miss Jessica, lie on top of her with your head past her feet. There, that is the exact position I found them in when I entered the bedroom."

"Chelsea," John said, "there must have been some kind of struggle just before the gun went off."

"Mr. John, the master was much too weak to struggle with anyone."

"Jessica, John, what if Quigly lunged at Mr. Thorndike? Jason, you said Mr. Thorndike kept a gun in his bedroom. Where did he keep it?"

"There is a push-in compartment at the head of his bed. One presses here and the covering collapses inward. See, here is the storage area for his pistol."

"Jason," Jessica asked, "show us where you touched Quigly." Jason bent over me and placed his hand around the lower part of my neck. He said the best he could remember was that Mr. Quigly apparently had opened his shirt. When Jason reached for him, he dug into Quigly's neck and upper chest as he moved him.

"Jason, think. Did you see a gun when you entered the room, or when you pushed Quigly's body from Mr. Thorndike?" John was very determined to have Jason describe every detail of what he observed.

"Mr. John, I was not really concerned about a weapon. I became very excited when the master was buried under this giant of a man. I admit, in my haste to remove Mr. Quigly, I could have caused marks upon his upper torso."

"Jason, you said Mr. Thorndike was alive when you came to the bedroom ... "

"Yes, Miss Jessica. He spoke to me as I lifted him back to the head of his bed. I placed a pillow under his head and asked if I could make him comfortable."

"What did he say, Jason?" John asked.

"The master directed me to call his physician and the police and then travel to Miss Chelsea's office. I immediately responded to his commands, Mr. John."

I could see Jessica and John were very concerned that Mr. Thorndike would direct Jason to leave him if he were injured or thought he might

81

be dying. I hoped the subject of the tape would not come up again, but if it did I would have to take them into my confidence. I would not tell them anything of my past life. The only way I thought I could avoid disclosing the entire contents of the tape was to deal with Quigly's blackmail threat within the corporation. I thought a good offense could stop their inquiries.

"John, Jessica, the tape recording keeps coming up. Let me briefly say what was on the tape … "

John interrupted me and said firmly, "Chelsea, is the tape recording important to Jason's case?"

"I don't think the contents are important, but let me explain. I recommended Quigly for employment with Thorndike several years ago. Quigly thought he could blackmail me to have him promoted to a director's position. I did recommend him for one position, which I know I shouldn't have, but I did. I discussed the matter with Mr. Thorndike and he said he would meet with Quigly and 'take care of the matter.' You know the rest of the story. We're trying to determine what happened here in Mr. Thorndike's bedroom when Quigly was killed."

"OK, the way I see things is that we must build our case on the exact actions of Mr. Thorndike and not be concerned with any motives he may have had. I have a gut feeling that the old man did Quigly in," John said.

"Yes," Jessica joined in, "a couple of things are really important now. We must find the second gun, if there was one. And we must get Dr. Benoni's tests of Mr. Thorndike's and Quigly's hands and clothes."

"Chelsea, I am very surprised that the police did not find a second gun — only one bullet was fired from Mr. Thorndike's gun. Let's tear this bedroom apart and find that gun."

"John, I am surprised, too. Maybe the second gun was picked up by someone who was here before the police arrived — think that is a possibility?" Jessica responded.

"OK, who was here before the police arrived? I mean everyone."

"Well, Miss Chelsea, the doctor and the ambulance carriage drivers arrived just as I departed for your office."

"John, have you questioned each one of the drivers about seeing guns?"

"No, Chelsea. One of the drivers was a temporary just in from the North. I have not been able to locate him, but the other drivers are helping. I hope to hear something about him soon."

"Keep on it, John. When we finish here, get back on his trail. If he was a temporary he may have something to do with the missing gun.

"John, Jessica, look this room over, and don't miss anything. The main evidence the police have are the traces of paraffin and powder and the hair and skin under Jason's nails. The coroner testified Quigly was already dead when the marks were made on him. It is apparent Jason may have scratched Quigly when he lifted him from Mr. Thorndike."

Suddenly John called our attention to a large picture hanging to the left of the head of Mr. Thorndike's bed. It was a picture of Mr. Thorndike's father, measuring about four feet by four feet. The older Mr. Thorndike was dressed in a dark suit. On the side of the left lapel was a hole. We carefully examined the hole without disturbing the puncture marks. John lifted the painting from the wall. Embedded in the wall was a piece of lead, possibly a bullet from a gun. We were elated to find something the police had overlooked. John replaced the painting and I called the district attorney's office and reported what we found. Soon a forensic investigator arrived to view our findings. Before he removed the lead from the wall he took measurements and did triangulation drawings of the angle of entry. He surmised that the bullet came from the area of the foot of Mr. Thorndike's bed. A two-by-two-foot section of the wall was cut away to avoid damaging the slug. The forensic investigator took the wall section to the laboratory for analysis of the lead buried in the wood.

The police laboratory technician guessed the spent lead came not from Mr. Thorndike's gun, but from another .38 revolver. The missing gun! ... and one we hoped Quigly owned.

Quigly was killed by a single shot from a .38 caliber pistol registered to Mr. Thorndike. The finding of the spent lead indicated the second gun was in the bedroom and possibly fired from the foot of Mr. Thorndike's bed. We had to wait for the aging of the spent lead. It could have been there for years, possibly discharged when someone was cleaning a weapon. But we now had new clues on which we could build another set of circumstances to ponder over.

We went back to the corporation to review what we had found and to try and find answers to what had become a giant puzzle. I instructed John and Jessica to continue with the search for the second gun. Jessica was to check purchase receipts in the gun shops to see if Quigly might have purchased a .38 revolver. Police registration also had to be checked to determine if Quigly might have had a permit to carry a weapon. John was to find the fourth ambulance attendant and question him. I had to leave the team to get back to the corporation before Mr. Putman tried to depose me again.

2 When I reached my office Linda gave me an urgent message from the district attorney's office. I was to contact them as soon as possible. I called and identified myself and was overwhelmed with the news.

"Ms. Carodine, the district attorney is ill and will not be able to continue with the trial for a few days. He must know your views on a request for a continuance until next week."

"I am sorry Mr. Hightower is ill. Yes, the defense will agree with a continuance until next week." I could hardly contain my excitement. *Lord! Thank you!* We needed more time to cement our case, especially the results of the spent lead dug out of Mr. Thorndike's wall. I must call J.C. and see what he has found in Dr. Benoni's safe about the paraffin and gunpowder tests of Quigly's and Mr. Thorndike's hands and clothes.

"J.C., can you come to my office to talk about the case?"

"Yes, Chelsea, I'll be right there." J.C. rushed to my office.

"What's the story on the tests from Benoni's office?"

"I'm glad you're here, I tried to reach you at the mansion but you had left. I secured the court order to obtain the tests, but I'm being delayed by the people in the hospital. They will not respond until their lawyer reviews the case. I should have the test results by Thursday or Friday at the latest."

"That will be fine, J.C. The good Lord helped us a little: we have a continuance until next week."

"Great, Chelsea! How does the defense team see the case thus far?"

"Well, the prosecution completed its case and we are set to go with ours when court reconvenes next week. We discovered what may be key evidence to the puzzle in Mr. Thorndike's bedroom. A .38 slug was found in the wall and we are waiting for the results of the test on the lead. We hope it is from a recently fired pistol that Quigly owned."

"Then you don't have the second gun yet?"

"You're right, J.C. That would really be the clincher — if we could only find that weapon. Jessica and John are beating the bushes for it now."

84

"Chelsea, I must tell you something that came from some of my inside sources. The district attorney's office is delving into something about a blackmail scheme in the corporation involving Quigly. Do you know anything about it?"

"Well, that rotten Hightower. He's not ill — he lied to the court to get more time to dig up some dirt about the corporation."

"Chelsea, I have a feeling I am being kept in the dark on this subject. If this is anything that will affect the corporation, I must know about it before it hits the news media. Do you know, Chelsea?"

"Yes, J.C., I know about it!"

"Well, do I get to share the information?"

"J.C., this whole mess is beginning to get to me. The blackmailer was Quigly. He knew about some wild parties we had in Mexico after the Parker buy-out. After he was hired, on my recommendation I might add, he thought he could use the information from the Mexican trip to further his position in the corporation."

"And all this happened before you became the CEO ... "

"Yes, J.C., and Quigly continued with his plot after I became the CEO. But Mr. Thorndike knew the entire story because I told him about it personally."

"Chelsea, since whatever happened seems to be personal I am not really interested in the events. I do want to be assured that the corporation will not be affected if the information becomes public."

"J.C., what Quigly had was conjecture on his part. He saw me in the company of several people while I was in Mexico. Matthew Glyndon acted as an interpreter and I was a witness for Quigly and Magda to get married while we were in Mexico. We were all partying and having fun. J.C., a few of the people on the trip were married and without their spouses. I am sure things happened throughout the group that would not bear close examination by their husbands or wives without some emotional damage to their relationships."

"Face it, Chelsea! Material like that could be damaging to you and Jason, if Jason knew about it before Quigly came to the mansion. Watch it carefully!"

"J.C., the subject of blackmail was also introduced in the prosecutor's opening statement. He tried to use Karen King's tape of Quigly's voice that suggested he 'had me where he wanted me.' The judge discussed the tape in his chambers with the prosecution and John, and the judge threw it out. The prosecution may try again with one of our witnesses."

"Well, whatever happened really shouldn't affect the case since both Glyndon and Quigly are dead. What can be said?"

God, did it hurt me when J.C. reminded me that Matthew was dead. I had to turn away to the window to keep from showing the emotion that was plainly clear in my face. I can't stand it when anything is said about Matthew. What a situation I'm in. I'm trying to protect the reputations of two men whom I loved dearly and who are both dead.

"Chelsea, wait a minute! You said Mr. Thorndike knew about Quigly blackmailing you. The prosecution could use a motive of Jason protecting the reputations of you, Thorndike, and the corporation. But now it is conceivable that Mr. Thorndike killed Quigly! Not Jason!"

"No! J.C.! Oh, I don't know. I really don't want to believe Mr. Thorndike killed Quigly, but that seems to be the only logical explanation."

"What about self-defense! Chelsea, that second gun must be found. If Quigly owned the gun and had it with him when he visited Mr. Thorndike, he may have threatened the old man."

"J.C., can you meet with John, Jessica, and me this afternoon? I'll have Linda find them and we can try and build a new approach to the case."

"Sure, Chelsea. Let me know when you are ready."

"Linda, track down John and Jessica and get them here by 4:00 P.M. today."

"Will do, boss lady. Any ideas where I can find them?"

"Use your resources, lady!" We both laughed, comic-type relief.

John arrived shortly after the meeting with J.C. He didn't find the paramedic attendant. He did find a pawn shop where the missing gun had been pawned. He paid the pawn ticket and recovered the gun that was supposedly pawned by the attendant. Now the gun must be test fired and comparisons made with the lead from Mr. Thorndike's wall. What a piece of luck — really, hard work on John's part. Shortly after 4:00 P.M., Jessica arrived. The gun registration with the police revealed that Quigly had a permit to carry a concealed weapon. If he had the gun with him, why didn't he have a gun holster? Jessica also traced the purchase of a weapon by Quigly. Now we had to match the serial number of the gun John recovered from the pawn shop with the .357 magnum we think

86

Quigly owned. God, I thought, You must be helping me. Things are beginning to come together to clear Jason.

I asked J.C. if he would try to build a scenario for the defense so we could all be well-versed in what we had to present when we went back to court next week.

The three of them went to work immediately.

3 Linda, my trusted executive assistant, had all my correspondence lined up and ready to be reviewed so I could decide what action was required. Putman had sent a memo stating that the expansion of the southern plant should be delayed for a few months. His rationale seemed like a personal problem rather than a business decision. I dictated a response to Putman.

"Mr. Putman, I have reviewed your memo of the 15th. I appreciate your concern for the problems we may encounter with the southern plant expansions.

"In order to be sure we cover all areas, I am establishing a committee to review the expansion of the plant and product lines. I shall expect this committee to investigate all areas of the proposed expansion and report to the CEO and the board of directors with its findings within thirty days.

"Your vast experience with the corporation and knowledge of the specific projects makes you an outstanding candidate to chair this committee. Therefore, Mr. Putman, I ask that you become the chairman, complete the task at hand, and report to me and the board by the end of next month. Please let me have your decision by next Tuesday."

After I signed the memo I had a kindly thought that Mr. Thorndike would be proud that I am employing his tactics in dealing with the opposition. He always said, "Chelsea, when you are faced with opposition, divide it. After you divide it, then make your opposition a part of the solution rather than the problem. One's view is greater from the top looking down than from the bottom looking up."

Mr. Thorndike was a wise old man. I miss him so much! With Putman as the chairman, the committee findings will come. I will be able to keep ahead of the crest of the wave. Putman may put me on trial along with Jason if I am not careful.

J.C. had placed the offer to buy the $5 million in stock, and the two board members had withdrawn their offer. Putman was very upset that he had been outmaneuvered. He was still trying to muster support from the rest of the board members who owned bits and pieces of Thorndike stock. I don't feel he is as much a threat as before, but I will definitely not let my guard down with him again.

Morgan, as the director of Engineering and Plants, would have a direct involvement in the expansion of the southern plant and the additional product lines. I wondered if Putman's motive in trying to divest me of the power of the CEO's office may have been to remove Morgan's approval authority of the project. Morgan would have the final approval on any physical expansions, including location and size of the plants. Maybe Putman had friends who wanted to benefit from the expansion and that's why he wanted to delay it. My conjectures were kept mostly to myself. Since I have been in the man's world as a woman executive I have learned to be very cautious in dealing with men. I feel deeply inside that I am resented every time I have to do battle with the opposite gender. But, I have made up my mind: I will be professional, I will not be forced out of the CEO position. I feel I owe that to Mr. Thorndike. After the stock is released I will realign the board of directors, and only those who are willing to be professional will be retained. I don't have time for gender bickering.

There are eight Thorndike Corporation senior managers, two are women and six are men. It's strange, but the most loyal and proficient are the group of men managers. I feel myself bending more toward the women because I can understand how difficult it was for them to reach senior management positions on the basis of only their professional talents. We should be closer, if for no other reason than because we suffered through the same struggle.

I still feel good about myself! I am doing what I really want to do and I am not catering to what society nor the industry demands of women. I am at peace with myself. But I understand what the realities are for me, a woman, being the CEO of an industry like Thorndike. There may be other directions I will choose to take later in my life, but for now I am well satisfied. Thorndike is continuing to profit — as much or more than before I became the CEO. I realize my plans for Thorndike Industries will be challenged every time I propose them. The allies I am building on the board of directors and the support of my senior managers will help carry my plans through. I haven't even considered the fact that in a couple of weeks I will own the controlling stock in the corporation.

Mine is a dream world for a woman! A strong business position, never any money worries, a loving and supportive husband and three lovely children, and no outside disruptions any longer. Yes, *mine is the best of all worlds.*

4 Linda interrupted my thoughts with a buzz on the office intercom. "Boss lady, Pastor Clayborne is asking for you. Will you take his call?"

"Yes, Linda, I'll talk with him." I wondered why Abel would be calling me. We hadn't talked about how we should contact each other after Chelsea Lyn left his home to live with me. I was a little nervous when I answered the phone.

"Hello, Abel. How are you?"

"Chelsea, hello to you! I'm just fine. How are you and your family? And Chelsea Lyn — is she well and happy?"

"Thanks for asking, Abel. They are doing very well. And Chelsea Lyn seems to be a very happy young lady. I am surprised to hear from you."

"Chelsea, I hope my call is not disturbing to you. I miss Chelsea Lyn very much. Tell me, how has she adjusted to you and your husband and her new life?"

"Abel, she has made a wonderful adjustment. She seems happy and is doing very well in school. She is attending a Christian school close to where we live."

"I am happy to hear she is in a Christian school. Chelsea, do you go to church with her?"

"Abel, this is strange. She asked me last weekend if we could go to church as a family. I guess I have been to busy with my work and a criminal trial we are going through to have much time for my family. But, Abel, to answer your question, yes, we are all going to church beginning next week."

"Does Chelsea Lyn ever ask about Kersi and me?"

"No, that is, not directly. She referred to you both when she asked if we could go to church."

"Chelsea, what are you going to tell her when she questions you about both of her parents?"

"Chelsea, what are you going to tell her when she questions you about
both of her parents?"

"Oh, Abel, I really don't know. I think about it all the time. I don't know if I should tell her before she asks me, or what? I know I must tell her, but I just don't know how I'm going to do it."

"Chelsea, if you need my help, let me know. Maybe I can help you explain things to her."

"Abel, you understand that Morgan does not know who Chelsea Lyn's parents are."

"Chelsea, I can't believe that Morgan doesn't know that you're Chelsea Lyn's biological mother."

"Abel, I tried to talk with Morgan about what happened to me, but he refused to listen. I was going to tell him about Chelsea Lyn but he said he didn't want anything to disrupt the happy life he has with me and the children. No, I will not try again to explain about Chelsea Lyn."

"How are you going to keep Chelsea Lyn from talking with him after she finds out that I am her biological father?"

"Oh, Abel, please don't complicate things for me. I will have to face that situation when it happens — that is, if Morgan questions me."

"I am happy that Chelsea Lyn is doing fine. May I see her one day?"

"Yes, Abel, I will meet you some place with her. I don't think you should come to our home to see her."

"Whatever you say, Chelsea. Please call me when it is convenient for you and Chelsea Lyn to have lunch with me and talk for awhile."

"Are you still at the same telephone number?"

"Yes, it's the same number. Please call when you can. My schedule is very flexible. And thank you, Chelsea, for our child."

Abel recognized "our child" for the first time. I feel as if Abel and I are divorced. I don't really have any emotional feelings for him even though he is Chelsea Lyn's biological father. Morgan is her real father now. The two of them love each other as much as any biological father and child can love each other. Abel is right: it may not be too long before Chelsea Lyn will ask about her father. I knew that Kersi and Abel always told Chelsea Lyn that I was her real mother, but neither of them ever told me about how they may have discussed her father. I will have to talk with Abel and ask what they told Chelsea Lyn before she and I ever discuss the subject of her real father. God, don't let this discussion come up now. My mind and emotions are so filled with the business and the trial. I don't think I could stand any more.

J.C. left a message with Linda that the defense team had come up with a few new strategies and needed to talk with me about them. The trial is set to resume next week. We have a few days to get everything we need done before we present our case.

5 The prosecution's case hinged upon the gunpowder residue on Jason's clothes and the hair and skin pieces under his fingernails. Before we can build our case we must counter every bit of evidence presented. Jason admitted to moving Quigly's body. The question is, how did he get gunpowder residue on his clothes?

The coroner testified the marks made on Quigly's body were made after he was dead. In Jason's concern for Mr. Thorndike he could have used much more force than was necessary to move Quigly. The prosecution intimated in questioning that Jason may have carried through with the idle threats he made in the presence of the gardener, and killed Quigly and then disrupted the crime scene to cover up his actions. We have work to do before next week!

"Chelsea, we have worked out a couple of scenarios we need to discuss with you."

"OK, J.C. Hello, John, Jessica. So you all have been hard at work and now you have the possible solutions to the crime, right?"

"Well, I wouldn't go that far, Chelsea. But we do have a couple of plausible scenarios to discuss."

"Well, let's hear the first one."

"We know Jason called Quigly's secretary to make the appointment for him to see Mr. Thorndike," J.C. began, "so Jason knew the time of the meeting. Jason let Quigly in and Quigly must have angered Jason in some way."

John continued the story. "Jason waited outside the bedroom and listened as the two men talked. When the yelling started, which was near the end of the tape, Jason rushed in to protect Mr. Thorndike. Jason saw Mr. Thorndike with his gun out, pointing it at Quigly. Jason's presence startled Quigly and he went for Mr. Thorndike. As Quigly lunged at Mr. Thorndike the gun accidentally fired, striking Quigly in the chest. Jason grabbed Quigly and jerked him very hard away from Mr. Thorndike, which explains the deep scratches and cuts on Quigly and the hair and skin fragments in Jason's fingernails."

"OK, I'll play the devil's advocate. What about the hot tea found in the room? Did Jason go for the tea after the shooting? Jason said he heard two loud noises but he couldn't say they were pistol shots — but he said there were definitely two loud bangs. Is Jason lying to us about where he was and what he heard? No, I don't believe that description of what happened will fly. And, people, you have not even considered the second sound, the second gun, and the fact that Quigly may have fired his gun into the wall."

John said, "Chelsea, the motive for the killing could well be what was on the tape Mr. Thorndike recorded and you heard."

"What motive would that be, John?"

John replied, "Something said by Mr. Thorndike may have angered Quigly so much that he was going to use his hands to kill the old man, but Mr. Thorndike pulled the gun out of the compartment, fired and killed Quigly. If Quigly had a gun, it could have discharged as he was being shot. It is not uncommon for a person in shock from a gunshot wound to react physically. Jason was where he said he was, in the kitchen. When Jason went to the bedroom he found Quigly lying on top of Mr. Thorndike and violently pulled him to the floor. Mr. Thorndike intended to kill Quigly when the appointment was made the day before. After all, what could Mr. Thorndike lose? He was near death in any event."

"Chelsea," Jessica said, "we believe the contents of the tape, if it had not been destroyed, would clearly show Mr. Thorndike's motive for killing Quigly."

"What you all have said may prove to be what really happened. But, again, what about the two loud bangs Jason heard? And what if the bullet taken from the wall was fired from a gun that Quigly took with him to the meeting? Maybe Quigly didn't take the gun to shoot anyone, but took it for his own protection. Remember, Jessica found that Quigly had purchased a .357 magnum and he had a police permit to carry a concealed weapon. What if Quigly had pulled his gun out, and Mr. Thorndike reacted with fright and pulled his gun from the compartment in the bed and fired without thinking?"

"Chelsea, I think you are giving Mr. Thorndike too much credit for quick action. He was 93 years old. Even if he were in excellent health I don't believe he could have been quicker than the much younger Quigly, if Quigly did have his gun out. No, I can't believe that part of the scenario," J.C. exclaimed.

"John, when did the police say the test on the .357 magnum you recovered from the pawn shop would be completed?"

"Sergeant Smith said the test and comparison would be completed by Thursday evening," John replied.

"How about the classifying and aging test on the bullet recovered from the wall?"

Jessica replied, "The police recovered a slug they say probably came from a .38 caliber, possibly a revolver. Aging of the bullet won't be required if the comparison tests show the bullet came from the gun John recovered at the pawn shop."

"Thanks, Jessica." I said to John and Jessica, "Then our immediate next move is to prove that the gun was owned by Quigly. We also must prove that it was in Mr. Thorndike's bedroom and was removed. The big question to answer is 'Who pawned it?' John, you must locate the fourth paramedic who was in the Thorndike mansion that evening."

"Chelsea," J.C. said, "I got the court order for the paraffin and gunpowder residue test taken by Dr. Benoni and it has been certified by the coroner. The results will be admissible in court."

"Thanks, J.C., that's wonderful. What did the test reveal?"

"Both Mr. Thorndike and Quigly had considerable residue on their hands and clothes. It is safe to conclude that either or both of them fired a weapon, or one of them grabbed a weapon when it was fired."

"J.C., your notion that Mr. Thorndike might have killed Quigly may be plausible, but please remember Mr. Thorndike is not on trial. If someone other than Jason is to be tried for murder, let it be another trial. I don't want Mr. Thorndike's name brought into the trial as a participant in any manner."

"I don't know if we can keep his name out, Chelsea, you understand … "

"J.C., the defense team must prove that Jason did not kill Quigly. We are not really interested in trying to solve another crime during Jason's trial."

"I understand how you feel, Chelsea," J.C. replied angrily, "but we may not have the final say on whether Mr. Thorndike is brought into the trial."

"J.C., John, Jessica, please go along with me on this. If Mr. Thorndike did fire the gun that killed Quigly I am sure it would be justifiable, self-defense. But what I am saying is this: our efforts must be concentrated on Jason's trial alone."

I don't think I solved any trial issues by trying to exclude Mr. Thorndike and I certainly didn't convince any of my co-counsels.

"Chelsea, I was wondering what you're going to do about the ... ?"

"I have a feeling you all are wondering what I'm going to do about reconstructing what was on the tape Jason brought to me."

"Chelsea, that is your decision," J.C. said. "I agree with you. Jason is on trial for second-degree murder plus several other related charges. If the contents of the tape has a bearing on his acquittal, then yes, you must try and remember. It may be to our advantage to put you on the stand to talk about the tape if it becomes an issue or if we need its contents to clear Jason."

"Yes, I know you are right, J.C. I'll do what we must do to clear Jason."

It was late Friday when we completed our meeting. We still had several things to get done before court reconvened the following week. I wondered if my past would ever leave me. The tape clearly indicated blackmail, and even though my name was not mentioned, the CEO position was. Linda also heard the tapes. Between Jason, Linda and myself, maybe we could put together enough of what was said to appease our defense team. If I could convince them the tape's contents had no bearing on Jason's defense, maybe the issue would die.

6 Linda remained in the office until the defense team meeting was over. She works well with the senior managers, in fact she could probably do my job as well as I do. She came in with an apologetic look on her face and said, "Boss lady, about that tape. My recorder was on when it was played here in the office. I have a complete copy of the conversations — if you need it."

"Linda! That's wonderful! But please just sit on it until we see if we need it. OK?"

She tucked the tape in her briefcase and said, "Don't worry, boss. It will be safe and sound with me if you need it."

Stacked among the large files of correspondence was a letter from the U.S. Embassy in Ankara, Turkey. I picked up the letter and began to read.

"Dear Ms. Carodine," it began. "Approximately three years ago several American manufacturers' representatives were reportedly killed in a Turkish Air Force military transport between Ankara and Dyerbikier, Turkey. According to the files here in the Embassy, the Turkish government stipulated all members of the aircraft had perished and subsequently issued death certificates based upon the aircraft's manifest. Listed in the manifest was one Matthew Glyndon, an employee, at the time, of Thorndike Industries. Several U.S. military members who currently are assisting the Turkish Air Force in training reported to have talked with an American who possibly could be the Matthew Glyndon listed as killed in the aircraft.

"Ms. Carodine, as the chief operating officer of Thorndike, you are requested to dispatch personnel who knew Matthew Glyndon to Ankara to assist with the proper identification of this person who possibly could be your employee. This matter is not urgent. Reports about the person who may be Matthew Glyndon indicate he is in good health and working with several Turkish villages north of Dyerbikier. Your contact at the Embassy will be Mr. Charles Keen, Deputy Director of Turkish Affairs. His address is the U.S. Embassy and he may be reached via international telephone at 704-775621. If you are near a military installation you may use military communications directly to the U.S. Embassy. Sincerely yours, James V. Knight Jr., Chargé d'Affaires."

I sat and stared at the letter. I couldn't read it again. I *just couldn't believe Matthew could be alive!* I began to cry uncontrollably. Linda heard me crying, came in, closed the office door, and sat with me. She had known Matthew but she never questioned me about our relationship. I suspected she knew that Matthew and I had been lovers, but she never said a word. She was in Mexico with the team from the Parker buy-out shortly after Matthew was hired from the old Parker Corporation by Mr. Thorndike. God, I thought, my feelings for Matthew are not as strong as before but I know I still love him. He is the father of my son Caesar and he will always have a place in my heart. But what am I to do? I must not let Matthew interfere with Jason's defense. My total being must be for Jason. I had accepted Matthew's death. I can't even think about the possibility of Matthew being alive. *No!* I can't! Linda was very sympathetic and offered to help in any way. No, I thought, I cannot let Matthew come back into my life and compromise what I have found with Morgan and my children. Matthew never knew about Chelsea Lyn. I can't

96

imagine confiding in him about my life with Abel and Kersi and having a baby for them.

His Castillian background and strong Catholic beliefs would probably be cause enough for him to never admit that he and I had a son. I won't let him back into my life. I keep telling myself, I'm over Matthew Glyndon. I made that decision when I finally accepted his death. *No! ... No! ... He cannot come back!*

God, am I being punished for my past? All of my energy must be directed toward Jason's defense; I cannot let my personal problems interfere with clearing Jason.

7 John called me at home to tell me he had located the paramedic who had taken the gun from the crime scene. I wondered what John had to do to get the paramedic to confess he had taken the gun. I learned later that John had taken him to the district attorney's office and bargained for him. The district attorney reluctantly consented to accepting the confession, but insisted the paramedic be charged with removing evidence from a crime scene and grand larceny for stealing the gun. John's price in the deal was to defend the paramedic if he were charged. The district attorney knew the paramedic's testimony could wreck his chances of winning a conviction of Jason. John apparently had backed him into a corner with this new defense finding.

We were back in court at 9:00 A.M. on Monday. John, Jessica, J.C., and I were seated at the defense table. As the judge entered, the clerk called for people in the courtroom to rise. The sharp sound of the gavel indicated the court session had begun. The judge asked, "Is the defense prepared to present its case?" John rose and responded, "We are, Your Honor." The judge asked John to call his first witness.

John asked permission to approach the bench. John and the district attorney approached the judge.

"Your Honor, the defense requests permission from the court to change our order of witnesses. We would like to reserve our decision to call Mr. Jason."

The judge responded, "I believe you have scheduled to call Mr. Jason to the stand."

"Yes, Your Honor, but we have uncovered additional evidence which has a direct bearing on the case, and we would like to reconsider our request to call Mr. Jason after we hear the witnesses."

The judge looked at the district attorney and said, "Does the prosecution have any objections to this realignment of the witnesses?"

"Your Honor, we are aware of additional findings by the defense, and in the spirit of fairness we pose no objections."

"Counselor, you may proceed with your witness."

"Thank you, Your Honor. The defense calls Mr. Joe Styles."

"Mr. Styles, you are still under oath," the judge said. "Proceed, Counselor."

"Mr. Styles, did you remove a slug from the wall of the bedroom where Mr. Quigly was killed?"

"Yes, sir. A two-by-two-foot section of the wall was removed and the slug was extracted from the wood."

"Will you please tell the court what the condition of the lead slug was and whether you could identify the type of weapon used to fire the slug?"

"The slug was recently fired and the markings were easily identified. The slug was probably fired from either a .38 pistol or a .357 magnum."

"Mr. Styles, could the slug have been fired from a .357 magnum pistol?"

"Yes, sir, it could have been, but … "

"Then you agree it could have been fired from a .357 gun."

"Yes, sir, but … "

"That will be all, Mr. Styles. Your witness."

"The prosecutor only has one question, Your Honor. Please clarify for the court the difference between a .38 caliber and a .357 magnum pistol."

"Yes, sir. The .357 magnum pistol can easily fire a .38 slug. But I would never fire a .357 magnum slug from a .38 caliber pistol."

"And why wouldn't you fire a slug as easily from either gun?"

"In my opinion, the difference in the powder of a .357 magnum slug and a .38 caliber slug is too much for a .38 caliber pistol to safely fire. It could damage the pistol and would be dangerous for the person who is firing it."

"Thank you, Mr. Styles. No further questions."

"Call your next witness," the judge sounded.

"We call Mr. Tom Pate."

"Mr. Pate, will you please state your name and inform the jury what you do for a living."

"My name is Tom Pate and I own the Pate Firearms Assembly and Testing Laboratory."

"Mr. Pate, do you do any business with the district attorney's office or the sheriff's department in this county?"

"Yes, sir. I am under contract to test and make comparisons of any weapons involved in police business or crimes."

"Did you test a .357 magnum pistol which was delivered to you by the sheriff's office?"

"Yes, I personally tested that weapon."

"And what did you find?"

"The .38 slug dug out of the wall at the crime scene matched the rifling from the .357 magnum delivered by the sheriff."

"Mr. Pate, let me understand what you are saying. A .357 magnum pistol can also fire .38 caliber ammunition?"

He quickly added, "Yes, that is correct. But you should not fire a .357 magnum load from a .38 pistol because the person and the pistol could be damaged from the high powder charge of the shell. I agree with the previous witness on this subject."

"Objection, Your Honor. This material is irrelevant and the defense is wasting the court's time."

"Counsel, what is your point?"

John replied, "Your Honor, the defendant stated he heard two loud noises which he identified as gunshots. The prosecution discounted his statements. We are establishing the fact that two weapons were fired in the bedroom. We are not attempting to state who fired the weapons."

"Overruled. Continue, Counselor."

"Mr. Pate, can you approximate the firing age of the slug which was dug from the wall?"

"Yes, sir. The estimate is that the slug was fired within an hour of the time of the reported crime. It was definitely a fresh slug."

"Mr. Pate, did you test-fire the .38 pistol found at the crime scene?"

"Yes, my laboratory did."

"Did the slug taken from the wall come from the same .38 gun found at the scene?"

"Definitely not. The slug which was removed from the victim's body came from the .38 caliber gun found at the scene. The slug from the wall came from the .357 magnum I personally tested."

"The defense has no further questions."

"No questions, Your Honor," replied the prosecutor.

"Counsel, do you have any more witnesses?"

"Yes, Your Honor, defense calls Doctor Joseph Hinds."

"Doctor Hinds, raise your right hand. Do you swear the testimony you are about to give in this case will be the truth, so help you God?"

"I do," the doctor answered. The clerk directed him to the witness stand.

"Doctor, please state your name and occupation for the record."

"Doctor Joseph Hinds, County Coroner."

"Doctor Hinds, did you examine Mr. Jason's hands for evidence relating to what may have happened in Mr. Thorndike's bedroom?"

"Objection. Leading the witness. The facts are clear; a murder was committed in Mr. Thorndike's bedroom."

"Objection. Move to strike the witness's testimony as nonresponsive."

"Sustained. Rephrase your question, Counselor."

"Doctor Hinds, is it possible to ascertain whether the segments of skin and hair the prosecution claimed to have recovered from Mr. Jason's hands came from a dead person or a person who was still alive?"

"Yes. It is fairly easy to make that determination."

"Doctor, will you please explain, in layman's terms, how this determination can be made?"

"Well, in layman's terms we may say the heart is a pump that maintains a certain amount of pressure in our body. When one is alive and receives an injury, blood will flow out at the point of injury. After the pump ceases to operate there is no pressure, and therefore a cut or injury will not result in the flow of blood."

"Are the differences between skin and hair samples taken from a deceased person and a living person very noticeable?"

"Yes, of course. The body receives all of its nutrients and oxygen supply through the blood. The heart pumps the blood, and when the heart stops, death occurs — and, of course, the blood flow ceases. The cells are subsequently starved of oxygen. In this particular case, blood pooled in the cavities of the body as soon as death occurred."

"Doctor, did the samples of skin and hair found under the fingernails of Mr. Jason come from a deceased person?"

"Yes, I can say that with a fairly high degree of confidence."

"Doctor, let me turn to the powder residue tests of Mr. Quigly and Mr. Thorndike. What did you find?"

"Powder residue and particles of nitrates released when a gun is fired tend to adhere to any human flesh, and to the clothes of the person who fired the weapon and anyone close by. There were sufficient amounts of both substances to indicate that both men either fired a weapon or were in contact with one when it was fired."

"Doctor, if there had been a struggle and only one weapon was fired, would you find about the same amount of residue on both persons?"

"No, if only one weapon were fired there would have been many fewer blast elements and much less residue."

"Then you are confident that you found sufficient quantities of blast residue on Quigly's and Thorndike's skin and clothes to indicate two weapons were fired?"

"Yes, I believe so. The tests ran by Doctor Benoni used the neutron activation analysis, or NAA, tests. The tests are about 99% accurate. Powder residue and traces of nitrates were contained on their skin and clothes."

"Now, Doctor, did you find the same concentration of powder residue and traces of nitrates on Mr. Jason's hands and clothes?"

"No. We did find traces, but not sufficient to document that Mr. Jason actually fired a weapon — but traces were there."

"No further questions. Your witness," John said to the prosecution.

"Doctor Hinds," the prosecutor began, "would you agree Mr. Jason could have had some type of cover over his hands and clothes at first — that is, to lessen the concentration of powder residue and nitrates?"

"Yes, it is possible, but not very likely since we removed skin and hair from Mr. Jason's hands."

"Doctor Hinds, would you agree the powder residue and nitrates found on Mr. Jason could have occurred when he fired a gun?"

"Yes, that is possible, but I would say ... "

"Doctor Hinds, how long after death does the discoloration of the skin and hair take place?"

"The outer layers of the skin are the first areas to lose life support and therefore discoloration occurs rather quickly — I would say within five to seven minutes."

"Dr. Hinds, what degree of confidence do you have in your last statement?"

"Well, sir, it is possible to make mistakes with regard to the exact time of death. Therefore, three to five minutes is what I would describe as my best estimate. But the other methods of determining death are ... "

"Thank you, Doctor, no further questions."

"Yes, but ... "

"No further questions, Doctor. You are excused."

District Attorney Hightower requested the judge to adjourn the court before additional witnesses were questioned. The judge agreed and said the court would reconvene at 1:00 P.M.

"John, you're doing excellently. You presented all our evidence and Hightower couldn't challenge much of it ... "

"Excuse me, Chelsea. I have a question for Jason. Jason, think about the time just before you heard the shots. Tell me exactly what you were doing. Did you speak with anyone? Did anyone see you from the pantry?"

"Mr. John, I have wracked my brain and the only thing I can remember is Mrs. Richardson's maid ringing the rear doorbell and asking for a loan of lump sugar. But Mr. John, I explained this meeting to the police when they questioned me at the mansion."

"Jason, was that when you heard the shots? Did she hear the shots? *Think hard, man!* Did the maid say she also heard the shots?"

"Why, yes, of course she did. She is from the lower English class. Her comments about the loud noises were something like, 'Blimy, it's almost like being back home in Lancaster with all that loud noise.' Yes, by George, those were almost her exact words."

John took Jessica's arm and said, "Jessica, get a subpoena and get out to the Richardson's — and bring that maid in before court reconvenes after lunch."

"John, I met Mrs. Richardson, I'll call her and have her bring the maid here. We won't need a subpoena."

When court reconvened John and I approached the bench with Hightower to explain we'd located an additional witness who would testify that Jason was with her when the gunshots were heard. Hightower

102

objected and wanted to know when we were going to get our act together. The judge permitted the maid to testify. The oath was administered and the maid took the stand.

John began, "Ms. Reiggley ... "

"Beg your pardon, governor, my name is *Reg-in-ly*, that's with a hard 'R'."

"Ms. Reginly, were you with Mr. Jason on September 10 at about 3:45 P.M.?"

"Objection, Your Honor. The defense is leading the witness."

"Overruled. The witness will answer the counselor's question."

"Well, mate, let me see, that was a Wednesday as me mind recalls. Oh, yeah, I was at Mr. Thorndike's conversing with me friend Mr. Jason. That's the gentleman sitting right over there at that table. A fine gentlemen he's."

"Ms. Reginly, did you and Mr. Jason notice anything unusual that day?"

"I don't rightly know what you mean, governor."

"Were you and Mr. Jason disturbed by any loud noises?"

"Why, yes. You see we work in a high-class neighborhood, I mean our employers have, you know, are very wealthy people ... "

"Ms. Reginly, please answer the question. Did you hear any noises that normally were not heard in your neighborhood?"

"Well, sir, please give a lady time to get it straight in her head. As I was saying, Mr. Jason and me were conversing about the lump sugar I was borrowing when, *all of a sudden*, mind you, these two loud bangs sounded."

"And you are sure there were two loud bangs?"

"Well, that's ... what I believe I said, governor."

"Thank you, Ms. Reginly. Your witness," John said as he turned to Hightower.

"Ms. Reginly, how did you know what time it was when you were with Mr. Jason?" Hightower asked.

"*It was tea time, matey!* Every afternoon tea is served promptly at 4:00 P.M. in the Richardson mansion. I remember me shopping list had lump sugar listed on it, but I hadn't been to the market. I needed some more lumps of sugar for Mrs. Richardson's tea. She doesn't take to granulated sugar, says it's too fine."

"And when you were conversing with Mr. Jason, you said you heard unusual noises?"

"Yes, that's what I told the other gentleman. I commented to me friend Jason about how it was like being back in Lancaster, I mean with all that noise."

"And would you please describe for the court, just what type of noise did you hear?"

"It was two lightning-quick sounds like one of those American autos misfiring its sparks, that's what it sounded like."

"No further questions."

"Does the defense have any additional witnesses?"

"Yes, Your Honor. We call Joe Dozzer." The clerk administered the oath and directed him to the witness stand.

"Please state your full name for the court."

He responded, "Joe Dozzer."

John continued, "Mr. Dozzer, are you employed, and if so where do you work?"

"I don't have a regular job at this time."

"Mr. Dozzer, did you ever work for the High Flight Ambulance Service?"

"Yes, sir, but only as a temporary."

"Mr. Dozzer, were you working for the company on September 10th?"

"Yes, sir. I started to work for them on September 8th, I think."

"Were you part of a crew who responded to an emergency call from the Thorndike mansion at 1660 Rue Hill here in Lewisburg?"

"Objection. The defense is leading the witness," Hightower said as he stood up from the prosecutor's table.

"Sustained." John acknowledged the judge's ruling with a nod of his head.

"Mr. Dozzer, please tell the court where you were on September 10th, at about four in the afternoon."

"I was at that rich guy's mansion, where you just said … up on Rue Hill."

John said, "Let the record show Mr. Dozzer identified Mr. Thorndike's home at 1600 Rue Hill here in Lewisburg." John continued his questioning. "Mr. Dozzer, I want you to think carefully about my next few questions. Did you notice a gun in the Thorndike bedroom?"

104

"Yes sir, I did." John had cautioned Dozzer about incriminating himself before he began his questions.

"Mr. Dozzer, please tell the court about the gun you saw in the bedroom."

"Well, it was a .357 magnum. You already know that I took the gun from the bedroom and pawned it."

"Mr. Dozzer, do you have a pawn ticket for the gun?"

"Yes, sir. Here it is."

John said, "Your Honor, defense would like to have this pawn ticket become a part of Exhibit Number 10, along with the gun previously identified." The judge so ordered.

"Mr. Dozzer, do you have anything further you would like to tell the court about the gun?"

Dozzer twisted his face in a questioning look and replied, "I just want to say I'm sorry for taking the gun from the rich guy's house."

"Your witness," John said. Hightower seemed very angry when he began his questioning.

"Mr. Dozzer, have you made some kind of a deal with the defense for your testimony in this case?"

"Objection, Your Honor. Mr. Dozzer's statement concerning his appearance in this court is a matter of record."

"Sustained. I caution the prosecutor to restrain himself."

"Yes, Your Honor." Hightower continued, "Mr. Dozzer, are you aware that it is against the law to remove evidence from a crime scene?"

"Yes, sir, I know I shouldn't have taken the gun … "

"Mr. Dozzer, if you face charges because you removed the gun from the crime scene, can you pay for an attorney?"

"I already have an attorney who will help me if anything happens to me."

"And Mr. Dozzer, will you please tell the court who that attorney is?"

"Objection. Irrelevant and immaterial!" John shouted as he stood up.

"Overruled, Counselor. You may proceed, Mr. Hightower."

"Mr. Dozzer … then I can assume that you have made a deal … "

"Objection, Your Honor. Immaterial! The statements I previously referred to contain Mr. Dozzer's sworn statement. The prosecution agreed to its inclusion in the record of this court. The prosecutor has made his point."

"Sustained."

The prosecutor showed his anger by saying, "Nothing further, Your Honor." The judge asked John if he desired to redirect.

"No, Your Honor," John replied. The judge excused the witness.

"Does the defense wish to call any other witnesses?"

"No, Your Honor. We had reserved the right to put Mr. Jason on the stand. We relinquish that right. We do not feel Mr. Jason needs to testify on his own behalf."

"Very well. The court will recess for 30 minutes. Will the prosecution be prepared for closing statements?"

"Yes, Your Honor."

Shortly the judge reconvened the court and directed the prosecutor to deliver his closing statements.

"Very well, Mr. Hightower, proceed."

"Ladies and gentlemen of the jury, the evidence presented by the prosecution can leave no doubt in your minds that Mr. Jason killed Luther Quigly. Let me put his actions in perspective. The defendant had been a loyal servant and friend of Mr. Thorndike for twenty-five years. He, in fact, was the old gentleman's physical protector, a bodyguard in a sense. The defendant made the appointment for Quigly to be at the Thorndike mansion on September 10, the afternoon he was killed. The defendant also knew why Luther Quigly was to be at the mansion. We believe he suspected the deceased was to make demands that Mr. Thorndike could not defend against. It is the prosecution's contention that the defendant placed himself outside the bedroom and listened as the two men began to exchange angry words.

"When the voices indicated violence might occur, the defendant rushed into the room, took the .38 caliber pistol from where he knew Mr. Thorndike kept it, and killed Quigly. After he had committed this act of murder he altered the crime scene by moving Luther Quigly's body to cover up his actions. In the process of moving the heavy deceased Quigly, the defendant's fingernails dug into Quigly's skin, scratching and bruising him. Dr. Hinds, testifying as to the condition of Quigly's body, stated he could not accurately determine whether Luther Quigly was alive or dead when he was moved. The prosecution contends that Luther Quigly was alive when the defendant assaulted him.

"A late witness, the Richardson's maid, testified at the ninth hour: very suspicious. To say that Jonathan Jason was in her company when they thought they heard two loud noises, described as sounding like

106

automobile backfiring, is totally unbelievable. If Ms. Reginly was with the defendant at any time, the noises they heard could have easily been an automobile backfiring. These noises, the state contends, really occurred after the defendant had committed the crime of murder and was now seeking a witness to help build an alibi.

"Skin fragments and hair from Luther Quigly's body were found under the fingernails of the defendant. One may ask, 'why would the defendant Jonathan Jason go to so much trouble to create an alibi?' Ladies and gentlemen of the jury, Jonathan Jason's acts could have been honorable. If he, in fact, was protecting his employer from harm, his actions could be justified as self-defense. But that was not the case. The state produced a witness who said the defendant Jonathan Jason had previously made statements to the effect that he wanted to 'extinguish that man,' meaning Luther Quigly.

"The so-called second gun, allegedly found in a pawn shop and registered to Luther Quigly, was another defense maneuver designed to confuse you. We ask that you vote your conscience and find Jonathan Jason guilty of murder in the second degree and of destroying evidence at the crime scene to cover up his guilt. Thank you, ladies and gentlemen."

"Is the defense ready to deliver a closing statement?" the judge asked.

"Yes, Your Honor. Our closing statement will be presented by co-counsel Chelsea Carodine." My mind flashed back to the Casey trial, when Mr. Thorndike was watching. I felt his presence with me as I began the closing statements.

"Ladies and gentlemen of the jury, it is difficult to fight the state when one is accused of a crime he did not commit. Only with hard facts and credible witnesses can a victim overcome the insurmountable odds of the power of the state. Mr. Jonathan Jason is not a citizen of the United States. His loyalty remains with the Queen and his England. He longs to return to his home and to enjoy his retirement. He cannot understand the American justice system accusing an innocent man and placing him on trial for a crime he did not commit.

"Ladies and gentlemen of the jury, let me review the facts with you:

"Fact one. It has been proven that the defendant was in the company of Ms. Reginly who testified as to the date and time of the two loud noises, later identified as gunshots. The defendant did not go to the bedroom until about five minutes or so after hearing the loud noises. If he had suspected the noises were from a gun and from Mr. Thorndike's bedroom, he would have run the halls to investigate. That was not the case. The defendant could not have been even close to the bedroom. It has been shown the defendant was in the kitchen in the company of a neighbor, Ms. Reginly.

"Fact two. The skin and hair found under Mr. Jason's fingernails came from a deceased person, as testified to by Doctor Hinds, the county coroner. The fact that time of death estimates can vary does not always pertain to specific parts of a deceased person's body such as the skin. Dr. Hinds was very specific when he estimated the time of decomposition of the skin.

"Fact three. Two slugs were recovered from the bedroom. One, a .38 caliber slug, was taken from Luther Quigly's chest. The other, a .38 caliber slug that came from a different gun, was found in the wall directly behind the head of Mr. Thorndike's bed. Thus, if the sounds did not identify two gunshots, the slugs found at the crime scene certainly did. Two guns were involved in this crime.

"The prosecution certainly cannot believe that the defendant had planned the murder of Luther Quigly in the bedroom of his employer. Luther Quigly was killed by a person unknown to this court. That person may have been acting in self-defense. It is not this court's responsibility to seek out others who may have been involved.

"Fact four. Both of the deceased persons had strong evidence of gunpowder and nitrate on their skin and clothes. A slight amount was found on the defendant's hands and clothes. Evidence was presented to substantiate that the small amounts of gunpowder and nitrate found on Jonathan Jason's hands and clothes actually came from the deceased, Luther Quigly, when Jason lifted him from his employer. The gunpowder and nitrate residue found on the defendant were not sufficient to substantiate the claim that he had recently fired a weapon.

"Fact five. The state has not proven any of its evidence against Jonathan Jason. We in the defense surmise that the defendant did move the deceased, but only to free his employer from the weight of the deceased Quigly, and nothing more.

"Ladies and gentlemen of the jury, the state has not proved beyond any doubts you have in your mind that Jonathan Jason committed any crime, except that of attempting to protect his employer from the weight

108

of a deceased person. We ask that you find Jonathan Jason not guilty of all charges."

When I completed the closing statement, the judge began his charge to the jury.

"Ladies and gentlemen of the jury, you have heard the evidence presented by the state and the rebuttal of that evidence by the defense. It is now your task to render an impartial decision based solely upon the evidence presented during the trial. You are cautioned to deal only with the evidence and facts presented during the trial and not be influenced by opening or closing statements by either party. The charge is murder in the second degree. You must find the defendant, Jonathan Jason, either guilty or not guilty of this and the related charges. You may now retire to the jury room and consider your decision."

The judge continued, "This court is adjourned until the jury has reached its decision. The state and the defense will be notified when a decision has been reached."

Now the wait begins! After the trial, we met in my office to review the case and what we could have done and didn't do. Jason was placed in a holding cell in the courthouse to await his fate. J.C. seemed pleased with the presentations made by John and commented on the excellent closing statement I had made. He didn't need to polish any apples, so I took it as a compliment.

"Chelsea, I believe all the facts necessary to win the case were presented. If the prosecution had picked up on blackmail as a motive, I was ready to push you into the full-blown excusable homicide with Thorndike as the culprit."

"Yes, J.C., and you would have been right to do so — but I'm very pleased we didn't have to bring Mr. Thorndike into the case. If, and that is a very big *if*, he killed Quigly. And J.C., we may never really know just what happened.

"John, Jessica, you two were very professional. Thanks for being a part of the defense team."

John replied, "Hey, it's not over! We haven't heard the fat lady sing yet."

I agreed with John's statement.

"I suggest we all go back to work until the jury is in with its verdict. Let's all say a prayer for Jason. We know he did not kill Quigly. Our prayer should be for the jury to find him innocent of the charges. I'll talk with you all when court is reconvened."

8

I went back to the office, called Linda in, and closed the door. I had to talk about the telegram from Turkey. Linda had come in with a large file; I asked her what it was.

"Boss lady, I recovered Matthew Glyndon's file from permanent records. I hope you don't mind. I just knew you would want to discuss the telegram and decide what to do next."

"Linda, after Jason's trial is over, whatever happens, I must decide how I'm going to deal with the possibility of Matthew Glyndon being alive somewhere in Turkey."

"Boss, if you don't mind me saying so, I think you should go and take someone along with you to help."

"Yes, Linda, you're probably right. I'll need assistance, but who could I take with me?"

"May I suggest someone ... ?"

"Linda, please stop being so apologetic. You know how much I depend on you. Of course you can make your suggestion."

"Do you think Dr. Olga Doubreski could go with you?"

"Linda, that's a wonderful idea. You're just great. See if you can reach her and I'll propose it to her. Wait, Linda, I must talk with Morgan before I make any plans to go to Turkey. But if I do go, Olga is an excellent choice to go along."

The telephone rang and Linda answered it from my desk.

"It's for you, boss, from the court." I hurriedly grabbed the telephone, but was hesitant to hear what the caller had to say.

"Ms. Carodine," the court clerk began, "the jury has reached a verdict and court will reconvene this afternoon at 2:00 P.M. Please be prompt."

"Linda, get J.C., John, and Jessica. Tell them to come to my office and bring their files on the case." We all had a great deal of confidence when we left the court, but one never can outguess a group of citizens who make decisions that affect lives. Shortly, the group reached my office. Linda called on the intercom and I said to send them in.

"Well, John, what is it you said — 'It's not over until the fat lady sings'? Well, the jury has reached a verdict and court will reconvene at two this afternoon. Do we have any stones to kick over?"

110

"Chelsea, Jessica and I have been reviewing the case. In the event the verdict goes against Jason, I think we have a couple of very strong areas of appeal."

"Fine, John. If we don't win, get the appeal package completed and filed as soon as possible. Jessica, look into bail for Jason. Just remember, we must be ready to go with our plans, just in case we don't win a clear decision."

We all waited anxiously for the court to reconvene. I can't even think of not winning the case. I know we had evidence we didn't use, but that would have meant an open trial not only of Jason, but also of me and Mr. Thorndike. God, will my life ever settle down to something resembling normalcy?

The clerk asked the court to rise as the judge made his entrance. The jury had already been seated and we were all sitting on pins and needles. The gavel sound was especially loud as the judge convened the court. He surveyed the courtroom to check for the presence of the defense and the prosecution, and then addressed the jury.

"Ladies and gentlemen of the jury, have you reached a verdict in the case of the state versus Jonathan Elmer Jason?"

The foreman, a lady, rose and said, "We have, Your Honor."

"Please give your verdict to the clerk." The clerk took the verdict and delivered it to the judge. The judge reviewed the verdict silently and returned it to the clerk. The clerk then gave the verdict back to the foreman. Heavens, please get on with it, I thought. We can't stand this silly maneuvering.

"The foreman will please read the verdict." I took Jason's hand and squeezed it very hard.

"We, the jury," the foreman began, "we find the defendant, Jonathan Elmer Jason, not guilty."

The prosecution interrupted our jubilation by requesting a poll of the jurors. As the clerk called their names, each juror answered "not guilty."

We all hugged, patted backs, and congratulated each other for the win. When I looked at Jason I thought, he's got another American cold — his eyes are very teary.

Jason came to me and very stiffly put out his hand and said, "Miss Chelsea, how can I ever thank you and the others for what you have done for me? I believe this lesson will enable me to respect the American justice system a slight bit more. Thank you all."

Something I had not expected came out in the Lewisburg Herald the next morning. Big headlines read, "Thorndike CEO Successfully Defends Employee of Murder." The news spread was all about the trial, step by step, and near the end several lines were speculations about my future. The story told of a woman who had worked her way to the top of the corporation and now needed more excitement in her life. The article read, "Not content with her role as the Chief Executive Officer of Thorndike Industries, Chelsea Carodine took on the defense of her boss's butler who was accused of second-degree murder. We asked Ms. Carodine, what is your next challenge? Have you ever thought of jumping into the world of politics?" I thought, no, not politics. I am happy with my CEO role.

Morgan attended a few sessions of the trial and he constantly supported me in what I was doing. He felt that I needed a cause, something other than just being the CEO. As we talked, he said he is beginning to see a restlessness in me.

I thought this would be a good time to talk with Morgan about Matthew and what I need to do. Morgan went back to my office with me.

"Morgan, dear, read this telegram. I need to discuss it with you." I had no idea what his response might be. He finished the letter and took my hands in his very gently.

"Chelsea, you must be the one to go! You worked with Matthew and you know him. If Thorndike were here he would probably order you to go ... "

"But, Morgan, what about our children?"

"Sylvia and I can take care of them. Anyway, when you leave, I will have more time with them."

"Are you sure you want me to go, Morgan?"

"Of course. No one else is more concerned about Matthew than you. To everyone else he was an executive with Thorndike. I know you are concerned and I want you to go and do what you can for him, if it is really Matthew."

"Linda suggested I ask Olga if she would go with me. What do you think?"

"That's great! I would feel much better about the trip if Olga went with you."

"If you are sure, Morgan, dear ... "

"Chelsea, I am sure. You are the only one from Thorndike who should go."

"Well, we do have people in Turkey on the contract who speak Turkish. I'll use them if I need help while in country."

"I suggest you call Olga, do some planning, and set a date to depart."

"Morgan, do you realize how much I love you?"

"Not really! I can't even remember the last time you told me you love me."

"Morgan, you, … you know how much I love you. If I haven't told you often enough I will have to change my ways. But Morgan, don't you remember last night?"

"Gee, was that you I made love to last night? I thought it was a new and exciting woman I just met. My, I just can't seem to keep my girlfriends apart."

"Morgan, you silly boy! Darling, thank you for understanding how I feel about going to Turkey to look for Matthew."

"Just remember one thing, pumpkin, you and I have the most complete love between two people that ever existed. I cherish our times alone and also with the children. We'll say prayers for your trip and a safe return to us. We love you very much, Chelsea."

"And I love you and the children with all my heart. Yes, we do have something very wonderful."

Linda rang and said she'd called Olga and asked her to call me as soon as possible. As Morgan was leaving, Linda announced that Olga was on the telephone. Morgan kissed my cheek and said he would see me at home.

"Olga, how are you, dear?"

"I am very fine, Chelsea. Is Jason's trial over? Is he free?"

"Oh, yes, Olga. *We won the case!*"

She screamed over the telephone. "That is wonderful, my dear. Is Jason all right now?"

"Yes, Olga. He is doing just fine. Thanks for asking about him."

"I have interest in his welfare also. And how are you? Is everything OK with you and Morgan and the children?"

"Yes, thank you, dear. Olga, I received a telegram from the U.S. Embassy in Ankara, Turkey that stated an American had been observed by the U.S. military trainers in the area where Matthew's plane went down three years ago."

113

"Is it Matthew?"

"No one seems to know, Olga. I am going to Turkey. I have to know if it is Matthew. Olga, can you go with me?"

"When do you want to go, Chelsea?"

"I want to be in Turkey by the end of this month, that is, about 14 days from now. Can you arrange to go with me?"

"I can do anything I must do to help you, Chelsea. I have agreement with doctor friend of mine to cover my patients. Yes, I can be ready. I will come to Lewisburg two days before we leave for Turkey."

"Oh, thank you, Olga. Linda will make your travel arrangements to Lewisburg and ours on the overseas trip. Olga, you are my dear, dear friend and I love you."

"Yes, my dear Chelsea. You are like the daughter I never had. *You are really my daughter!*"

I couldn't wait to see Olga. She has been a very important part of my life and I know she will always be there for me — when I need a confidante to talk about those things in my past life that are shared only between the two of us. I called Linda to my office.

"Linda, *make our travel arrangements to Turkey!*"

1 After Morgan insisted that I to go to Turkey I realized there were a million things that had to be done before I left on the trip. The deputy CEO position had been vacant since I was promoted. I never bothered to fill the position because I didn't think a second senior person in the CEO's office was necessary. The battles with Putman and a couple of the board members made me cautious, and I felt now was the time to select someone I could trust. All of the senior male managers have been very encouraging; I could probably choose any one of them and feel comfortable. But wait! Chelsea, I thought, where is your brain? The one person in the entire organization who has enough backbone to tell you like it is, even if you don't agree, is J.C. Kippins, the chief of the law division! I knew J.C.'s loyalty to me was probably greater than anyone else's in the entire organization. He was very close to Mr. Thorndike and I knew they had shared opinions of me over the past several years.

I asked Linda to make an appointment for J.C. to spend about an hour or so with me as soon as possible. She set the appointment for 9:00 A.M., the first one on my calendar for the day. Good, I thought, I can begin the discussion with J.C. about the deputy CEO position before the day becomes so hectic.

J.C. was in my office when I came in. Linda already had delivered hot coffee and danish.

"Come in, J.C. How are you today?"

"I'm just fine, Chelsea. I didn't know the subject of our meeting, so I must confess I am totally unprepared to discuss whatever it is we are going to talk about."

"J.C., believe me, you are definitely prepared for this discussion."

Linda served the coffee and danish, and I sat in a chair across from J.C. We engaged in casual conversation while we ate. Finally J.C. couldn't hold back his curiosity about why he was called to the "front office" without notes or backup information.

"Chelsea, it's nice having danish and coffee with the CEO, but would you mind telling me why I am here?"

"J.C., how do you feel working for a woman?"

"Chelsea, are we revisiting the gender question?"

"Why, no, J.C., have we discussed this subject before?"

"Yes, of course we have. Don't you remember when you were first hired we had a conversation relating to women and gender in my office. I remember you thought I was probing to have you expose your views — which, incidentally, you did. Remember?"

"Oh, yes, I remember that conversation. No, J.C., that is not my purpose! I believe I understand how you feel about women in the workplace. And believe me, if you didn't share the same views as I, we wouldn't be talking today."

"Well, now that the ground rules have been established shall we discuss what's on your mind?"

"J.C., you remember Mr. Thorndike had a deputy CEO before I was selected for the position. Did you know much about what he did?"

"You're speaking of Kit Jamison. Chelsea, he was the old man's right-hand man. He was professional and knew the manufacturing and legal aspects of the business like the back of his hand. And he was an excellent people manager."

"J.C., I need a deputy CEO ... "

He responded very positively. "Chelsea, if you don't mind me saying, that is an excellent idea. Do you want me to draw up a list of the candidates I would recommend?"

"No, J.C. I know who I want."

"Excellent. Then I can do some preliminary interviews or something ... "

"J.C., I want you to take the deputy position."

"Chelsea, you what? *You want me as your deputy?* I'm overwhelmed! I never dreamed you would consider me for the position. I just don't know what to say."

"Say you will accept the position, J.C."

"Well, of course, I will. I just have to get over the shock of being offered such an opportunity without warning. I mean, for you to consider me is a real honor."

"Then you think you can work for a woman boss?"

"Chelsea, let me say I am very thankful for the differences in men and women. I think we need beauty, femininity, kindness, and all those qualities that belong to women almost exclusively. But, I believe if a woman is qualified, competent, and professional she should be

"Chelsea, you what? *You want me as your deputy?* ... Well, of course I will accept."

considered for positions of authority and responsibility. Gender should have nothing to do with it!"

"Gee, J.C., I didn't mean to get you on a soapbox ... "

"Chelsea, I believe we understand each other. Yes, I will be very happy to become your deputy."

"Good. I would like to have you in your new office by the end of tomorrow."

"Boy, you move fast when you make up your mind."

"One thing, J.C. We need a strong, well qualified person to take your law division position. Any candidates?"

"Yes, a very professional woman! Susan Rosco has been my deputy for the past two years. She knows the corporation and is an outstanding lawyer. She can easily take over with little or no transition. I recommend her for the job without any reservations. She can handle the position."

"Yes, I know Susan." I asked Linda to have Susan join J.C. and me in the office. In a few minutes Linda rang the intercom and said, "Boss lady, Susan is on her way."

"Thanks, Linda. Tell her to come into the office when she arrives."

Susan Rosco was the lawyer I worked with during the Parker buy-out program. She reviewed all the contracts and prepared briefs for me and the committee. She always came through in a pinch. Susan is very mature for her age. She's about 32 years old, light brown hair, a beautiful face, and a smile that wins hearts. She was married for about three years to another lawyer. It seemed their differences in law led to their divorce. She stands about 5 feet 8 inches, is slim, and has a very beautifully curved body which she de-emphasizes with professional-looking business suits. At cocktail parties, however, she definitely dresses the part of a beautiful woman who is well aware of her effect on men.

In a few minutes a light knock on the door sounded and Susan came into the office.

"Susan, come in. How are you?"

"Just fine, thank you, Chelsea. Hello, J.C."

"Hello, Susan. How's your workload?" J.C. asked.

"It's heavy, J.C., but I can always take on one more case."

"Susan, this 'case' is the Chief of the Law Division," I said as I looked directly at her.

"I don't quite understand. What has happened in the chief's office that I am not aware of?"

"Susan, J.C. has recommended you to take the law division chief's position. How do you feel about it?"

"May I ask, is J.C. being moved out of the chief's job?"

"Yes, Susan. J.C. has accepted the Deputy CEO position. He takes over that position tomorrow. If you feel you can handle being chief of the law division, then the job's yours."

"Well, I guess this is the first time lightning has struck me this year. Yes, of course, I am thrilled to be considered ... yes I *accept*." She seemed to be thrilled to get the job.

"Excellent. That is settled. You take over tomorrow. J.C. will be available to discuss anything he has been working on that you may not know about. Get moving, troops!"

I called Linda and dictated a memo to the board and the senior managers of the corporation explaining the changes of positions with the names of the new appointees. I expect Putman may have something to say, but I am within my authority as CEO to make changes in the senior officers. I can't be concerned with the egocentric male mentality of people like Putman.

2   I called Morgan and suggested we have dinner at Hoffman's. As always, he was elated. My womanly curiosity and suspicions about Morgan's suggestion that I was obviously the one who should go to Turkey was bothering me. I wonder if Morgan knows about Matthew and me. He wouldn't listen to me, but I've had a feeling for a long time that he was aware of my closeness to Matthew. Is he testing me? God, I wish I could stop being so uneasy about him wanting me to go to Turkey.

Out of the silence of my mind I heard a voice say, "Hi, beautiful. You are my lovely wife, aren't you?"

"Hello, darling." I thought, how could I ever doubt such a loving person as Morgan. He is very sincere in everything he says to me.

"Yes, my dear Morgan, I am your wife."

"Chelsea, sweetheart! I know I was the one who suggested you go to Turkey. And I still believe you are the only one who must go from Thorndike. But, honey, I'm going to miss you terribly."

"Oh, Morgan, I am going to miss you and the children so much. I just wish I didn't have to go. We all accepted Matthew's death three years ago. It's difficult to try and resurrect a person you have accepted as deceased."

Little did Morgan know the terrible hurt I was feeling. What if the person is really Matthew? What will I do if he wants to come back and be with me and his son Caesar? Oh, God, if you have any blessings left for me, please help me to solve this puzzle before it destroys me. Morgan accepted my past life by refusing to listen to me. Please don't let anything happen to my marriage and my family, my children. I must have appeared to be in a daze. Morgan snapped his fingers before me and said, "Hey there, you with the stars in your eyes. Are you with me tonight?"

"Oh, Morgan, I'm sorry. I guess I am preoccupied with the trip and what may happen."

"Yes, my dear, I realize you are. But tonight, sweetheart, try and put it out of your mind and be here with me, OK?"

"Forgive me, Morgan. Do you realize how much I truly love you?"

"Of course. In measurement, about half as much as I love you."

"Morgan, that's not true. You can't love me any more than I love you. There are just not words powerful enough for me to express my complete love for you. So there, smartie."

"Well, another family discussion ended. Shall we have dinner?"

"Yes. And you know what I want. You can order it for me while I go to the ladies' room."

We had a wonderful dinner. Afterwards we took a walk through the park near the restaurant. The night was clear and the big bright moon just hung in the sky like a giant piece of cheese. We stopped and Morgan embraced me and kissed me several times, very passionately. He placed his hands under my coat and reached around my body and pulled me to him. I felt we had to go home to bed or get a motel room. He apparently felt the same way. We dashed home. Sylvia had put the children in bed and she was in her quarters watching TV. Morgan picked me up and carried me through the living room directly to our bedroom in the back of the house. Our house sits on a hill about three hundred yards above a large lake. Our bedroom window was illuminated by the bright rays of the moon as its beams reflected from the lake. Morgan began to undress me. I knew he liked to be the aggressor so I relaxed and let him have his way. Soon we were naked and our embraces continued. As we lay on the bed the moonbeams streaked across our bodies as the giant weeping willow branches danced in the wind. Morgan made love to me for a long time. His lovemaking is always so complete for me. He doesn't stop until he feels I have been completely satisfied. I guess that is another reason I love this man so much. He has so much loving consideration for my feelings as a lover and woman.

Afterwards, as we lay in each other's arms, my mind wandered back to Matthew. How I had agonized with myself every time I came back to Morgan after being with Matthew. I kept telling myself that Matthew was temporary, but I never really believed it. I often thought I must be two people in one. When I was with Morgan, he was my complete life. Later when Matthew and I were together I had such an exultant feeling, like being on a cloud high in the heavens, all alone. But I always had a hard landing when I returned to Morgan. My conscience became so heavy with guilt that I often wished I would get caught and punished somehow. I must keep telling myself I will not permit Matthew back into my life.

The day after a love session, Morgan always told me how wonderful the woman in his lovemaking was. He often joked with me about me being a "new woman." My suspicious mind questioned whether he really didn't identify with me while he was making love to me. Just another quirk of a woman's mind, I thought, forget it.

Morgan was very pleased with the selection of J.C. to be my deputy. He also agreed that Susan Rosco was probably the most qualified to take J.C.'s position. I asked Morgan how he knew so much about Susan Rosco's qualifications.

"Morgan, how well do you know Susan Rosco?" God, I thought, my jealous mind.

"Well, let me remember. She is the curvy one with the brown hair and the bright white smile, isn't she?"

"Morgan, will you please be serious? How do you know Susan?"

"Susan worked on the three overseas contracts for Turkey, England, and Spain before the team left to renegotiate. She also reviewed our efforts before the team briefed you, our grand CEO, after the trip. Remember the trip?"

"Oh, yes. So she is the one who discovered all the problems with the contract in Turkey that Matthew had negotiated while he was with Parker."

"True, my lady. She is the gal."

"Morgan, how do you mean the 'gal'?"

"You know, a woman, and a very pretty one at that."

121

"Morgan, please stop teasing me. Oh, let's just forget I ever asked."

Morgan and I had three days with our children before Olga was due to arrive. Chelsea Lyn had her wish about church. We went to church for the first time as a family. Morgan was pleased to show off his family. We were greeted as visitors and made several acquaintances. Chelsea Lyn developed instantaneous friendships with several of the young people her age. Our boys also got lost with new friends. Morgan and I watched our children in their new world. Within a few days, Chelsea Lyn would want to have her newfound friends visit her home. Later on Sunday afternoon we cooked hamburgers and hot dogs on the grill and entertained several of her new friends. As I watched her mingle, I wondered what her reaction will be when she learns that her biological father is Abel Clayborne. I know she must know one day. I only hope she is mature enough to handle the emotions I am sure will result. Morgan didn't want to listen to me when I wanted to tell him about my past. I wonder what will happen when he learns that Abel is Chelsea Lyn's father and that I am her true biological mother? I had to put that problem out of my mind, along with the trip to Turkey and what I may find with Matthew Glyndon.

3 Olga arrived two days before we were to leave for Turkey. Linda made the travel arrangements and updated both our passports. Olga also insisted we take the necessary immunizations before we departed. Those shots seem to always make me sick. I fought her about it but Olga is both my doctor and my loving friend, so I lost the battle.

We all enjoyed Olga's visit. She is a very real part of our family. I am sure she will help me to decide what should be done about Matthew before we reach Turkey. I am still at a loss. I don't know how I will act when I see him for the first time. Somehow I must set my mind that "we are divorced" and I am only meeting him to discuss our son and nothing more. Olga and I didn't talk about what we may find. She reviewed my clothes and suggested I take warmer suits and a coat. She had been to Turkey in the late fall and knew how cold it can become.

As the time grew near to our departure I began to feel the pent-up emotions I had been suppressing. God, don't let me say or do anything that will jeopardize my relationship with Morgan. Help me to keep calm and in control, *just one more day!* We had our last evening meal at home. Sylvia prepared a wonderful dinner. After dinner we sat around the fire and talked with the children. Soon night came and Sylvia prepared the children for bed. Morgan always went to them and listened to their prayers. I hoped they would be praying for their mother this time. I tucked them in one by one and had a special prayer with each one. Caesar didn't know that I was going to see his father but he said in his prayers, "Dear God, take care of my mother and help my father too!" I knew in my heart he was praying for Morgan, but I hoped the prayer would also be for Matthew.

4 The day of departure came. The family drove us to the airport and remained with us until we boarded the airplane. Once on the airplane I looked desperately for them, but the airport windows were shaded and I could not see my family. Olga and I settled back into our seats and prepared for the takeoff.

It wasn't long before Olga began to talk about what we may find in Turkey.

"Chelsea, my dear, do you know if this American in Turkey is really Matthew?"

"No, Olga, I don't. When the search parties were looking for him after the airplane crash three years ago, his description was given to a number of people. The U.S. Embassy also had photographs of him."

"Then it is not certain the American is Matthew?"

"No, I guess not. Sometimes I pray the person is not Matthew."

"How do you feel about Matthew now, Chelsea dear?"

"*Oh, Olga, I really don't know!* I want to know if this person is really Matthew. But then again, I am so frightened that it may be Matthew and I won't know what to do."

"Chelsea, I think you may still have love for Matthew, but you are trying to deny it."

"*Olga, I just can't accept Matthew back into my life!* He died three years ago and I went through my grieving for him. He can't come back now."

"Then, my dear, why are you the one to go to Turkey and determine if this man is Matthew?"

"I don't know, Olga. My heart told me to go and my mind said no, I shouldn't go. I suppose Morgan influenced my mind and so here we are."

"Now, Chelsea, I think we should play the game we played about you telling Morgan about your past life, da."

"Olga, I am too confused about Matthew. With Morgan it was to tell or not tell. That was a clear decision. This one is not."

"Well, my dear Chelsea, you must think and plan what you are to do if this person turns out to be Matthew."

"Olga, you're the doctor with psychiatric training. *Suppose you tell me what I should do.*"

"You have doctor's role wrong, Chelsea. We listen while you open your mind. Somewhere, as you talk about your problem, *you begin to see a solution!* We doctors don't make your decisions."

"I'm sorry, Olga. I realize no one else can make decisions for me. What to do in this situation is heart-rending. If this person is Matthew, I don't think I will know what I should do until I actually see him."

"I must tell you, Chelsea, that will be too late. I think you must plan what you are to do before you see this person. You said you cannot take Matthew back into your life. That decision must be part of your plan. Do you understand me, dear?"

"Yes, Olga, I know you are right. May I sleep for awhile?"

5 The flight from New York consumed seven hours. We landed in Ankara, Turkey, and our contact at the U.S. Embassy met us at the airport.

"Ms. Chelsea Carodine," the loudspeaker sounded, "please come to the visitors' center in the central part of the airport. Your escort is awaiting you."

A tall, nice-looking, well-dressed young man approached us at the desk.

"Pardon me, are you Ms. Chelsea Carodine?"

"Yes. And this is Doctor Doubreski. She is with me."

"How do you do? I am Charles Keen, assigned to the U.S. Embassy. We have hotel reservations for you at the Hilton. I hope that is all right with you."

"Yes, I do believe my office assistant may have made reservations for us at the same hotel."

"Please come with me and I will help you clear customs. The Turks are very strict as to what comes into their country. You must list all your

124

valuables and the amount of foreign currency you are bringing in. Here are the forms. Please complete them and I'll take care of them."

"Thank you very much. Can you tell me much about the American thought to be Matthew Glyndon?"

"No, madam. I haven't see him. We have several reports from the U.S. Military Training Mission in Turkey. One of the members did identify a photograph he thought was the man in our records."

"Mr. Keen, what will be the procedure? Will someone from the embassy accompany us to the village, or do we go alone?"

"No, Ms. Carodine, you can't go to the village unaccompanied. Two of Thorndike's employees have your schedule and they will contact you at the hotel. They will go with you to the village. They both speak Turkish very well."

In a short time we arrived at the Hilton Hotel in Ankara and the escort from the embassy departed. He stated we should stay in contact with his office in the event we encountered any diplomatic difficulty. Olga and I shared the same room. We unpacked our bags and sat in the room with a relaxing drink. Neither of us are heavy drinkers, but after the long flight we thought a few drinks would settle our nerves. Our flight had arrived early in the evening. A message awaited us and advised us the two Thorndike employees would meet us for breakfast. We were glad we didn't have to deal with anyone our first evening. We had an excellent dinner and decided to retire early in the evening. Tomorrow's problems would get here soon enough.

Morning came too quickly. We both were fatigued from the flight. When we went to the hotel restaurant the two Thorndike employees were there. They both greeted us as if they knew us.

"Ms. Carodine, I am Tom Demenski and this is Raoul Carover. We are your Thorndike employees here on the Turkish contract."

"How do you do? Tell me, how did you know I was from Thorndike?"

"Your executive assistant, Ms. Linda Jamison, faxed photographs of you and the doctor so we would know you."

"Well, that's wonderful Linda." I thought, she does think of everything.

"Gentlemen, will you have breakfast with us?"

"Yes, thank you. We can discuss what you desire to do while we have breakfast."

125

"Yes, that will be just fine." We went into the dining room and ordered our meals.

"Mr. Demenski, may I call you Tom?"

"Yes, of course, please do, Ms. Carodine."

"Then call me Chelsea. And this is Olga. Tell me, Tom, what do you know about this American who may be our presumed-lost Mr. Matthew Glyndon?"

"Well, I met the gentleman, but he didn't recognize anything about the Thorndike Corporation. That is, he gave me that impression."

"Does the man look healthy?" I asked anxiously.

"Yes, he seems healthy. He's about 5 feet 10 inches tall, with black hair and a dark complexion, and a number of scars on his face. We thought he was Turkish when we first saw him. And, Chelsea, this may be a wild goose chase for you. He may not be this Matthew Glyndon." I wanted to get there and see for myself.

"When can we see him?"

"I have arranged for a Turkish Army escort to the village. These people don't like strangers. The Army escort is at your service. I can make a quick telephone call if you are ready to go."

"OK, Tom, give us about an hour. We should be ready to go by ten this morning. We will meet you at the hotel entrance."

"Fine, Chelsea. We'll see you in about an hour. I will have the escort ready and waiting. The trip by aircraft will take about an hour. We'll go to the village from the landing strip in an Army jeep."

I attempted to reach Morgan by telephone but I was not successful. I left a message for him about our trip to Dyerbikier, saying that I would call him when we returned to Ankara. Olga and I headed to the hotel room to freshen ourselves and change clothes. We packed our bags and checked out.

I thought, the time is near. I should know if the person is Matthew by late afternoon today. *God, please give me strength and keep me calm!* Olga asked if we should talk before we took the trip to the village. She made it sound like a matter of life or death that we have a plan before we met the man.

"OK, Olga. If this American is not Matthew, I have no problems. We just simply come back here and get the next flight back to the States."

"Chelsea, my dear, you choose the easy course first. Suppose the man is really Matthew? What will you say when you meet him?"

"I will ask how he has been and tell him how hard we searched for him after the aircraft crashed. I shall also talk to him about returning to the States."

"My, my, you are going to say all that as soon as you meet him, are you?"

"Well, Olga!" *I screamed.* "What do you expect me to say?"

"You are losing control of your emotions, Chelsea, and you aren't even near the person. Do you think you can have control of yourself when you come face-to-face with him? That is, if he is really Matthew?"

"Olga, I am petrified. I really don't know how it will be. I just know I must do it. Shall we go and meet the escort?"

The trip from Ankara to Dyerbikier took a little over an hour flying time. The Turkish Air Force aircraft could have been the same type that went down with Matthew. Tom said it was a C-119 given to the Turkish Air Force by our U.S. foreign aid program. It looked like something we would give away. Its seats were made of canvas and were hung by straps along each side of the rear part of the aircraft. It was a very real troop carrier aircraft. The cabin was not pressurized and the noise of the engines and wind shrilling through unseen openings in the fuselage was rather unnerving. As the aircraft circled to land we could see the many outlying villages. Each village seemed to contain a series of small mud-type huts with brush fences to contain the farm animals. *God, I thought, is this where Matthew lives?* I couldn't believe it.

Finally we landed at an airstrip outside of the remote city of Dyerbikier. The view from the air was much more picturesque than from the ground. This part of Turkey is about as remote as one can imagine. Two Turkish Army Jeeps met us, and an officer identified as a third lieutenant in the Turkish Army was to accompany us to the villages where Matthew was supposed to be living. I was happy to have Tom and Raoul along to handle the conversations with the Turkish troops and the villagers. No one spoke enough English to be understood. Once we got off the main highway, we found the roads were rough and muddy. I could see why we needed Jeeps to reach the villages. The dirt and mud roads were almost impassable even with the Jeeps. Finally the village where Matthew was reported to be living came into view. We entered the village and were greeted by the entire population. It was apparent they didn't receive too many visitors from America. The children held out their hands

127

for candy and anything else we had for them. Luckily, Tom had brought several bags of candy and small gifts for the villagers.

As we stepped out of the Jeep Tom pointed out the person suspected of being Matthew. It was difficult to identify him at a distance. As he came closer I felt my heart skip a beat. He walks like Matthew did. He is about the same weight and height as Matthew. Oh, *God*, I said to myself, *it is Matthew!*

Tom greeted him and brought him over to Olga and me. The tears began to flow. I turned away and wiped my eyes and hoped I wouldn't begin crying in front of him.

Before I could speak his name he greeted me with a polite, "How do you do, madam? I am Asher Gaspar." *I was shocked beyond belief!*

"Matthew! You are Matthew Glyndon! Remember? I am Chelsea, Chelsea Carodine!" My voice reached a high-pitched squeal and tears formed in my eyes again and ran freely down my cheeks.

"Madam," Matthew said, "are you hurt? You seem to be crying. Is there anything I can do for you?" Oh, God, Matthew doesn't remember me or Olga. He has lost his memory.

Olga tried to talk with him. She asked anxiously, *"Matthew, do you remember me?* I am Olga, you remember? I am Chelsea's doctor." He stared at us while he frowned, apparently trying to place us.

"No, I am sorry, madam. I do not believe I know you. Did we meet before?"

"Olga, this is horrible! I never expected something like this. What can we do?" I continued to cry and my emotions were about to burst.

"Chelsea, please be calm. I think we should return to the hotel and talk about this."

"No! I do not want to go back to Ankara! We will find a place in Dyerbikier. I want to help Matthew remember me and his life. Olga, if you want to return to the States, please go ahead. *Don't worry about me!"*

"Chelsea, I will remain here with you. Maybe exposing Matthew to us over a few days will help him to remember who we are and something about his life. No, I will not leave you!"

"Matthew, please sit here so we can talk."

"Madam, my name is Asher Gaspar. I do not know who you think I am ... "

"No!" I screamed, "You are Matthew Glyndon! You are an American who worked for Thorndike Industries. You were in an aircraft crash three years

128

"Matthew! You are Matthew Glyndon! Remember? I am Chelsea, Chelsea Carodine!"

ago. Do you remember any of this?" I cried, *"Oh, Matthew, please remember!"*

"Madam, please calm yourself. I know who I am. I am not this ... Matthew Glyndon you think I am. Please excuse me, I must return to my village."

"No! I mean, please, Matthew, *or ... Asher ... please stay with us for a while!"*

"Madam, if you like I shall meet you again another day. I must go."

"Can you meet us in Dyerbikier at the local hotel? The day after tomorrow?"

"Yes, that will be fine. I shall be there early. Good-bye, madam."

As Olga and I were driven into Dyerbikier, I remembered her trying to make me work through scenarios of what I would do when we met Matthew. Never in a million years would I have thought he would not remember us. I must help him regain his memory. I asked Olga if she could contact a local psychiatrist who could help Matthew. Olga responded, saying she didn't want to sound cruel, but ...

"Chelsea, this may be the best chance you will ever have to leave Matthew as he is. He seems to be happy and healthy, do you think you should alter his life ... ?"

"No! I will not leave him as he is! He needs my help. I am the only person who loves him enough to help him regain his memory and live a normal life."

"Chelsea, my dear. I ask, why do you want to continue to have these terrible crises in your life? At this point, here in Turkey, you can be in control. Why must you be everyone's savior? Do you hear me? Da?"

"Yes, Olga, I hear you and I appreciate your concern. Frankly I don't know why I feel I must help Matthew regain his memory and learn who he is. If he does recover his memory I realize I may have a gigantic, unmanageable problem. I just don't know. Something is driving me to help Matthew."

"Chelsea, please think very carefully what you are doing. Do not think only of what you feel you must do, but think of Morgan and your children. What will their lives be like if you ... "

"I'm sorry, Olga. I know my life has not been a shining example for anyone to follow, but I can't simply go away and let Matthew remain in this Godforsaken place."

"I don't know how you reason, Chelsea. You seem to be one who wants everything in life without paying the costs. In Russia our decisions sometimes meant one life exchanged for many other lives. These were difficult choices, but many families had to make them. Once we accepted our decisions, we asked God to forgive us if we made poor decisions, and to help us to forget."

"Olga, thank you. I know you're trying to help me make a decision. Finding Matthew with his loss of memory makes me think of an abused wife. She loves her man, but he beats her. Then he apologizes and treats her like a queen for awhile. She remains with him. Then he beats her again and again, and the same pattern continues ... "

"Or, Chelsea, until she becomes a mature person who finally discovers her own identity and stands up for her rights. It is then when she becomes her own person! But the process is painful because she must give up someone she believes she loves with all her heart."

"Olga, would you really have me just leave Matthew as we found him?"

"I cannot make your decision, Chelsea."

"Maybe it is my paternal concerns. How will I answer Caesar when he asks about his biological father?"

"Let me ask you, Chelsea: *How many fathers have been lost in the wars?*"

"Are you suggesting I lie to my son about his father?"

"What you do in life must always be your own decision. Only you will answer for your sins, not anyone else."

"Olga, I just can't leave Matthew as he is. I must help him if I can. *I know I must try!*"

"Then the question is settled. You and I will help Matthew to regain his memory, if that is possible."

"Thank you, Olga, for your support. This decision may not be the right one, but I feel in my heart that I must try to help Matthew. *I just can't walk away!*"

After our discussion, Olga began looking for a local doctor who could help us with Matthew. Her efforts proved fruitful. Her search uncovered a group of psychiatrists and psychologists who were in Turkey on government and private grants to study the local population. The doctors discovered that a large number of the older population had exceptional memories of almost everything that had happened in their lives. What a strange place to find specialists on such a subject! Later we learned the

131

doctors had been in the region for several years, on grants to study several tribes of the Turkish locals who had exhibited long-term memories of every aspect of their past. I thought, what a wonderful find! The good Lord must be in my corner again.

Olga arranged a meeting with two of the doctors who agreed to review Matthew's situation. We talked for most of the day and discussed almost all we knew about Matthew. When they asked how well Matthew knew us, I had to confess that he and I had been lovers and had a son. I hoped my secret would be safe with them here in Turkey. The doctors suggested that we not identify them as doctors until after they had an opportunity to observe Matthew and to listen to our conversation. One doctor told Olga the fact that Matthew was willing to meet again was a good indication that he had concerns about his past.

Matthew arrived shortly after seven in the morning. He did mean early!

"Good morning, Asher. It is nice that you would come to the hotel to talk with us. How do you feel today?"

"I am well, madam. How is your health and yours, Madam Olga?"

"Thank you, Matthew ... I mean Asher. You remembered my name."

"We are fine. Asher, may I introduce you to two of our friends? This is Michael Smyth and Kenneth Hill. These gentlemen are from England. They are here working for their government, helping your people."

"I am very pleased to meet you, gentlemen. I am Asher Gaspar. I live in Village Kishmier, which is east of here."

"Asher, are you a Turkish national?"

"If you mean am I a citizen, the answer is yes. I signed for the draft like all other Turkish men of eighteen and older."

"How long have you lived here, Asher?"

"I have been here all my life. I have a wife and one small child, and Allah has blessed me with a forthcoming son."

Oh, *God*, I thought, *Matthew is married to a Turkish woman!* He said "thanks to Allah." Matthew was Catholic. How could he have changed so quickly to some foreign religion?

Doctor Smyth asked, "If you have lived here all your life, how in the name of the Queen did you learn to speak such perfect English?"

"I am not sure. I think I must have been born with a keen ability to grasp language. I also speak Spanish and Turkish," Matthew responded.

"May we ask what you do for a living?"

"I am a farm advisor and a construction engineer. I work for the government, helping the villages to produce the kinds of crops that will grow in the tundra."

"Where did you learn how to do what you do? Did you attend a college?"

"I can't seem to remember where I learned my trades. I believe my father must have taught me. Many of our people learn languages and trades from their fathers."

"Mr. Gaspar, do you ever wonder whether you had another life before you came to Turkey?"

"I do not know what you mean, sir! I do not know of any other life."

"Then you do not recognize nor remember either of the two ladies, Chelsea or Olga?"

"I had disturbing thoughts about Chelsea during the past two days. But I cannot remember who she is. Do you think she is an important person I should know?"

"Yes, Mr. Gaspar. *She was a very important person in your life at one time.*"

"Then I ask, gentlemen, how can I recall a person or events I do not have in my mind?"

"Asher, would you be willing to let us help you regain your memory?"

"Gentlemen, I do not know that I have lost my memory. Madam Chelsea and Olga have said I am a Matthew Glyndon. I believe them to be in error. But I will submit to your questions and tests to learn if I do have another identity."

"That is wonderful, Asher." I was excited that Matthew at least would let us try and help him although he didn't realize his needs.

Doctor Smyth suggested Matthew return to Dyerbikier on a regular basis for the next several days in order to continue to talk and be tested. Matthew agreed. I was elated he was going to cooperate. I was totally confused as to why I so desperately wanted him to remember me. Even if he recovers his memory I cannot accept him back into my life. He has a wife and a child, with another child soon to be born. No! I must begin to accept the fact that *Matthew Glyndon is lost to me forever!* His son Caesar must accept Morgan totally as his father, and I can never tell Caesar about Matthew.

Matthew came every day for the next seven days and met with the doctors. When he was not being tested Olga and I had opportunities to

133

talk with him. I touched him several times, hoping he would remember my touch. But no, there was no recognition and he would pull away from my hand every time I reached for him. He asked if it was an American custom for women to touch strange men. I was at a loss. I thought, Matthew you will begin to remember and when you regain your memory I know you will want to hold me!

6

After every type of test the doctors had at their disposal was administered, they both were amazed that all the tests they tried apparently had no effect upon Matthew regaining any of his memory. Doctor Smyth recommended that Matthew be taken to the U.S. for a more complete medical review at the Mayo Clinic.

I thought, just how are we going to convince him to leave his family and travel to the States to try and regain memories of a life he doesn't want and never knew existed?

I had to have time to work this problem out. We talked at length with Matthew about coming to the States and submitting to more tests. He indicated he would cooperate but he could not travel until after the birth of his second son. His wife was at the end of her seventh month of pregnancy. Olga suggested we have one of the Thorndike employees come to visit Matthew every few days and bring items and equipment he needed to do his job. She thought this would soften his attitude toward the trip to the States. We met with Matthew one last time before we departed for Ankara for our return to the States.

"Asher, may I please call you by the name I know you?"

"If it will make you comfortable then I do not have objections. I know who I am. Names are not so important."

"Thank you, Matthew. I do feel more comfortable speaking with you as Matthew."

"May I ask you, ladies, are you very serious about a trip to your country for me to be studied by your doctors?"

"Oh, yes. I am very serious and excited about the trip."

"Then you must understand, I do not have funds to pay for travel or living ... "

"That is not a problem," I responded excitedly. "The Thorndike Corporation will pay all of your expenses including the medical examinations. You should not worry about the funds."

134

"I must also have funds for my wife and children while I am away. My relatives will see to my family, but I must not burden them with providing food for them."

"Yes, yes. All expenses will be paid for you and your family."

"Then it is agreed. I shall come to the United States when you have made the arrangements for me, only after the birth of my son. Is that the understanding?"

"Yes, Matthew. That is the understanding. Mr. Tom Demenski and Raoul Carover will visit you regularly and will provide you with whatever you require for your family. They will also help you in your work if you desire."

"Yes, thank you very much. That would be very kind and I thank you personally."

We said good-bye and Olga and I returned to Ankara for the return trip to the States. Once we arrived in Ankara, I called Morgan to tell him what we had found. We had a terrible time getting through the international circuits, but finally I could hear Morgan saying, "Hello."

"Morgan, this is Chelsea. How are you, darling? How are the children?"

"Chelsea, my love. Where are you? We are all just fine. Are you OK?"

"Yes, darling, Olga and I are well. I am calling from Ankara, Turkey. I was not able to call internationally from Dyerbikier. We were there for eight days. Morgan, we found Matthew!"

"Wonderful, Chelsea. How is he?"

"Morgan, that is the sad part. *He has lost his memory totally.* He didn't recognize me or Olga."

"Gee, that's sad, darling. So tell me, what happened?"

"Matthew looks the same except he has a few scars on his face and neck. He seems healthy and he did talk with us during the eight days we were in Dyerbikier. But, Morgan, we also found a group of doctors who examined Matthew ... "

"Chelsea, I thought you said Dyerbikier was the end of the earth. How did you find doctors with any expertise in memory loss in a remote place like that?"

"Honey, I'll tell you all about it when I return. There is one thing I want to say. Morgan, the doctors recommended Matthew be brought to the Mayo Clinic for evaluation."

"You said he doesn't remember anything of his past. Chelsea, how did you talk him into coming back here to the States?"

"The doctors seem to think he wants to remember his past. I frankly don't know. He talked with Olga and me over the eight days we were with him, and he never did recognize us nor anything we said."

"Well, did he agree to come back to the States?"

"Yes, but there's one complication. He is married to a Turkish girl who is pregnant. He won't come until she delivers his 'son.' How he knows the child will be a son, I will never know. The medical facilities here are sort of ancient."

"Honey, hurry back. We all miss you terribly. We'll talk more when you return. Have a safe trip back. We will be praying for you."

"Yes, Morgan dear, I miss you all very much. Kiss the children for me. Olga sends her best to you and the children."

I hoped Morgan listened to the part of my conversation concerning Matthew's marriage. If he had any thoughts about Matthew's and my past, the fact that Matthew is married may put them to rest. Chelsea, I thought, please stop thinking Morgan is jealous of you. He is the most accepting and loving man you will ever find.

7
The trip from Ankara back to New York was long and tiring. I asked Olga to remain with me at home for a few days and rest before she returned to Boggsville. She was happy to accept. I didn't know if she wanted to rest or to continue talking to me, still pressing me as to what I would do if Matthew gets his memory back. A short commuter flight took us into Lewisburg. Morgan and the children were at the airport to greet us. As we entered the passenger gate I could see Chelsea Lyn standing at the edge of the crowd. She has grown so much. I can still see the strong resemblances to Abel, especially in her eyes. Abel had such bright and shining but serious eyes. The first time he looked at me I felt he was looking directly into my soul. And now I am looking across the crowd to a beautiful slender fifteen-year-old who, like her mother, looks more like eighteen than her age.

"Mom, Mom!" the boys shouted as they ran and jumped into my arms. I remember when I could scoop them up into my arms. I had to kneel down to hug them. They both have grown so tall. I thought, Caesar dear, I was just with your father yesterday, but he doesn't know you exist. Morgan came to me and hugged me and kissed me very passionately, as if he hadn't seem me in several months. We had been gone for twelve days, but it did seem like a longer time to both of us.

"Chelsea, my love. I missed you. Are you OK?"

"Yes, Morgan, I'm just fine. *Oh, Morgan, no, I'm not just fine!* I'm so distressed to find Matthew in the condition he's in. He is a completely lost man but he doesn't even realize it."

"Hey, you're doing all you can do. Give him time. Maybe the doctors at Mayo can help him."

"Morgan, I just can't believe a person can lose his total memory and yet function as well as Matthew seems to be doing. *I simply can't understand it!*"

"Did he sound as he did before the aircraft accident?"

"Yes, that's the unusual thing. His speech is far superior to the people in the village where he lives and yet he seemed to blend in with them."

"What were the findings of the doctors who saw him in Turkey?"

"Neither of them could quite understand how he could remember his languages, especially the Spanish, and not remember anything else about his past."

"Well, honey, we will have to wait and see. Hey, your dad should be at our house when we arrive. He called and I told him when you were returning. I invited him to come down for a few days."

"Oh, Morgan, you are about the nicest person in the entire world. Thanks for inviting him."

"Well, you know your old man and I get along pretty well. And I thought since Olga was coming back with you, maybe we could get her to hang around for a couple of days and visit."

"Morgan, are you trying to plan something that I don't know about?"

"Never in a thousand years, my sweet. I just thought you would like to see your father. And I knew Olga would like to see him!"

"Olga, Morgan invited Dad for a few days. Do you mind?"

"My dear, that is very wonderful news. I like your dad's company. I will enjoy my few days of rest with you and your family."

Dad was waiting at the house when we arrived. He had walked to the lake and was coming up the hill when he saw our car pull into the driveway. Sylvia was home so I thought she would have seen to his needs. Dad waved wildly at us and the kids. The boys took off like horses to

137

jump into his arms. Dad is capable of picking them both up and they enjoy the rough-and-tumble play with him.

Olga extended her hand to greet him and Dad pulled her into his arms and gave her a real "Russian Bear" hug. She eagerly responded. I wondered if something had been developing between my dad and Olga.

It was early afternoon and the cool November weather was exhilarating. Almost all of the leaves had dropped from the trees and covered the ground. The piles of dark orange, brown, and yellow colors covered the ground and the walkway as if a giant hand had dropped them. The large oak trees, with their branches bare, looked like true giants reaching for the sky. Even without their leaves they blocked out much of the sun's rays. We all pulled our lawn chairs into the warm sunlight as we sat on the patio enjoying our drinks. The boys were on the lawn playing football with their grandfather. This is when I really love my dad. He always takes time with the boys and Chelsea Lyn to play and talk about what's happening in their lives. Chelsea Lyn is at that stage where she needs to talk with the male population. Between Morgan and Dad she has two very receptive people who love her and have willing ears for her to expound on what she wants to do in life.

During the three days Dad and Olga were with us I noticed the closeness they seemed to have developed. They took several walks around the lake. I could see them holding hands and occasionally stopping and embracing. I wondered if they were kissing. They were too far away for me to see any details of their embraces. Morgan also noticed their actions and commented.

"Chelsea, I do believe your dad and Olga are getting along exceptionally well. What do you think?"

"Yes, Morgan, I think you are right. I think they are good for each other. Olga doesn't have anyone she is serious about and neither does Dad."

"Well, maybe they're the perfect match. Two lonely people meet, fall in love, and get married!"

"Oh, Morgan, *I don't think it's that serious.* Do you?"

"Could be, my love. We may never know until the time comes for them to confess they have been holding hands and hugging and even kissing ... "

"Morgan, would you please be serious. I mean, so what if they do want to get married, they don't have to ask me. They both are over twenty-one."

"Then no worry, my dear, until they choose to tell us."

The three days of rest with my family ended and I knew it was back to the office for me. I didn't think much about what was happening in the corporation since J.C. had accepted the deputy CEO position. I knew he could handle any situation that came up. I asked Morgan if he had noticed any major occurrences since I was gone. His answer was that things seemed to be running very smoothly. He said J.C. visited several of the plants and renewed his acquaintances with the senior managers. I felt very comfortable with J.C.'s ability to run the corporation. On my way to the office, I drove Olga to the airport for her trip back to Boggsville. She was still very concerned as to what would happen when Matthew came to the States.

"Chelsea, are you going to expose Matthew to people in the corporation to try and help him regain his memory?" I didn't know. I had not thought about it.

"Only if the doctors who treat him think it would be a good idea," I responded. "No, I will not do it on my own."

"Well, my dear. You have about two months before Matthew will be here. Are you going to think about what may happen before he arrives — if his memory comes back to him?"

"Olga, I feel very strangely toward Matthew. I don't think I love him as I did when we were together and when we had Caesar. But I feel I owe him all the help I can give him. You remember he left me five million dollars when he was declared dead. I must contact the insurance people about the policy they paid when Matthew was declared officially dead. He also left me his town house and two expensive cars. The money I got from selling his property is still in the bank, drawing interest. I have not touched a cent of it. It all belongs to him and somehow I must get it back to him."

"Chelsea, how you explain your feelings now is good. I see your love being replaced with sympathy and concern. Da, that is very good for you."

"Do you really think so, Olga? Is that what you think is happening to me?"

"Yes I do. But I must say to you, Chelsea, *be careful with your feelings!* If Matthew does get his memory back he may want to begin things again with you."

"But Olga, he is married. And he has a son and is expecting another. I don't think he would leave them and want to come back to me."

"Medicine does not know enough about what causes the mind to block out part of its existence. Maybe Matthew will remember you and his life here in the States and forget what happened to him in Turkey."

"Olga, that can't be possible, can it?"

"My dear, we will know only after Matthew is subjected to the tests at Mayo Clinic and what happens there. We keep up with what happens there every day."

"Olga, could you serve as Thorndike's medical advisor when Matthew comes to the States? I mean, be there with him all the time and see what they do to him."

"Yes, my dear, that would be possible. I will arrange my patients so I will be available when Matthew comes for examinations and evaluation. When do you expect him?"

"Once he lets the embassy know his baby has been born, they will notify me when he will be available to travel. I suspect it will be sometime during the next three months. Linda will call you when she is ready to make the travel arrangements for him."

"That is good. I will talk with you often. Chelsea, please consider what is to happen if Matthew regains his memory and wants to make demands on you."

"Yes, I have already thought about that possibility. Olga, before you go, will you answer a question for me?"

"Of course, my dear. What is it?"

"Are you and my father getting serious about each other?"

She smiled and said, "Chelsea, I am beginning to feel very dear with your father. He is coming to visit me at the end of next week. I will tell you how I feel when we are together for awhile. Do you approve of us seeing each other?"

"*Oh, Olga, I think it's wonderful!* If you and Dad were to get married you would be my mother. Wouldn't that be just grand?"

"Well, Chelsea, I don't know if you would be a good daughter to your mother ... "

"Olga, you have been around Morgan too much. Would you please stop joking with me. You would like me to be your daughter, wouldn't you?"

"My dear, you couldn't be closer to me even if your dad and I did get married. I consider you as my daughter and I have since I first met you."

"Thank you, Olga. I am very happy for you and Dad."

I waited as Olga's airplane taxied down the runway and lifted into the sky. What a thrill it would be if she and Dad did get married. I must talk with Dad and see if he is really serious about Olga. God, Chelsea, now you are the one concerned with who your father goes with. Kind of a turnaround, isn't it?

8 As soon as I reached my office Linda said I had several calls from John Capps, the lawyer who handled Mr. Thorndike's estate and will. He said he could speak only with me. I wondered, what would Capps be calling me about? I wondered if it were about Mr. Thorndike's will. I asked Linda to get him on the telephone.

"John, this is Chelsea Carodine. What can I do for you?"

"Chelsea, thanks for returning my call. I am concerned about the five million dollars Mr. Thorndike left to a person you were going to identify. I believe we need to disburse the funds as soon as possible. Do you want to give me the name or should I transfer the funds to you for disbursement?"

"John, I would like to have you disburse the funds. Neither Mr. Thorndike nor I must be identified as the benefactor. Do you understand what I mean?"

"You mean you don't want whoever is to receive the funds to know where they came from. Is that correct?"

"Yes. Can you arrange that?"

"Chelsea, that may be a little difficult if the funds are going to an individual. It would be much easier to place the funds in a trust."

"Well, John, can you work it out and give me a call in a couple of days? You understand what I want to do, don't you?"

"Yes, of course, Chelsea. I'll give you a call near the end of the week with my recommendations."

"Thanks, John. I'll expect to hear from you at the latest by Friday, this week."

I can't have the likes of Stan Jones pestering me as to why he didn't get more money from Mr. Thorndike's will. I don't want anyone knowing that Stan Jones is the illegitimate son. If Mr. Thorndike had wanted to acknowledge Stan as his son he would have done so many years ago. I wondered if Stan ever really thought about where the money came from that supported him through life and put him through law school? When he worked for the corporation, Stan certainly never suspected that Mr. Thorndike was his father. If he had known, Stan would have been the most unpleasant and obstinate individual a person could imagine. I fired him because he couldn't follow instructions, not because he hated women in positions of authority. I'm hopeful that John will work out the disbursement of the funds without Stan ever discovering their source.

J.C. came to my office to brief me on the events that had taken place while I was gone. The first thing he said was, "Chelsea, the holding period on the stock has ended. You now officially own 60% of Thorndike Corporation."

"How about the five million in stock Mr. Thorndike left the city? What's the status on my offer?"

"Yours was the only offer, so that stock was also freed for purchase at the same time. Shall I negotiate a price or do you want the entire five million face value to go to the city?"

"Let the city have the entire amount, J.C. We don't need to bargain with them. The city fathers are very supportive of Thorndike; let's keep it that way."

"The first interim report from the committee that Putman is heading came in. Things look pretty good for the expansion of the southern plant and the additional product lines."

"What's the scuttlebutt about Putman? Is he still up to his tricks of trying to control the corporation?"

"He has really surprised me, Chelsea. His interim report was very positive. When you appointed him chairman of the committee he may have taken it as a gesture that you wanted him on your side. It seems to have worked. He's really supportive of your directions from the last board meeting."

"Well, J.C., give the credit to Mr. Thorndike. He taught me that strategy."

142

"What do you think about letting John Capps handle the negotiations as a lobbyist for the corporation on the national health care issue?"

"I don't know, J.C. Give me a few days on that one. John is doing some research for me now on Mr. Thorndike's will. Let me see how he handles that matter before we send more business his way."

"Sure, Chelsea. I have several other law firms we can go to anyway."

"J.C., let me tell you how comfortable I felt with you in charge while I was away. I never even once concerned myself with the matters of the corporation."

"Well, tell me about what you found in Turkey. Was the American Matthew Glyndon?"

"Yes, I'm afraid so, J.C."

"What do you mean, Chelsea? Was it Matthew ... "

"J.C., all I can say is that it was Matthew's body, but his memory of who he was seems to be gone."

"You mean to say he didn't recognize you or Olga?"

"That's right, J.C. He doesn't have a clue as to who he was three years ago."

"You do realize, Chelsea, the corporation should fund any care he may require."

"Yes, and I have committed the corporation to pay. He should be coming to the States in a couple of months for evaluation and treatment at the Mayo Clinic."

"Tell me, how did he look? Did you recognize him?"

"Yes. He was rather unkempt but he was clean shaven and looked almost the same as when he left here three years ago. He was broken-up in the crash. We didn't get into his medical history. I don't know what injuries he received except the loss of his memory."

"Is he coming back to the States for good? Why is he waiting another three months?"

"He is married to a young Turkish girl. They have one son and are expecting another one in a month or so. He is coming back only to see if the people at Mayo can help him remember any part of his past life."

"Do we need to set up a schedule for his trip and care at the Clinic?"

"I think Linda can handle the arrangements. She'll keep us up to date on the progress."

"I am terribly sorry for Matthew, Chelsea. You worked with him during the Parker buy-out. As I remember you recommended him to Mr. Thorndike for hire by the corporation."

"Yes, that's right, J.C. I knew Matthew very well. We negotiated over long periods of time during the buy-out."

"Well, boss, you're up-to-date on the events that took place while you were gone. I'll get back to work. By the way, Chelsea, welcome back and I'm very pleased to be working with you."

"Thanks, J.C."

Linda came into the office and closed the door. I knew she wanted the real story about Matthew. She never interfered in my personal life, but was always there for me when I needed to talk with someone confidentially. I have no doubt that she knew Matthew and I were lovers.

"Tell me, boss lady, how are you doing?"

"Linda, I can't explain how I felt when I saw Matthew for the first time in three years. My heart almost jumped from my chest. When I realized he didn't recognize me, I got so mad I began to scream."

"That must have been awful for you, boss. I don't know how you felt, but I can sympathize with you. How disappointing to find him — and not to find him."

"He is married. He has one child and his wife is expecting another. He will come to the States only for the time it takes for the folks at the Mayo Clinic to try and help him recover his memory."

"I know this may sound harsh, boss, but it may be best for you that he not remember his past."

"Yes, that's what Olga said also. I just don't know if he can be helped to recover his memory. And I certainly don't have any idea what will happen if he does remember his past."

"I checked his pay records and he is due pay for the past three years. Boss, at the $125,000 per year with raises plus interest he was earning, that's not chicken feed."

"Linda, follow up on his pay. Check with J.C. and make sure a check is cut for the entire amount of his earnings and interest before he arrives. And be sure he remains on the payroll at the same level as his last active pay period until he decides what he is going to do."

"OK, boss, I'll take care of that. I'm a little nervous about him coming back. I mean after we went through his memorial service and funeral."

144

"Yes, it is a strange feeling to find him alive. It's so disappointing to see him without his memory. I'm going to do what I can do to help him. What he does after that is his decision. If he gets his memory back he may not want to return to Turkey — even with a wife and children. We'll have to wait and see what happens."

9

We had been back from Turkey for about ten days when Linda rang the intercom and said Olga was on the telephone.

"Hello, Olga. Did you recover from the trip?"

"Yes, my dear Chelsea. I am quite recovered and I returned to work just yesterday."

"Well, Olga, why have you been playing hooky for the past week?"

"Your father has been here with me. Chelsea, my dear daughter, we have had so much fun together. We have been out every night, dancing and going to the theater. I feel so young again."

"That is wonderful, Olga. I must tell you, I thought about getting you and Dad together once before, but I just didn't."

"Chelsea my dear, how do you feel about your father and me being together? As you Americans would say, 'an item'?"

"Olga, I think it is wonderful that you and Dad found each other. I am very happy for both of you. Is this the beginning of something great?"

"My dear, one never knows. I don't believe in love at first sight, as you Americans do. No, nothing that either of us can't walk away from at this point."

"Olga, will you promise me one thing?"

"What must I promise you, my dear Chelsea?"

"If you and Dad do decide to make a permanent arrangement, let Morgan and I host the event."

"Why, of course, my dear. That is very gracious of you to offer. I shall remember to tell 'my daughter' before anyone else — that is, if a solid union should happen."

"Thanks for calling, Olga. I'll talk with you again soon."

Linda came to the door as I hung up the telephone and said, "Boss lady, John Capps is on the telephone for you. Do you want to talk with him or shall I take his number?"

"Oh, it's OK, Linda, I'll talk with him." I picked up the phone. "John, what can I do for you?"

"Chelsea, I would like to talk with you about the five million bequest from Mr. Thorndike's will. When would be a good time?"

"John, have you solved the problem? It is vital that the person receiving the bequest not know where it came from."

"I do have a couple of solutions. When can we meet?"

"I'll get Linda, my assistant, back on the phone. She will set up a meeting for us." I called to her, "Linda, pick up the telephone and give John Capps about an hour within the next couple of days."

I asked Linda to call Susan Rosco, our new chief of the law division, so I could talk with her about the meeting and ask her to be prepared to meet with us. Susan said she didn't particularly like John. I thought, she may help to keep John Capps honest about his propositions. John had handled Mr. Thorndike's personal accounts for a number of years. He worked for the corporation for about six years, then went on his own. Shortly after he left his position he suddenly began to manage Mr. Thorndike's personal accounts. Susan apparently knows things about John the rest of us don't know.

John was prompt. His appointment was for 1:00 P.M. and he was in the outer office at 12:30 P.M. I heard Susan greet him rather coolly as they were escorted into my office for the meeting.

"Hello, John, Susan. So John, how are we going to handle this matter of disbursing the five million to a person who must not know where it came from?"

"Well, Chelsea, I believe the simplest method will be to establish a temporary escrow trust account in one of our local banks, then have the bank send a registered letter to the person who'll receive the funds. The bank trust department's letter would tell the person that the money is available to him or her, providing certain agreements are executed."

"And what would the agreements be, John?" Susan asked.

"Susan, the person or persons receiving the funds would have to agree not to pursue the source of the funds on condition that he or she would forfeit the entire amount of money if the agreements are broken."

"That will work, Chelsea," Susan said.

"OK, John, draw up the estate agreement, open the account, and transfer the money. I hope this will be the one and only time I will have to deal with this subject."

"That will work, Chelsea. Let's go with it."

"Chelsea, may I have the name of the individual for the bank?"

"His name is Stanley Jones. He worked for Thorndike at one time."

"I remember him," Susan said. "He was a real woman-hater. He didn't think women had brains. J.C. never gave him a case to handle if a woman was involved because of his hostility. He had problems, as I remember."

"Yes, I remember he exhibited a very unprofessional attitude with me one time. OK, John, thanks for coming by. Keep me informed."

I hoped the problem of Stan Jones and the money Mr. Thorndike left him would finally be put to rest. My intuition tells me to keep my guard up and be prepared for anything where Stan Jones is concerned. God, when will I be able to settle down to a normal life and enjoy my husband and children?

Linda buzzed me on the intercom and said Pastor Abel Clayborne was on the telephone and wanted to speak with me. I wondered why Abel was calling. We'd talked just last month. Abel said he was going on an overseas mission and would be gone for at least two years. He wanted to know if we should talk with Chelsea Lyn before he left the States. Oh, God, Abel is leaving the country. I wonder, *is it time to tell Chelsea Lyn about her biological father?*

CHAPTER FIVE

CHELSEA LYN COMES OF AGE

1 Abel's last telephone call caught me off guard. Heavens, I thought, isn't it enough that I have to deal with the emotions Matthew has brought back to me? If Abel goes overseas on a pastoral posting I won't have his help with Chelsea Lyn. I just don't know if I can talk with her on my own. I must talk with him again about this terrible situation. I asked Linda to get Abel on the telephone. Soon Linda said, "Chelsea, Pastor Clayborne is on line one."

"Thanks, Linda. Abel, what is this about a foreign mission?"

"Hello, Chelsea. It's nice you called. I was just about to leave the church for the day."

"Well, Abel, what's happening with you? Are you really thinking of going on an overseas posting?"

"Yes, Chelsea. The church needs experienced pastors in several countries. I have a choice of the Middle East or Africa."

"But, Abel, is it really necessary for you to take one of these assignments?"

"No, not really, Chelsea. But since Kersi died and Chelsea Lyn went to live with you I have been rather depressed. My church is well established and has three pastors. I don't think a senior pastor is really needed here."

"How long will you remain overseas? Do you get home leave any time during the tour?"

"I don't know much about the program since I have just been asked to consider a posting. The tours are for two years. I don't know about return trips during the tour."

"Abel, if you take one of the posts, how much time will you have before you depart?"

"I am told I could be processed and in a country within 30 to 45 days from the date of acceptance."

"Abel, if you go away and can't help me ... I'm frightened about telling Chelsea Lyn that you are her real father."

"That's why I called you, Chelsea. It may be advisable for you and me to meet and talk about the problem before you tell Chelsea Lyn. My offer to help is still there for you."

"Well, if you have made up your mind to go overseas I suppose we should meet as soon as possible."

"Yes, almost any time would be fine with me. You tell me when and where, and I will arrange my schedule accordingly."

"Let me call you, Abel. I will make it soon. Is that all right with you?"

"Yes, Chelsea, just let me know. It's been nice talking with you. God bless you until we meet again."

"Thanks Abel, and God be with you also."

Chelsea Lyn will be sixteen years old next week. She has been with us for three years. Never once during that time has she even suggested that we talk of her real father. I wonder if it is even necessary to discuss the subject with her. Then I ask myself, "How would you feel if you never knew who your real father was?" My heart tells me it would be unfair not to talk with Chelsea Lyn about Abel. But my very logical mind says to let things be as they are. Deal with the issue when, and if, it comes up. Abel is right. If I'm to talk with Chelsea Lyn about him, he and I should decide how and what we are going to say. Maybe Abel, with his pastoral experience, can better explain the situation. I know I haven't thought of any answers if Chelsea Lyn were to question me about her real father. Yes, I think Abel and I should meet and discuss the situation before he leaves for an overseas pastoral posting.

2 Linda buzzed me on the intercom and said John Capps was on the line.

"Good afternoon, John. How did things go?"

"Chelsea, everything went just fine. Stanley Jones signed the agreement not to attempt to discover the source of the funds. The document was witnessed and signatures notarized, and he said he fully understood the conditions for receiving the five million dollars."

"John, did he question you at all before he signed the document?"

"He said he just couldn't understand who would leave him that much money. He tried to make small talk about my law practice. He was probably 'fishing' for information about my clients. But, Chelsea, I have no doubt that he clearly understood the conditions of accepting the bequest."

"John, I just don't trust the man. Were you listed on any of the documents?"

"No, Chelsea. The trust department of the First National Employees Bank and Trust handled the entire transaction. Only bank officials' signatures appeared on any of the documents."

"OK, just cover your tracks with Stan. I don't want any trouble from him at some future date."

"Yes, I quite agree with you. I believe the transaction was handled discreetly and confidentially. I don't see how he will be able to discover the source of the funds. He set up an account and the bank transferred the money to his account."

"Thanks, John. Keep an eye on Stan Jones for me. Good job, John."

Well, I hope that is the last I will hear about Mr. Thorndike's generosity to Stan Jones. I don't know if Mr. Thorndike felt an obligation to Stan or to the woman who bore him. It would have been more productive to establish a college scholarship in the name of his devoted love than to give the money to the likes of Stan Jones. I just hope he takes the money and disappears!

Linda buzzed me and said Morgan had called. His message said to either call him or to leave word so he could take Linda and me to lunch. I rang for Linda.

"Well, Linda, should we take Morgan up on his offer for lunch?"

"Sure, boss, sounds great! I never pass up a free lunch. It's been a long time since I've had lunch with my boss and her husband."

"Good! Will you call Morgan and tell him we will meet him at Hoffman's?"

"Yes, boss lady, that would be my pleasure." A moment later I heard her on the phone, joking with Morgan.

Morgan was waiting at the door for us when we arrived. He smiled and said, "This is great! Lunch with two of the most beautiful women in the Thorndike Corporation. Hello, ladies." He hugged and kissed me and gave Linda a peck on her cheek. We ordered wine with our lunch. As we waited Morgan talked about Chelsea Lyn.

"Next week is Chelsea Lyn's sixteen birthday. Any ideas about presents?"

"She doesn't need any clothes. Maybe a new watch or jewelry. I don't know, Morgan. We need to include the family in the celebration," I said.

"Of course, Olga and Dad for sure. Linda, can you come to her party?"

"Oh, yes, boss lady, I would love to help celebrate her sweet sixteenth! A surprise party would be something she'd remember for a long time," Linda responded.

"Hey, that's a great idea," Morgan said. "Chelsea Lyn has a number of friends at school and now she also has church friends."

Linda added, "I can help with the deception. I'll bring her friends at the stroke of the hour," she laughed.

Morgan accepted her offer and said, "Her birthday is on Friday. What do you think of a party Friday evening? And, I'm not finished yet. Afterwards, let's all go to the mountains and let her take along a few friends."

"Oh, Morgan, that sounds just great. And Linda, please come to the mountains with us. I'll have Sylvia prepare something very special for Chelsea Lyn's dinner party. And Linda can call Olga and Dad." Linda was very excited and pleased we included her.

We enjoyed our wine and lunch as we continued talking about the party.

"I just love invitations from beautiful women. Thank you, ladies, for sharing lunch with me."

"Thanks, dear, it's decent of you to take time for us."

3 Morgan had not suggested a birthday present for Chelsea Lyn. I wondered what he might be thinking of getting for her. I thought we could meet for dinner tomorrow evening and talk about the last-minute presents for Chelsea Lyn. Morgan seemed to always get to Hoffman's before me. He was waiting for me at the front entrance. As usual he was talking to one of the girls who had worked at the restaurant for a number of years. I told him if he could tear himself away from the beautiful woman he could have dinner with me. I don't think Morgan gives the girls a second thought. He has always been an extremely friendly person who talks to everyone. He never meets a stranger. If people aren't already in his circle of friends, once they meet him they soon become his friends.

"Morgan, what are we going to give Chelsea Lyn for her birthday?"

"I was thinking of a little sports car ... "

"*No! Morgan!* Honey ... please. She is not ready to take on the responsibility of a car. She's too young." Oh, he can't give my little girl a car! I can't have anything happen to her. I have only had my daughter for three years. No, we will not give her a car!

"My dear, you realize she has had driver's education and has her learner's permit. We have driven together for the past six months. She drives to school, and when I pick her up she drives home. She can have her license once she is sixteen."

"*No! Please, Morgan, not a car this year.* Let's wait for her seventeen birthday at least. Please ... please, go along with me on this, dear."

"OK. You win. She can wait for another year. But I want her to get some experience with one of our cars during this year. Is that all right with you?"

"Yes, dear. But please only with supervision for awhile, please?"

"Well, we're back to square one. What do we get her for her birthday?"

"We could get her new clothes ... "

Morgan interrupted me and said, "Not exciting enough. Hey, how about a three- or five-day cruise aboard a ship!"

"Now that is unique," I responded. "Yes, she would like that. Does the family go with her?"

"I was thinking of paying for a few of her friends and a couple of parents from the school. Besides, she may want to be away from her family for a few days after she reaches the golden age of sixteen."

"Good. I will ask Linda to make the arrangements."

"How about sending Linda along on the trip?"

"Morgan, you get smarter and more considerate every day of your life. I'll ask Linda if she can go along as one of the chaperons."

"I think I will have the steak. I need some protein for tonight's activity."

"Oh, is that right? And what activity are you speaking of?"

"I know this beautiful girl who is an easy mark. I thought I would take her to a motel and make love to her for awhile."

"Why go to a motel? Come home with me to my place."

"Boy, that's an offer I can't refuse. And since I love this girl very much I guess that will be all right."

"Morgan, I love our date nights. You're so much fun to be with. I do love you very much." Later when we arrived home Morgan took me directly to the bedroom and began to undress me. I thought, our lovemaking gets better every time. I don't think any two people could

153

love each more than Morgan and I. As we lay in each other's arms with the moon streaming through the skylight my mind drifted to Chelsea Lyn and Abel. I had a terrible feeling that it wouldn't be too long before the subject of her real father would come up between us. I cannot hurt her. But how am I going to explain that Abel is her real father unless I tell her the truth? Morgan moved closer to me and we drifted into a deep sleep.

4 We took Raynor and Caesar into our confidence about Chelsea Lyn's surprise party and they were very excited to be included in a secret from their sister. Everyone got into high gear and helped to prepare for the party.

I told J.C. I would be out of the office from Thursday through Monday and he could handle any emergencies that may come along. He was very pleased I was spending time with my family. And I was happy to have someone like J.C. to take over the operation.

Chelsea Lyn apparently was suspicious about possible preparations for her birthday. She seemed excited about turning sixteen.

Thursday evening, she and I sat on her bed and talked about her school and friends and things in general. She said she was very glad to be growing up. She took my hands in hers and looked directly at me with those soul-searching eyes Abel had given her and said, "Mother, I have a very special, secret request I want to ask for my birthday."

"Oh, sweetheart. What can possibly be a secret we can give you for your birthday?"

She responded as she continued to focus those shining eyes into my soul. "Mother, this gift cannot come from Papa Morgan. This gift must come from you," she said as she took my face in her hands and continued looking into my eyes.

"What is it, my dear Chelsea Lyn?"

"Mother, Father Abel and Mother Kersi always told me you were my real mother. But Mother, neither of them ever told me who my real father is."

She stunned me! I knew this would happen but I asked, why now, Lord?

"Chelsea Lyn, my darling daughter. May I ask that we wait until next week to talk about that, please?"

154

"Mother, please! Please! I would like to know for my birthday. Please promise you will tell me who my real father is. And, Mother, can you tell me why neither Father Abel nor Mother Kersi would ever tell me?"

"My dearest, did you ever ask them?"

"No, Mother. I didn't ever think of anything like that when I was with them. I didn't know you then. I accepted them as my real mother and father, that is, until you came for me."

"Chelsea Lyn, does it bother you not knowing who your real father is?"

"Mother, I have matured quite a bit over the past three years. I am a young woman now. It will not be long before I shall be going to college."

"Do you remember your childhood with the Claybornes?"

"Yes, Mother, I had a wonderful childhood with Father Abel and Mother Kersi. And Mother, I have been so very happy here with you and Papa Morgan."

"Are you very concerned not knowing who your real father is?"

"Yes, it does bother me very much. I feel I need to know more about me. And Mother, that includes knowing who my real father is."

"Chelsea Lyn, my dear, since you want to know who your father is before your birthday I will have to let you know when we can talk about it, OK? By the way, Morgan has suggested you can take a few friends to the mountains from Saturday until Monday if you wish."

"Mother, do you promise me with all your heart that we can talk about this before my birthday?"

"Yes, dear, I promise with all my heart. We shall have our discussion."

"Then, Mother, it will be just grand to take my friends to the mountains. How many can I take?"

"Darling, if your friends bring extra sleeping bags you can bring the entire neighborhood. You girls can have the family room to camp out in."

"Oh, *Mother, that is wonderful!* I shall make a list and call them."

"Chelsea Lyn, do you know that I love you very much and I am very proud that you are my daughter?"

"Yes, Mother, I felt your great love for me the moment I first saw you at Father Abel's house a long time ago. And Mother, do you realize I love you and Papa Morgan very, very much ... and Mother, I'm proud to be your daughter."

"*Mother, please! Please!* I would like to know for my birthday. Please promise you will tell me who my real father is ... "

5 As I walked into my office the next morning, I asked Linda to please call Pastor Clayborne for me. In a few minutes she rang and said he was on the telephone.

"Good morning, Abel. Well, it finally happened. Chelsea ... "

"Morning, Chelsea. What finally happened?"

"Chelsea Lyn asked me to tell her who her real father is. And, get this! This is what she wants for her sixteen birthday."

"Oh, Lord. What did you say?"

"*I was so stunned I didn't know what to say!* I was able to postpone the discussion for a couple of days."

"My dear Chelsea, I sympathize with you. What a terrible predicament!"

"Abel, we need to meet and talk about what I'm are going to say to Chelsea Lyn. And Abel, could you plan to be with us, if I need you?"

"Chelsea, I'm free of any appointments today. I can meet you when and where you say. And yes, Chelsea, I shall always be there to help you when you need me."

"Can you come here to my office, Abel?"

Abel hesitated a moment and said, "Are you sure, Chelsea? I don't want to complicate matters for you."

"Yes. It is quite proper for me to talk with a pastor in my office. When can you be here?"

"I will be there within the hour. Shall I come directly to your office?"

"Yes, I'm on the fifteen floor of the Thorndike Tower. Do you know where that is?"

"Yes, I know your building. I will see you in about an hour."

I called Linda into my office and told her Pastor Clayborne was coming to meet with me and to hold all appointments and calls until we concluded our meeting.

"Well, boss lady, I am finally going to get to meet the pastor with the famous telephone voice."

"Oh, Linda, that's right, you never meet him. But you've had many telephone conversations with him, haven't you?"

"Sure have, boss. Do you want refreshments?"

"Linda, you could get our lunch for us. I'm sure our meeting will take two or three hours. Yes, that would be nice. Thank you."

Abel arrived as promised, about an hour from the time we talked. Linda met him and introduced herself. I could hear her say how nice it was to finally meet the voice on the telephone. Abel followed Linda into my office. I met them at the door and asked Abel what he would like for lunch. Linda took our orders and excused herself.

Abel looked weary. His normally bright, shining eyes did not show the happy confidence he always seem to have. He said he was depressed and it showed in his personality. I now know he was trying to go overseas to escape his depression and unhappiness. Abel had never appeared so down.

I asked, "Abel, are you well? You don't seem like the high-spirited Abel I know."

"Yes, Chelsea. I'm OK. I just can't seem to renew my interest in my work at the church. Maybe I am not challenged enough."

"Abel, I am sorry. You were always such an uplifting person. I know how you helped me when I lived with you and Kersi in the parish. You pulled me up from depression several times in my early life."

"Thank you, Chelsea. I am happy that I contributed to your well-being. I suppose we should try and plan a way to tell Chelsea Lyn about me."

"Yes, Abel. I realize she must know, especially since she was the one to ask. But, I am at a complete loss as to how she can be told and not be hurt."

"What about your husband, Morgan? Does he know?"

"*No!* Morgan never questioned me when I brought Chelsea Lyn home. He trusted me with the adoption papers. He signed the papers without even looking at them. We both are on the papers, but I was listed as her mother. Morgan is the only one who really adopted her."

"Well, Chelsea, that is another problem you must deal with. But let's talk about Chelsea Lyn. I am sure she is mature enough to know the truth about her birth."

"How do you think we should tell her, Abel?"

"Let me do it, Chelsea. I want you with us, of course. But let me tell her what happened with Kersi and me before you came along."

"Abel, I'm willing to try any approach. I just hope you are right about her being mature enough to handle the truth. Abel, we need to talk with her in the next day or two, before her birthday."

"How about Monday afternoon in my church office?"

"I suppose that would be a proper place for her to learn the truth. She is a very religious young lady."

I knew telling Morgan the truth was my responsibility. I couldn't have Chelsea Lyn share my problem with Morgan. I wish Abel could help me decide how to deal with Morgan. Before Chelsea Lyn left for school I told her I would pick her up at the end of the day, that I had someplace to take her. She didn't seem too surprised. I was sure she suspected I was going to take her to buy birthday presents. Oh, God, please help me through this terrible ordeal. I couldn't imagine how Abel intended to talk with her. I know it's my place to tell her what happened with me, and I will. I just don't have a clue as to how I'm going to do it.

6 Chelsea Lyn was waiting for me at the school entrance. She came to the car and asked if she could drive. I consented and she slid behind the steering wheel, adjusted her seat, the mirrors, inside and out, and said, "Where to, Mother?" I gave her directions as we drove to the church. I felt I should get her prepared for our discussion before we reached the church. I asked how her school day had gone. She said she always had a good time in school. Learning seemed to be so important to her.

I finally began, "Chelsea Lyn, remember I promised you we would talk about your early life this week before your birthday?"

"Yes Mother, *you mean the subject of 'who my real father is'?*"

"Yes, dear. We are going to Father Abel's church to meet him. We three are going to talk about it."

"Oh, that's grand. Father Abel has always been so wonderful to me. I love him dearly."

In a few minutes we reached the church. Abel was standing outside the main door waiting to greet us. His church is one of the oldest in the city. It looks like a king's mansion. The giant doors have early religious designs carved into the heavy wood. Big brass rings adorn the center of the doors and at one time were probably used to open them. Modern technology has replaced them with golden door knobs and a pneumatic motor to assist in swinging them open. Abel took our hands in his and said we could go to the side entrance near his office.

"Well, Chelsea Lyn. Tell me, how are you doing in school?"

"Father Abel, I am making all A's this semester. You realize I will complete high school next year. I am almost two years ahead of my peer group."

159

"That is wonderful. What do you intend to study in college?"

"I really want to be a doctor. I am beginning to think about pediatrics. I love children and I think it would be great to take care of them as a doctor."

"Chelsea Lyn, did your mother tell you why we wanted to meet you here?"

"I'm not sure. Mother and I were going to discuss a private matter … is that why I'm here in the church?"

Abel said, "Chelsea, Chelsea Lyn, may we say a prayer before we begin our discussion?"

Chelsea Lyn responded with a resounding, "Yes, of course, Father Abel."

Abel began, "Lord, we come to you today with heavy hearts. You created little Chelsea Lyn and she has been a Godly blessing to her family during her entire life. We are before you today, Lord, to ask your guidance in what we must say today. Please, Lord, know that we have sinned in your eyes. But we asked and received your forgiveness many years ago. We must now confess again to this young girl so that she may know herself. We ask this in the name of God the Father, the Son, and the Holy Spirit, Amen." Chelsea Lyn made the sign of the cross as she passed her hand from shoulder to shoulder and then to her head and heart.

"Chelsea Lyn, do you remember Mother Kersi talking to you about your real mother?"

"Yes," she said as she squeezed my hand.

"Can you remember when she first began to tell you that your real mother would come for you one day?" Abel's penetrating eyes seemed to be looking into her soul.

"Yes, I think so. I was in the third grade and I remember Mother Kersi was very ill. I remember bringing things to her in bed. I sat with her on the bed and she helped me with my homework."

"Yes, that was about the time I remember also. Chelsea Lyn, that was about eight years ago, wasn't it?"

"Well, I was seven years old, Father Abel — about nine years ago, I think."

"Did Mother Kersi ever tell you that your mother lived with us?"

"Of course, she did. You should remember that. She said it was when you lived in that big German-built house on the north side of Lewisburg."

160

"My, Chelsea Lyn, you do have a good memory. Did she tell you that you were born in that house?"

"Yes, she did. Of course, I don't remember that," she laughed nervously.

"And did she ever tell you why she was not your natural mother?"

"She said she couldn't have a child because she was in an accident."

"Abel, let me! Chelsea Lyn, did you ever know that Abel and Kersi and I loved each other very much when I lived with them?"

"Yes, I think so. Well, Mother Kersi always talked like she loved you very much. She said the Lord had sent you to them. I couldn't understand what she meant then and I don't really know now."

"Chelsea Lyn, I don't know if you are going to understand what I am about to say to you, but I pray to the Lord that you will be patient and try to understand."

"Father Abel, why do I think I'm about to be told a fairy tale?"

"Chelsea Lyn, what your mother wants to say to you is no fairy tale. It is real life as we lived it." Abel's voice became very stern.

"What is it, Mother? What do you want to tell me?"

"Chelsea Lyn, *Abel is your real father!*"

Chelsea Lyn's beautiful little face took on a shocked expression as she sat and looked from me to Abel and back again. The silence was deafening. I started to speak and she stopped me and said, *"No, please, Mother, don't say anything!* May I go into the church for awhile?"

"Oh, my darling Chelsea Lyn, I have hurt you so ... "

"Mother, Father Abel, please I must be alone for a few minutes."

She rose from the chair and walked into the main church. She went to the altar and knelt before the crucifix and raised her beautiful shining eyes to its face. We could see her, but we couldn't hear what she was saying. We couldn't hear her prayers. Oh, God, please help her to understand that what we did in bringing her into the world was your work. We know we broke your covenants, but you have forgiven us. Please help our daughter as she struggles with this new discovery in her life. Abel knelt at the door entrance and began to pray. I continued to pray for our Chelsea Lyn. We must help her to win the struggle she is going through here in the church.

After what seemed to be hours, but was really not more than thirty to forty minutes, Chelsea Lyn came back to the church office. She had been crying and her pretty teenage face was streaked with mascara that had run down her cheeks. She looked into Abel's eyes ... and then turned to me ... and stared without saying a word. Tears were still running down my cheeks and ... *I couldn't control my sobbing.* I reached out for her and she pulled away. She sat down and pulled her legs into her stomach and sat in a tightly drawn fetal position. Her chin rested on her knees and the tears continued to flow down her cheeks. I knelt beside her and began to tell her how sorry we were that we had not told her about her real father long ago.

She looked at me without saying a word. I don't really know if she even heard what I was trying to say between my tears and sobbing. Abel knelt next to her and began to pray again. He gently stroked her head as he asked God to help her understand what had happened to her. Finally she sat up in the chair and said she had something to say. We waited.

She looked first at Abel and then to me and said, "Mother, how could you and Father Abel do what you did? Mother Kersi was his wife. You two broke the Lord's rules. You had sexual intercourse to have me. Oh, no, *don't try to tell me that I was another immaculate conception!* You two not only cheated on Mother Kersi, but you also *cheated on the Lord!* ... How could you?"

"Child," Abel said, "there are things you must understand about Mother Kersi. You were aware that she could not have children ... "

She interrupted and said, "Father Abel, did you and Mother use that as an excuse to make love ... ?"

Abel took her hands in his and said, "No, my dear little Chelsea Lyn. We prayed to the Lord for years to give us our own children, but somehow the Lord did not grant us that prayer."

"Then you say to me, Father Abel, that it was all right for you and my mother to have a baby?"

Abel responded with more force in his voice. *"Chelsea Lyn, we are not trying to justify what we did!* But you must listen to why it happened."

I followed his words and said very loudly, "Chelsea Lyn, please listen to what Father Abel is saying to you."

"Mother Kersi had reached the end of her patience when she was told that she would never have a baby of her own. We tried to adopt two different children, one a little girl born to a teenage mother, only to fail at the last moment."

"Chelsea Lyn, my daughter," I said, "you didn't know what Mother Kersi had gone through trying to have a child. When I came to their home, she took it as a sign from the Lord that somehow I was there in answer to her prayers."

"You mean, Mother, the Lord sent you to have a baby by Father Abel. *Please don't expect me to believe that story!*"

"Well, whether you believe it or not, that is what your Mother Kersi believed. She told me if she could not have a child of her own then she would not live. Chelsea Lyn, *my child, do you know what I am saying?* Mother Kersi would have taken her life if we had not agreed to have a child — *to have you for her!*"

Hearing Abel talking so forceful to her made me want to tell her how I felt for so many years, knowing that I had a beautiful little girl that I could not see. I began the story.

"Chelsea Lyn, you must now listen to how I felt. You were born to me but I didn't even get to see you or to hold you when you were born. Mother Kersi was afraid if I held you that I would not keep my word and let them take you. She was right. If I had held you, *I would have never given you to them for adoption!*"

"Then, Mother," she said through her tears, "*you are saying you gave me away when I was born ... ?*"

"*No! Chelsea Lyn!* You are not being fair to your mother. She gave her word to live by the adoption ... ," Abel said very loudly.

"And Chelsea Lyn, you have no idea how much I cried for you. My world was empty. Every time Abel would call my first words were '*When will I see my daughter?*' and '*when will she be mine?*'" I tried to explain to her how ... only a mother would feel.

"Chelsea Lyn," Abel continued, "you remember when Mother Kersi and I were divorced, don't you?"

"Yes, I ... remember. Why did she take me from you, Father Abel?"

"I don't know, child. She became very ill before the divorce. Maybe her illness drove to what she did. Later, when she was very ill, you remember living with me and going to the Christian school down the street?"

"Yes, I remember that."

"Well, it was then that I learned that Mother Kersi was near death and could die at any time. I called your mother to come to see her before the Lord took her. Chelsea Lyn, do you know what a wonderful thing Mother Kersi did as she was dying?"

163

"No! Chelsea Lyn! You are not being fair to your mother. She gave her word to live by the adoption … "

"Oh, Father Abel, I'm so sad. I can't think of that time. I loved her so much and yet I knew the Lord was going to take her. Why did he take her?"

"Chelsea Lyn, my daughter. You must understand, we are not in control of our lives. We gave our lives to the Lord to do with what he would. The Lord probably told Mother Kersi to give you, my daughter, back to me before he took her. You were the last person on her lips as she died. You were almost thirteen when I came for you. Do you remember?"

"Mother ... and Father Abel, I am really ... trying to understand why both of you broke the Lord's commandants when I was conceived. Maybe I need some time to pray and maybe I need to understand why adults do what they do. *I don't know!* I am so confused. I know I am a good Christian and I would never do anything against my Lord. Why did you and Father Abel sin against the Lord?"

"Chelsea Lyn," Abel began, "all we can ask is that you forgive us as the Lord forgives sinners. We sinned and we have prayed many times that we would be forgiven by the Lord. And now we are asking you to accept what has happened in your life and to forgive us if you have it in your heart to do so."

"Oh, Father Abel, Mother, I will try. I will really try!"

Abel took us both in his arms and held us for a few minutes. He said, "May we have a prayer before we leave? Can we go to the altar?"

We walked into the church, down the aisle, and knelt at the altar. Abel began to pray, "Father, we ask that you give Chelsea Lyn the understanding to know that we love her and that you love her. And that all we have done in our lives has been for her. We ask your guidance in this desperate hour. Help us all to love one another and to forgive each other for any sins we may have committed. We pray in your name. Amen."

Chelsea Lyn and I left the church. Neither of us spoke during the ride home. When we arrived I asked how she was and she replied, "Mother, I'm not sure. This day has taken a great deal of my strength. And, Mother, my beliefs have been shaken terribly. I must be alone for awhile, please."

"Yes, my dear. I understand."

"No! Mother, I don't think you do understand! You can't possibly feel what I have felt this day. Learning Father Abel is my real father is quite a shock. Please give me time, and maybe I will understand. I don't know."

As I stopped the car in the driveway, Chelsea Lyn opened the door and ran into the house and directly to her room. I thought to myself, this little sixteen-year-old has a great deal on her mind. She is such a lady. I am sure she will hide her emotional hurt and put on a good face for her birthday weekend.

Morgan was in the kitchen and yelled at her to come and say hello to her father. He came to the door and asked, "What happened to our happy girl?" I was not prepared to discuss what had transpired. I told him she was upset with female problems. He didn't question my answer.

7 Chelsea Lyn didn't come down for supper. Morgan fixed a plate and took it to her room. He knocked and asked, "Angel, it's your old man. Can I come in? I have a plate of wonderful food for you."

"Papa Morgan, I'm really not hungry. I really don't feel like talking to anyone either."

"My dear, you realize I have a long line of beautiful teenage girls waiting to have something to eat with me and to listen to my stories of the day. Do I have to take the second in line?"

"Oh, Papa Morgan, you can come in. Maybe I will get hungry when I see what you have brought me."

"Well, that's better. I haven't seen my angel all day. Don't you feel well, sweetheart?"

"Papa Morgan, this has been a very trying day for me. I am very tired."

"Want to talk with your old man about it, angel?"

"Papa Morgan, will you call Mother for me? Please ask her to come to my room. I want to talk with both of you." I heard Morgan call for me to come to Chelsea Lyn's room.

"Chelsea Lyn, sweetheart, are you all right?" I didn't know why she wanted me and Morgan together in her room. *Was she about to tell Morgan what happened today?* I almost could feel her emotional pain. Lord, tell me how I can help my daughter. I will do anything to help her get over the hurt she must be feeling. It's not an everyday occurrence when a young lady is introduced to a man she thought was her adopted father only to learn he is her real father.

"I think so, Mother. Can I talk with both of you about today?"

I was really not prepared for Chelsea Lyn to tell Morgan about what happened at the church today. I didn't know how I would keep her from talking if she chose to talk. I recalled what Morgan said when I brought Chelsea Lyn home for the first time. He was so happy to have her join our family. Later he said he was not really interested in who her parents were. He just said he thought they were wonderful, intelligent, and Christian people. He didn't want to know any more. As I remember, he *never* really understood that I am Chelsea Lyn's biological mother.

Well, if Chelsea Lyn is going to tell him about Abel, it is her choice. I will have to suffer the consequences of trying to explain to Morgan about Abel and me. I took Chelsea Lyn's face in my hands and looked into her beautiful eyes and said, "Darling, you can talk about anything. I am sure Papa Morgan wants to hear what you have to say."

She placed her lips on my cheek and whispered, "Thank you, Mother. I want Papa Morgan to know my real father."

Morgan said, "Hey, what's going on between you two, female secrets or something?"

"Papa Morgan, I want you to know that you are my father and I'm going to remain with you as long as you want me as a daughter."

"Chelsea Lyn, that sounds heavy. Have I done something to disturb you"?

"Oh, no! Please don't ever think that I don't love you. I know you love me and I think you always will. But I guess always is a long time. But you do love me, don't you?"

"Of course I love you. Hey, we're getting very serious about something. What is troubling you, angel?"

"Papa Morgan, I would like you to meet my real father! I mean if it wouldn't upset you. Would it?"

"Angel, that would not upset me. It would be wonderful to know the real father of such a beautiful and loving young lady. But I must tell you if we have to fight over you, I'll win." Morgan was trying desperately to lighten the conversation.

"Oh, Papa Morgan, there's not going to be any fight. You're just kidding me."

"Of course, I am, angel. Yes, sweetheart, I would love to meet your real father."

"Mother, would it be possible to invite Father Abel over for my birthday?"

167

"Darling, you can talk about anything. I am sure Papa Morgan wants to hear what you have to say."

Well, lightning struck again! I wondered what would happen next in my life. Morgan, unsuspecting, will be meeting my first lover and Chelsea Lyn's father. I can't believe this is happening! How can I get out of this dilemma without causing a scene that will return to haunt me? I looked at Morgan and he shook his head approvingly in response to Chelsea Lyn's question. I managed to say, "Well, I guess it is all right with me if Papa Morgan agrees."

"Please, Papa Morgan, may we invite him for dinner or something? I want the two most important men in my life to know each other. Is it OK, Mother?"

"Yes, of course, sweetheart, if that is what you want. It's your birthday!"

8 When I reached my office on Tuesday morning I called Abel immediately.

"Hello, Abel, this is Chelsea. Are you sitting down?"

"Good morning, Chelsea. Yes, I'm sitting at my desk. What do you mean?"

"Chelsea Lyn *is inviting you to her birthday party Friday.* Well, it is really a surprise party — she doesn't know about it."

"Chelsea, *are you serious?* Chelsea Lyn wants me to come to your home?"

"Yes, I am serious and you heard what I said. Your daughter wants you to meet the man who adopted her."

"*Chelsea, I can't come!* I mean, I don't think it is the proper thing to do. I certainly don't want to embarrass you."

"Abel, I have resolved there is nothing I can do to hide anything about my life any more. I will just have to trust the Lord as I did when I consented to have Chelsea Lyn for you and Kersi."

"May I ask, what is your husband's view toward our meeting?"

"Abel, let me tell you exactly what Morgan said when Chelsea Lyn asked if she could invite her real father for dinner to meet him. He said 'wonderful.'"

"Chelsea, I don't quite understand all this. Am I missing something in our conversation?"

"What do you mean, Abel? Chelsea Lyn simply wants the two of you to meet."

"Please tell me, does Morgan know our entire story?"

"No, he doesn't know that I am Chelsea Lyn's mother! And Abel, if he did, Morgan is a Christian who has made mistakes, but truly lives a Christian life now. I think his heart is big enough to forgive what we did in bringing Chelsea Lyn into the world."

"Chelsea, I am just a little frightened to come to your home. But if that is what you and Chelsea Lyn want, then I will come. The Lord will have to be with us. Yes, tell Chelsea Lyn I would be delighted to help celebrate her sixteenth birthday."

"Abel, you and I can't really do anything else. We both should be with our daughter as she becomes this lovely sixteen-year-old lady."

9 Friday was a long day. I had not intended to work, but I couldn't be around Chelsea Lyn and Morgan all day, then greet Abel at dinner. I buried myself in the affairs of the corporation and worked like a demon was in my soul. I waited as long as I could before departing for home. Abel was to arrive at 6:30 P.M. I guess it is proper for the lady of the house to officially greet her visitors even if one of them is her first lover. Oh, dear God, give me the strength to get through whatever is awaiting me this evening.

I had arrived a few minutes ahead of Abel and was upstairs refreshing myself when I heard Sylvia greet him at the front door. Before I reached the door, Chelsea Lyn dashed through it and landed in his arms. I was happy to see her smiling and enjoying the evening after her ordeal yesterday. I hoped this concession of having Abel come to our home on her very important sixteen birthday would help her solve the problem of discovering her real father. Chelsea Lyn escorted Abel throughout the lower part of the house. Morgan and Linda had gone to pick up the several girls and boys who would come in at the proper time to begin the surprise party. I greeted Abel and welcomed him to our home. Chelsea Lyn seemed to watch our reactions to each other. I didn't know what my emotions would do when Abel and Morgan meet for the first time. *I would soon know!* Chelsea Lyn's disappointment in Abel and me when she learned Abel was her real father seemed to have subsided.

Morgan called to check whether the time was right to bring the other teenagers in and begin the surprise party. Abel and Chelsea Lyn were sitting on the patio looking down toward the lake. I told Morgan to bring them on and "Let's get on with the party."

Before Morgan and Linda came with the teenagers, Olga and Dad arrived. Introductions and greetings were made and Olga raised her eyebrows and said to me, "So, my dear Chelsea, *this is the father of Chelsea Lyn!* What is he doing here in your home, may I inquire?"

"It's a long story, Olga. We can talk after the party. Please help me get through this evening. Morgan and Linda are on their way with the teenagers for the surprise party ... "

"Abel, this is my father, Mr. Thomas Carodine. Father is a professor at City College."

"I am very happy to meet you, Mr. Carodine. Sir, I must apologize to you."

"Why, may I ask, Pastor Clayborne?"

"When I received your letter addressed to Chelsea concerning your wife's — her mother's — death I did not deliver it immediately. For that I must apologize. It was my decision because of Chelsea's condition at the time."

"Pastor, that is long past. But if it will help your conscience, I accept your apology."

"Abel, you met Dr. Olga Doubreski. Olga has been my doctor for a long time. And, I might add, *my confidante and loving friend.*" I hoped Abel noticed the "confidante" part of my introduction. He should understand that Olga knows all about my life with the Claybornes.

Chelsea Lyn came to me very excited and asked where Papa Morgan was. "Mother, you didn't go back on your word, did you? Papa Morgan will be here, won't he?"

"Yes, of course, he will. Go say hello to your grandfather and Doctor Olga."

"Grandfather and Dr. Olga," she shouted, "I'm so happy you came to my birthday dinner. Did your meet my real father?"

"Yes, dear, we did. Chelsea Lyn, are you happy to have reached the golden age of 'sweet sixteen and never been kissed'?"

"Grandfather, you don't know if I've been kissed. Maybe I have and maybe not. You just don't know, do you?"

"Well, my dear granddaughter, are you playing games with the senior member of this family? Sixteen may not be to old to spank where I come from."

"Oh, Grandfather! No, I have not had nor do I have a serious boyfriend. So does that answer your question?"

171

"Then you're still my girl, right?"

"Yes, Grandfather. I will always be yours, Papa Morgan's, and now Father Abel's girl."

Suddenly the evening quiet time was interrupted with a loud blast of car horns. Morgan and Linda drove into the driveway with two carloads of teenagers ready for the surprise party. As the teenagers began to climb out of the cars, they were shouting to Chelsea Lyn, "Surprise! Surprise! Happy Birthday to Chelsea Lyn."

Chelsea Lyn was very surprised! I didn't know how the surprise party would affect the introduction of her two fathers, but I hoped the occasion would be much lighter with the arrival of all the teens. Chelsea Lyn greeted her friends with shouts of joy and jubilation. Each came to her bearing a gift. Soon the hearth at the fireplace was covered with birthday gifts. Chelsea Lyn was flitting about thanking everyone for coming. She came to me and asked who had planned such a grand surprise for her birthday. I wanted to say, *"Daughter, dear, you planned what may be the main event!* The party preparations were minor." But of course, I would never bring attention to her desire to have both fathers together. I waited until Morgan had settled the teens down to a semblance of quietness and asked the adults if they wanted to adjourn to the patio.

10 Chelsea Lyn jumped up from visiting with her friends, excused herself, and said she would return in a few minutes.

"Wait, Mother! I want to go to the patio with you. I want to be the one to introduce my two fathers." I thought, what is she planning now?

Chelsea Lyn took Morgan by the arm and escorted him to where Abel was standing. She said proudly, "Papa Morgan, I want you to meet my real father, Father Abel."

For the first time Morgan seemed surprised. I didn't know if it was because Abel was a pastor or that he was much older than Morgan. Morgan extended his hand and said, "It is indeed a real pleasure, sir, to meet the father of such an outstanding young lady. I thank you from the bottom of my heart for permitting me to become her father."

Now it was Abel's turn to be surprised and shocked. He was almost lost for words. He finally said, "Morgan, thank you for your kind words.

I don't know quite what to say. I have never been in a situation like this before ... "

"Morgan, Abel, let me get you drinks!" My conscience was at me again. I wanted to be with them as they discussed Chelsea Lyn — and anything else they had to say. I hoped Morgan wouldn't get into any embarrassing questions. Abel was being very cautious with his answers. Soon I felt it time to get the two of them away from each other. I took Abel back to Olga so she could question him in any manner she chose. I felt she may have a few choice words to say to Abel anyway.

Chelsea Lyn's group had reached the peak of the party with loud music and dancing in the large family room that overlooked the lake. I could see her looking for Morgan and Abel as she danced with her partner. I didn't really want her to be alone with Morgan and Abel. Her innocent conversation could introduce something that Morgan would wonder about. I stopped the music and announced it was time for the birthday gifts to be presented and opened. Morgan had talked with the parents of the teens who were to accompany Linda on the cruise. Linda was excited to be going and she made the announcement, "And now, ladies and gentlemen, one of the presents of the evening: Chelsea Lyn and four young ladies will accompany me to the Caribbean on a five-day cruise with the good wishes of her parents, Chelsea and Morgan."

"Oh, *Mother! Papa Morgan! How wonderful!* How did you think of a birthday gift like that? It is just grand. I'm so excited!" The four teen girls at the party had cleared the trip with their parents. They were as excited as Chelsea Lyn was.

Morgan then announced that the birthday party that began this evening would last through the weekend at our cabin in the mountains. After the weekend in the mountains, the five girls will be on their way to the ship cruise. The excitement of the evening kept Abel and Morgan involved with the teens and other guests. About eleven o'clock, Abel said he should be departing. I rescued Chelsea Lyn from her friends. Abel extended his good wishes to the crowd. Chelsea Lyn and I walked him to his car. He hugged Chelsea Lyn and said, "My dear daughter, that was a very brave thing you did. I hope your new father loves you as I love you. You must understand you will always be in my heart, *you will always be my daughter.*"

"Mother, Father Abel, this evening with Papa Morgan and Father Abel helped me to understand part of what happened when we talked a couple of days ago at the church. I don't know what I would have done, Mother, if you had not permitted them to meet."

"My little girl! If having your two fathers meet will help heal your hurt then the Lord has answered my prayers. Chelsea Lyn, I am very proud of you."

"Chelsea, I will let you know what happens with the foreign posting."

"Chelsea Lyn, we didn't tell you before. Father Abel may be taking a foreign pastoral posting to help people to become Christians."

"Oh, Mother! Father Abel! *You wouldn't leave* ... I mean after you and Papa Morgan met? I want you to know each other better."

"We will, my child. I will come again before I depart," Abel said as he drove away.

Chelsea Lyn and I stood for a long few minutes watching Abel drive away. Chelsea Lyn then hugged me and through the flow of her tears said, "Thank you, Mother. Thank you very much for this wonderful evening. My two fathers have met each other and I am very happy!" She hugged me tightly and said, *"This is the happiest birthday I could ever have!"*

CHAPTER SIX

THE PRODIGAL SON RETURNS

1 Chelsea Lyn's sixteenth birthday party finally ended. Her four girlfriends remained overnight for the trip to the mountains. Father, Olga, Morgan, Linda, and I sat on the patio and talked about the party. Morgan seemed to be in deep thought. Finally he said, "You know, it was kind of strange meeting Chelsea Lyn's father."

"How do you mean, Morgan?" Father asked.

"I was surprised that he is an older man."

Olga responded to Morgan. "But, Morgan, my dear, Chelsea Lyn is sixteen years old. You should subtract sixteen years to know he was a much younger father. Da?"

"Da, Olga. I suppose I was a little shocked when she asked if she could invite her real father to her birthday party."

I tried to calm him. "Morgan, dear, that was the only thing Chelsea Lynn asked for, to have her real father here. She thought the evening with her fathers would be a quiet dinner."

"I share Morgan's concern," Father said. "I found her request rather odd. But I'm happy the evening turned out so well for her."

"Frankly I'm quite relieved we had such a nice evening. Morgan, dear, thank you so much for being the wonderful person you are." I reached over and kissed him on the cheek.

"Well, lady, I'm only returning a small part to my family. I will say I was not too surprised that he is a pastor. I can see where Chelsea Lyn developed her strong Christian beliefs."

I thought, it's about time to move away from talking about Abel. I turned to Dad and said, "Well, Dad, Olga, I'm so happy you two are seeing each other ... "

"You mean, my daughter, we have your approval to date?" Father laughed as he took Olga's hand.

"Oh, Dad, I didn't mean it that way ... "

"I know what she meant," Olga said as she laughed.

"Ladies, have you two been talking about me?"

"Well, Dad, I had to warn Olga about you, didn't I?"

Linda had been rather quiet during the family discussions. She said, "Well, folks, I thought we had a wonderful surprise party for Chelsea

Lyn. And with those words I believe I'll retire for the night. Chelsea, I presume we will get an early start for the mountains?"

I responded with a laugh. "Yes, my dear. We usually start out about six thirty or so. Sylvia isn't going with us but she will have our food and supplies ready, including breakfast at about six A.M. Can you handle that, Linda?"

She laughed and said, "I can handle anything since I'm on vacation for the next several days. Good night, all!" We all said good night and she went to her room.

Morgan rose and said he was rather tired. He excused himself and went to our bedroom. I didn't want to be a wet blanket for Olga and Dad, so I told them good night and joined Morgan in our bedroom. I had to tell Morgan how much I loved him for accepting Chelsea Lyn's real father.

"Morgan, thank you again, darling, for being nice to Abel. Chelsea Lyn had her eyes on you two for most of the evening."

"Yes, I knew she was watching us. But, honey, I didn't put on a act for her. Abel does seem like a fine person."

"Well, your daughter loves you even more for agreeing to be with her real father tonight."

"You know, honey, his wife must have been a wonderful person. Chelsea Lyn has such gentle ways, sort of like you." Oh, God, help me. Please don't let Morgan question me about Chelsea Lyn's mother. I can't continue lying to him. If he wasn't shocked about meeting Abel he would be shocked if he knew that I am Chelsea Lyn's real mother. I waited for the next shoe to fall. Morgan reached up and pulled me into his arms and kissed me very hard and passionately. I would be the aggressor tonight. The conversation about Abel will be drowned in our lovemaking. Morgan had taken his shower and was dressed in his pajamas. I pulled the drawstring on his pants and they fell to the floor. He removed my clothes, one piece at a time, and as he did he kissed my exposed body. Our bodies seemed to mold to one another. We made love for a long time. I was more passionate tonight because I was so thankful that our love remains strong. I hope it can withstand the stress when I must explain about Abel and me … about Chelsea Lyn's real mother. I silently said my prayers.

2 Dad and Olga elected to remain in our home rather than go to the mountains with us, Linda, and the boys and young girls. We left Sylvia at home to care for their needs. Once we were set to go Linda explained that all members of the party, except the parents, would take care of the meals and cleaning. Linda listed the duties they would all have since Sylvia was not going with us. The girls were put into cooking and cleaning crews of two each. Over the three-day trip, each one would have a different partner for their assigned chores.

The drive through the countryside was very beautiful. In the lower elevations we could still see the remnants of multicolored leaves on the trees. The leaves had lost their bright colors, and many had turned to a light or dark brown as they fell from the trees. As we drove into the mountains we could see snow on the higher elevations. The snow and evergreen trees created a beautiful, breathtaking view of the mountains. The girls wished for snow all the way to the cabin. The wind was blowing and bending the bare trees toward the ground. As we drove nearer to the cabin, we could feel the cold air of the early afternoon. Snow had not started to fall, but the weather forecast indicated the snow would begin later in the evening. What a beautiful sight it would be in the morning with white powdery snow covering the leaves and laying on the evergreen branches. Once inside the cabin, Morgan started a fire and the girls immediately began toasting marshmallows. The little boys joined in with their girl visitors and became a part of the crowd. I thought, this is going to be a very challenging weekend.

Linda took over the supervision of the girls and our sons, and Morgan and I had time together. The teams of girls performed their assigned duties cheerfully and sang songs most of the evening as we sat by the hot sparkling fire. Chelsea Lyn and her friends cared for Raynor and Caesar. During the morning Morgan, Linda, and I took several long walks through the nature paths near the cabin. I thought that with Linda along Morgan would not ask any more questions about Chelsea Lyn's real mother. I walked on eggshells for the first day, thinking he might want me to describe her mother. Linda sensed my discomfort and she remained with Morgan and me when we were outside the cabin away from the girls and our sons. I was relieved when we began packing up Monday morning for the drive back home. Linda and the girls would leave for the airport later in the afternoon, headed for their cruise.

177

The entire family drove to the airport in two cars to see Linda and the girls off on their trip. Olga and Dad were to depart about an hour later, so we all remained in the airport until their flight took off. Dad was flying to Boggsville with Olga. His university was on winter break from the Thanksgiving holiday until the first week in January. I wondered if Dad was going to stay with Olga for the entire time. "Chelsea," I said to myself, "your father is over 21 and he can make his own decisions. And Olga can take care of herself. Stop worrying about them." I confessed to myself that my worry was not about them being together. My worry was about Olga telling Dad about my past. I hoped she wouldn't talk with him about me without first asking me. *I can't have anything come between my father and me, ever again!*

3 It seemed strange being in my office without Linda. She had arranged for one of the director's secretaries to cover her job while she was gone. Despite Linda's absence, my job was much easier with J.C. as my deputy. The tons of correspondence about corporate operations were now being handled by him. He scheduled a daily meeting with me, either morning or afternoon, to brief me on the important issues I should be concerned about. J.C. said Putman was still doing a fine job with the committee on the analysis of the plant and product line expansions. J.C. chuckled every time he talked of Putman. The Putman "tiger" who was hell bent on being a thorn in my side had become one who couldn't do enough support the CEO's directions. I wished so desperately that I could manage my personal life as efficiently as I have managed my professional life. It's difficult sometimes to keep the two separated.

I still have the problem of bringing Matthew to the States to try and help him recover his memory. I can't understand myself sometimes. This desire to help Matthew is ... *so all-consuming!* But in the same breath, I have the terrible fear of what may happen if he regains his memory. What will happen with his Turkish wife and children, and what kind of relationship would Caesar and I have with him? Fear grips my throat and my heart seems to stop beating when I think of what the future holds for me.

The secretary rang to say a Mr. Jason was on the telephone for me.

"Jason, how nice to hear from you. How are you?"

I can't have anything come between my father and me, ever again!

"Good day, Miss Chelsea. I am fine, thank you. How is life with you?"

"I'm fine, Jason."

"Miss Chelsea, I desire to make a trip back to London and I thought I should check with you before I depart. Is all of this terrible situation with Mr. Quigly over for me?"

"Of course, Jason. The jury cleared you of all charges. You are free to go anywhere you choose."

"Oh, that is wonderful news, Miss Chelsea. I must tell you there have been several persons coming by the mansion asking me questions about Mr. Thorndike's early life."

"What people, Jason? What kinds of questions?"

"Well, Miss Chelsea, I was asked if I had any records of the master's college days. They asked if I knew where Mr. Thorndike lived then. And another question frequently asked was if I knew he had lived with a woman."

"Jason, did you get a business card or any identification from them?"

"No, Miss Chelsea, but I was informed at least one of the gentleman was a private investigator."

"Did he say what he was investigating, Jason?"

"Not really, Miss Chelsea. He was very elusive when I questioned him as to why he was inquiring about Mr. Thorndike since the master had deceased."

"Jason, if anyone else comes to you with questions about Mr. Thorndike, please refer them to me. And, Jason, please get a name or a business card, OK?"

"Yes, Miss Chelsea, I shall do as you have instructed me. I shall make arrangements to travel to London for a fortnight if you have no objections."

"You can go anywhere you choose, Jason. Thank you for letting me know about your trip. Have a safe one and enjoy yourself. You realize you are a very wealthy man now, don't you?"

"Yes, Miss Chelsea. I just cannot imagine how much money the master did leave me. Thank you for your assistance. I shall call when I return."

4 I asked the secretary to have Susan Rosco come to my office as soon as possible. In a few minutes Susan knocked on the door, asking as she entered, "What's up, Chelsea? You sounded anxious."

"Susan, you, John Capps, and I are the only people who know about Stan Jones and the five million dollars Mr. Thorndike left him. You haven't mentioned this to anyone else, have you?"

"Heavens no, Chelsea! And I'm sure John would never betray his client's confidentiality. Why do you ask? Has something happened?"

"I'm not sure, Susan. Jason called me earlier today and said several different people had been asking him questions about Mr. Thorndike's history."

"You're suspicious of Stan Jones, aren't you?"

"Frankly, yes, Susan. I just have a funny feeling that he's up to something."

"Chelsea, you don't think he would be so stupid as to try to discover the source of his bequest, do you?"

"I don't know. He would be a fool to violate the terms of the agreement he signed. He could lose the five million dollars if these people are trying to dig up information about Mr. Thorndike for him. He may be trying to break the will.

"Susan, get John Capps in for a meeting with us. I also want J.C. in on the meeting. Make it soon, say within the next couple of days."

"Sure, Chelsea. I'll call John right away."

As Susan was leaving the office, Morgan popped into the reception area. He greeted her with a smile and hug and asked how she was doing as the new law division chief. She took his arm and squeezed him in response. Her big smile let Morgan know she loved his touch. Morgan knocked as he strolled into my office. He asked the secretary if I had any appointments during lunch.

"No, Mr. Gage, Ms. Carodine is not engaged over the lunch period."

"Good morning, Ms. Carodine. I was wondering if you'd like to have lunch with your Director of Engineering. Of course, we'll discuss business!"

"Yes, Morgan, lunch with you would be nice. Give me a moment."

We went to a small restaurant near the office. I hoped Morgan would discuss business — or anything other than Chelsea Lyn's real mother.

We ordered our lunch and as we were waiting I decided to be the aggressor again.

"Morgan, do you my remember me talking with you about the five million dollars Mr. Thorndike left Stan Jones?"

"Yes, Chelsea. I thought John Capps took care of that for you."

"He did, Morgan. That is, he took care of the transfer of the funds to Stan Jones. But I sense another problem with Stan Jones."

"What would that be, sweetheart?"

"I talked with Jason this morning ... "

"Great! How is the old boy doing?"

"He's doing just fine. He wanted to let me know he is going to London for a couple of weeks. A fortnight is two weeks, isn't it?"

"Yes, as I remember my British history, it is."

"Well, what I am trying to tell you is that Jason said he's been questioned by several people claiming to be private investigators, questions about Mr. Thorndike's early life."

"That is interesting. But, didn't you tell me that Stan had to agree not to try and discover the source of the five mil he received?"

"Morgan, you have the same suspicions I have. You think Stan may be behind this. The investigators may have been hired by him ... "

"Honey, the guy is nuts. If he is trying to find out who left him the money, he is violating the agreement for sure."

"Yes, that's what I think. But how do we find out if Stan is the one who hired the investigators?"

"Hire investigators of your own to check on his investigators," he laughed.

"I'm to meet with Susan, John, and J.C. within the next couple of days. I'll let them help decide if this may be a threat and how we should handle it."

"Good idea, sweetie. Boy, this lunch is tasty. How's yours?"

"Oh, mine is very good. Morgan, thanks for taking me to lunch. It's nice to be with just you. I love Linda but I don't think we will take another woman to the mountains with us again. And maybe not our children, either."

"Your propositions get better all the time. When are we leaving?"

"I'll see you at home tonight. Bye, dear."

5 As I entered the office Linda was phoning in from aboard the ship. I suddenly felt very anxious about her call. I ran to my desk and picked up the telephone.

"Linda, is everything all right?"

She responded, "Yes, boss lady. I just wanted to call and let you know that we all got aboard the ship and are having a wonderful trip. No one is seasick yet."

"Oh, that's wonderful, Linda. When I get a call like this I immediately think that something bad has happened. I'm so happy you all are enjoying the cruise."

"OK, boss, just wanted to check in with you. We'll see you on Friday."

Linda is such a thoughtful person. I would never trust anyone else with my daughter Chelsea Lyn as I do Linda. The other parents were also impressed with her as the chaperone for the girls on the cruise.

Susan Rosco called and said she would set a meeting for later in the afternoon if I were free to discuss the Jones case. John and J.C. joined us in my office.

"Chelsea, Susan said you think Stan Jones may be trying to investigate the source of the money left him by Mr. Thorndike."

"Yes, J.C., that is what I think. I know I may be wrong, but I just don't want to take any chances. And another thing, I think Mr. Thorndike's reputation should be protected."

Susan said, "What do you propose we do?"

John Capps answered her by saying, "I can hire a couple of investigators to run down what is happening, before we get too involved."

J.C. responded, "I think that's our best bet, John. OK with you, Chelsea?"

"Before we get too involved, take another look at the legal ramifications of anyone trying to break Mr. Thorndike's will."

"Chelsea, the will is ironclad. It has been reviewed by two trust departments and one legal firm. Mr. Thorndike made his intentions very clear. I don't think anyone can break it."

"Then why are Stan and his investigators checking on Mr. Thorndike's college life?"

"I don't have a clue about that, but I'll get a couple of private investigators to find out."

" ... I can hire a couple of investigators to run down what is happening, before we get too involved."

The meeting ended. John was to get going on the investigation as soon as possible. I felt I needed to talk with Jason as soon as he returns from London. I don't know much about Mr. Thorndike's life except what he told me, but I am beginning to have a number of questions that need answers.

The cruise ship's last stop was in New Jersey. Three carloads of parents drove to the dock to meet Linda and our girls. The ship docked on time while the girls waved frantically from the deck. It seemed like hours before they disembarked. Chelsea Lyn came down the gangplank and jumped into Morgan's arms. The other girls went from one parent to another with tales of the wonderful adventures they'd had on the cruise.

I hugged a well-tanned Linda and thanked her for chaperoning the girls. She said, "Hey, boss lady, you can add this to my job description any time. The girls had a wonderful time, as you can see."

"Thank you, Linda. You must have kept the girls on a leash."

"No, boss. These ladies are very responsible young adults. I don't think their parents will have any problems with them, any time."

Once we were home Chelsea Lyn asked if Father Abel had selected his foreign pastoral posting. I said we had not talked since the party. She was very worried that Morgan and Abel would not have enough time to get to know each other. I wondered why this young girl was so worried about her two fathers getting together. She asked if it would be possible to invite Abel for dinner again. I hesitated and said I would have to check my schedule.

When Morgan and I were alone I asked him how he felt about having Abel back to our home.

"I don't object to him coming … "

"But, if you had a choice you would rather he didn't come back? Is that what you're intimating?"

"No, honey. Let's leave it this way. If that is what Chelsea Lyn wants, then I'll go along with her."

"Chelsea Lyn did ask. I told her I would check our schedule. I didn't want to commit to having him over unless you agreed."

"Can I ask how long will this go on? I mean, having dinners with her real dad?"

"Didn't I tell you? Abel is planning to take an overseas pastoral posting in either the Far East or the Middle East."

185

"Then his visits here will only be for a short while … "

"Yes, Morgan, only while he makes preparations to go overseas."

"OK. Tell Chelsea Lyn she can plan to have him over as often as he can come. I just don't understand her motive in wanting us to know each other so well."

"Morgan, she's young. She was very sheltered growing up. Maybe she is just trying to spread her wings a little."

"Maybe you're right. Enough said about the subject."

I thought, thank heavens, maybe Morgan will not press the issue about Chelsea Lyn's real mother. This subject could be very embarrassing for Abel and me.

I never had an opportunity to talk with Olga about Abel. She had seemed very concerned that Abel was in my home when she and Dad arrived. I guess I owe her the courtesy of a telephone call, she's so dear to me. I asked Linda to ring her for me.

"Hello, Olga." I waited. "Hello, Olga … "

"This is Olga. Are you there, Chelsea dear?"

"Yes, Olga. How are you? Is Dad still there with you?"

"My dear," she laughed, "are you inquiring about my health or checking on your father?"

"No, Olga. Don't be silly, I'm not checking on Dad. You had asked about Abel when you met him at our home. I thought I would give you an opportunity to say what you wanted to say that night."

"Well, my dear, I was rather surprised to find Abel there. Tell me how that happened."

"It was Chelsea Lyn's idea. She wanted her two fathers to meet each other."

"Chelsea, my dear one, I realize Morgan accepted your past life in silence. Don't you think you are pushing the situation a little far by bringing Abel and Morgan together?"

"Olga, I am worried to death that Chelsea Lyn would, quite innocently, say something about me being her real mother. I'm sure Morgan would be embarrassed. But, Olga, I don't know what to do about it."

"I will tell you, dear. If I were making the decisions, I would not have Abel and Morgan together any more."

"It's not that easy, Olga. Morgan was not overly receptive to having Abel visit too often, but he did say Abel was welcome until his pastoral appointment comes through."

"Then I would suggest you tell Abel to get the papers done and go to his posting."

"Olga, I think Abel is as uncomfortable as I am about coming to my home. But we are all catering to Chelsea Lyn because Abel is leaving and she won't see him for a couple of years."

"Chelsea, I do not want you to hurt. But I must admit that Abel is a father who kept his word. When his wife Kersi died he could have just kept Chelsea Lyn and not given her back to you. I think since Abel is leaving he should have the opportunity to visit Chelsea Lyn. And I, too, can understand how Morgan feels."

"Thank you, Olga. I love you for your consideration. Things will work out."

6 John Capps called a meeting to discuss his findings about the investigation of what we all thought were Stan Jones' efforts to uncover the source of his inheritance. J.C., Susan, John, and I met in my office for John's briefing. Linda served coffee and tea and said she would hold all calls until we had finished.

"Well, folks, you were all correct. Stan Jones hired the detectives to try and discover his parentage. Right now, I don't know if we can prove he broke the agreement he signed, but his investigators are busy."

"So just what did your investigators find, John?" I asked anxiously.

"For one thing," John began, "Jones' people are trying to discover who Stan's father was … "

"John, isn't that proof enough that he's trying to break the agreement?"

"Not really, Chelsea. He may be just using his money to find his roots."

"Chelsea," J.C. said, "does anyone know who Stan's father is or was?"

"J.C., what I am about to tell you all must not leave this room." Everyone nodded their concurrence. I thought to myself, I didn't really know if it is the proper time to expose Mr. Thorndike as Stan's father.

I began the story, "In legal terms what I am about to tell you is hearsay: I am repeating what Mr. Thorndike told me. I do not have any proof, except his word, of anything I say."

"And what you are going to tell us relates to what Stan is doing?" J.C. said as he looked at John and Susan.

"Yes, J.C." I wondered to myself if Mr. Thorndike would think that I was betraying his confidence and trust by telling other people about his personal life. I felt it had to be done to stop Stan. He could do far greater damage to Mr. Thorndike's reputation if he discovered that Mr. Thorndike was his father. I told the group what Mr. Thorndike had told me about him and his girlfriend, and what she did when she learned she was pregnant. When I finished the story I could see tears rolling down Susan's cheeks.

She wiped her eyes and said, "That was the most unselfish thing a woman could do for a man. I really don't know if I could have gone away and had a baby without any emotional help."

"Susan, Mr. Thorndike didn't abandoned his love. He was with her when Stan was born. He didn't know at the time that she had not listed him as the father on the birth certificate."

"If I understand the situation," J.C. began, "Stan Jones really does not know that Mr. Thorndike was his father nor can he prove it through a recorded legal document. Am I correct about … "

"Yes, J.C., I may be second-guessing Mr. Thorndike, but instructions in his will clearly indicated that Stan was not to know that he was his father."

"Then what we need to do is to keep track of Mr. Stan Jones and find out what he's trying to do. Is he really looking for family members or is he attempting to discover who left him the money? What do you suspect he's trying to do Chelsea?" John asked.

"*I think he would like to try and break the will!* He already knows that Mr. Thorndike left the corporation to me. If he thinks he has a fifty-fifty chance of breaking the will, his greed will lead him toward that objective."

John said excitedly, "Chelsea, there was a report of movement of his money from his bank account, the one he set up when the trust was paid."

"John, that may be our prime lead in determining what he is trying to do. Have your investigators get all they can on the money transfer," J.C. directed.

"Does anyone else have anything else to add to what we must do about Stan?"

"I think we need to know about the money transfer and we should find out immediately," Susan said very sternly.

"Yes, I quite agree. John, get your investigators to find out what Stan is doing and get back to us as soon as possible. We will be available to hear what you find." I dismissed the meeting, thinking to myself, well, Mr. Jones, just what do you think you can do this time?

7 I asked Linda to put her secretaries on the alert for any request for information from an outside source, especially private investigators, about Mr. Thorndike or the corporation. I'd discovered the most efficient way of hearing rumors before they became facts was to include the women who "manage" the offices for their bosses.

As Linda delivered correspondence for my review and instructions, she said, "Boss, I think one of these letters is from Matthew. It's from Turkey."

"Let me see," I said excitedly. My blood pressure shot up and my cheeks flushed bright red.

Linda asked, "Boss, are you all right?"

I said with a shaky voice, "Yes, Linda. I'm OK. I don't know why I get so excited about the possibility of Matthew coming here."

"Boss lady, I think I understand how you feel about Matthew. If you need to talk about it, I'm here for you."

"Thanks, Linda," I responded. "My world gets so confused too often. This thing with Stan Jones is going to cause me problems. And along with that problem, Matthew is coming to the States to try and regain his memory."

I opened the letter and began reading:

"Dear Ms. Carodine,

"I find it most difficult to begin this letter to you. My son was born, but Allah did not give him breath. Allah gave and Allah took away! I am without my expected son. My wife Ishisk is very ill and I believe that Allah may also take her. I have faith that when I visit your States Allah will favor me and restore what he desires me to remember about any life you say I previously lived. I will not come to your country until my wife

189

is well. Ishisk desires me to go, but I cannot leave her. I shall correspond with you when it is possible for me to plan.

"Your friend, Asher — or if you prefer, Matthew."

I showed the letter to Linda and tears formed and ran freely down her cheeks. "Chelsea, I'm so sorry for you. Just remember when you need to talk, I'm here."

"Thanks, Linda. You're very kind and I love you for being so considerate."

J.C. came in a few minutes later to brief me about corporate matters. I can't imagine how I managed without a deputy. Sometimes I think J.C. would like to treat me like his daughter. I sense the same fatherly instincts in him as I did in Mr. Thorndike.

"The board meeting is next week, Chelsea. Are you anticipating any personnel changes on the board?"

My response was very confident. "You know, J.C., when I was having difficulty with Putman and his cronies, I couldn't wait until I owned the corporation stock so I could sweep my opponents away. Now, I'm not so sure I want to make any changes. Putman seems to have become my best support on the board."

"Yes, I am very surprised about that. But, I have known Putman for a long time. If he feels he is being put out to pasture, he gets into battle gear. I think you gave him the pasture when you made him chairman of the Planning Committee."

"Thanks to Mr. Thorndike! J.C., that man had a very calming effect on me. I hope I can live up to his 'down-home' philosophy." I laughed as I remembered how I hoped his management philosophy would not tie my hands when I prosecuted the Casey suit. "What a true gentleman."

"Yes," J.C. responded, "he was a kind, considerate, but a very determined man when it came to the people in his corporation."

"J.C., I would really like to do something in his honor. The corporation has a benevolent fund we could draw from. Maybe a fund or something everyone could make contributions to, would be the thing to do. What do you think?"

"Of course, anything is possible. I favor contributions from our people. Maybe we should ask for suggestions from the employees. They'll have more pride in something they help build," responded J.C.

"OK, but until we decide what to do, push it to the back burner."

"Sure, Chelsea. Let me know what type of endeavor you may want to consider when you're ready." J.C. is a true and loyal friend to me.

"Thanks, J.C. We'll talk about it sometime in the future."

"Well, Putman's latest report, which he will present to the board, is very sound. Morgan and Putman met about the southern plant expansions and new product lines. Morgan agreed with Putman's recommendations in the report. I don't think he is trying to give anything to his buddies in the south."

"Tell me, J.C., has Putman said anything about dealing with Morgan on the expansion — you know, since he is my husband?"

"Not that I have heard, Chelsea. Putman seems to be completely aboveboard with his committee and the study prepared by the group. I don't think you need to worry about him."

"Thanks, J.C. Is there anything else I should know about?"

"Not really. I can take care of the minor fires. You have enough to worry about with Stan Jones and having Matthew come back to the States."

"J.C., will you follow up on Matthew's back pay? Make sure a check is cut before he arrives."

"Yes, I'll have it calculated. Do you have a firm date yet?"

"No. Matthew's told me in a letter that his son was born dead. That may complicate his trip. I don't have any idea when he may get here, but my plans are for early January."

"Chelsea, I'm sorry for him. Did you get a feeling from his letter how he took the death of his newborn son?"

"No, J.C. Matthew's personality is much calmer than when he was here. I think he has a more moderate outlook. I just don't recognize him as the Matthew I knew. And something else is very disturbing to me ...."

"What's that, Chelsea?"

"Matthew seems to have forgotten that he was Catholic. He appears to have adopted the Islamic religion."

"Well, maybe one day the entire puzzle of Matthew Glyndon will be solved. Let me know if I can help in any way."

"Thanks again, J.C. Matthew has to work out his problems in Turkey on his own. Maybe we can help him when, and if, he comes here for treatment to try and remember his past. At times I don't think he wants to remember, but he is curious."

191

"One last item. John Capps tells me he should have the investigation about Stan Jones wrapped up in the next few days. I'll set up a meeting when he says he's ready. I'll keep you up on this." J.C. left the office and I looked again at Matthew's letter. One line of the letter stood out like a bright light.

"My wife Ishisk is very ill and I believe Allah may take her." I wonder what will happen if she dies! Will her death prompt him to get his memory back? Has Matthew become so immersed in his newfound religion that he can predict what will happen? I am becoming very nervous about what may happen. One thing I must do is to call the insurance company and get the insurance Matthew left straightened out. Morgan was led to believe the money was left by my grandmother. Luckily I have not spent much of it. The interest would have kept the principal intact.

I told Linda I would be away from the office for a couple of hours, then called John Davis, the lawyer who handled Matthew's estate, and made an appointment. Once in his office, I explained what had happened. Davis couldn't believe it. He checked his files on Matthew. He said, "Chelsea, the policy to you was five million dollars. Do you still have most of the money?"

"Of course, I do. The principal is still there. I did use some of the interest. But, no worry, I can repay anything I need to put back into the settlement."

"I'll get with the insurance company and let you know what our course of action should be … "

"John, this must be very confidential! Make that clear to whomever you talk with at the insurance company. I cannot have this leaked to the news media, either."

"Of course, Chelsea. I have a person I can call immediately. I'll get right back to you with what we have to do."

8 When I returned to the office, Linda said Olga had called. Linda got Olga on the telephone for me.

"Hello, Olga! How are you? Is Dad still there with you?"

"My, so many questions, one at one time, da? I am well. No, your dad went back to Lewisburg last evening. My dear, I must ask a question."

"Oh, so I'm going to give you advice now. Da?"

"Da, my dear. Maybe you can tell me how to do something."

"Well, what is it, Olga? What great advice can I offer you?" I laughed as thought I was about to become an Ann Landers.

"Your dad thinks we should move in together in one house. I don't think two professional people in the United States who are not man and wife can live together. That is what I need to know from you."

"Well, Olga, people who are not married live together all the time here. But I don't think you and Dad can live together … "

"Do you object to us living together in the same house?"

"No, it's not that, Olga. I mean, well, Dad lives in a small town."

"I don't understand. What does living in Lewisburg or Boggsville have to do if your dad and I want to move into the same house?"

"Did Dad say anything about retiring from teaching?"

"No. He will stay in teaching job in Lewisburg."

"Then are you going to move your practice to Lewisburg?"

"We do not know. One problem at one time. Do you object to your dad and me living in the same house together?"

"*Oh, Olga, of course not!* You two can do what you want to do. It's just that, well, people talk in small towns. I just don't want anyone saying anything bad about you or Dad."

"Then you say if we live together, it is bad?"

"No, Olga! How can I make you understand what I am saying?"

"I want to find out if you, his daughter, think it is good idea."

"Olga, as you say to me, that is yours and Dad's problem to work out. I like the idea that you and he are seeing each other. I never really thought about you two living together."

"My dear, we are growing older. We must make our decision what we are going to do. Your father has not suggested we marry. Would that please you, Chelsea?"

"Do you love my dad, Olga?"

"My dear, lasting love will come, I am sure. We are both concerned with our economic well-being at the present time."

"Olga, I don't understand. Don't you know if you love my dad?"

"Chelsea, you are young. I am sure you will learn that love is only part of a true relationship. I enjoy being with your father. We talk and laugh and I think he likes being with me … "

"Has Dad told you he loves you, Olga?"

193

"*No, of course not!* I believe he looks at life as I do. If we live together and become accustomed to each other, maybe love will come. Who knows?"

"Olga. May I ask something of you ... "

"Of course, Chelsea. What is it?"

"Olga, *please don't tell my father about my life with the Claybornes and Matthew!*"

"My dear Chelsea, that is something you must suffer with. If you want to tell him, then you must. *It is your business and I shall say nothing!*"

"Oh, thank you, Olga. I hope you and Dad do work out something. But remember how small town people talk!"

I am sure I didn't get through to Olga about American small town gossip. Dad will have to explain it to her when she talks with him about it. I feel better now that *she assured me she will not talk to Dad about my past.* Maybe their situation will work out for them. I have been very nervous with the two of them together so much. I was sure Olga had told him what I shared with her about my past. If they do get married, my secrets, my past life, will be around my neck for a long time. As much as I fear Dad finding out about my past, I really have too many happenings in my present to be too concerned about it.

9 Immediately after I talked with Olga, Linda said John Davis was on the telephone for me and needed to speak with me right away. I answered his call.

"Chelsea, I have the information about the insurance. Can we talk over the telephone?"

"Sure, John, what did you find?" I waited for instructions to repay the money.

"I spoke with a Mr. Alex Johanus, who is a senior vice president of the settlement division. Here's the story. The file shows a death certificate was issued by the Turkish government. It clearly stipulated that no one survived the crash of the aircraft Matthew Glyndon was on. The insurance company had a good contract with Matthew and you were listed as his beneficiary. The contract was fulfilled when the insurance company received the death certificate."

"What does all this mean, John?"

194

"Chelsea, what this means is that you do not have to return the money you received upon Matthew's declared death. The only way the company could reclaim the money is if they could prove fraud in faking a death of a person who later turns up alive." I couldn't believe what I was hearing. I remembered contract law, but a situation like this was never discussed. *I was shocked!*

"OK, let me make sure I understand what you have said. Since Matthew was officially declared dead by a competent authority, the insurance company cannot reclaim the money. Is this what I am hearing, John?"

"Yes, Chelsea. You're hearing it right. The company told me they would not attempt to recapture the money. The money is yours. I will officially notify the insurance company in writing and get a total release, just in case. I'll get it to you as soon as possible." Well, what a strange set of circumstances. Morgan will still think the money came from my grandmother and I don't have to deal with it! If Matthew could only remember, I would either share it or give it all to him.

I checked my appointments with Linda. I called to her and asked, "Linda, who is this Gabrielle Snowden on my appointment list?"

"I'm not sure, boss. I thought you knew her. She sounded as if you two knew each other. Shall I call her and find out what she wants?"

"No, don't bother, Linda. She should be here soon." I kept wondering who she was. The name "Gabrielle" sounded familiar, but I couldn't place her.

Linda called and said, "Boss lady, Ms. Snowden is here. Shall I bring her in?"

"Sure, Linda, show her in." I could hear Linda leading her to my office.

"Boss, this is Ms. Gabrielle Snowden." I looked her over very carefully. No, I can't remember ever meeting her. Her plain face had been skillfully made up to emphasize her quiet beauty. Her beautiful white teeth and bright red lips emphasized a smile with a "come-on look" that probably pulled men to her like a magnet.

She looked as if she had been poured into the form-fitting dress which highlighted her curvy figure and very shapely legs. I took her hand and said, "Ms. Snowden, I'm Chelsea Carodine, and I am pleased to meet you. What can I do for you?"

"Ms. Carodine, I have never met you, but I do know who you are. I am recently divorced and need a job very badly. I thought if I came to see you directly, rather than going through Personnel, you could help expedite the process of hiring me."

"Tell me, Ms. Snowden, why would I make an exception for you?"

"Well, Ms. Carodine, I do know your husband. I worked for him during the Parker buy-out program." The cogs in my brain begin to mesh.

I thought, yes, Gabrielle, you are the one Morgan told me about during the Parker buy-out. I wonder if you think you are going to worm your way into a position in Thorndike because you had a "sexual encounter" with my husband Morgan. This is the most ridiculous thing I have ever heard of. Stay calm, Chelsea, I said to myself. Handle this matter as you would handle any other disruption to the Thorndike family.

I leaned forward and looked her directly in the eyes and said, "Ms. Snowden, I will have to consult with my personnel chief. Could you please come back tomorrow, say about this same time?"

She parted her lips in a coy half-smile and said, "Of course, Ms. Carodine, that will be fine. I shall return tomorrow. And Ms. Carodine, thanks." Well, this is about the most outrageous case of silent blackmail I have ever witnessed. I smiled to myself as I thought, yes, Ms. Snowden, please come back tomorrow for your surprise.

Morgan and I like to have a before-dinner drink on the patio overlooking the lake. He greeted me, as always, with a tender kiss and a long hug. As we sat looking over the beautiful lake with the huge weeping willow trees slinging their arms in the wind, I thought, well, Morgan, let's talk about Gabrielle.

Morgan looked puzzled and said, "Tell me, lady, what is that brain of yours doing? Settle down, love, and enjoy the scenery and the man who loves you very much." My mind kept saying, let's talk about Gabrielle, Morgan. I hoped I had really forgiven and forgotten the matter so that we could talk about it as two intelligent adults.

I began, "Morgan, do you ever think of Gabrielle Snowden?"

He really looked puzzled. "Chelsea, are you talking about the 'Gabrielle' who worked for Parker Industries … ?"

"Yes, that 'Gabrielle,' Morgan."

He looked at me, angrily at first, then said, "May I ask why we are talking about Gabrielle? I thought she was a dim spot in your memory bank that you were never going to recall."

"Morgan, I'm not looking for an argument. Quite the contrary, I am rather amused at what happened today." His expression changed from a puzzling look to a 'what the hell is going on' look.

He said, "Chelsea, will you please tell me what the devil is going on?"

"Well, dear, Ms. Gabrielle Snowden came to my office today and asked me for a position in Thorndike … "

"You're joking, Chelsea! *What is she trying to pull?*"

"That's what you and I are going to find out tomorrow, dear. She will be in my office at 10:30 A.M. Will you please be there to help me greet her?"

Morgan leaned back in his chair and began to laugh uncontrollably. He said, "Is she in for a shock! She came to confront you, and now she has to deal with us both." He continued to laugh at the situation as if it were a big joke.

"Why, Morgan, dear, don't you want me to give her a job as a director or some other high position?"

Morgan was still laughing as he said, "Honey, you're the boss. Do what you like. Just don't put her in my directorate." I thought, it's wonderful to be able to joke about an old affair. Sometimes I wish Morgan had listened to the horrible story of my past. This incident with "Ms. Gabrielle" is a real joke to me. I am not threatened at all by her approach. Morgan was honest with me immediately after the incident took place. In fact, I thought I would give her a job — that is, if her story is sad enough.

Morgan rode to work with me the next day, and we joked about Gabrielle. We wondered what she would say to us when she saw Morgan and me together. I asked Linda to have Morgan in my office by 10:10 or 10:15 A.M. He was prompt! We were having coffee when Linda announced that Ms. Snowden had arrived. I asked that she be escorted into my office. Linda brought her in, and when she saw Morgan she stopped in her tracks. It was apparent she was as nervous as a cat on a stove. She had on another skintight knit dress that clung to her like glue.

"Good morning, Ms. Snowden," I said with a coy smile.

"Good morning …." She looked at Morgan and back to me as if she were at a loss for words.

Morgan greeted her and said, "How have you been, Gabrielle?"

"I … have been fine … just fine, thank you, Mr. Gage."

"Ms. Snowden, may I ask why you came to me about a job? You knew Mr. Gage. Why didn't you go to him?"

"I didn't think he would see me," she said as she looked at Morgan.

"But you didn't answer my first question. Why did you come to me? I don't even know you."

She seemed to regain her composure, looked directly at me, and said, "Well, I thought ... I would have something to say to you about your husband. *But apparently you two have already talked!* What I have to say would not be news to you, Ms. Carodine."

"Gabrielle," Morgan said, "did you come here to pressure my wife for a job because of what happened between you and me several years ago?"

"Well, I can see your wife is not too excited about your escapades! I thought she would be interested in what happened. But, I see that is not the case. Please excuse me." She left the office in a huff. Linda said she was cursing under her breath as she left the outer office.

"Morgan, come here and give me a kiss. I feel great! That is how the 'other' woman' ... "

Morgan said, " ... and the 'other man', should be handled. Right, my love?"

I quickly agreed. "Yes, Morgan, my dear husband. I love you very much." He took me into his arms and kissed me for a long time. Every time he kisses me like that I get all excited.

"Morgan, keep the fire burning until tonight, sweet." He released me and planted a kiss on my cheek as he left the office.

10 J.C. came into the office in his usual happy mood and said, "Chelsea, you will simply not believe what that Stan Jones has done." I thought, wrong, J.C., I wouldn't be surprised at anything he would do.

I asked, "Has John Capps completed his investigation?"

"Yes. I scheduled a meeting for 10:00 A.M. tomorrow. I do not have all the facts of the case so I suggested John brief all of us on his findings." Linda confirmed the meeting and called Susan Rosco to inform her.

Linda had coffee and danish ready for the meeting. Susan and J.C. came into the office before John arrived. Susan reported that any legal cost incurred to counter Stan Jones' actions can be paid from the corporation. The terms of the agreement also stipulated that the winner of any action could collect from the other side. Soon John arrived with his charts and briefing materials.

"Sorry I'm a bit late folks," John said. "I had to stop at the courthouse and set up a hearing before Judge Tinnus on this matter. His clerk found an opening, and he is set to hear our argument on Thursday this week."

"Well, John, we're all eager to hear what you've found."

"Stan Jones has definitely broken the agreement not to search out the source of the five million dollars from the trust. The administration of the trust is still technically under the jurisdiction of Judge Tinnus's court. That's why I set a hearing to review the terms of the agreement and Stan Jones's actions."

"John," J.C. asked, "how strong is your evidence that Stan broke the agreement?"

John handed J.C. an official-looking document and said, "These papers are sworn affidavits from two people Stan used to transfer the trust money from his own name."

"OK. John, give us the whole story. What did Stan do?" I was anxious to hear just how much of a scoundrel Stan turned out to be.

John began to unravel the story. "We have evidence that Stan hired three investigators to search out the source of the trust money. J.C.'s friends in the police department persuaded the three to 'talk about their arrangement' with Stan Jones. Something was said about violations of ethics that would affect their licenses."

"So, John, you've learned to use our 'inside sources' to pin Stan Jones?" J.C. said, laughing.

John nodded and continued with his findings. "Stan apparently moved the trust fund money from his name to those of several other people, whom he 'thought' he could trust."

Susan stopped John and asked, "Are you saying that Stan's actions show that he was trying to find the source of the funds?"

John responded, "Yes, it's my conclusion that Stan transferred the money to avoid any action against him as a result of his breaking the agreement. And," John continued, "I think he suspected action would be brought against him to recover the funds if he didn't have the money in his name."

Susan stood up and said, "Well, that is where Mr. Stan Jones is wrong. Chelsea, we need to have the court of jurisdiction freeze the funds to whomever Stan transferred the money ... "

John responded, "Susan, I think we have that well in hand. Injunctions have already been issued against all parties — two of whom are named and the others listed as John and Jane Doe — freezing the assets."

J.C. looked at me and said, "Good work, John. What is our next step with Mr. Jones?"

John responded, "Stan Jones was served yesterday with notice to appear in court this Thursday to respond to the charges that he broke the agreement."

Susan said to John, "I will be with you in court as a co-counsel." John looked at each of us and asked if we had any further questions. He asked that we meet after the court session on Thursday to consider the corporation's next action against Stan Jones. We all agreed to be ready for John's call.

After the group left my office, Linda came in to say that Chelsea Lyn had called from school and asked if I could pick her up and drive her home. I wondered why she called me. Morgan normally swings by her school and drives her home two or three times a week. I drove to the school and Chelsea Lyn was waiting for me.

"Hi, Mom. Thanks for picking me up." She seemed such a happy teenager. I waited to hear why she had asked me to drive her home.

I asked, "Honey, are you all right?"

She smiled and said, "Mom, how soon is Father Abel going overseas?"

Oh, I thought, here we go again with her two fathers.

I responded, "I'm not sure, honey. I haven't talked with him since your birthday party."

"Mom, would it be possible for you and me to go to the church and visit Father Abel?" My mind was racing a mile a minute. Why does she want to be with Abel and me?

"Yes, Chelsea Lyn, if you like. Let me call on the car phone and see if he is available this afternoon. Do you want to go today?"

"Yes, Mother, that would be just fine."

I called the church and Abel answered the telephone. I asked if we could come and see him. He was surprised, but said he would wait for us at the church. In ten minutes we drove up in front of the church. Abel was at the entrance waiting for us. As he approached the car, he said, "Hello, ladies. Whom do I owe for this visit by my two favorite people?"

"Father Abel, Mother, I need to talk with you both."

Abel took our arms and led us into his office. Once we were seated, he said, "It is wonderful to see you both. I hoped we could have a couple of days together before I go overseas."

Chelsea Lyn responded, "Yes, Father Abel. That would be fine, but that is not why I wanted to see you both today." I looked at Abel and he looked at me, both of us with questions on our faces.

"Chelsea Lyn, dear, has something happened? Why do you want to talk with us?" I asked as we sat in Abel's office.

She looked directly at each of us and said, "*I owe you both an apology.*" She began to cry very softly. Abel and I were shocked! Has our daughter suddenly become an adult?

He asked, "Chelsea Lyn, may I ask why you feel you need to apologize to us?"

"Mother, Father, I didn't ... have a right to ... judge either of you, I mean, because you brought me into the world ... " I tried to console her but she said, "*Please, Mother, let me finish what I have to say!* I have been praying about my harsh words to both of you. I know that Jesus forgave his enemies and gave his life for our sins. I asked myself, how could I judge my parents for what they did in giving me birth?"

"Chelsea Lyn, when you spoke the other day, you spoke as a young emotional person. Today I see a young adult woman who has reconciled herself with her Lord," Abel said.

"Chelsea Lyn, darling, we love you very much. We realized the shock of learning that Abel was your real father hurt you very much. Neither of us could help you over that hurt. I agree with Father Abel, you have truly become a responsible young adult today."

"Mother," she said as she dried her tears, "may we have ... Father Abel to our home before he leaves us for such a long time?" Tears formed in my eyes. Chelsea Lyn, Abel, and I hugged each other and I could feel the tears flowing down the cheeks of my daughter and her father Abel.

I assured her that he would visit her when he could before he departed for his overseas pastoral assignment. Morgan had already agreed Abel should visit.

11 The court hearing ended early in the afternoon and J.C. called for a meeting to review the results. Linda scheduled the meeting for four in the afternoon. John Capps, Susan and J.C. came to my office and they all seemed very pleased with themselves. Their attitudes indicated a favorable decision was rendered by Judge Tinnus. J.C. and Susan waited for John to tell the story.

He began, "Chelsea, Judge Tinnus found Stan in contempt of court in that he willfully engaged in actions that bordered on fraud. He ordered all trust funds received by Stan be returned to the corporation with you as the trustee of the funds, unless of course, you decline." I thought, so Stan was going after the source of the funds. Apparently he could not prove that Mr. Thorndike was his father. Stan is such a vindictive man. He would go for me and what Mr. Thorndike left me in his will if he had found any proof.

I responded to John, "You did an excellent job. Can you have Stan Jones come to see me?"

He looked at me with a questioning stare and said, "Why on earth would you want to meet with Stan Jones?"

"I have my reasons, John. Can you arrange for a meeting here in my office?"

"Yes, of course. When do you want it?"

"Right away. And John, is there any further action Stan can take to attempt to overturn Judge Tinnus's decision?"

John answered very positively. "Not a thing, Chelsea. He has no legal recourse. He accepted a gift from the court of jurisdiction and then insulted the court by his actions."

"Good. Set the meeting here in my office and call Linda and give her the time."

When Linda set the appointment for Stan Jones she burst into my office and said in a very emotional voice, *"Boss lady, I'm very disappointed in you!"* She caught me by surprise.

"Linda, what on earth for?"

She stood with her hands on her hips and said, "That Stan Jones is the worst scoundrel I have ever known. You wouldn't believe what he said about you when you fired him during the Parker buy-out. And now you are going to meet with him about the trust fund left to him. Come on, boss ... "

I shared her opinion of Stan being the worst scoundrel we knew but said, "Linda, when Stan arrives I would like to have you sit in on the meeting. I am sure you will understand my reasons after we meet."

Stan arrived a few minutes early. I could hear Linda being very short with her replies to his questions. Apparently she had the same difficulty with him as most women had, but she overcame them. By the time Linda escorted him into my office, he looked like a whipped dog and his attitude was almost civil. He tried to be friendly.

"Chelsea, how have you been?"

"Stan, let's dispense with the friendly greetings. I wanted to meet with you for a very specific reason. I don't want to waste any time exchanging greetings neither of us mean. Please sit there, Stan."

"Chelsea, it's your meeting. You're calling the shots."

"Stan, you were left five million dollars by a benefactor who did not want you to know who he or she was. You stipulated that you would not attempt to determine where the funds came from. You violated that agreement. Not only did you violate the agreement, but you attempted to hide the funds in other people's names in the event you were discovered ... "

"Chelsea, that is all a matter of record, I really don't have to sit here and listen to you recite it to me again. Listen, Chelsea, I'm without a job. I may be disbarred by the state because of what happened, and now you want to give me a swift kick in the pants." He rose and started toward the door.

"*Wait, Stan. Hear me out!*" He turned and stood looking at me.

"OK, Chelsea, I will hear what you have to say, just don't repeat what has already happened to me."

"Stan, I am the official trustee of the, let me see ... four point two million dollars originally left to you. I can use this money in anyway I choose to use it."

"And may I ask, *what in the hell does that have to do with me?*"

"Stan, I'm going to make that money available to you ... "

"*You're going to do what?*" He stood up and looked stupefied.

"I said I'm going to let you draw from the trust fund, but under very strict conditions with which you must agree."

His expression changed from anger to a questioning look. He said, "You mean you are going to give the money back to me? The balance of the five million dollars?" I had never seen Stan so humble.

I responded, "Yes, Stan. And here are the conditions! You may draw money for necessities of life up to an amount which I will set. Any money you may require above the set amount *for any reason*, must be personally approved by me."

"Chelsea, you really know how to kick a man when he's down, don't you?"

"*Stan, I don't have to give you a damn cent!* Whether you believe it or not, I'm trying to give you another opportunity to prove to yourself that you can keep your word. No, Stan, I'm not trying to kick you while you're down."

Linda couldn't sit still any longer. She looked at Stan with anger in her eyes and had her say. "Mr. Jones, you really have a chip a mile wide on your shoulders. What good have you ever done in your life? Why do you think the world owes you a living? Stan, you've got a lot to learn about life *and, I might add, about women, too!*"

"OK, OK ... Maybe I do need to look at myself. But, Chelsea, don't hold the money over my head. If you are sincere in letting me draw from the trust account, then I am appreciative. I just never expected anyone to do anything for me.

"Chelsea, Linda, I apologize to you both for any discomfort I may have caused either of you. Please accept my apology." *What a shock!* Stan agreed to the conditions.

I asked Linda to work out an amount he could draw from the account without approval. She seemed more conciliatory after Stan had apologized. But she still had that look: We got you, *you scoundrel!*

I thought, *the problem with the Prodigal Son may finally be over!*

"Mr. Jones, you really have a chip a mile wide on your shoulders ...
Stan, you've got a lot to learn about life *and, I might add,
about women, too!*"

CHAPTER SEVEN

THE GIFT OF LIFE

1 I was sitting at my desk thinking about Chelsea Lyn's insistence that her two fathers get to know each other better before Abel left for his overseas assignment. Her emotional outburst when she learned that Abel is her biological father reminded me of my attack on Morgan when he told me about the Parker secretary, Gabrielle, and his "sexual encounter." His words just didn't sink into my mind for a very long moment of time. My anger quickly turned to hurt and distrust.

Logically, the situation should not have disturbed me. My past wasn't too rosy. After I became pregnant with Abel's child I wanted him to continue our lovemaking. Kersi stopped us when she insisted that he and I would hurt the baby. My love for Abel was at Kersi's pleasure. I knew I loved him for myself but I could never have destroyed their marriage. After Morgan and I were married, I never thought that he would break our marriage commitment. When I was in Mexico with Matthew I realized how vulnerable a person could become after a few drinks in a party atmosphere. My marriage to Morgan was never threatened until Matthew and I had the affair in Mexico. The consequences of that affair continue to haunt me when I look at Caesar and think of Matthew's present condition. He is without any memories of his past. I had prayed that his heart would command his mind and tell him who I was. But that was not the case.

J.C. interrupted my thoughts when he walked into my office to present his briefing on the state of the giant Thorndike corporation. Linda served coffee and asked if she should stay to take notes. I asked J.C. if he had any earth-shaking items that needed action by the directors. He said he would give Linda the notes. J.C. reminded me that I wanted to talk about a remembrance for Mr. Thorndike. He said a statue in the courtyard wouldn't be a good use of the corporation's money. I agreed and we tossed around several ideas. We both favored something that would be a lasting tribute and one that would provide a service to the community. After awhile, it was clear we weren't getting anywhere, so I suggested we postpone trying to make a decision. J.C. continued his briefings. He said the state of the corporation was excellent. With the holidays near he suggested we discuss bonuses for the employees. I asked that he give the directors an opportunity to recommend bonus rates for the employees. He agreed. J.C. said the city was grateful for the money left by Mr. Thorndike and would build a youth park as he had recommended in his will.

After J.C. completed his briefing and left my office, Linda came in and said she was still angry about Stan Jones. She just couldn't understand why I had returned the four million dollars to him.

"Boss lady, I wouldn't give that woman-hating rat a red cent! He would have had you fired if he could have. There," she said, "I've had my say. But I know he will be irritated every time he must draw on the account." I could appreciate Linda's views.

"Linda, I'm trying not to be vindictive with Stan, even through his conduct was very unprofessional most of the time. I just won't crawl down to his level. Do you understand what I mean, Linda?" She still looked angry.

"Sure, boss, I can understand your views, but I wouldn't have been so generous."

I hope Stan gets heartburn every time he needs money from the fund. He will not be able to draw any money, except for necessities, without careful scrutiny — first by Linda and then by me. It will be punishment enough every time he is forced to ask for any money for the pleasures of life. And the rules by which he will be able to draw from the fund will be changed as I see fit. He may draw from the account only for as long as he abides by my rules.

2 "Boss lady, Morgan is on the telephone for you. Can you take his call?" Morgan often called the office to talk with me. I always ask if it is company business or if he wants to talk just because he misses me.

"Hello, Morgan. Is this business or can I talk with my husband?"

His voice sounded very disturbed. Uh oh, I thought, what's going to hit me next?

"Chelsea, can you take off for a couple of hours and take a walk with me in the park?" What is bothering him? He never asks me to take off in the middle of a work day unless we both have scheduled to be away.

I responded, "Sure, honey. Is something bothering you?" His answer told me to be on my guard: he has something on his mind. I told Linda

I would be away from the office for awhile. Morgan didn't offer to pick me up and I wondered why. I drove to the park and Morgan had just pulled into a parking spot ahead of me. He came to the car as I opened the door. His face was drawn. Yes, he is worried about something.

"Morgan, hi, honey!" I said as I stepped out of the car.

"Hello, darling. I'm sorry I took you away from the office, but I need to talk with you." I was becoming very anxious.

"That's all right, sweetheart." He took my hand and led me along the walkway. Thanksgiving Day had just passed and the weather was beginning to turn to the dreary overcast that precedes the snow. We bundled ourselves up in our winter coats and walked along the path, hand in hand. I knew that when Morgan had something on his mind, he had to be the one to start the conversation. Anyway, I didn't want him to think I was worried about what he might say.

The trees had long since lost their leaves. The tree branches looked cold. Their coats, the leaves, were not there to clothe them, and the wind whipped through and bent the branches skyward and then back to earth. I thought, wouldn't it be wonderful if humans could throw off their troubles as easily as the branches seem to, bending with the wind.

Morgan squeezed my hand and said, "Chelsea, do you realize that I love you with all my heart?" I thought, when did I hear that emphasis on "love with all his heart" before? The same thoughts I had earlier in the day about his "sexual encounter" crept into my mind.

"Chelsea, I must talk with you, but I don't quite now how to begin."

"Morgan, dear, we love each other. You can tell me what's on your mind." I was really afraid to hear what he was trying to say. I had no idea what it was, but I knew it must be something that could affect our marriage.

He looked at me and said, "Chelsea, it's about Chelsea Lyn ...." *I screamed!*

"What is it, Morgan? What has happened to Chelsea Lyn?" He took me by the shoulders and tried to calm me.

"She's OK. I mean she hasn't been hurt. Nothing has happened, she's all right." I looked at him and didn't know what to say.

"Morgan, what are you saying to me?"

"Chelsea, do you talk with Chelsea Lyn about girl-boy relations very often?"

209

"Why, yes, we talk now and then, about a lot of things. I'm not sure I know what you mean, Morgan." Morgan seemed very uncomfortable. I couldn't understand his hesitancy.

"Well," he said, "I think she has been getting too close to me … I mean as a man and woman." My expression must have prompted him.

"I don't understand what you mean, Morgan. Will you please just tell me what you are trying to say? *What about Chelsea Lyn?*" I could tell he was still uncomfortable.

"Chelsea, our daughter is getting too emotional with me."

"What has she done?"

"Well, when she sits on my lap, she acts more like a young woman than a daughter. She makes me feel uncomfortable … she has become very bold in talking about boy and girl relationships."

I looked at him very sternly and said, "Morgan, have you told Chelsea Lyn how you feel? Have you told her to act like a young lady and not a daddy's girl?" He looked at me, obviously wondering why I was becoming angry.

"Chelsea, I don't want to fight about this. I need your help. You're the mother, you can talk with her about things like this better than I can." I felt ashamed of myself.

"I'm sorry, Morgan. Of course, I'll help. I really had no idea that Chelsea Lyn was *'coming on' to her father?"*

He responded very loudly, *"Now wait a minute!* She is not coming on to me." I wondered how long this had been happening.

"Morgan, honey, please explain what you think she is doing. Has Chelsea Lyn been doing whatever she has been doing very long?"

He looked at me and said, "Chelsea, believe it or not, Chelsea Lyn's behavior, as you say, 'coming on to her father' has occurred since Abel's visit on her sixteenth birthday."

I couldn't believe what I was hearing. Is Chelsea Lyn trying to get to me with her behavior with Morgan? I couldn't understand what Abel's visit had to do with her behavior. I began to understand how Morgan felt. Something was happening in his family that he could not control. I wondered if Morgan had tried to correct Chelsea Lyn when she pushed herself on him?

"Morgan, have you talked with Chelsea Lyn about her conduct?" He looked puzzled.

210

"Yes, of course. But, Chelsea, when she hugs me she begins to breathe heavily and gets excited. I push her away and I get very angry with her. She ignores what I say and pressures me as if she knows what she is doing. Do you think she is sexually active?"

"I don't know, Morgan. Honey, I'll have a long talk with her tonight. Maybe I can find out what's going on in her overactive brain." Morgan was relieved to have me take charge. I only hope I can communicate with her. This is a very difficult time of her life. I remember the events with my dad and my boyfriends. I don't want anything like that to happen with my daughter.

The rest of the day at the office dragged on. Today was the senior managers' quarterly meeting. Each manager presents a "state of the department" report and the meetings seem to go on and on. I couldn't keep my mind on the presentations. I whispered to J.C. to continue the meeting and that I had to leave. He asked if I felt OK. I assured him I was not ill, but that I had a very pressing situation at home that needed my immediate attention. I quietly excused myself from the meeting.

The drive home gave me time to think about an approach to Chelsea Lyn. I remember how difficult it was to talk with my father when I was her age. The combination of my rebellion against him and pressure from my peers drove me to do things I normally would never do. After I spent a weekend with a married man, my father would not believe me when I told him we didn't have sex. I really didn't know the meaning of trust and respect when I tried to tell him the truth about the weekend. My challenge to him was to have me examined by a doctor to prove that I was still a virgin. He said I had violated his rules of decency and if I could not follow his rules then I was to leave home. So, I was on my own shortly after my seventeenth birthday. *Oh, God, please give me the wisdom and patience to listen to my daughter!*

Chelsea Lyn had not come from school when I arrived home. Sylvia had gone for the boys and I was alone in the house. I took a cup of coffee to the patio to think about what I was to say to Chelsea Lyn.

When Sylvia returned with the boys, they ran to me. Both of them were trying to tell me about their day at school at the same time. I hugged them and said, "Hey, wait a minute. One at a time. And remember, when one is talking the other does not interrupt, OK?"

Caesar said, "Mom, I'm first."

211

Raynor chimed in, "Mom, Caesar always gets to go first and he tells some of my story."

"Caesar asked first. And no, he will not tell your story, will you, Caesar?" He responded with a frown on his face.

"Well, Raynor, I will try not to tell any of your story, so there." Raynor seemed satisfied so we listened to Caesar's tales of his day at school.

"We had … I mean a great big bear came to the school today and some of us got to pet him," Caesar shouted.

"Yes, Caesar was one who got to touch the bear … " Raynor replied.

"You were a fraidy cat. Even the dumb girls put their hands on him."

"Caesar, you shouldn't talk about your classmates like that. Girls are not dumb!"

"I'm sorry, Mom. I didn't mean dumb like spelling and reading … just about the bear."

"OK, we will accept your explanation. Go on with your story so Raynor can tell his."

Caesar continued, "The bear was ten feet tall or something like that … "

Raynor shouted, "No, he wasn't ten feet high! The man with him said he was only seven or six feet tall."

"Raynor, we agreed not to interrupt each other. You will have your turn."

He countered, "But, Mom, Caesar will talk all day and we will have to eat dinner and I won't remember what happened."

"OK, boys, we will let Caesar talk for two more minutes and then you can have your turn."

Raynor admonished Caesar, "Then I will watch the clock and count the minutes!" Caesar seemed undisturbed by his brother's antics and continued.

"The bear's keeper said we could go to the zoo and see lots more animals. Can we go, Mom, please?"

Raynor said, "Your time is up, Caesar. Now it's my time to talk."

"All right, Raynor, it's your turn. Tell us about your day."

He frowned and said, "But I can't tell about the bear because Caesar already told that."

"Well, what else happened in school that you can tell us about?"

Raynor chimed in, "Mom, Caesar always gets to go first and he tells some of my story."

He thought for a moment and shouted, "Yes, I remember, we got to look at a Disney movie about a big lion! He was big, but I wasn't scared of him."

My boys, how happy they are! I love them so very much. Morgan's enthusiasm is always evident in Raynor. Caesar reflects Matthew's careful attention to details. Two boys by two different fathers seem so very much the same. I promised we could all go to the zoo on Saturday and see the other animals. That seemed to make them happy and they dashed off to the yard to play.

The long driveway is clearly visible from the patio. Morgan's car turned into the driveway and I could see Chelsea Lyn on the driver's side. Please, dear Lord, help me to keep their relationship intact. Chelsea Lyn needs a father figure in her life so much. I just hope she is not torn between Morgan and Abel. She may be reaching out with her emotions to reassure Morgan of her love.

In anticipation of their arrival Sylvia had prepared refreshments and brought them to the patio. The boys came running as she came out. Morgan and Chelsea Lyn greeted the boys with hugs and kisses and did the same with me. *What a loving family we have!* Nothing must spoil our relationships. I must listen to Chelsea Lyn rather than reading the "riot act" to her about her conduct with Morgan.

The other side of the story, of course, is Morgan's perception of her conduct. Her innocence is so obvious in everything she does, I can't believe she has any other intentions when she is close to Morgan. Chelsea, I thought, keep an open mind until you hear the complete story — and don't get too emotional, even if you feel anxiety over the situation. We all sat on the patio and enjoyed Sylvia's refreshments. Shortly, Morgan sensed my need to be alone with Chelsea Lyn so we could talk. He grabbed up the boys and said, "Hey, gang, do you two think you can beat your old man in wrestling?"

They both shouted, "Yes, we can. We can beat you any time." Off they went to one of the bedrooms to practice their mayhem on each other.

Chelsea Lyn leaned back in her chair and said, "Mom, I'm so happy here. Sometimes I can't wait to get home and just enjoy the beauty of the trees and the lake. My mind becomes so clear when I sit here on the patio." I looked at this beautiful sixteen-year-old and thought she looked closer to twenty than the teenager she is. She is about five feet, six inches tall and has a beautiful breast line and figure. Her legs are beautifully

"Mom, I'm so happy here. Sometimes I can't wait to get home and just enjoy the beauty of the trees and the lake … "

structured, and when she walks she attracts attention of both women and men. She has my facial structure. We both are fortunate to have small dainty noses. She has Abel's deep blue, soul-searching eyes. When she looks me directly in the eyes I can see Abel so clearly. His eyes always seem to smile and talk, even when he is silent. Chelsea Lyn's disposition is the same. She is normally cool and calm under trying circumstances. Her loss of emotional control when I told her about Abel being her real father was so unlike her. I wondered how I was going to open the conversation, especially after she expressed such happiness. I thought, here goes!

"Chelsea Lyn, we haven't talked about the boys in your life. What's going on in that department?"

"Oh, Mom, I don't know. Most of the boys in my school seem so immature. I've been asked out several times, but I'm not going to date until I'm at least seventeen."

"Yes, dear, I know what you mean. I always liked older men. I remember being attracted to my French teacher because he spoke broken English and I thought the way he talked was so cute."

Chelsea Lyn sat up and said, "Mom, how old was your French teacher?" I thought, look out, Chelsea, don't lead into you and Abel. After all, Abel was almost twenty years older than you when you two had sexual relations and Chelsea Lyn was conceived.

I quickly responded, "Oh, he was not that much older than I was. Maybe four or five years. He was in the United States studying for his Ph.D. and he taught French at my high school."

"Oh, Mom. That's not an older man. I think of an older man … I mean not really old, but much older than I am. You know, someone like Papa Morgan." I thought, this may be my opening.

"Chelsea Lyn, how do you feel about your Papa Morgan?"

"He's my father, that's how I feel about him." I thought, I'm not getting to the core of the subject.

"Then, how do you feel about your biological father, Abel?"

"Well, Mom, that's when I really get mixed feelings. You said Father Abel was my real father, but I don't feel the same about him as I do Papa Morgan."

"How do you mean you don't feel the same … ?"

She quickly responded, "I mean I accepted what you said about Father Abel being my real father. But he seems so remote to me. That's

216

why I wanted to get him and Papa Morgan together so they could get to know each other better."

I wondered what her logic was and asked, "Honey, I don't seem to grasp your reasoning. How will that help you to relate to either of them?"

She responded with her teenage logic, "Well, Mother, Father Abel is rather cold and besides, he is leaving for overseas and I won't be able to see him or talk with him until he returns. Papa Morgan has such a happy and warm personality and he's so close to me. I think I have really accepted him as my real, that is, *my only father!* Oh, I don't know, Mother. Sometimes I get so confused about both of my fathers. I almost wish you hadn't told me about Father Abel." I thought, *My child! Now you tell me.*

"Remember you pleaded with me to tell you who your real father was — for your sixteenth birthday?"

"Mom, I know I asked about my real father, but I never thought it would be Father Abel."

Maybe my little girl is going through her "first love" with her Papa Morgan. Most girls do seem to associate their first male "puppy love" with their fathers. I was just beginning to think Chelsea Lyn was going through one of the "growing up" stages of youth.

I asked her, "Chelsea Lyn, how do you feel when you hug and kiss your Papa Morgan?"

She looked at me with a shy look and responded, "Mom, I do get flustered when Papa Morgan and I hold each other. I really don't know what is happening to me. He is my stepfather, not my real father ... I just don't know what happens to me, Mom."

I had to be careful with my response. I thought back to when I was so attracted to Abel. He was twenty years older than I. I was completely in love with him before we had sex. I don't know what I would have done if Kersi had not had her *"directions from God"* for me to have a baby with Abel. Her approval seemed to make everything all right for Abel and me to make love. Oh, *dear Jesus!"* I thought, please don't let Chelsea Lyn have my thoughts of the past. I tried to make light of her attachment by reminding her who Morgan is.

"Yes dear, I understand. But, Chelsea Lyn, Papa Morgan *is your real father now!* He loves you very much and we both want you to be happy in your life."

"Mother, I am happy. I have wonderful parents and two little brothers who are the sweetest kids in the world. What else could I want?" I felt

Chelsea Lyn had not revealed her innermost emotional feelings about Morgan.

"Chelsea Lyn, dear, have you been close to a boy ... I mean have you ... ?"

"Mother, if you are trying to ask me if I have been intimate with a boy or a man, the answer is no! *Mother, I'm not one of those 'sexually active' teenagers!*"

Well, I thought, thank you, daughter, for being so honest with me. Now I can be more candid in what I ask you.

"Chelsea Lyn, has a man ... fondled you, or tried to take advantage of you?"

She looked at me with a puzzled frown and responded, "No, Mother! *I am a virgin, and I shall remain a virgin until I meet that 'very special man' of my life! Does that answer you question?"* What a determined, direct response from my little girl!

"Chelsea Lyn, you will come to me if you need to discuss anything personal, won't you?"

She took my hands and kissed them gently and said, "Mother, I love you for being so honest with me. I confess, I do have terribly frustrating feelings about Papa Morgan when we are close. Maybe if he were not so good looking and my stepfather I wouldn't be so embarrassed ... I mean, if he were just another guy I wouldn't feel that way. I'll always be honest with you and Papa Morgan. And yes, Mother, I know I can come to you if I need to talk about real private things."

I was thrilled! Our conversation ended on such an upbeat, positive note. I think our mother-to-daughter channels of communications are working. I hope I can explain to Morgan that Chelsea Lyn has a teenage crush on her stepfather without upsetting him too much.

3 Christmas was near and the boys had been busy making up their lists for Santa Claus. Morgan still wanted to give Chelsea Lyn a new car, but she had not even hinted that she wanted one. She continued to drive our cars at every opportunity. Maybe she wanted to be sure she could safely operate a car by herself before she asked for one. Her Christmas list included clothes and a new watch.

Morgan and I treated every day of the year as if it were Christmas.

218

We want our family to understand the true meaning of Christmas and not that it is just a time when everyone receives presents. Our church commitment continues to grow and I can see the *"Christ-like"* conviction and devotion of our beautiful teenager, Chelsea Lyn. I wondered why I ever doubted her integrity. At sixteen she is more mature than most of her peers. Her views on almost everything we discuss seem so grown-up. She may still get a little flustered when she and Morgan hold each other, *but that, too, is a part of growing up.*

Sylvia, our wonderful housekeeper, requested a leave of absence so she could travel to Poland for Christmas with her family. We had two temporary housekeepers during her absence, neither of which could match Sylvia's boundless energy. Jason called to express his happiness for our Christmas. I asked what he was going to do for Christmas.

"Miss Chelsea, I shall be at the summer home my dear Master Thorndike left me in his will. I shall prepare an English Christmas dinner and have a glass of sherry ... "

I interrupted him and asked, "Jason, would you please come to our home for Christmas? My father and Olga will be here and we would love to have you join us on Christmas Eve and remain until your English Boxer Day. Isn't that the day after Christmas?" He was surprised that I remembered my English history.

"Miss Chelsea, I shall be most happy to share Christmas with you and your family. But I insist that I bring one of my English Christmas dishes."

"Yes, of course, Jason. Bring whatever you like. It is wonderful that you can come and be with us at this time of the year. Jason, I have missed seeing you."

"Thank you, Miss Chelsea. I have been rather sad that our contacts have not been more frequent. It would be a pleasure to see you more in the coming year."

"Yes, Jason. We should remain in close touch. We look forward to seeing you for Christmas Eve." He was very grateful to be invited for Christmas. I should have called him first.

Dad and Olga arrived two days before Christmas loaded with presents for the boys and Chelsea Lyn. After the Christmas greetings were over Olga pulled me aside and asked, "Tell me, Chelsea dear, is Abel going to come to your home for Christmas?"

219

I looked at her with a shocked look and said, "Olga, I did not even think of asking Abel. And, since you mentioned his name, Chelsea Lyn has not asked for him to be here. I wonder why?" Olga seemed relieved.

"Chelsea, my dear, I do not feel too comfortable with Abel and Morgan together. I have bad feeling that one day one of them will ask about Chelsea Lyn's real mother. I don't want Morgan to be hurt."

I sighed as I responded, "Olga, I share your concern. I really don't know what to do if Morgan discovers that I am Chelsea Lyn's natural mother. I think about it almost every day. But, Olga, what can I do?"

She took me by the shoulders and looked directly at me and said, "My dear Chelsea, since Chelsea Lyn knows Abel is her father, I think Morgan should know the truth. But it is your life and if anyone is to tell him, it must be you … "

"But Olga, I tried to tell him about my past and he wouldn't listen."

"This is different. Chelsea Lyn is here living with you. She knows you are her real mother. Tell me, do you have a secret pact with Chelsea Lyn not to tell Morgan?" I knew Olga was right. Even though Morgan wouldn't listen to me before, he must be told that I am Chelsea Lyn's natural mother. I just don't know how I'm going to explain it to him. I didn't want to have to deal with the problem during the Christmas season. I'll talk with Morgan later.

Jason arrived early on Christmas Eve. He took his culinary creation into the kitchen. I felt really good about introducing Jason to Dad and Olga and my family. Morgan knew him from the corporation. When he was introduced to the boys they laughed at his English. Chelsea Lyn was very ladylike and commented how she enjoyed hearing a real Englishman speak. We all gathered in the family room with the Christmas tree and decorations. Everyone was to help decorate the tree. Morgan put the Christmas music on the tape recorder and we all sang Christmas carols as we strung the lights and hung ornaments. Jason was very happy to be with us and his voice filled the room — and we all tried to match his volume. We all were in a festive mood when the front doorbell rang. I went to the door, and there stood Abel with his arms full of Christmas presents.

"Abel, how nice you could come." I wondered if Chelsea Lyn had invited him.

"Father Abel," she shouted, "you did come to our Christmas party. How wonderful." She hugged him and helped him with the Christmas presents. Chelsea Lyn took him to the family room to greet our guests and to introduce him to Jason.

"Father Abel, this is Mr. Jason. He worked for Mr. Thorndike for a long time."

Jason didn't know who he was greeting when he said, "It is very nice that a pastor could come for a visit on Christmas Eve. I am very happy to meet you, sir." Abel looked surprised when Jason greeted him.

"Yes, Mr. Jason, it is my pleasure to meet you. I must say I am not just a pastor. I am Chelsea Lyn's father." It was Jason's turn to look surprised.

"I am very sorry, sir, I didn't mean to exclude you from your family."

About that time Olga stepped in and said, "I need some help in the kitchen to complete the preparation of the food. Jason, will you please help me?"

"Yes, of course, madam. I shall be very happy to assist you." Olga took Jason to the kitchen. I thought, thank you, Olga, for saving the family from an embarrassing moment. Morgan greeted Abel and took him to the wet bar for refreshments. Dad joined Morgan and Abel. Chelsea Lyn, the boys, and I finished the decorating the tree.

Chelsea Lyn whispered to me, "Mom, thanks for inviting Father Abel. I completely forgot to call him. Mom, you're just wonderful." I thought nothing could be gained if I confessed that I had not invited Abel. Olga and Jason rolled tea carts loaded with food into the family room so we could snack as we enjoyed our fellowship. Chelsea Lyn asked Abel if he would pray over the food.

Abel began, "Heavenly Father, thank you for the wonderful day of your Son's birth. We are grateful that we can gather here as *family* and celebrate this event. We thank you for all your blessings through this year. Bless this food, may it nourish our bodies as your Spirit nourishes our souls. Amen."

Abel's prayer seemed to emphasize the *family*. Maybe it was just my imagination. We all ate and drank Christmas cheer and the boys flitted from one person to another asking what they were getting for Christmas. Soon it was bedtime for the boys. We all selected one present to open before bed. The boys chose the biggest boxes they could find.

They shouted with joy, "Look, everybody! A real computer game with Mickey Mouse. Oh, boy, are we going to have fun with these."

Chelsea Lyn selected a Christmas card. She read it and screamed, "Thank you, Papa Morgan and Mother." Olga asked if the card contained a car inside. Chelsea Lyn answered, "Much better than a car, Olga. It entitles me to a multimedia computer system with all the attachments. *It is wonderful!* Oh, thank you again and again." Abel handled Chelsea Lyn a package and asked her to open it. She took the package and opened it very carefully.

"Oh, Father Abel, it is beautiful. Look everyone. *My own statue of Jesus!*"

Soon the Christmas Eve presents had all been opened and Chelsea Lyn took the boys to their rooms to prepare them for bed. When Sylvia was busy, Chelsea Lyn often took care of the boys. She said good night to all and hugged Abel very dearly and thanked him for coming and for the present. I looked at Abel and detected a tear as it rolled down his cheek. I put my arms around both of them and asked God to take care of them. Abel said he would be leaving about January sixth of the new year. He would be going to Turkey for his overseas assignment. I wondered if he would be going to where Matthew lived. I was afraid to ask.

Olga, Dad, Morgan, Jason, and Abel and I sat around the fire and talked. Olga asked Jason what he had been doing since Mr. Thorndike's death. He said, "Ms. Olga, I have been sorting out the master's personal items and disposing of the more commercial ones. Miss Chelsea, there are a number of items I think you should have from Mr. Thorndike's home. If you could come by one day I would sort them out so you could inspect them."

I was rather shocked and responded to him, "That's very kind of you, Jason. I'll be glad to come by and look at the items. Any day next week will be just fine for me. Things are very slow at the office this time of year." He seemed glad that I accepted his offer.

"Thank you, Miss Chelsea. Would Tuesday immediately after noon be suitable for you?"

"Yes, Jason, that will be just fine."

Dad asked, "Jason, I understand Mr. Thorndike had a granddaughter who was killed at a young age. He said Chelsea reminded him of her."

"Mr. Carodine, Mr. Thorndike never had any grandchildren of his own."

I said to Jason, "But Jason, Mr. Thorndike talked to me several times about Nada, his granddaughter ...." I thought, he was never married!

222

Jason interrupted me and said, "I beg your pardon, Miss Chelsea. Mr. Thorndike often provided for young people whom he referred to as his grandchildren. Nada was a very special young girl in Mr. Thorndike's life. When he saw you at your college he returned elated. He told me that when he met you, he felt as though he had just visited with the 'spirit' of his adopted granddaughter, Nada." I wondered why Mr. Thorndike never told me that Nada was not his granddaughter. I guess when he told me about his illegitimate son, Stan, I could have figured he never had a wife so he could not have had any blood relatives.

"Mr. Thorndike," Jason continued, "did the same for me. He discovered me when I was a mere lad of sixteen years of age. I had been in foster homes since I was twelve. Mr. Thorndike educated me through English middle school and then asked what trade I would prefer. I told him I would prefer to become his butler and serve him. He then sent me to the exclusive Thomas Hooks Butler Training Academy. When I completed the training, he brought me to America and I was with him for nearly twenty-six years."

Jason continued, "Miss Chelsea, I have established a scholarship at the butler academy for young people who do not have funds but desire to become home managers and servants. It is my way of keeping my master's spirit alive."

"Jason, your life story would make a good book. Have you thought of writing about your life?"

He began to smile and replied, "Ms. Chelsea, I am currently writing a book for an English firm about a butler's life." We all applauded.

"That is wonderful," Dad said. "Will you include what happened here in the past several months, I mean the tragedy?"

Jason responded, "No sir, Mr. Carodine, this book will only cover the training and life of a butler. I could never include anything about Master Thorndike."

The evening was getting late and Abel said he should say good night. I walked him to the door and thanked him for coming. He said, "Chelsea, I was rather embarrassed at first, but I am more comfortable visiting your home now. Thank you. Good night." I asked him to please come again.

When I returned to the family room everyone was saying good night to each other. We hugged Olga and Dad and shook Jason's hand and retired to our bedrooms. When Morgan and I were alone I felt I had to tell him about Abel and me. We were sitting at the bedroom window overlooking the lake. The air was cold. We bundled up in our coats and walked out on the second floor patio. Morgan was holding me very close. I asked if he was trying to keep warm or was he showing me that he loved me. In the standard joking Morgan manner he said he was just trying to keep warm. I thought, how should I begin? If I continued to wait for the right time I would never tell him. He would probably learn the truth from Chelsea Lyn.

"Morgan, do you remember when I asked if you were ever curious about Chelsea Lyn's mother?"

"Yes, but what does that have to do with me trying to keep warm by snuggling up to you?"

"Morgan, please listen to me and be serious, just for a moment."

"Should I stand at attention or can I continue to lean against you?" I thought, how am I going to tell him if I can't get his attention for a moment?

"Morgan, I have things that I must tell you … "

"Are you sure it can't wait until we are just a little warmer?" I thought, the best way is to just tell him.

"Morgan, I am talking about Chelsea Lyn's mother. Don't you want to know more about your daughter's mother?"

He took my face in his warm hands and said, "My darling Chelsea, I already know all I need to know about my daughter's mother."

I was shocked! What is he saying, *he already knows?*

He continued, "She is very pretty, just like you. She has a cute little turned-up nose, fair complexion, striking figure, and likes to make love to her husband. Am I close yet?" What is he trying to say to me? Does he really know or is he guessing?

"Morgan, how can you describe Chelsea Lyn's mother? You don't even know her?"

"But, my lady, I do know her. *She is the love of my life!*"

I didn't know what to say. I stammered, I tried to find the words to question him … all I could do was break down and cry. My sobbing and gasping became uncontrollable. Morgan eased me back into the bedroom, removed my coat, and held me very close as he told me he loved me very much. I continued to cry. How could he have known? He has never even hinted that he knew I am Chelsea Lyn's mother. His only remark about Abel was why Chelsea Lyn felt the two of them had to meet. I couldn't understand what was happening. Morgan already knew what I was trying to tell him. I slowly began to gain control of my crying. Morgan gave me his handkerchief and I walked away from him.

I turned to him and said, "Morgan, do you really understand that *I am Chelsea Lyn's biological mother?*"

"Yes, my love. I have suspected you were her mother for a long time. When I look at Chelsea Lyn and then at you, I see a carbon copy of my daughter. Do you remember when I said Chelsea Lyn's mother had to be very intelligent and pretty?"

"Yes, I remember you saying that. Is that when you knew I was her mother?"

"I'm not sure when I actually realized you are her mother. Somehow I just knew it." I couldn't believe what Morgan was saying. He has never approached me about the circumstances of my being Chelsea Lyn's mother. I thought he could have at least screamed at me as to how I could have a baby by a pastor. *But, no, never a word!* I began to wonder *What kind of man is Morgan?* Another man would have divorced his wife if he even suspected her of being unfaithful, before or after marriage. I had to talk with him.

"Morgan, don't you want to know how it happened?"

"Chelsea, dear, you had a life before you met me. I have never questioned you about your past nor did I want you to tell me about it. *You are my wife today.* That is what is important to me. I know you love me and I love you with all my heart … "

I stopped him and said, "Morgan, would you listen if I just started talking about how it happened with Abel?"

"Darling, if it will make you feel better, yes, tell me about it. I assure you it will not change my feelings for you. What is important to me is today. You and my family."

I have never met a person with the control that Morgan has over his feelings. But now, I knew I had to tell him what happened. I began, "Morgan, I never told you that my dad asked me to leave home when I was seventeen, but he did — but that is all forgotten now. I found a job in a pastor's home. I was to help keep house and work in the church office. The people I lived with were Abel and Kersi Clayborne. Kersi could not have a baby. Abel and I believed she would kill herself if she could not have a baby of her own. Some people would say I was brainwashed into having Chelsea Lyn. But Morgan, I wasn't. I had their baby because of the great love I felt for Kersi and Abel. I'll make it short. Kersi planned

225

when Abel and I would be together. The rest is self-evident. Chelsea Lyn was born and Kersi took her and left the day she was born. I never saw her until I went for her when she was *almost thirteen years old!*"

Morgan said, "Yes, I remember when you went for her. Darling, you were the happiest woman in the world when you brought that little girl home with you. You could have said she belonged to you then. It wouldn't have made any difference."

"*Oh, Morgan, you are so wonderful!* I just can't believe you."

"Honey, I hope you never fully understand me. Maybe I am different from most men. But, honey, I have found love and caring in you and my children — yes, all three are my children. Most men never find the kind of love I have, but are always searching for."

"Morgan, would you *please* take me to bed and make love to me?"

"Then I can conclude that our conversation is finished, for good?"

"Yes, darling, finished for good!" He took me in his arms and I melted like I have never melted before. I know I am totally his lover and wife. *Another man will never touch me again!* He gently kissed my face, first each ear and then my eyes, nose, and finally my mouth. I pulled him to me and we lay on the bed. In a few minutes we were kissing each other passionately, each responding to the other's emotional needs. He very gently and slowly massaged my body until he knew I wanted him with all of my heart. Our passion simply exploded and the emotions of the lies I had lived with drained from my mind. Shortly I snuggled up to him and we fell asleep.

4   Christmas Day was simply wonderful. Chelsea Lyn and I prepared breakfast and had an opportunity to talk. I told her that Papa Morgan and I talked about her and her father Abel last night. She looked at me with a shocked look on her face and said, "Mother, I have been very careful not to say anything about you being my real mother. Did Papa Morgan discover our secret?"

I smiled as I said, "Darling, Papa Morgan and I had a long talk about it. He has known for a long time that I am your biological mother."

She screamed and said, "You mean he knew and never said anything about it to you?"

"That's correct, dear. Your Papa Morgan is one in a million and he loves us all with all his heart." Chelsea Lyn hugged me and began to cry.

"Oh, Mother … I was always afraid that … *I would be the one to slip and say something about you … being my mother!* I am so glad he knows."

I stroked her hair and responded, "My dear, I'm sorry to have put you through the ordeal of keeping our secret. When you feel you can talk about it, please talk with Papa Morgan about us, you and me, OK, sweetheart?" She remained in my arms crying ever so softly for several minutes.

She looked at me with those penetrating, shining eyes and said, "*Mother, I love you very much!*" She dried her eyes and went to work preparing the breakfast. I could almost feel the stress flowing away from her mind.

"Mother, we have a group of hungry people out there waiting for their breakfast. We better get going or they will be clamoring for service."

After breakfast Jason apologized but said he must leave. He had planned to stay with us until after Christmas. He didn't say why he was leaving but said good-bye to everyone and thanked us for his stay and the wonderful friendship. We walked him to his car and invited him to come more often. We sat about the dining table having coffee and continuing our talk about our wonderful Christmas, the first one with all of our family.

5 Dad and Olga remained with us for a few days after Christmas. Olga was still concerned about Abel's visit on Christmas Eve. She asked if the subject of "*the real mother*" came up during his visit. When I told her about my conversation with Morgan, she cried. It takes a lot to make Olga cry. She must have been really moved by Morgan's response to me when I told him about Abel and me. Finally, through her tears she said, "Morgan is a man with a true Christian heart. I think he carried much guilt about the onetime affair with the secretary."

"Yes, Olga. I just simply can't believe Morgan's outlook on life. He is more than a puritan, *he is a saint!*" Olga dried her eyes and hugged me.

"You have wonderful family, Chelsea. You must remember that when you try to help other people. Do not become too emotionally involved or you will lose."

"Olga, are you are talking about Matthew?"

227

"Yes, I did have Matthew in mind. Chelsea, my dear, you must be careful. You owe your energy to your family. Do not neglect them to help Matthew. I do not believe Matthew wants to remember who he was … "

"Olga, *that's not true!* Why would he want to come to the States if he didn't want to remember his past life?"

She looked at me sternly and said, "I will be harsh with you, Chelsea. I believe Matthew is responding to your insistence that he come to the States to seek his identity. I really don't believe he wants to come on his own." I was stunned that she would say such a thing.

"OK, Olga. *I won't contact Matthew again!* But … if he contacts me, on his own, then I will do what I can do to help him regain his memory. After he recovers his memory, what he does will be his decision."

"And, my dear, what if his decisions include being with you, whom he may remember as his wife?" Olga knew Matthew and I were never legally married.

"Olga, I'll deal with that situation …." Dad came in with a cup of coffee and interrupted our conversation.

"Good morning, my dear Thomas. Happy holidays to you," Olga said to Dad. He bent over and kissed her on the cheek and turned to me.

"And how is my dear daughter this morning?"

I hugged him and responded, "Dad, I'm just fine. Oh, I love it when you two are here with us."

"Yes, it's grand to have such a wonderfully happy family," Dad said.

"My dear Thomas, do you have something to clear with your daughter Chelsea?"

"Yes, Olga, I remember. Chelsea, Olga tells me you said we shouldn't move in together. Did you have a specific reason, dear?" Dad's statement surprised me.

"Dad, I think I may not have made my point. I believe I said that two unmarried, professional people living in a small town like Lewisburg would cause gossip that may harm your reputations. At least I think that's what I said."

Olga looked at Dad and said, "Da, Chelsea said people who live in town would talk about you and me. Is that bad in America?" Dad smiled at her.

"Olga, my dear, Chelsea expressed concern for our welfare. She was not withholding her approval for us to move in together. Do you understand, dear?"

"Da, I understand now. So how do we have people not to talk about us?"

"Well, one way is to get married."

Olga looked at Dad and said, "Thomas, my dear one, I think I love you very much, but maybe I am not ready to marry you." Dad laughed and looked at me with his response.

"Chelsea, what do you think of a woman who says no to a marriage proposal before one is made?"

I hugged both of them and gave my opinion, "Dad, I think Olga is correct. She has to get to know you … "

"I suspected this would happen, so I took measures."

Olga said, "What measures did you take, Mr. Thomas Carodine? Did you get another woman to move in with you?" Dad continued his jovial mood.

"*No, Ms. Olga!* I purchased the condo next to mine. You can become my renter until you decide what is best for your future."

"Thomas, you bought condo for me to move into to have people not talk about us?" She had a puzzled look on her face as she took Dad's arm.

"Yes, my dear. But only until I propose to you and you say yes!"

Morgan joined us for coffee. The boys were racing through the family room with their new Christmas toys. Soon Chelsea Lyn, our 'sleepy head', came in her pajamas and greeted everyone with hugs and kisses on the cheeks. She sat next to Morgan and he cuddled her in his arms. She said, barely above a whisper, "Papa Morgan, you are the greatest dad a girl could ever have. Thank you for being so wonderful to Mother and me." The shock of her tenderness brought tears to Morgan's eyes. He hugged her to hide his tears.

"Sweetie …, I'm the lucky one. I have two beautiful, talented women in my life who love me." He wiped his eyes and continued. "What other man in the entire world can make that statement?" I went to them and hugged them both. I couldn't hold back my tears. I am so happy! … I have my family. *I have regained my life!*

CHAPTER EIGHT
SAVE A LOVE

1 *God must be on my side!* My fear of Morgan's learning that I am Chelsea Lyn's biological mother threatened my sanity for so long. Olga was right: Morgan had to know. And my dear, sweet Chelsea Lyn had been carrying the burden of secrecy for me. Lifting that burden from her had to be done. I'm glad it's over. I had a terrible dread of the consequences of my secret when Morgan learned the truth. I am still truly amazed at his depth of understanding and forgiveness. It is his wonderful gift from God. His acceptance of my confession didn't create an emotional gap between us. If anything, the truth brought him and me and Chelsea Lyn closer together as a family. The secrets of my past seem to be unfolding, a page at a time. I wonder what will happen when Morgan learns that Caesar is Matthew Glyndon's son. I pray that this last secret will be accepted. But all my fears of everything that ever happened to me are magnified in my mind. I must be the one to reveal this one last secret to my dear husband, Morgan. I just don't know how much he can take. I only hope when he does learn the truth it will not be the one that breaks him emotionally. The revelation of my relationship with Matthew rests entirely upon Matthew's shoulders, *and he doesn't even know it yet!*

Not contacting Matthew, as I'd promised Olga, could easily solve the problem. If Matthew does not want to come to the States for tests and medical help to restore his memory, only Olga and I will know that Matthew is Caesar's father. I hope my conscience can withstand the stress and tension of waiting for Matthew's contact, if he decides to make the trip. I must maintain control of my emotions and thank the Lord for my life and my wonderful family. *I can't, I won't* let Matthew Glyndon destroy me and my family if he chooses to come to the States for examinations and evaluation.

Chelsea Lyn asked if we could have Father Abel come to dinner before he departed for his overseas pastoral posting. I told her I would talk with Morgan and if he did not object, then yes, Abel could spend a last evening with us.

The holidays are over and now I'm going back to work. I was in the bedroom fixing my face when I decided this would be the time to talk with Morgan about Abel.

"Morgan, Chelsea Lyn asked if Abel could come for dinner before he leaves for overseas. How do you feel about it, dear?"

Morgan shrugged his shoulders and said, "I don't have any objections to him coming for dinner. After all he is Chelsea Lyn's biological father. I suppose we can't deny her one last visit with him before he leaves." I couldn't tell if he was accepting or objecting.

"Morgan, would you feel uncomfortable with him here?"

He looked at me and replied, "Chelsea, I consider Abel your divorced husband. But he is Chelsea Lyn's father. He was the only father she had for the first twelve years of her life. Yes, I think she should have a chance to be with him if she feels the need." I still wasn't satisfied.

"Morgan, dear, I could take Chelsea Lyn to a restaurant for dinner with him if that would please you."

"Chelsea, *I'm not uncomfortable being with Abel!* I realize you must have feelings for him, but he is not a threat to me. I know you love me and your family. Besides, one of us may have to make a telephone call to him if anything ever happens to Chelsea Lyn, or to you for that matter." I thought, what a wonderful Christian outlook he has.

"Thank you, Morgan. I'll tell Chelsea Lyn to ask him for next Friday evening. His departure is scheduled for Monday afternoon."

Morgan looked up and said, "You will take Chelsea Lyn to the airport to see him off, won't you?"

"Why, yes, if you think it's all right."

"Honey, it's the only thing you can do. We don't know how his prolonged absences will affect Chelsea Lyn." This man, so concerned about others!

The first of the year in the office is always hectic. The corporation's fiscal year begins in January. It's the time when all new expenditures for the year must be reviewed and funded. It seems each senior manager has more projects than funds. Linda had arranged the first meeting for 10:00 A.M. She and I always took the first thirty minutes or so to go over the schedule and match it to the hours of my day. We talked about the holidays and what each of us had done. She couldn't believe me when I told her what happened between Morgan and me when I told him about Pastor Abel and Chelsea Lyn.

"Boss lady, I'm learning more about you every day. Did you tell him about Matthew and Mexico?" Linda never knew for sure what had happened between Matthew and me. She had suspicions, but we never talked. I wonder what she suspects?

"What exactly are you referring to, Linda?" Her embarrassment was obvious.

"I'm sorry, Chelsea. I didn't mean to imply anything. I just thought that you had nice feelings for Matthew. I remembered that you cried when you thought he had been killed in Turkey." I smoothed over the discussion.

"Yes, Linda, I still have feelings for Matthew. But he doesn't remember anything about his past. I doubt if he and I will ever talk about us again."

She looked puzzled and said, "But, boss, is he still coming to the States for treatment?"

"I don't know, Linda. I have decided not to encourage him to come. It's his decision entirely."

"But if he does come here, are you going to help him?" I thought, yes, Linda with all my heart.

"Of course, I will do anything I can do to help him remember who he is."

"Sorry to take your time on personal things. You have a full schedule today, beginning with the funding meeting at 10:00 A.M. and lasting until 6:00 P.M., unless you feel we should cut it short." I thought, what a way to begin the new year.

The managers gathered in the conference room and our meeting began. The allocation of money to projects went smoothly until we discussed the new product lines in the plumbing division. Parnella Verbena, one of the senior woman managers, made her presentation on incorporating a new line of women's bathroom fixtures. Many of her ideas came from Europe. Her presentation began very professionally.

"Ladies and gentlemen, Thorndike Corporation can be the leader in manufacturing women's bathroom fixtures *if we begin this year!* Blueprints and details have been worked out so that we can begin as soon as the tooling and assembly line is completed in the new southern plant." She explained this expansion of the product line would consume about three-fourths of the funds allocated for the southern plant. Karl Torley, the manager of the established product line of tools for the automotive market, objected to the possibility of cutting his funds.

He pleaded, "If the 25% increase for the women's bathroom fixtures is to come from this year's allocation, I will have to close part of the automotive tooling operation. We have an established market. I do not agree that we should take from what we know sells and dive into an unknown consumer market in women's bathroom fixtures."

Parnella responded, "Where is your nerve, Karl?"

He replied angrily, "I beg your pardon, Ms. Verbena. It's not nerve, it's experience and common sense." I could see there was about to be a battle between the sexes if I didn't step in.

"Ladies and gentlemen, I suggest you make this presentation to Mr. Morgan Gage in manufacturing. I will table any further discussion until after the Director of Manufacturing has a cut at your presentations." Everyone knows that Morgan and I are married. I hope they didn't get any ideas of me "passing the buck" or influencing his decisions. After the meeting was over, Parnella stayed behind to talk with me.

Standing defiantly before my desk with her hands on her hips, she said, "Ms. Carodine, I have worked on this concept of the women's bathroom fixtures for a long time. *I just know it will sell!*"

I attempted to calm her. "Parnella, I think it needs more discussion. Your estimate that the automotive tooling operation would lose about 25% of the funding this year will require other decisions to be made."

She walked over to the window and paused as she looked over the city. She turned and looked directly at me with anger in her eyes and said, "*Chelsea, can't you see what's happening here? This argument is not about product lines. It's about men against women!*" Oh, no, I thought — lady, don't bring sexism and woman power into this management decision.

"Parnella, I think you should cool down. You're acting like a feminist who is trying to win her argument at any cost ... "

She quickly replied, "Well, maybe I am concerned that we women are not getting our share. Someone has to stand up for our cause." That did it! I thought, try again, Chelsea.

"Parnella, may I suggest you personally follow this product line through with briefings to each director who is affected by it. Sell your idea, don't force it on unwilling managers." She glared at me and responded as she pounded her fist on my desk.

"Chelsea, I'm getting damn tired of working my ass off and not making a dent in this corporation's chauvinist pig male managers ... "

I stopped her and replied, "Parnella, please don't bring sexism, gender, or 'chauvinist pigs' into this conversation. You're not going to get anywhere with an attitude like that in Thorndike. And you are certainly not going to win any friends."

She snapped back, "Chelsea, I don't need friends. I'm a professional woman but we women don't have a chance against the damn males ...." That was about all I could take from her. I asked her to cool down.

"Parnella, we have a strong human rights program. If you feel any sexual discrimination I suggest you to talk to the chief of that division." She picked up her charts and hurriedly exited my office.

Linda came into the office and said, "Boss lady, I could hear that argument in the outer office. Do you have a problem?" I couldn't believe that one of the two senior woman managers could have become so emotionally involved that she would scream "sexual discrimination."

"I don't know what her problem is. Call the chief of our Human Rights Division and tell him I want to talk with him in my office."

"Sounds serious! I'll get him immediately."

In a few minutes David Cromwell came to my office. He sounded anxious.

"Linda said we may have a problem. What's going on?"

"David, go talk with Parnella Verbena. Don't say anything about me asking you to see her. Find out what's bothering her. She's an excellent manager, in fact I recommended her when she came to us from the Parker buy-out program. She's got some kind of a beef. Help her work it out. And David, get back to me as soon as possible."

"Sure, boss. I'll take a look at her file before I speak with her."

I asked Linda to get in touch with J.C. Just a few minutes later, he stuck his head in the door and said, "Good morning, Chelsea. You need me?"

"Yes, J.C. Parnella came to see me after the funding meeting. She was quite upset over the fact that I did not approve her new product line. Keep close tabs on the situation and help resolve her problem. Morgan will hear the presentation about the women's bathroom product line and he should get back to you or me within a week or so. J.C., stay on top of this. I don't want a senior woman manager yelling 'sexism'." J.C. was surprised but said he would follow it closely.

Well, I suppose situations like this occur all the time. Stan Jones's was the last case of sexism in Thorndike and I fired him! I hope Parnella thinks about her demands and realizes it's not a woman versus man issue that is keeping the new product line from being adopted.

J.C. came back into my office to say he had talked with John Capps. I quickly asked, "Has Stan Jones created another problem for us?"

He smiled and said, "No, I think John is interested in getting our lobbying contract. He didn't mention Stan Jones." Well, what a relief, I thought.

"What do you think about the lobbying contract, J.C.?"

"I think John's firm can handle it. He has handled Thorndike's business for a number of years. He has to be well qualified or he would have been gone."

"OK, set up a meeting with the principals and we'll discuss the contract."

2 Linda's voice on the intercom announced that Mr. Tom Deminski was calling long distance from Ankara, Turkey. Oh, heavens, I thought, what next?

"Hello, Tom. How are you? ... Yes, we're doing well. What is happening?"

"Ms. Carodine, I have been in contact with the man you believe to be Matthew Glyndon. He would like to speak with you over the telephone. If you want to talk with him I will fly to his village and make the arrangements."

"Yes, of course, Tom, I'll speak with him. Can you arrange his call during my office hours? I realize there's a considerable time difference, but I would prefer talking with him from my office."

Tom responded, "Yes, Ms. Carodine, I will arrange it. I anticipate it will be the day after tomorrow before I can get him to a telephone. Will that be all right?"

"Yes, Tom. That will be just fine. I shall expect your call on Thursday." I felt an overwhelming need to talk to Olga.

"Linda, please get Olga on the telephone for me." She dialed Olga's office.

"Olga, this is Chelsea. How are you, dear?"

She seemed happy to hear my voice. "I am fine, my dear daughter. How are you and your family?"

"We are doing well, Olga. Olga, I had a call from Tom Deminski in Turkey today. He said that Matthew wants to talk with me. I expect the call on Thursday. And Olga, *I didn't call him!* He wants to talk with me."

"What do you think this means, Chelsea dear?"

"I don't really know, Olga. But if Matthew wants to come to the States I must talk with you before he arrives. I want you on the team that will do the medical evaluation."

"My dear, if he is to come to the States this may be a good time for me. I will be moving to Lewisburg in about two weeks. We must talk about what you desire me to do before I open my medical practice there in Lewisburg."

"Olga, I will have a contract drawn up for you to be Thorndike's medical liaison between Matthew and the medical team. Can I have my contract people talk with you about terms?"

"Yes, Chelsea, I will talk with them when you say." This is wonderful. Olga will be able to watch every development and keep me abreast of Matthew's progress.

I didn't sleep Tuesday or Wednesday nights. I told Morgan about the telephone call from Turkey. He suggested I wait for the call before drawing any conclusions as to what it may be about. He said, "If Matthew has decided to come to the States then we have to help him. But don't worry about the call until you know what it's all about, OK, honey?" Morgan is always in control — I envy him! I am so glad he is supporting me in my decision to help Matthew.

3 David Cromwell, the director of human relations, was in my office about to brief me on the situation with Parnella when Linda announced the telephone call from Turkey was coming through. I asked David to excuse me while I took the call. It seemed like a very long time before I heard Matthew's voice.

"Ms. Carodine, this is Asher, or Matthew to you. I have decided to accept your offer and travel to the States for a review by your doctors. Is there a good time that I should arrive?" Oh, what a question! I thought, no, Matthew, there is no good time for you to try and come back into my life.

"Whatever arrangements you make to arrive in the States will be just fine. Olga, the doctor you met in Turkey, will be with you all during the examinations and evaluations. At least you will know one of the team."

"Yes, that will be just fine. How do I get tickets for the airplane?"

"Is Mr. Tom Deminski there with you?" Matthew responded affirmatively. I asked to speak with Tom.

"Tom, will you please make the arrangements for a visa and airline tickets for Matthew? Charge all expenses to the corporation's travel account."

Tom was very helpful and said, "Sure, Ms. Carodine, I'll be happy to make the arrangements. It will take about ten days to get the visa. If all goes well, Matthew should be on the airplane in ten to twelve days from now. Is that all right with you?"

I thought, that will give me time to get Olga prepared and under contract.

"Yes, Tom, that will be fine. Will you please call the office with the flight information when Matthew departs?"

He responded, "Yes, I'll call your assistant when the arrangements have been made. I will also call the day he departs." I thanked him and ended the call.

4 I called David back into the office to conclude his briefing on Parnella's problem. He took out a large personnel file and began, "Chelsea, are you aware that Ms. Verbena has had a number of encounters with her male subordinates and counterparts?" I was surprised by what he said.

"What do you mean, David?"

"I have had four cases within the past two years involving Ms. Verbena's promoting what appeared to be 'less qualified women' in preference to 'allegedly more educated and experienced men.'" I thought, what do we have here?

"And what happened in those cases, David?"

"Three of the men were permitted to transfer to another division, in grade, and the fourth man is still in Parnella's division. This fourth case was the last one I handled."

"Were each of the cases investigated and disposed of within the EEOC guidelines ... "

238

"Oh, yes. We always have our lawyers review our actions and then consult with a member of the federal EEOC to be sure we are in compliance with the law."

"In that man's case, do we have a disgruntled employee waiting to explode?"

"I'm not sure. The issue was an efficiency report that Parnella gave him, a report in which she gave him a rather low rating. After the complaint was filed Parnella agreed to rewrite the report and raise the rating."

"David," I asked, "how many other employee complaints have we had in the past year?" I can't let Thorndike get into a contest with the EEOC. Being a woman in the CEO position makes me a clear target.

David looked through his records and said, "The only employee complaints, all from men, are in Parnella's division." What is this woman trying to do? She can't be allowed to tear down Mr. Thorndike's philosophy of employee fairness regardless of gender. I asked David to schedule a meeting with J.C. and Parnella to discuss each case and give me a complete report within forty-eight hours. *David knows how important this matter is to me!*

Chelsea Lyn called later in the afternoon and was excited about her father Abel coming to dinner on Friday. She had gone shopping with Sylvia and said she would help prepare the meal. "Mom, I want this to be a very special dinner for Father Abel and I'm helping Sylvia prepare it." She sounded very happy. My talk with Morgan about being her real mother probably released her from the stress of keeping our secret. I love that young lady with all my heart.

5 Linda rang to say that Morgan was in the office to see me. He knocked lightly and entered, saying, "Chelsea, this is business. I don't want any monkeying around from the CEO."

I responded, "Is that right, Mr. Gage? Don't you enjoy being attacked by women in high places?"

He laughed and said, "Only on high stools. Not in positions of authority." Morgan suggested J.C. join us. He wanted to discuss the southern plant product lines. Linda called J.C. into my office.

"Well, Mr. Gage, what's on your mind?" Morgan pulled out a chart to explain his point.

"I understand the last senior managers' meeting generated a tiff about the product lines in the southern plant."

J.C. laughed as he replied, "Yes, I would say *just a tiff!*" Morgan had the entire Engineering Directorate's product lines detailed on his chart.

He said, "We can't schedule the new women's bathroom fixtures to begin manufacturing tooling until the fall of next year. It will take about six or eight months after the tooling to produce the first products — if we choose to produce them."

J.C. reviewed the chart and said, "Parnella Verbena seems to be planning for this fiscal year."

"No, way, J.C.," Morgan said. "Even if we had the extra capital investment funds, time is against us."

I looked at Morgan and asked, "Why do you suppose Parnella made such a pitch about a product line that can't go until next year?"

J.C. looked at me over his glasses and said, "Chelsea, I think we may have a woman who is rearing her head on the gender issue." It didn't surprise me after her outburst in my office.

"Morgan, as the director of engineering, how do you see this women's bathroom fixture product line?"

He looked at the graphs and responded, "Here is the picture. November or December of next year for the tooling, and product production six months later. That's the best we can do."

"OK, gentlemen, I'm satisfied with your plans." I rang Linda and asked her to call Ms. Verbena to my office for a discussion of the women's bathroom fixture product line. In a few minutes Parnella walked into my office with a big smile, until she saw Morgan and J.C.

She said very angrily, "What is this, a woman lynching?" I ignored her remark.

"Ms. Verbena, your recommendation for the new product line has been reviewed by quality control and engineering. The question is not the reallocation of funds but the time required to tool up for the product. The earliest date we can plan for is May or June next year."

Frowning, she said, *"Well, I can see the women have lost out again!"* I stood up from my desk and asked Morgan and J.C. to please give me a few minutes with Parnella.

"Parnella, what's the chip on your shoulder about men against women in this corporation?"

She placed her hands on the corner of my desk and said, "Well, Chelsea, that is just how it is. I've worked my buns off for the last three years and the first time I come up with a big seller for the company *I am shot down by a man — your husband, no less!*" I thought to myself, stay cool, Chelsea. This woman has a very distorted view of her importance to the company; deal with her gently.

I responded, "Parnella, look at this chart. This is the best possible timetable for the women's bathroom fixture product line ...." Her anger was still evident.

"Chelsea, did you *instruct your husband to shoot down the product line ... ?*"

"Ms. Verbena, I suggest you calm down and look at the facts."

"*No, Ms. Carodine*, I don't have to look at the timeline. I can see what is happening. All the big guns in the corporation are shooting at me because *I'm a successful woman, and they are frightened of me!*" I couldn't believe what I was hearing! Is this a feminist gone power hungry? Try again, Chelsea.

I tried to get her attention and said, "Parnella, I'm sorry you feel the way you do. The product line will be scheduled as the director of engineering has planned ... "

"Oh, if you can't do it on a woman-to-woman basis you turn your men dogs loose on me ... "

I stood up and said, "*That will be enough, Ms. Verbena.* If you cannot accept the decision then I suggest you look for another position."

"So it finally comes down to you firing me. *You, a woman, firing me!*"

"Ms. Verbena, I am not firing you! I am trying to give you a logical reason why that product line can't go until next year."

She took hold of my desk and said angrily and very sarcastically, "It's too bad that you had to line up all of your top dogs to get to me. Let me tell you, Ms. *Chelsea Carodine, it won't work* ...." I thought, remember, Chelsea, you're a professional — don't lose your head.

"Ms. Verbena, I will give you a week to cool off. If at the end of that week you can come in here and discuss this problem logically, you may remain ... with Thorndike ... "

She very rudely interpreted me and said, "*Don't do me any favors, Mrs. CEO!*" *That does it*, I thought.

"Ms. Verbena, I wasn't going to fire you, *that is, until I saw that you are not interested in being logical!*"

241

She screamed back at me. *"Fire me, bitch!* You will not hear the last of it!"

"Yes, Ms. Verbena, you are getting your wish. *Your services are terminated as of this date.* I suggest you clean out your desk and leave the company today. I will send my deputy to accompany you."

She stormed out of the office, saying, *"Ms. Carodine, you will regret your actions today!"*

I called to Linda to have J.C. accompany Ms. Verbena while she cleared out her desk and personal items. "Linda, bring your pad in for a memorandum of the meeting with Ms. Verbena." Linda recorded the events of the meeting in an official memorandum with date and subject. I also wanted the other participants' notes on the subject. "Linda, take a memo from Morgan and J.C. about their observations of the meeting before they left my office. Get David Cromwell back here." I wanted everything that happened to be recorded in official files.

"David, I have just terminated Ms. Verbena for insubordination and conduct unbecoming an official of Thorndike Corporation. Complete a case file on what occurred today. Arrange for an exit interview with Ms. Verbena. Get a copy of the interview, and send her file over to Susan Rosco and the EEOC for review.

"I don't want any flak coming back about what took place with Ms. Verbena today." David is a very positive people manager. I can count on him to make sure our actions are legal.

"Don't worry, Chelsea. I'll take care of this."

I was glad when the day ended. Just as I was about to leave the office, Linda buzzed me and said Morgan was on the telephone.

"Hi, dear. What can I do for you?" He responded in his usual happy way.

"Well, beautiful, I think you need a cocktail and dinner with one of your suitors. By the way, I'm available."

"That sounds great, Morgan. I'll meet you at Hoffman's. And thanks, honey."

6 Linda called Sylvia to tell her Morgan and I were eating dinner out and that we'd be home around nine. If the children want to see us tonight, they have permission to wait up for us. Linda is such a dear. I would be lost without her.

242

"Fire me, bitch! … Ms. Carodine, you will regret your actions today!"

Morgan arrived before I did and met me at the door. He had already ordered drinks and I was glad to sit down and relax with him. He commented on our day.

"Boy, Ms. Carodine-Gage, I hope all of your days are not like today."

"Yes, I agree with that statement. It was a very emotionally draining day for me. I really didn't want to terminate Parnella but she pushed me beyond any reasonable limits ...." Morgan interrupted me and assured me he felt my actions were fair.

"Honey, I've had a couple of run-ins with Parnella. She is for the woman at all costs. I approved transfers of three of her male subordinates because they couldn't work for her, she was so bossy and demanding."

"Then you think I did the right thing in terminating her?" Morgan shook his head approvingly.

"Honey, you did what you had to do." I suppose I was seeking Morgan's approval because Parnella is the first professional woman I have terminated.

"Thanks for your reassurance, Morgan. I needed that."

"Honey, what's the latest on Matthew? Linda said the call came through."

"Yes, I talked with him yesterday. Tom Deminski will make the arrangements for Matthew to travel here. Tom said he should be here in about ten or twelve days."

Morgan took my hands and said, "Honey, have you thought out what you are going to do to help him regain his memory?" Oh, heavens, I thought, my husband is concerned about what I should do to help *my former lover!*

I responded, "I'm going to put Olga under contract as the Thorndike medical advisor. She will be with Matthew during his tests and evaluations. Linda will call contracts tomorrow and start the ball rolling." Morgan seemed to approve of my initial actions.

"Well, babe, if we are to have any time together we should try and get away within the next few days, before Matthew arrives. I know he will consume all of your time once he arrives." I thought to myself, Chelsea, you're the luckiest woman in the world with a man like Morgan who loves you in spite of what may happen with your former lover.

"So, my dear, what do you feel like eating tonight?"

"I think I'll have a nice, juicy steak. You know how I want it cooked. I'll be right back." I went to the powder room to freshen my face.

Our dinner was very relaxing. Morgan seems to sense when I need a break from the pressures of the office. He always answers my needs, even before I really know what they are. That thought reminded me of Matthew. He also felt my moods and consoled me when I needed relief. And now he will be here in Lewisburg in about ten days. I am still afraid of what will happen if he regains his memory. *But I can't back out now!*

7

Olga moved into the condo in Lewisburg that Dad purchased. I didn't know why she wouldn't marry Dad and move into his condo. It seemed silly to buy a separate one until she makes up her mind. But, that's their business, and they are both over twenty-one and certainly don't answer to me.

Olga called the office and said she was ready to meet with me and the contract people. I had Linda arrange a meeting with J.C. to ensure what we were doing didn't violate any corporate policies. The meeting was set for 9:00 A.M. and Olga was a few minutes early. As I came into the office she and Linda kidded me about being the boss with "banker's hours." I greeted them and asked Linda to bring coffee and hot rolls in for the three of us. We were talking about "woman" things when suddenly Linda asked, "Olga, I understand you have moved here to Lewisburg. Are you going to set up your medical practice here?"

Olga smiled and replied, "Da. I was persuaded by Mr. Carodine to move here. I will rent a condo from him for awhile."

Linda looked puzzled and said, "Olga, aren't you and Mr. Carodine going together?"

"Yes, he does take me to dinner and we dance sometime."

I broke into their conversation, hoping to save Olga from any embarrassment. "Linda, will you please check on the contracts people and be sure J.C. is here for the meeting?"

"Sure thing, boss, I'll get on it right away."

I looked at Olga and said, "Olga, did Linda embarrass you about Dad?"

"What do you say? I am never to be embarrassed about your father. I will answer questions about what we do. I am truthful person." What a lady!

J.C. came in with his usual happy smile and greeted Olga and me.

"How are you ladies this morning?"

Olga responded, "I'm just fine, Mr. J.C. I also think Chelsea is fine for today." She said that right. Soon my days may not be "right." I explained what I wanted Olga to do for the corporation. The contract representative, Joe Keen, didn't see a problem with her being under contract as our medical advisor.

He said, "Matthew Glyndon is still an employee of Thorndike. The corporation's medical plan will defray his medical costs and the contract will be paid directly from the corporation."

Once the legal details were concluded, Olga and I left for lunch. I needed to talk with her about Matthew. "Olga, before Matthew arrives, can you get his medical records from the hospital in Turkey?"

"Da. I don't think that will be a problem since I am to be his doctor. How do I find out which hospital treated him?" One of the doctors who reviewed his case while we were in Turkey had discovered that the Ankara General Medical Center had been where Matthew received his reconstructive surgery and medical treatments. I told Olga how to request the records. I thought, one more thing.

Matthew had been in a severe aircraft crash. He was terribly injured. The doctors in Turkey indicated he received extensive injuries to his head, jaw, and teeth. His fingers were also burned completely at the tips. I wondered if his fingerprints were destroyed? My concern was for a complete identification of this person whom I thought to be Matthew Glyndon. I hoped Olga could perform tests that would positively identify the person as Matthew Glyndon. I had no idea as to why I doubted his identify. He looked like the Matthew whom I loved and had a son with. *Why was I wondering at this point?*

Maybe I was rationalizing that he was not Matthew and my problems would be solved. My mind raced and my face became flushed. What is this conflict about Matthew's identification? I wanted Olga to perform whatever medical tests were necessary to confirm his identity.

"Olga, do you still have your copy of Matthew's medical records?"

"Da, Chelsea dear. I have medical records when I treated him and I have also samples of his blood when I took blood test for you."

"Olga, is it possible that you can have a DNA test performed on Matthew's blood? I mean, since you still have his blood sample."

She asked, "Da, I think that would be possible. May I ask why would you want a DNA of Matthew?"

"I don't know, Olga. I just want to be absolutely sure this person is Matthew Glyndon."

She seemed genuinely puzzled and asked, "My dear Chelsea, I thought you were sure this person was Matthew when you met him in Turkey. Tell me, are you having doubts about who he is?" My confusion was obvious to Olga.

"I don't know, Olga. I have such confusing thoughts. Maybe I am hoping that the person coming in from Turkey is not Matthew Glyndon."

"Da, I think your emotions are working overtime. Please be calm until he has gone through the medical examinations, and then ask questions."

"I know, Olga. I am such a wreck. I want to help him, but then again, I want him to just disappear. Maybe that is why I want the person to be someone else, not Matthew."

Olga said she still had the slides of blood she took from Matthew when she was trying to determine Caesar's parenthood. With new blood samples, she could send them to a laboratory and have them compared. The results should show whether the person is Matthew or an impostor. I asked myself, why are you doing this, Chelsea? Olga said if I had doubts we shouldn't have Matthew come to the States.

"Chelsea, I can send the slides to Turkey and have the comparison tests made there. If this person proves not to be Matthew, your problem will be solved."

"*Olga, please do as I ask!* Are there other tests you can perform to check his identity?"

She explained, "Da, his fingerprints, his dental records, and other physical markings on his body can help to show if he is Matthew Glyndon."

"Olga, we were told that he was in an airplane crash that caused extensive damage to his face, arms, and hands. What if the crash caused damage to the extent that we cannot identify him by his previous records? What then?"

"Chelsea, I ask you to be patient. You should meet face-to-face with this person and try to determine if you really believe him to be Matthew. If you do believe he is who you think him to be, then the tests you suggest are not necessary." I couldn't convey to Olga the strange feeling I had about this person who may be Matthew.

Morgan was very supportive. He suggested we invite Matthew to our home for dinner to help him reacquaint himself with America.

Morgan, I thought, I love you with all my heart, but please, *don't do me this favor* of asking Matthew to our home.

Olga signed the contract as Thorndike's medical advisor on the Matthew Glyndon case. She was to be with Matthew during every phase of his medical examinations and evaluations. Luckily, she would report his progress directly to me. I would know what happened to Matthew and his reaction to all the tests. Some people would call this "dirty pool," but I have to know what Matthew's reactions to the tests are before anyone else knows. *My marriage could depend on his memory!*

Olga received Matthew's medical records a few days before he was due to arrive. After reviewing the records, she came to my office to brief me on the findings. Her first remark was that, "Matthew should have died." She said, "The injuries he received would have killed a normal person." I wondered how Matthew had lived through such a crash. His entire face had been crushed and he was burned so badly about the hands, arms, and chest area. Olga couldn't understand how anyone could have lived after such injuries. I thought, so, Olga, you now may have doubts too!

An English plastic surgeon, who was on assignment to the Ankara General Medical Center, had performed the restoration of Matthew's face and burned areas of his body. Olga said his medical reports were very detailed. She said the restoration of his facial area was a miracle. Bones and skin from various parts of his body had been transplanted to his face. The records indicated the operations occurred over several months.

"Olga, could the surgery and the pain killers he was given have affected his memory?"

She was very positive when she said, "Of course, my dear. The trauma to the body and mind during a series of operations could have damaged his capacity to remember. Many of medical findings in cases like Matthew's are speculations." Olga went over every detail of Matthew's medical file with me. She carefully explained the procedures the doctors had used in operating on Matthew.

"Olga, have you talked with the doctors at the Mayo Clinic who are going to treat Matthew?"

She nodded and said, "I will drive out in a couple of days with these records and meet the doctors and medical personnel of the team. I will also make arrangements for your corporation to pay for his care. I have a voucher to give to the clinic."

8 I called home to check on Chelsea Lyn's dinner for Abel. She and
Sylvia said everything would be ready for a seven o'clock sit-
down. I wondered if Chelsea Lyn had invited her grandfather and
Olga.

"Chelsea Lyn, who all is going to be at your dinner for your father
Abel?" She responded with laughter in her voice.
"Mom, this dinner is only for Father Abel and our family. I didn't invite
Olga and Grandfather because I don't think Olga likes Father Abel."

"Oh, sweetie, I don't think Olga dislikes your father Abel ... "

"Well, Mom, if you don't mind, can this dinner be just for our family
— I mean just the boys, you and Dad, and Father Abel?" I thought, this
is her special way to say good-bye to Abel.

"Yes. That's just fine, dear. It's your dinner, so I guess you should
invite who you choose."

She responded rather quickly, "Mom, you're not angry with me, are
you? I mean, for not inviting Grandfather and Olga this time?" I assured
her I wasn't mad with her.

My car was in the shop for repairs so Morgan arranged to come to
the office to drive me home. I thought this would give us a few minutes
together. I think Morgan is more uncomfortable with Abel now that he
knows that Abel and I are Chelsea Lyn's parents. Morgan called on his
cellular telephone as he approached the office.

"Mrs. CEO, are you about ready to leave your office?"

"Yes, Mrs. CEO's husband. I'll meet you at the front entrance." In a
few minutes he drove up in his red Mercedes convertible and honked
his horn as he pulled to a stop.

"Hey, good-looking, you need a ride?" That's Morgan, always
kidding.

"I certainly do. A girl would never pass up a ride in a hot car like
this." Morgan took the long way home. He said we weren't spending
enough time together, just he and I.

"Honey, do you know a pretty girl who would like to go away for a
weekend with a lonely guy?" *What a wonderful idea!* I thought.

"Yes, sir! Where are you going to take me?"

He cut his eyes at me and said, "I want to take you to this cabin I
have way up in the hills. Only you, me, and Mother Nature!" I didn't
know if he was trying to lighten up for the evening with Abel or not.

"Morgan, let's get through tonight and we can leave early in the morning, before anyone is awake. I'll tell Sylvia and Chelsea Lyn tonight."

"I suppose this is *Abel's last supper,* so to speak!" He laughed.

"Yes. I understand he departs on Monday for his overseas posting."

"Do you know where he is going?" I tried to remember what Abel had said.

"No, I'm sorry, Morgan. I can't remember where he said the assignment is."

"Oh, well, I'm sure he will tell us tonight."

Chelsea Lyn was at the door as we drove up the driveway. "Dad, Mom, you just have time to shower and dress. Father Abel will be here by six o'clock. Please hurry!" Morgan looked surprised.

"Princess, I thought we were going to eat in our bathing suits by the pool!"

She yelled at him, "Oh, Dad! *No one can swim in an outdoor pool in the winter!*"

"Well, in that case, will my bright yellow shirt with my red tie be formal enough for you?"

She took him by the arm and said, "Dad, will you stop kidding and get upstairs and get ready? I have already laid out your tuxedo. And Mom, your blue evening dress and matching shoes are on your bed. Now, will you please hurry?" Chelsea Lyn had planned this evening and she was taking charge of everything, including selecting what she wanted us to wear. We rushed upstairs and hurriedly dressed so we could meet Abel when he arrived.

Abel arrived promptly at six. He was dressed in a tuxedo and presented Chelsea Lyn with long-stemmed roses.

"Oh, Father Abel, they're beautiful. I'll ask Sylvia to put them in water and we will have them on the table."

"Good evening, Abel. It's nice that you could visit before you depart."

"It is my pleasure. And, Morgan, thank you very much for permitting me to have this last evening with your family and Chelsea Lyn." I could feel the stiffness in both Abel and Morgan. The atmosphere was very formal. Both men were acting as if they had met for the first time and were being "polite" to each other.

Morgan served drinks and we sat in front of the fireplace. The flicking flames and their shadows seemed to hold our eyes as we stared at the fire. Our conversations were laced with comments about the pictures we

250

imagined being painted by the flames as the logs burned, snapping and popping as they did. Chelsea Lyn came in and announced that dinner was served. What a proud young lady! Once seated, Chelsea Lyn said she would say the prayer. My mind wandered as she prayed for the safety of her father Abel in his new calling.

It was about eighteen years ago that I had my first meal with Abel and Kersi. I remember Kersi had said the prayer. Her prayers were mostly for me. I wondered if Kersi had already *decided then that I would bear their baby!* Morgan stood up and brought me back to reality as he said, "Let me offer a toast to Abel on his new overseas posting. Good luck and may the Lord look over you." We all raised our glasses of wine and punch to Abel and wished him well. Abel complimented Chelsea Lyn for the tasty and delightful dinner.

Soon after dinner, Morgan took the boys to their rooms to get them ready for bed. Chelsea Lyn was in the kitchen preparing a dessert. Abel and I were alone sitting by the fire. He asked, "Chelsea, are you going to tell Morgan that you are Chelsea Lyn's mother?"

"Abel, he already knows. He and I had a talk after your last visit."

"Chelsea, why didn't you tell me he knew about us! I am terribly embarrassed! And I would think Morgan is also." I thought Morgan had handled himself rather well.

"Abel, I'm sorry I didn't inform you that Morgan knew about us before you came tonight. But, Abel, I wouldn't worry about Morgan ..."

Abel looked hurt. "I'm sorry, Chelsea, but I do feel very bad about Morgan knowing about us and me not being aware that you had talked with him." I couldn't believe Abel, a pastor, could be reacting the way he was. I said to myself, Abel, Morgan was a great deal more forgiving than you are. He accepted the truth and forgave me.

"I cannot believe a husband could be told that you had a child by another man, then invite that man to his home and merely accept it."

"Then, Abel, you don't know Morgan. He is a truly Christian person. He lives by his beliefs." Abel shook his head in disbelief.

"Chelsea, if Morgan is not embarrassed by my presence in his home, then I am embarrassed for him. I had hoped you would not discuss our situation until after I had departed." I was seeing another side of Abel Clayborne tonight!

"Abel, our daughter Chelsea Lyn carried our guilt by trying to keep her mother's identity a secret from the man who adopted her and who

251

loves her very much. *I had to talk with Morgan!* I couldn't expect Chelsea Lyn to forever be on her guard when she was with Morgan."

Abel took my hand and said, "Please forgive me, Chelsea. I was thinking only of myself. I must say that you have a very understanding and forgiving man in Morgan. I think I would protect this marriage at all costs." I hugged him and wished him well.

"Abel, take care of yourself. Please write to your daughter often. She is growing up so quickly. She needs your spiritual strength."

"Yes, I shall write to her frequently. Will you please say good night to Morgan for me? I would like a few minutes alone with my daughter."

"Yes, of course, Abel." I called Chelsea Lyn to come and say good night.

"Chelsea Lyn, I pray that you will continue to be the fine young girl who lived with me and Mother Kersi for the first twelve years of your life."

"I will, Father Abel. I feel so sad that you are going so far away. When will I ever see you again?"

Abel took her in his arms and patted her shoulders and said, "I shall never be too far away from you. My spirit shall always be with you. I will write. And, little lady, I shall expect letters from my beautiful daughter — with pictures — very often."

"Yes, Father Abel, I'll write to you every day!"

"Now dry your eyes and let me remember you with a smile." Abel drove slowly out of the driveway, waving his hand through the car window.

Chelsea Lyn turned to me and said, "Oh, Mother, I feel so sad to see him leave. It will be such a long time before I will see him again." I held my little daughter as the tears rolled down her cheeks.

9 Tom Deminski phoned from Ankara to tell me Matthew was on his way. He had given Linda the flight information earlier in the day. Matthew was to arrive in Lewisburg tomorrow afternoon, about four P.M. *My heart ached!* The secret with Abel was out and Chelsea Lyn would not continue to feel guilty with Morgan. But now Matthew Glyndon may disrupt my entire life. *All over again!*

I wondered, how many more of my secrets will Morgan be able to take before it becomes too much!

252

Before Chelsea Lyn left for school on Monday I arranged to pick her up there. Abel's airplane was scheduled to depart at 3:35 P.M. from the Lewisburg airport. I told Morgan that Chelsea Lyn and I would have lunch with Abel and then go on to the airport. Morgan's only comment was to be gentle with "his little girl." Abel and I had a few minutes alone at the church while his bags were being placed in the car. He took me in his arms and held me for a few minutes and said, "Chelsea, my love is so much stronger for you. But my feelings are more spiritual now that I see you with your family. You have a very peaceful nature. I see happiness in your eyes and I feel the gentleness you share with your family." I wanted to tell Abel how deeply in love with him I had been at one time.

"Thank you, Abel. You know I share your feelings. We must always communicate because we also share our wonderful daughter."

He grasped my hand and said, "Yes, we shall. Chelsea, I am sorry for my emotional display last Friday evening ... "

I stopped him and said, "Abel, it was my fault. I should have told you that I had spoken with Morgan about you and me."

"Well, the story has been told. Our commitment now is to ensure Chelsea Lyn understands what happened in our lives when she was born. You will talk with her about Kersi and me now and then, won't you? The first twelve years of Chelsea Lyn's life will always be a part of her."

"Abel, Chelsea Lyn will always remember you and Kersi. And yes, *we will talk!*" We left the church to pick up Chelsea Lyn. She was waiting for us at the front entrance of the school. At first she seemed so excited to see us. In a few minutes, though, the sadness of Abel's departure was apparent in her pretty face. She was fighting back the tears as she flitted from one subject to another.

"Father Abel, I have a gift for you." She handed him a small package wrapped with red ribbon.

"My, a present for me. Let me open it!" He tore away the paper and for a long moment he stared at the present. Chelsea Lyn had framed a picture of her and me.

She said, "We are the only two women in your life now, Father Abel. You will just have to carry us with you wherever you go!"

Abel's eyes filled with tears and he sobbed unashamedly. The three of us hugged. Chelsea Lyn said through her tears, "I shall miss you ... terribly, Father Abel. Please take care of yourself and ... *and come back to me!*"

He caressed her shoulders gently and said, *"I love you very much, my wonderful little daughter!"* Abel pulled away and went through the gate to his waiting airplane.

CHAPTER NINE
CLOSURE!

1 Abel had been gone for three days when Olga, Morgan, and I found ourselves back at the airport to greet Matthew Glyndon. *Another bizarre happening for me!* One man in my life had gone, another was reentering, and my husband Morgan is here in the middle of this emotional turmoil. He is not aware that Matthew is Caesar's father. *This is the final dark secret of my past!*

Olga visited the Mayo Clinic, and the doctors and therapists are ready to begin work with Matthew. During her visits the doctors had recommended that Matthew be exposed to as much of his past as possible. Morgan was not well acquainted with Matthew, but he had met him several times during the contract problems in the overseas areas. Morgan offered to help Matthew in any way possible to remember who he was.

The relationship of these two men in my life could become an explosive emotional issue if Matthew suddenly remembered our past. I could not control what he would say, but I do know *he should not be the one to tell Morgan about our past!*

Olga suggested that Morgan and I greet Matthew and then depart. She would escort Matthew to his quarters in the clinic and prepare him for his first examinations. The airplane was late! We stood around in the terminal and I felt my emotions begin to build. My mind played the "what if" game during the wait. What if Matthew regained his memory on the flight and he greets me with a very long passionate kiss? Oh, *God, please don't let that happen!* My mind continued playing games: What if Matthew remembers Olga and the situation when he thought his baby had died? Olga's explanation about selective memory returning to people who had received injuries like Matthew's frightened me. Finally, after what seemed like hours but were only minutes, the announcement of Matthew's flight sounded over the speaker system. The three of us gathered at the gate and watched every passenger disembark. Olga said, "One last thing I must say. Please do not build any relationships for Matthew. Do not tell him you two are married!" I wondered, why?

Finally I could see Matthew making his way along the ramp. He still carried himself well. He was dressed in a dark suit. I remembered, he almost always dressed in dark suits or clothing! As he approached he recognized Olga and then me. He extended his hand to greet us.

"It is very nice to see you again, Doctor Olga. And you, Chelsea. Thank you very much for meeting me. Otherwise, I am sure I would have become lost in a short time." Olga directed him toward Morgan and introduced him.

"Matthew, this is Morgan Gage. He is an executive with the Thorndike Corporation."

Matthew didn't recognize Morgan. He shook his hand and said, "I am happy to meet you, sir. Are you a friend of Doctor Olga and Chelsea?"

"Yes, you can say that. I have known them for a long time." I thought, *Morgan, what a nice way to avoid saying that I am your wife!*

"I think Matthew and I should go ahead to the clinic and let him get settled and rest for today," Olga said. "Tomorrow he will begin physical examinations."

Morgan went for Olga's car and drove it to the airport entrance. I looked at every detail of Matthew's face. Yes, he is Matthew! Even with the skin tightened from surgery he looked the same as when we were together. I asked Olga to stop by the office when she had gotten Matthew settled. I needed to talk with her.

Morgan and I drove back to the office in his car. He looked at me and said, "I pity that poor man. I wouldn't want to be in his shoes. I can't imagine a person losing his memory so completely." I was so emotional about Matthew being introduced to Morgan, I couldn't talk. I could almost hear Olga say, "Morgan, Chelsea's husband, meet Matthew, Chelsea's former lover." How strange I felt. The two men I loved with all my heart had just met each other and neither of them was aware of the real situation. I have felt for a long time that Morgan realized I had strong feelings for Matthew. I had to talk with Olga about my appearance when he and Matthew were introduced.

When I returned to the office, Linda was eager to hear about Matthew. She asked, "Boss, how did Matthew look? Did he remember anything about the area, the airport, or Morgan?" Linda seemed as anxious now as I was before Matthew arrived.

"Linda, one question at a time, please. Matthew looked well … "

"I mean, does he look the same as he did when he worked for us?"

"Well, he does have a few scars and drawn skin from his operations but, yes, I think he looks about the same."

"Did he remember that you and Olga were in Turkey?"

I had to calm her. "Linda, please bring us some coffee and we will have a nice long talk. Ask someone to answer your phones." She smiled and hurried out of the office. In a few minutes she brought coffee, and we sat and talked.

"Now, boss, tell me all about Matthew. What did he say when he met Morgan? Did he know Morgan before his accident?" I thought, Linda, slow down!

"Linda, Matthew seems to be the same to me, except he can't remember anything about his past nor the people he knew. He met Morgan when we were working on the overseas contracts. You remember Morgan took a team to England, Spain, and Turkey. The Turks were the only ones who wanted Matthew to return to renegotiate the contract. God! If he had not responded to their request, he would still have his memory." I told her Olga had taken Matthew to the clinic to get him settled, and that Olga would be coming by the office when she returned from the clinic.

About four in the afternoon Olga came to the office while Linda and I were talking. She knocked lightly and came in. Linda brought coffee and wanted to hear if anything else happened with Matthew. I asked Olga, "Well, my dear doctor, did you get the patient checked into his quarters?"

"Da. Everything went well. He is in special room which is viewed by an attendant at all hours."

Linda interrupted, "Olga, do you mean Matthew is going to be watched twenty-four hours a day?" That did seem a little strange to me also.

"Olga, does he have any privacy?"

"Yes, he cares for his personal needs without anyone viewing him. This is normal procedure until a patient such as Matthew is placed in a hospital." Linda was still excited about hearing every detail.

"Olga, does Matthew know he is being observed?"

"Yes, He was shown the camera and told he could talk with the attendant while in his room."

Linda said, "I certainly wouldn't want someone watching me like that." Olga explained what would happen with Matthew the first day or so.

257

"Matthew will first have very intensive physical examination. He then will be interviewed, by about three psychiatrists, I think."

I asked, "Olga, how long are all these tests going to take?"

She rolled her head and said, "I think, maybe, the physical examinations about three days. But he will also have CAT scan, an EEG, MRI, skull films, X-rays, and Ultrasound on his brain and skull."

Linda asked, "Will anyone be able to visit him while he is having the tests?"

"Yes, I will bring him out of the clinic to expose him to places where he worked and people he knew, to try and help him remember."

"Olga, come by the office as often as you can, and keep me informed of Matthew's progress. If I can help him, let me know."

She frowned as she said, "I think he will need more exposure to you if he is to regain his memory. Do you want me to bring him here to your office?" If Matthew was to be exposed to where he worked and the people he worked with, my office would be a good starting place. Matthew visited Mr. Thorndike in this office when he was hired.

I responded to Olga, "Yes, Olga. Let me know when you plan to bring him here, and I will schedule time for you and him. You can take him around the plant to expose him to the people he worked with." She nodded her head in agreement.

Morgan called and said he had to travel to the southern plant for a couple of days. The computer assembly line he and Casey invented had begun to break down. Morgan knew the details of the system to its finest degree. I asked Olga if she would like to have dinner with me at Hoffman's since Morgan would not be home for dinner. We left the office together.

2 I needed a drink to calm my nerves. Olga and I had cocktails while we talked about Matthew and what I would have to do if he began to regain his memory. Olga said, "Chelsea, my dear, *your problems are like Jack in the Box!* You tell Morgan about one and another one pops up."

"You're right, Olga. And believe me, you and I must keep track of Matthew's progress. If he appears to be remembering, I may have to talk with him privately about Morgan and the children." Olga said I had planned well, assigning her to the medical team so she can follow Matthew's progress daily.

"But, Chelsea, no one really knows when or how much Matthew may remember." I thought, there should be signs of recognition if he begins to remember places and people.

"Olga, won't you be able to recognize changes in Matthew if he does begin to remember?"

She shook her head negatively, "Not really, my dear. He could regain his complete memory and not tell anyone if he chose not to ... "

I was surprised. "Olga, if he does remember, don't you believe he will tell us? At least you and me."

"I do not know. It is possible that he already remembers some things but is keeping his secret." I told Olga to review his medical records again and take note of his head injuries.

"After you have conferred with the team doctors, Olga, and looked at his records, I want you to explain to me, again, in layman's terms, just how damaging his injuries were."

"Da, I can do that. I will bring his records with me tomorrow. Can you take a couple of hours to discuss them?" I couldn't wait to know for sure if his head injuries could have caused him to lose his memory.

I asked Olga, "Will the CAT scan and tests like that pinpoint his head injuries enough to determine whether they were the cause of his memory loss?"

"Chelsea, my dear, cerebral contusions can cause brain injury and bruising that result in hemorrhage and edema. The tests will detail his physical injuries. The EEG and cerebral angiography can help with the neurological diagnosis. But memory loss is very difficult, if not impossible, to determine. The history of the patient and the person's behavior give the best clues to recovery of memory."

"Then what you are saying, Olga, is that the doctors will not be able to determine from the test results whether the head injuries caused Matthew to lose his memory."

"Da, you are most correct. But if Matthew has a skull injury that shows on the films, it most likely would be the cause of the memory loss."

"*Olga, I'm frightened!* I mean ... with Matthew being here. What if he suddenly regains his memory and wants to pick up where we left off before he went to Turkey?"

Olga looked at me over her glasses and said, "My dear Chelsea, that is a possibility. Again, I say to you, plan what you are going to do before you have to do it!"

I sighed. "It's not that easy, Olga ... "

"But," she said, "you knew what the risks were when you convinced Matthew to come to the States. It is something you must deal with. I am sorry, my dear Chelsea. I cannot help you."

3 My early morning hours in the office without the day's panics are still my quiet times. Mr. Thorndike's office, now mine, is furnished in early American furniture. I kept his big old oak desk. His marks are still in the wood under the glass. I can sit in my high-backed desk chair and swing it toward the window and see the entire city of Lewisburg. About a mile to the east is our church, a giant old white stone building with three peaks reaching to the sky.

Chelsea Lyn needed her church family. Morgan and I have buried our lives in Thorndike and we have missed so much by not taking our children to church. I pray when I'm sitting here alone. Only God and me. He hears everything I say and sometimes I think he answers me. I have prayed so many times as I tried to straighten out my life. Morgan and I were so very happy before Matthew came into my life. Every time I tried to escape from that ordeal I only dug myself a deeper hole until I was snared permanently. When I thought Matthew was dead, I prayed just for him. And now I am sitting here praying again for Matthew. But this time my prayers are confusing to me. In one breath, I pray that he regains his memory but that he will not disrupt my life with Morgan and my children. In the next breath, I pray that he does not regain his memory and returns to Turkey and steps out of my life forever.

I cannot see an easy out for me! But I am committed to helping Matthew if I can. Whatever comes of my efforts for him, I must be willing to accept.

Linda knocked and entered my office, bringing me back to the world of panic of managing the Thorndike giant. She smiled and greeted me, "Good morning, boss. How are you today?"

I returned her smile and said, "I'm just fine, Linda." I thought, no! I am not 'just fine,' but I suppose the world doesn't have to know nor would it care how Chelsea Carodine feels. Show your smiling face to the world while your heart breaks!

"Boss, J.C. wants the meeting with John Capps about the lobbying position for ten this morning. Do you need any background information? Or do you want to speak with J.C. before John arrives?"

I nodded. "Yes, Linda, when J.C. comes in tell him to step into my office so we can talk a minute or two. And bring some coffee in with your note pad, please."

J.C. tapped on the door as he entered. This man is always happy. I don't think he would be disturbed if he knew the world was ending. He's a big man, about six feet tall. He has a muscular frame and somehow keeps his tan all winter. He plays golf every opportunity he gets. I often send him out with clients. He says he can conduct more business on a golf course than in a conference room any time. He is very efficient in everything he does and he's totally honest. One reason I took him as my deputy is his loyalty. He is willing to speak his mind, regardless of the wind's direction. He smiled and said, "Good morning, Chelsea. How are things coming along with Matthew?"

"Good morning, J.C. Olga said he began his physical examinations yesterday. No progress yet." He opened his briefcase and took out several papers.

"Chelsea, I have Matthew's salary checks. When do you want to give them to him?" Oh, I thought, this is definitely not the time to give him a large sum of money. He probably wouldn't know what to do with it anyway.

I responded, "J.C., please hold the checks. I'll tell you when the time is right, OK?"

"Sure, Chelsea. I'll keep them in my safe. Linda has the combination, so if you need them when I'm not here she can get them for you."

"J.C., is John Capps' law firm the right one for the lobbying contract in Washington?"

J.C. answered without hesitation, "Yes, I think he is, Chelsea. He's taken on a senior law partner who can manage his office here in Lewisburg while he takes care of the lobbying function."

"OK, if you think he can represent us, the job is his. Will you meet with him and have the contract drawn up and signed?"

He picked up his case and said, "Sure, Chelsea. I can take care of the details. I'll meet him in my office."

"Thanks, J.C. I will be out of the office after eleven o'clock today. I'm going to the clinic to speak with Olga and see how Matthew is doing."

"Chelsea, are you worried about Matthew's condition?"

"Oh, I don't know, J.C. It does worry me that his memory loss seems complete and total. I just can't imagine him not being able to even remember his name."

"Have you made any plans for him if he does recover his memory? I mean, here in the corporation?" Oh, I thought, I haven't planned for my personal problem yet.

"No, J.C., I really have not thought about where we could use him. If he recovers his memory he still may not be able to function in the corporation."

"Let me know if I can help in any way," he said as he left my office.

Linda came in to say Morgan had called and would be back in Lewisburg this afternoon. He fixed the problem with the computer conveyer system. He said if I could get away, he would buy my dinner at Hoffman's. I thought, that would be a grand idea. I need a night out with my husband. I need to devote some time to him and not be so consumed with the dreadful problems I may face with Matthew.

I arrived ahead of Morgan. I was sitting at our table when he came in. I thought, how many times had I watched him come through the restaurant door?

He still looks like a youth of sixteen years old who had parked his shiny red motorcycle and forgot to comb his hair before coming into the restaurant. His curly brownish hair lay over his brow. He swept it back with a stroke of his hand, only to have it pop back across his forehead. When he reached the table I took my comb and gently laid his hair in place. He was his usual cheerful self.

"Thanks, Mommy, I forgot my comb." I remembered when Morgan and I first met. Neither of us were willing to compromise with the other. We both were trying desperately to make our place in Thorndike. I admit I had a much easier time making my way than did Morgan — but not because of my gender. Lucky for me, Mr. Thorndike liked my grades at law school and thought he could mold me into the type of lawyer he needed for the corporation. *We both won!* And now I am so thankful and lucky to have Morgan, my love, my husband. I responded to his playful words.

"Mommy will buy you another comb so you can keep your hair out of your eyes."

"Hi, sweetie. Gee, it's so good to see you. Have I told you how much I love you lately?" Morgan and I both miss each other so much when we are away.

"Yes, Morgan, you always tell me how much you love me. And you show me in so many ways. I am so lucky that you love me."

He smiled and said, "Honey, I miss you when we're apart. I think we had better go home after dinner and retire to our bedroom for some intimate conversation."

"Is that what you are calling our lovemaking now?"

He turned his face up and said, "Who, me? No, really, all I want to do is talk very intimately to my wife."

"Well, if that's all you're going to do, maybe I better go some place else."

"OK. Enough lovemaking for the moment. What do you want for dinner, my love?"

"You know I like everything on the menu. Surprise me!"

Our dinners are always so nice in "our place"! Morgan brought me here on our first date several years ago. We never came here unless we had happy things to talk about. But tonight, Matthew Glyndon keeps coming back into my mind. Without warning, Morgan began asking questions about Matthew's progress.

"I was thinking, hon. If Matthew needs association with people to remember who he was, or is, we could still have him to our house for dinner. Maybe he misses his family and we can share ours with him."

My mind pleaded, oh, Morgan darling, please don't complicate my situation more than it is. If Matthew comes to our home and sees Caesar he may remember that part of his life. Olga said people with total memory loss will occasionally recapture segments of their past. *I don't want Matthew to remember that segment of his life, especially not in our home!*

"Morgan, dear, if you want to help Matthew, maybe you can escort him through the plant and reintroduce him to some of his former associates." I had to steer him away from the idea of bringing Matthew to our home. Leaving Matthew with Morgan could also complicate things, but maybe less so at the plant than at our home. I thought, Chelsea, you go from one crisis to another! Will there ever be any peace in your life? Morgan agreed the plant trip could be good for Matthew.

When we arrived home the children were waiting up for us. Chelsea Lyn, Caesar, and Raynor all jumped into our laps as we sat on the sofa in the family room. Chelsea Lyn was still hugging Morgan in a manner that I didn't like.

"Chelsea Lyn, sweetheart, sit by me and tell me about your day in school." She reluctantly left Morgan and leaned against me. "Any major problems with the boys who are always chasing you?"

She smiled and said, "Mom, really! I don't have boys chasing me. But I did meet this super senior who just transferred to our school. His name is Isaiah Moore."

Morgan said, "Hey, that sounds serious. I can't have a strange boy taking my little girl."

"Oh, Papa Morgan, no one could ever take me from you!"

I hoped she was joking. I said, "Chelsea Lyn, if he asks you out, you understand he comes here first?"

She responded immediately. "Mother, you know I would never go out with anyone without my parents' approval. When can I bring him home to meet you two?"

"How about next weekend? Ask Sylvia to cook a special dinner and ask him for Friday or Saturday night. Or Sunday after church would also be a good time."

"He goes to our church! I could have him come home with us for a mid-afternoon lunch, couldn't I, Mom, Papa Morgan?" We both agreed Sunday would be the day for his visit.

4 Wednesday morning Olga brought Matthew to my office. Linda greeted them and looked Matthew over from head to toe, as though with a magnifying glass. She tried to engage him in conversation but Matthew responded to her questions briefly, one or two words at a time. When Linda realized he wasn't going to talk with her she brought the two of them to my office. I asked Linda to bring refreshments and join us. I wanted her observations of Matthew. Matthew walked about the office, looking out at the city and lake from each window. When he sat down his first words were, "Ms. Carodine, do you work in this office?"

I smiled and said, "Yes, Matthew. This is my office. I am the chief executive officer of the Thorndike Corporation."

He seemed puzzled. "How do women get selected for jobs such as you have?" I thought, Matthew, have you forgotten everything about your life that was you, here in your own country? I didn't know how I should answer him.

"Well, being a woman made promotions more difficult, but I went to college and then to law school and became a lawyer. I joined Thorndike about eight years ago and worked hard ... "

He interrupted me and said, "Your father does not own this business?" I thought, oh, no, Matthew! And I don't own the corporation, that is, not all of it. Olga looked at me with a sidewise glance and motioned for me to keep him talking.

Linda brought the drinks in and served them. "Matthew, you don't take cream in your coffee, do you?" I thought, she is prodding him to remember.

"*No, I do not!* No one in Turkey drinks milk in their coffee." Well, I thought, that didn't work. Olga asked a more direct question.

"Matthew, do you remember this office?" He looked it over again and shook his head negatively.

"No. I do not remember this office. Have I been here before?"

Linda said. "Matthew, neither Chelsea nor I were here when you visited this office. Do you remember who was here?" Again he shook his head no.

"Olga, will you take Matthew on a tour of the offices? Be sure to include the contracts division. He may recognize the people who helped him on the Turkish contract. And also take him to meet Susan Rosco, the Chief of the Law Division."

As Olga and Matthew left the office Linda came in. I knew she wanted to say something.

"Well, Linda, have your say! What do you think?"

She made a funny face and said, "Boss lady, I just don't know if that person is Matthew or not. The Matthew I remember was a very personable man who was always smiling. I didn't see that guy's teeth one time." I thought, I haven't looked at any names of people he may have known from his personnel records. I wondered if his records would shed any light on his associates or people he worked with. I asked Linda to get his records from the vault. "His records have probably been placed in the permanent files."

Olga brought Matthew back to the office. She had watched his expression every time he was introduced to people. Olga whispered to me, "Chelsea, I am sure he recognized Susan Rosco. How did he know her?"

I remember Morgan saying Susan did the legal review of contracts for his team. She also worked with Matthew.

"Olga, Susan was the contracts review officer for the contracts in England, Spain, and Turkey. She was the one who worked with Matthew on the new Turkish contract he went over to renegotiate. What did Susan say?"

She thought a moment and said, "She greeted him like he had never been gone. But when she started to hug him, he pulled away."

I turned to Matthew who had been at the window looking out over the city and asked, "Matthew, did you recognize anyone you met today?"

He seemed to be in deep thought for a moment and then responded, "I have an inner feeling that I previously knew one lady. I think her name was Suzanne … "

Olga helped him. "That was Susan Rosco. Do you remember her?"

He looked at Olga and said, "Doctor Olga, I am not sure. I cannot tell where I saw her before, but I think I may have known her."

I looked at Olga and said to her and Matthew, "Olga, I think you should take Matthew back to the clinic. He's had a tough mental day. We can talk later about our next visit, to the plant or other areas he may remember."

Olga agreed and asked Matthew, "Young man, are you ready to drive back to the clinic so you can think about the day?" Matthew stood up and took my hand and thanked me for trying to help him.

"Ms. Carodine, maybe tomorrow or another day soon I will remember some places and people. I am sorry I cannot tell you I remember."

Soon after Olga and Matthew left, Morgan called to say he would pick me up in fifteen minutes if I were ready to go home. I told him I would meet him at the front entrance and to hurry. Morgan is so good for my spirits and morale. He arrived and I jumped in and reached across and gave him a kiss. He said, "Well, lady, I hope that is not all I'm going to get tonight!"

I pinched him on the leg and jokingly responded, "No, Mr. Gage, that is not all. You can have all of me if that will make you happy!" He turned and winked at me.

"Now you are talking, lady. But our time will have to be later. We promised the children to take them for a pizza dinner." How could I forget that!

"Yes, you're right. We will have fun with our kids tonight! I hope Sylvia remembered and didn't prepare dinner."

"I'm sure she will remember. I gave her tonight off."

Chelsea Lyn met us at the door. She was anxious to tell us she had the boys ready to go. "Papa Morgan, can we go to the new Pizza Place over in the Town Mall?" This young lady amazes me: the boys ready and the restaurant picked out.

"Well, I don't know," Morgan said. "Is there something special about the Pizza Place ... "

She interrupted and said, "That is where some of the kids from school go for pizza." Oh, I thought, are we going to meet someone there?

"Chelsea Lyn, have you taken a vote with the boys on where we are to eat?"

"Mom, this place has one of those indoor kiddie playgrounds. We can let the little monkeys loose!"

Morgan smiled and asked, "Chelsea Lyn, my dear young lady, is someone special going to be at the Pizza Place?"

She blushed. "Well, Isaiah Moore, who you said could come home with us after church on Sunday, just may be there. And if he is there, you can meet him."

"So, this is all a grand plot! You planned this so your mother and father would take you on your first unofficial date!"

She responded, "Well, since I am not going to date until I am seventeen I thought it would be nice to have my parents meet one of my male friends."

Morgan laughed and said, "Now the plot thickens. We will be meeting one of our daughter's many suitors tonight. Is that right, sweets?" Chelsea Lyn knew she could wrap Morgan around her little finger anytime she wanted to.

"Yes, Father dear. You caught me! But you will at least know who is coming home with us after church on Sunday for your famous hamburgers."

We had our pizza, and a short conversation with Chelsea Lyn's friend, and the boys played themselves out. Isaiah Moore was a handsome

267

young man. He was nervous when he was introduced to us, but he was polite and thanked us for the invitation for Sunday.

5 After the children were in bed Morgan and I sat in front of the fireplace and had a drink. We talked about our wonderful children and how responsible Chelsea Lyn had become. Morgan asked about Matthew.

"Sweetheart, is Matthew making any progress?"

"Maybe. Olga said he showed signs of recognition when he met Susan Rosco today. When he came back to the office we asked him about her. He admitted he might have known her some time in his past, but he couldn't remember."

Morgan said, "Wait a minute! Susan Rosco went to Turkey with Matthew. She was only there for about a week or so. I remember she went because I needed a legal review of a contract I had sent to her. I was told she wouldn't be back from Turkey for several days. Maybe she and Matthew had something going while she was in Turkey."

I almost became furious with Morgan for saying that about Matthew. *Matthew loved me too much to be with anyone else!* I thought, Morgan, you may have had a "sexual encounter" with a secretary, but Matthew would never have done anything like that. I had to bite my tongue to keep my thoughts to myself.

"Morgan, are you sure Susan went to Turkey with Matthew?"

"Well, kitten, it will be easy to check. The travel office keeps permanent computer records of all trips by Thorndike executives. The records come in handy with the IRS." I couldn't believe what he was saying. But, I thought, if Matthew were away from me why wouldn't he have an affair? He had an affair with me in Mexico. I'll check the travel records. I hope Morgan is wrong about Susan going to Turkey with Matthew. My mind kept racing. Why would Matthew think he may have known Susan "somewhere" in his past? I stopped myself. Why am I getting excited about the possibility that Matthew Glyndon may have had affair with Susan Rosco? I have already told myself that he is *not coming back into my life and destroying my marriage!* Remember, Chelsea, Morgan is the man you love and who loves you. Help Matthew regain his memory if you can, then send him back to Turkey or some place away from you.

I regained my composure and said to Morgan, "Well, if Matthew and Susan did have an affair, it may be one clue that helps him remember who he is."

Morgan smiled and said, "Well, lady, if I had an affair with a woman as beautiful as Susan Rosco I would certainly remember it. That is, if I had lost my memory!"

I pinched him and said, "Morgan, are you thinking of taking Susan out?"

He laughed and said, "Had you going for a minute, didn't I? Baby, there is no woman in the world who could entice me to leave my beautiful and talented wife." He took me in his arms and kissed me hard and very passionately. He picked me up in his arms and took me to the bedroom. I thought, Chelsea, he's going to make love to you tonight. *Forget Matthew!* Be with the man who loves you. Matthew died in your mind three years ago. *Leave him dead!* Enjoy loving your husband!

I expunged Matthew from my mind. My mind, body, and soul were Morgan's tonight. Morgan's muscular body crushed against mine as we made love. I kissed him as if this was the last time we would make love. I knew Morgan would always be the only man for me. After we had made love, for awhile we lay in each other's arms. I lay awake for hours wondering about my life. Only one more conscience-weighing thing between me and Morgan, and my life will be clear and clean. I thought, Chelsea, when your altruistic project for Matthew ends, your mind will be free of the shackles that have bound you for so many years. I will be one woman, one wife and lover to my husband, and the grandest mother ever to my children. *My destiny!* What is next for Chelsea Carodine?

6 Breakfast with the children normally begins our day. Sylvia caters to every family member's taste with her culinary skills. Tidbits of conversations between the boys and Chelsea Lyn about what's happening in their lives fill the air at breakfast. Chelsea Lyn, who has become quite a lady, scolds the boys not to interrupt the "adults" when they are speaking. Caesar rebounds with, "Some day I'm going to be so big that I will get to talk all I want to." And affirmative support comes from his brother Raynor, who shouts, "Yea, yea." So begins our day! We kiss our little dears and depart for the office.

Morgan and I began driving together when my car was being repaired. Being together for that thirty or so minutes in the morning was such a boost to us both that we continued to drive together. Morgan always uses our time to let me know how much he loves me and the children. This day, something else was also on his mind. He asked how Matthew's review was going and proposed, "Sweetie, have you thought about what I said about Matthew coming home with us? That is, if you think it will help him remember his former life?"

I was hesitant in replying. "I haven't thought about it, Morgan. Do you think an evening at home with our family will help him at all?"

He continued driving and said, "Well, he does have a family in Turkey. Maybe being around children will prompt him to remember something about his life here in the States."

"Can we wait for awhile on this … ?"

"Honey, Matthew Glyndon is your project. I'm willing to help if you need me."

Yes, he said that right! Matthew Glyndon is my project. Morgan's offer to help comes from his commitment to human kindness. I believe in my heart that he doesn't have any sinister motives for wanting to help Matthew. I should remember that when he offers. My concern is that Matthew may suddenly remember Caesar and the heavens will fall. What could I say or how could I explain to Morgan if Matthew did recognize Caesar and called him "son?" No! I must not bring Matthew to my home and expose him to Caesar.

"Morgan, thanks for helping with this 'Matthew project.' He still has a series of examinations before the doctors can say anything about the possibility of him recovering his memory. Let's wait for their findings first. OK, sweetheart?" He responded in his usual happy manner.

"Sure, babe. Life is full of webs, all tangled together. I hope he remembers who he is, or was, one day." We reached the office and I was relieved to have the conversation end. Morgan kissed me tenderly and said he would pick me up here when I am ready to go home.

Linda is somewhat like Morgan, always upbeat and happy. She greeted me with coffee for the two of us. She had begun to review the day's schedule when I interrupted her to ask if she could get a copy of the executive's travel record concerning Matthew's trip to Turkey.

"And, Linda, get the complete log for the day of Matthew's departure."

She responded cheerily, "Sure, boss. What are you looking for in the log?"

"I'm not sure, Linda. I just want to see what records are kept on executive travel."

Deceit again! I can't tell Linda I want the log to check whether Susan Rosco left for Turkey with Matthew! I stopped. Chelsea Carodine, as Morgan would say, '*What are you going to do with the information once you have it!*' It's funny in a way. I thought Matthew loved me so much that no one else in the entire world could entice him to do anything that would hurt me. If he went to Turkey with Susan, *I can just imagine what else they did!* What a distrusting, suspicious mind I have. So the two of them were on the same airplane to the same country. What does that prove? The fact that Matthew showed signs of recognizing Susan may be just a coincidence and nothing more.

Linda continued discussing my schedule for the day. "You have one item that may cause a little heartburn. Parnella Verbena put out the word that she is going to file a law suit with the Equal Employment Opportunity Commission, you know that famous EEOC crowd ... "

"And what does she expect to gain by doing such a stupid thing?"

Linda responded, "Well, at this point it is just a rumor. Do you want David to have a chat with her?"

"No, Linda. Let her do what she must do, and we will respond accordingly. Did David finish his review with the EEOC representative on her case?"

"I don't know, but I'll find out right away."

I asked, "What other little gem is on the schedule?"

She handed me Matthew's personnel record and said, "You may want to talk with Quigly's ex-wife. It seems Matthew knew Magda before Quigly married her. She may help him to regain his memory."

Oh, *no! Not another one of Matthew's girlfriends!* Chelsea, I thought, get hold of yourself. You are a happily married woman. Why are you so concerned about what Matthew *may have done* with any other woman? His past life, except for Caesar, has no meaning for you. Don't get yourself involved in trying to test his "past love" for you. I had convinced Matthew to come to the States to attempt to regain his memory. Whatever happens in the process is not my fault nor my responsibility. I must keep my mind focused on helping him and nothing more. After all, he had a life before he made love to me. What's my concern?

271

"J.C. also wants to bring you up-to-date on several corporate items. He said he can come in anytime you are free." I should be concerned with corporate matters and not my personal suspicions. I asked Linda to call J.C.

"Good morning, Chelsea," J.C. said. What a relief to have him take care of the pressing matters in the corporation. "How are things going with you?"

"All right, I suppose. Have you heard that Parnella may try an EEOC suit about her firing?" I asked. J.C. is never concerned with the threat of suits.

"Yes, I heard. Susan Rosco told me Parnella went to John Capps' law firm ... "

"J.C., *John can't represent her!*" I shouted.

J.C., in his calm manner said, "Don't get excited, Chelsea. That is how we got the word. Of course, John's firm can't take her case."

"Well, J.C., do you think the EEOC people will push her complaint?"

"No, at least I don't think so. But you can never tell about that group — after all, she is a member of the so-called 'minority'." I wanted to reemphasize to J.C. that she was fired by a woman, another member of the minority.

"Don't you think the EEOC will consider the fact that it was a woman who fired her? Will that fact have a bearing on her complaint?"

J.C. shrugged his shoulders and responded, "Chelsea, I don't think we should be too concerned about Parnella Verbena."

"Sorry, J.C., go on with your briefing."

J.C. took out his notebook and proceeded. "The construction at the southern plant is proceeding on schedule. I must complement your husband. Morgan is one of the most demanding executives we have. He's personally supervising the construction."

"Well thanks, J.C., I'll tell him."

"The city fathers expressed their thanks for the youth park donation and want a public presentation from you before they begin construction. I'll check your schedule with Linda." I cautioned him to remember that I am a woman and must have my hair done before any public presentations.

He laughed and said, "Yes, by all means, at least two day's notice." Then he continued. "John Capps also passed on the information that Stan

Jones is looking for a position with a law firm. John said Stan probably would come back to Thorndike if he could."

"J.C., that suggests an interesting possibility. If we hire him, we can control him. If someone else hires him, he may use their resources to try and trace his parents. But I think Thorndike will pass. I don't want him back in the corporation." J.C. nodded his head in agreement.

"We're on schedule with most production units. Morgan is also scheduling the next product lines. He says he has a number of recommendations from his managers. Before he accepts any of them, he wants to know about Parnella's recommendation on the women's bathroom products."

"J.C., get the production and markup figures on that line. Let's see if we can make any money on it." What a businessman my husband is. No business at home, only in the office.

"Chelsea, our department budgets are close to what was planned. One thing we didn't plan for was the expense of this year's lobbying efforts. John Capps came in with good figures for the balance of the year, but we must divert funds from other sources. I recommend we take a percentage from each department and put the item in next year's budget."

I responded, "That sounds fine, J.C. And tell Morgan he will have a decision on the women's bathroom product line after we review the figures." J.C. said he had one last question about Matthew.

"When do you want me to disburse Matthew's back pay?"

I said, "Hold it until I give you the word. He is still not ready to handle that amount of money."

"How's he progressing? Any recovery yet?"

"No, J.C. He is still undergoing examinations and tests. Olga is with him and I expect to hear from her sometime today or tomorrow. I'll let you know."

J.C. left the office. Linda brought the executive log in and said, "If you could tell me what you are looking for, maybe I could pull it out of this mess of files for you." I thought, no, Linda, I just want to know if Susan Rosco went to Turkey with Matthew.

"No, Linda, I'll check the files." She gave me the file and left the office.

I began looking for the names and dates of the time when Matthew left the States. Yes, here is his name. He left on June 9th. And, yes, two names below Matthew's was Susan Rosco. She left on the same flight for the same destination. I asked myself, "Chelsea, now that you have proof that Matthew and Susan went to Turkey together, what else can you prove? *And why bother?* I asked Linda to return the files to the vault.

Olga called to say she could bring Matthew out for another visit to the factory or any other location I thought they should see. I thought they should take a trip to Boggsville. He had lived in Boggsville with me. I said, "Olga, you know where Matthew and I lived. Take him to the apartment building and try to get him into his old apartment. That may jolt his memory."

"And then, my dear Chelsea, where else should I take him?"

"We always went to the Dolphin Restaurant for dinner. Go with him and talk about him and me being there. See if you get any reaction."

7   "Chelsea, my dear, in three days we should have all of Matthew's tests completed. The doctors would like to present their findings to you and me. Can I make a date for next week?"

"Oh, heavens!" I responded. "Yes, Olga but schedule it for Monday or Tuesday, OK?" She checked her schedule and said either day would be good.

"Chelsea, the doctors do not want Matthew present at the meeting."

"Why is that, Olga? Did they find something that he is not supposed to know?"

"I do not know at this time. But I think it to be a good idea also."

Olga and Matthew flew to Boggsville on the Thorndike jet. Matthew had been on it before, so we thought he might remember it. Olga and Matthew spent three days in Boggsville. She took him to every place I suggested. While they ate at the Dolphin Restaurant, she talked about me and him. She probed his mind at every location. I anxiously awaited her return to learn what Matthew may have remembered.

Finally! Olga came to the office to tell me about Matthew's reaction to the restaurant, his apartment, and the city of Boggsville. I blocked two hours off my schedule and told Linda not to let anyone disturb us. I asked Olga to start from the beginning and tell me everything. She'd taken notes at each location and recorded Matthew's reactions. She took out the note pad and said, "We landed at the same airport where he had landed many times and he looked about as if he may have recalled something. But he didn't say anything to me."

"What was next?"

She scanned down her book and said, "Yes, this was the day at the Dolphin Restaurant. He liked the fish tank in the lobby and said he may do something like it when he returns to Turkey. Does that tell you how much he remembered about your favorite restaurant?"

"So, he didn't remember anything about the restaurant?"

"Not a thing, Chelsea, my dear." I pressed her for his reaction when she talked about me and him.

"He simply said it must have been nice."

"But, Olga, didn't he remember anything about Boggsville?"

"My dear, if he remembered anything about any of the places we visited, he did not tell me."

"Did you watch his expressions … ?"

"Chelsea, please tell me, why do you want Matthew to remember you and him so badly? If he does recover his memory, you realize it will cause you many problems." I couldn't answer her. I knew she was correct. If he remembers and he is unwilling to accept my marriage, my life could be a total wreck.

"Thank you, Olga, for all you have done. I guess we're continuing to fight a losing battle with Matthew's memory." She reminded me we had a meeting with the doctors on Monday.

8 I told Morgan about Olga's and Matthew's visit to Boggsville and that he didn't remember anything about the places Olga took him. "Does this mean he has not regained any part of his memory?" "Apparently not. Olga said his expression never changed. He did not recall any place or person they met."

Morgan took me in his arms and said, "Sweetheart, shall we bring him here to the house for a last try?"

"Morgan, what is there in our home that could help him remember his past?" Suddenly, my mind began racing. Does Morgan know about Caesar? How could he? Does he want to bring Matthew to our home to test his memory of Caesar and me? I thought, Chelsea, you are letting your mind play games with you again. There is not the slightest possibility that Morgan knows about Matthew, me, and Caesar. He is only being the altruistic Morgan that he has always been. *Stop your suspicious mind!*

"Then what's next in his treatment? Will he simply return to Turkey if he doesn't remember his life here?" Morgan asked.

"Olga and I are meeting Monday with the team of doctors who have been treating him. Matthew will not be in the meeting. I haven't a clue about their findings. And I really can't understand why they don't want Matthew there either." Morgan ended the conversation by saying he would help if I wanted to bring Matthew home for an evening.

Olga and I drove to the clinic early Monday morning. The meeting was set for 10:00 A.M. and we had time to stop for coffee and a danish before the meeting.

"Olga, have you learned anything about what the team plans to present?"

"Yes, my dear. Their reports will be final on Matthew ... "

"Are you saying they have given up on trying to help him recover his memory?"

"No. That is not true. They have done everything they can do. Matthew does not remember any of his past!" I pressed for more information.

"But, Olga, *is there nothing else anyone can do for him?*" I began to cry. To think that Matthew must go through his life not remembering what we meant to each other, and our son, was just too much for me. Olga tried to comfort me.

"My dear, I feel as bad as you do. But you must accept the findings. We do not believe Matthew will ever recover his memory."

I sobbed and the tears poured down my cheeks. "Olga ... I feel so bad for him ... he's such a wonderful person. It hurts me to think he will never remember his son, Caesar."

Olga patted my shoulders and suggested we go to the meeting.

We were greeted by the several doctors. Each doctor had examined Matthew and administered specific tests. Doctor Kutz began the discussion with a report of his series of physical examinations.

"The client, Matthew Glyndon, according to his medical records, had undergone a series of extensive surgeries. His injuries came as the result of an airplane crash. His entire facial area, hands, arms, and legs were burned very severely. The degree ranged from first to third in severity. His facial skeleton was crushed, and there were severe injuries to the upper part of his neck. Restoration required about two years. Doctor King will now present his examination report."

"The client was administered an electroencephalogram, commonly called an EEG. The alpha and beta waves were normal. However, the thea and delta waves registered very high. The frequencies of these latter two waves indicated extreme emotional stress and the possibility the client suffered a degree of brain damage. The skull films also indicated several lacerations on the client's head that could have caused the high reading of the theta and delta waves. A CAT scan was also administered and did pinpoint the damaged areas of the skull.

"A cerebral angiography was also administered and revealed he suffered from a subarachnoid hemorrhage. A combination of these two injuries could have been the cause of the patient's complete loss of memory. The unexplained part with this patient is that he possesses all of the normal reactions except for those noted here."

I asked, "Dr. King, what does this all mean?"

"What we see is that the patient did suffer a sufficient amount of damage to his head and neck to have caused his loss of memory. However, he functions completely normally. We can conclude that the physical damage did cause brain impairment, that is clearly evident. Another major factor is the possibility of an emotional trauma that caused the patient to completely withdraw."

I asked, "Is there any treatment that may help him to recover his memory?"

He responded, "Ms. Carodine, frankly, we don't have a specific remedy. There is one drug that may help, but there are several side effects that the patient may or may not tolerate."

"And what drug is that, Doctor?"

"It's called Ketamine, the trade name is Ketalar. It is used in surgery. But in order to take it, the patient must understand its effects and agree to its use."

I asked him, "What specific side effects are you talking about, Doctor?"

"The effects may vary in severity between pleasant dreamlike states with vivid imagery to confusion, excitement, and irrational behavior. The duration of these states will vary among patients. I only recommend the use of Ketamine when all other efforts fail."

I said, "Doctor, I will respond for the patient. He will not be willing to have the drug administered."

"Then all I can recommend is a long stay in a rest home with familiar surroundings, but this method is definitely not a sure cure."

Dr. Kutz added, "The reason we didn't want the patient here today is that we think there is a possibility that he has regained part of his memory. We suspect he could be, shall we say, 'playing the game'."

I stood up and said, "Doctor, I disagree with you. I know this man. If he is in command of his memory, he could not hide his emotions for his loved ones nor for the places he has visited in Lewisburg and Boggsville."

The doctor apologized and said, "This last analysis is without medical foundation but merely an educated hunch. However, nothing in our physical, pathological, psychological, or emotional findings indicate that he could have completely lost his memory and still have functioned as well as he has thus far."

"Then, Doctor, what you really conclude is that Matthew could have lost his memory from an emotional trauma connected with the airplane crash or during his recovery period from the operations?"

The doctor replied, "Yes, it is entirely possible. Based upon our evaluations of the physical trauma his body endured in the operations and the possibility of an emotional trauma as a result of the drugs during the operations, together ... yes, these events could account for his complete loss of memory."

"Thank you, Doctors. Olga, shall we go?"

9 As we departed, Olga felt my emotions building. As we neared the car I broke down and cried hysterically. She held me and told me to let my feelings come out.

"My dear Chelsea," she said, "tears wash the soul and cleanse the heart. You will feel better after you have released your tensions. There, my dear, cry. I shall hold you."

"*What am I to do?* Do I just tell Matthew to go back to Turkey and forget that he ever existed?"

"The question is, my dear Chelsea, *what do you want to happen?*"

I spoke through my tears and said, "Olga, I can't just send him off without *his knowing that he has a son!*"

"Chelsea, please consider the consequences of telling him about Caesar."

"Olga, come back to the office with me. We can go to lunch or have Linda bring it to the office."

Olga is like a mother to me. She said, "Yes, I will go with you. I think it best to have lunch in your office. You are not in condition to go into public."

I looked at her and said, "Do I look that bad, Olga?"

"No, my dear, but you need privacy at this time."

Linda went to the coffee shop and brought each of us a hot lunch. She had a luncheon engagement and said she would have someone else answer the telephone. She said, "By the way, boss, there is a telegram from Turkey on your desk. The return address is the U.S. Embassy's. I didn't know if it was official or personal, so I didn't open it." I picked up the telegram as I began to eat my lunch. We often have cables about our contract personnel so I wasn't too concerned with it. It was from the embassy contact who met Olga and me on our trip to Turkey.

It began, "Ms. Carodine, please ensure this telegram is delivered to Mr. Matthew Glyndon, or Asher Archer, his Turkish name."

The telegram read, "I regret to inform you that your wife was killed in a fire in your village on January 24. Your son was injured and is recovering. The parents of your wife require your presence to properly bury their daughter. Please return to Turkey as quickly as possible."

I began to cry again. Olga looked over and said, "My dear, I thought you'd had your cry. Is something else troubling you?" I handed her the telegram.

"Oh, my, *this is terrible!* My dear, should I be the one to tell Matthew?"

"No, Olga, *I will tell him!* Will you go to the clinic and bring him here, please?"

She responded, "Yes, my poor Chelsea. I will call and have him ready to return with me." She called the clinic and left the office without speaking.

This is my fault. If I had not insisted that Matthew come to the States for treatment, his wife would still be alive!

I don't know how I'm going to tell him!

CHAPTER TEN
FINALITY

1 When Olga left for the clinic I sat at my desk and stared at the telegram. My tears continued to flow for Matthew. I have fought with myself about my feelings for him since he returned to the States. He lost his memory because I sent him to Turkey and now he has lost his wife because I brought him back to the States. *I prayed, oh, God, where is the justice in our lives?* I was making a mess of my face with all the crying ... but I just couldn't stop. My heart was breaking. Give me the strength to tell ... Matthew about the loss of his wife and his injured son. What can I say to a ... man I loved so dearly? He lost his life when he lost his memory ... and I lost him ... Give him the strength to accept Your will. *I felt as if my heart had been cut out of my breast!*

Linda returned from lunch and came into the office. When she saw me, her eyes grew watery, as if she felt my emotions for Matthew.

"*Boss, what is wrong? Are you all right?*" She came around the desk and placed her arms around me. I couldn't stop crying.

"Linda ... the telegram from Turkey ... please read it." She released me and picked up the telegram. As she read each line her voice began to quiver and in a few minutes we were holding each other and crying without shame.

"Oh, boss, I'm so sorry for you and Matthew. Has anyone told him? Does he know?"

I wiped my eyes and replied, "No, Linda, but I must be the one to tell him. *This is all my fault!* ... his memory of his past life lost, and now his wife. *What else can happen to him?*"

"Boss, it's not your fault. You didn't cause the airplane to crash. And you didn't cause the fire that killed his wife. *Please stop blaming yourself!*" I asked Linda to get Morgan on the telephone. In a moment she buzzed and said he was waiting.

"Morgan! Can you please come to my office right away?"

He was shocked. "Sweetheart, what's happened? Are you OK?"

I answered through my tears. "Yes, dear ... I just need you here with me."

"Honey, I'm on my way. Should be about twenty minutes. Chelsea, I love you very dearly."

"I know, Morgan, and I love you with all my heart ... I just need you here with me. Please hurry!" Linda brought hot coffee, and she and I sat and talked about Matthew.

"What's going to happen ... now, boss?" Linda asked as she continued to cry.

"Linda, I wish I knew. I don't know ... how Matthew is going to handle the news about his wife." Linda reminded me of the letter we received when his Turkish wife lost her baby.

"He apparently accepted that situation calmly. The letter he sent didn't seem to have much emotion or remorse in it."

"Yes, Linda, but that was an unborn child he'd never known, not his wife. Matthew was Catholic before he lost his memory. He now claims to be Islamic. And Linda ... I don't know a thing about his religion." Linda said she would get a book from the library if it would help. I thanked her. "Olga has gone for Matthew, so they should be here in a couple of hours. Maybe you had better get the book right away."

She responded, "I'm on my way. Be back in a few minutes!"

As she was leaving Morgan rushed into my office. "Honey, are you OK?" He took me in his arms and held me very tenderly as I began to cry again.

"Morgan ... Matthew's wife has been killed in a fire in their village ... Olga went to the clinic to get Matthew."

"My dear, dear wife. *The world seems to keep falling on you, doesn't it?*"

"Oh, Morgan, I feel so bad for him ... and I'm to blame for it!"

"Hey, wait a minute! Is this the chief executive officer of Thorndike accepting the blame for something she *could not control?* Don't be hard on yourself. *This is real life* ... "

I stopped him and said, "Morgan, you don't know how I feel about this situation ... Matthew and I ...." Linda came rushing back into the office and interrupted me.

"Oh, excuse me, boss. Hello, Morgan. Here is the book on Islam and Muslims, but I couldn't find anything in it about accepting a situation like this. Here, boss, you try."

"Thanks, Linda! Thank you, Linda ... more than you know." I was going to tell Morgan about Matthew and me! I said to myself, Get hold of yourself, Chelsea. You will weather this crisis. *Don't create another one!*

Morgan and I began to leaf through the book. He responded, "What specifically, are you trying to find in this book, Chelsea?"

"Morgan, it would help me if I knew how a follower of Islam, you know one who is a Muslim, accepts the death of a loved one before I talk with Matthew."

He responded, "I guess that's why you are a CEO. Doing your homework before you face the crisis!"

"Here it is. It says that death is somewhat of a reward during a holy war."

"I think this statement is more appropriate. 'A follower of Islam who is a Muslim accepts the will of Allah in all things. It is providence as decreed by Allah'."

"Let me see. Oh, Morgan, it really doesn't answer the question. I just hope Matthew can accept what has happened. Why didn't he remain a Catholic?"

2 Linda came into the office very quietly and said, "Boss, Olga and Matthew are here. Are you ready to talk with them?" I asked Morgan if he would mind if only Olga and I were with Matthew when I told him about his wife. Morgan agreed and left the office. Linda escorted Olga and Matthew into the office.

"Good afternoon, Chelsea. Are you well?" I must have looked a sight for Matthew to say that.

"Yes, Matthew. Thank you. How are you today?" I turned and wiped my eyes.

"I am very fine, thank you. Olga told me you desired to talk with me … "

Olga interrupted and said, "Chelsea, dear, should I wait outside? Do you want to speak with Matthew alone?"

I responded, *"No, Olga, please stay with us!"* I thought, here is a man whom I loved very much. And now, his former lover must tell him that his wife is dead. How did this happen to me?

"Matthew, how do you feel about your treatments at the clinic? Have you regained any of your memory?" He smiled and looked directly at me.

"No, Chelsea, I do not remember anything specific about my past life. I have had faint recalls with a few people. But no, not enough to even know who the people were or what part they played in my past."

"Matthew, I have very sad news for you from your village."

He responded, "May I ask, what is the sad news?" I picked up the telegram and spoke to him about it without reading the details. His first words were spoken in anger.

"*I should have been there to protect her!* And you say my son … is alive but is burned?" I tried to sound sympathetic.

"Yes, Matthew, your son is alive. He is in the burn center at the Ankara General Hospital." Again he sounded angry.

"If only we had a medical facility in Dyerbikier, his injuries could have been cared for sooner. The airplane to Ankara is more than one hour from my village."

He looked me directly in the eyes and asked if I would take him to a temple so he could offer his prayers to Allah. I rang Linda.

"Linda, please tell Morgan I need to use his car for awhile. Matthew has asked that I take him to a temple. Do you know where the nearest Islamic temple is?"

She said, "I'll find the nearest one from the telephone book." In a few minutes she came in and gave me directions.

"Boss, the temple is in the block next to St. Michael's Catholic Church. You can't miss it." She went to Matthew and placed her hand on his shoulder and said, "I'm terribly sorry about your wife, Matthew." He thanked her and as we walked into the foyer, Morgan took Matthew's hand and expressed his grief.

Matthew thanked him and said, "I have learned that Chelsea is your wife. You should be very proud of such a woman." Morgan gripped his hand and thanked him. Matthew and I left the office for the temple.

I remembered Matthew's back pay was in J.C.'s safe. I called Linda from the car phone and asked her to get the checks and arrange for them to be cashed and to set up an account for him by the time we returned to the office. She assured me it would be done.

I tried to pass the time by talking about the sights as we drove toward the temple. As we turned on to the street where the Catholic church and temple are located Matthew shocked me by saying, "*Wait, Chelsea! You are driving past my church!*"

I responded, "No, Matthew, that is the Catholic church. The temple is further down the street."

"Chelsea, I would like to go to *my church first!* Then I will go to the temple!"

"*Matthew!*" *I screamed.* "You remembered ... you are Catholic! What else do you remember?"

He looked at me and said without hesitation, "*You're Chelsea! Wait!* ... I am beginning to remember things in my past life. Yes, yes! *I am Catholic!* But I have also learned to be Islamic! Chelsea, I am starting to remember!" I stopped the car and we embraced.

"Oh, Matthew, I'm so happy for you ... "

"*Chelsea, I remember this street!* That church is where I went when I visited Lewisburg. Don't you remember?"

I responded thought my tears, "Oh, yes ... Matthew ... yes, I remember! This is wonderful. *Matthew, you are remembering!*"

He took my hands and said, "Chelsea, please wait here for me while I go into the temple to pass my wife's soul to Allah. Then I must also go my church to pray for her soul."

I was so happy! I continued to cry, but ... my tears were now tears of joy. I wanted to shout to the heavens and tell everyone that *Matthew remembers!*

Matthew returned a short time later with a very solemn look on his face. As he entered the car he took my hands in his and said, "Chelsea, my dear, we must go somewhere and talk."

I said, "Yes Matthew, we must talk!"

We stopped at a small uncrowded restaurant and ordered coffee and tea. Matthew looked me over as if he had only met me and needed to know everything about me. He took my hands in his. I felt he was about to ask how we could resume our lives. He looked into my eyes and said, "Chelsea, at one time in my life *I loved you with all my heart* ... "

"What do you mean, at *one time in your life* ... ?"

"Please wait until you hear what I must say to you." He continued, "And I love you today as I loved you then. But circumstances have changed in both of our lives ...." I couldn't understand what he was trying to tell me.

"Matthew, you must know that I am very happily married to Morgan now." I tried to give him an easy excuse to avoid embarrassment if he wanted us to pick up where we left each other three years ago.

"Matthew! ... You remembered ... you are Catholic!"

He looked at me tenderly and said, "Chelsea, you were always very impatient. Please let me have my say."

"Very well. I shall not speak again until you have *finished your sermon!*"

"Thank you, my dear. Olga has told me a great deal about you, Morgan, and your family. And yes, also my little son, Caesar. I didn't connect with anything she said until now. Chelsea, the past three years have had a great deal of meaning in my life. I was a crushed man and probably should have died in the airplane crash. This Turkish family — a father, his wife, and two daughters — rescued me and cared for me all during my many operations. Sometime during the operations and my loneliness I lost all recollections of my past life. I don't know just when, but it did happen."

Matthew seemed to have completely regained his memory. I wondered if the shock of losing his wife had traumatized him and brought his memory back.

"Matthew, when you were out of surgery, did you remember me and Caesar?"

"Yes, for awhile I remembered almost everything about my life with you and the Parker buy-out program. Yes, at first I remembered. But then one day while I was recovering from the last operation … my memory was suddenly gone. My mind seemed to be a complete blank."

"Matthew, the doctors couldn't find anything pathologically wrong with you that could have caused you to lose your memory. A traumatic condition was discussed as a possible reason."

He continued with his story. "I was taken into a Turkish village by this family and cared for until I had recovered."

"When did you marry the Turkish girl?"

"I am not sure how I became married to her, but she became my wife by Turkish law." My suspicious mind wanted to know more of the details of his life.

"Matthew, this girl. How old was she when you married her?"

"I really don't know. I think she was a teenager."

"What are you saying, Matthew? *You married a teenage girl?*"

"Chelsea, you don't understand the world in Turkey. Girls are expected to marry young … "

My jealous mind caused me to respond, "*So you married a teenage girl!* Tell me, Matthew, when was the baby born?"

He answered angrily, "Chelsea, please don't dig into the details of my life in Turkey. It is not important to what we must do now." My angry mind thought, oh, here it comes!

"*Well, tell me, Matthew,* now that your memory is returning, what are your plans?"

He took my hands in his and said very sweetly, "Chelsea, you have a grand life with Morgan and your children. Although I have not seen Caesar, I know in my heart he is well cared for and loved by you and your family. *I will not upset your life!*" He shocked me.

"Matthew, if you don't plan to come back into my life, what will you do?"

"The people in the Turkish villages depend upon me. I have taught them many things during the past three years. I must return to Turkey and continue my work."

"So it's your decision alone not to come back into my life. Well, Matthew, don't *you think I should have some say about what is to happen?*"

He responded in his kind and gentle manner. "Chelsea. I am a very changed man. At one time in my life, about all I wanted was success and pleasures for myself. I see myself in a completely different light now. What happened to me in Turkey has touched my soul in a way that *no one will ever understand.*"

"Matthew, you have *not even considered my feelings in your decision!* Don't you think I should have something to say about us?"

He looked at me and said, "Chelsea, it's your life with your family I am considering, ... but, if you like, you can divorce Morgan and we can have a legal marriage. *How does that sound?*"

Oh, my heavens, Chelsea, I thought. *What are you going to do now?* He caught you off-guard. He gave you an out, and now he sounds as if he wants you back. What next, girl?

I responded very weakly and uncertainly. "Well ... I really didn't mean ... I mean you were very considerate in your decision to return to Turkey. I'm ... sorry, Matthew. I just felt sort of left out. Do you understand what I am trying to say?"

He smiled and said, "Of course I do, Chelsea. You resorted to acting like a 'shunned woman' rather than accepting my decision because you didn't have your say."

I frowned at him and said, "Matthew, we had some really nice times together a long time ago. I would like to remember our good times. And Matthew, *I want to be your friend!*"

"Well, that's nice, *since we have a son!* I must remain in contact with you because I love my son and you are his mother."

"Matthew, what are people going to say when they learn you have regained your memory?"

He looked at me with his dark Castillian eyes and said, "My dear, when I went into the church there were many things for which I sought forgiveness. When I felt the flow of love from my God, I knew I had to include you and your family in my prayers ... "

I stopped him and said, "Matthew ... thank you ... "

He placed his fingers gently across my lips and said, "Let me finish, Chelsea. I prayed for guidance in what I should do. *Chelsea, in a flash of light* ... almost as quickly as I lost my memory, I began to remember my past life ... I was told to guard the life returned to me."

I didn't know what he meant.

"Matthew, I don't understand what you are saying."

He smiled and said, "Chelsea, *I have regained my memory!* I have a choice as to which life I may choose. I recently learned about you and Morgan and, of course, your family. When I asked the Lord what I should do, I felt his answer as if he were saying, '*Devote your life to others! Build, do not destroy!*' Chelsea, I know what that message means in my life."

I looked at him half smiling and responded, "Matthew, what will you do?"

He took my hands in his and gently kissed them. "Chelsea, my dear, no one except you and me must know that I have recovered my memory."

I insisted that Olga be told. "Olga knows about us; I must tell her. But if you are returning to Turkey, I don't think anyone else needs to know. And Matthew, thank you for being so considerate of my life, my family, and our son Caesar."

"Chelsea, I must go home as soon as I can get reservations ... "

"I'll have Linda get your tickets. And, Matthew, we have about $400,000 in back pay for you also ... "

He shouted, "*You have what? Four hundred thousand dollars?* Chelsea, do you have any idea what I can do with that much money in Turkey?" I was pleased that he was so excited about his back pay. He's the same Matthew I knew — generous with his assets. I thought it would be an appropriate time to tell him he also has about five million dollars in insurance money.

I smiled with so much love in my heart when I told him, "Matthew, when we were told that you had been killed, I received five million dollars in proceeds from the insurance policy you left me. I also have the money I got for the sale of your cars and townhouse. Matthew, that money is also yours."

He shook his head and said, "Chelsea, *I just can't believe what is happening!* God is answering my prayers. I must have made the decision he wanted me to make."

"Matthew, I'll set up a trust account for you with the money. It will be there for you when you want to use it." He couldn't understand why I didn't have to give the money back.

"Chelsea, *I am alive and now I have my memory.* Is it possible we can keep the money from the insurance?" I explained what John Davis, who was his lawyer, explained to me after he had talked with the insurance company.

"Matthew, don't you want to keep the money?"

He smiled and said, "Of course we can keep it, as long as it is legal. My mind imprisoned me for the past three years; I just don't want to live inside a physical prison."

"No, Matthew, that will not happen. It is perfectly legal."

He squeezed my hand and responded, "Chelsea, that is just wonderful! I may have enough money to build a small medical facility in Dyerbikier." I thought, what an opportune time to talk about a memorial for Mr. Thorndike.

"Matthew, we are going to build something in memory of Mr. Thorndike. Do you think we could help build that medical facility … in his honor?"

"Yes, yes … Chelsea, that would be just grand. I'll talk with you after I do the preliminary work, and maybe the corporation can help us build a medical center for our villages."

He reminded me again that we shouldn't talk about our situation to anyone other than Olga. I asked him if he would like to come to my home to see Caesar before he left the States. He was elated but said, "*We must be on our guard!* We can't let Morgan know that I have recovered my memory. Yes, that would be wonderful to see my son before I depart."

I called Linda from the car phone and asked her to get tickets for Matthew for a late flight tomorrow evening. I asked if Morgan was still in the office.

"Yes, boss. He's talking with J.C. I'll get him for you."

"Thanks, Linda," I said. "Morgan, I talked with Matthew about dinner at our house and he accepted for tonight. He will leave for Turkey tomorrow evening. Is that all right with you, dear?"

Morgan responded in his usual happy manner. "Yes, that will be swell. Shall I call Sylvia and have her prepare a special dinner?"

"You wonderful man. Yes, would you please? We are heading back to the office. See you soon."

3 Linda couldn't understand the rapid change in my disposition. When I'd left the office I was crying. Now, I tried very hard not to display my happiness and enthusiasm about Matthew recovering his memory. I greeted Morgan with a kiss on the cheek. He said hello to Matthew and told him he was welcome for dinner tonight. Then Morgan left for his office, and Olga followed me into mine. Matthew waited in the outer office with Linda in his "shy Turkish manner."

"What has happened to you, my dear! You are radiant. Tell me!"

I took her by both hands and looked into her eyes and said, "*Olga, Matthew has regained his memory!*"

She frowned and said, "Chelsea, my dear, *please be careful!* Does he want to come back to you? Does everyone know that he now remembers his past?"

"*No, Olga!*" I screamed in a muted voice. "And he doesn't want anyone other than you and me to know that he has regained his memory. Olga, he understands my situation and he has accepted it. He is returning to Turkey to be with his relatives and friends."

She seemed puzzled. "Chelsea, my dear, you are saying he does not want you?"

"*Yes. Isn't it wonderful?* He remembers, but he said he loves me and Caesar enough to accept what he found."

She hugged me and said, "My dear Chelsea, God has also answered your prayers. Be thankful and help Matthew to return to Turkey as quickly as possible."

"But, Olga, he wants to come and see Caesar before he leaves."

"And my dear, what does Morgan have to say about that?"

I smiled and said, "Oh, Morgan is very supportive. In fact, he greeted Matthew a while ago and welcomed him to our home for dinner tonight. Olga, can you and Dad be there with us?"

She nodded her head and said, "Yes. But I must call your dad. But, yes, I speak for him. We will be there. What time do we come?"

I hugged her and said, "You and Dad should be there before Matthew arrives. How about sixish?"

"My dear Chelsea, I hope you realize what you are doing. *Your husband and your former lover in your house at the same time!* Will you ever get out of the box?" I assured her this time everything would be different.

"Olga, only you, Matthew, and I know he has recovered his memory. And he is not going to tell anyone else."

Olga left the office to talk with Dad about tonight. Linda came in and asked for specific times for Matthew's flight. I told her as late in the evening as possible; he doesn't mind flying overnight. "And, Linda," I added, "will you get Matthew's checks from J.C. and go with Matthew to open a bank account before he leaves tomorrow?"

"Boss, are you sure he can manage that much money? Has something changed that I should know about?"

I knew I could trust Linda. I said, "Linda what I'm going to tell you can't leave this office. OK?"

She seemed puzzled but said, "Sure, boss lady. You know you can trust me."

"Linda, Matthew has recovered his memory ... "

She almost shouted. "*He what? You're joking! What happened? Did you wreck Morgan's car and give him another bump on the head?*" I was still excited about Matthew's recovery.

"No, silly woman! The word of his wife's death must have triggered something in his mind. We were on our way to the Islamic temple when he suddenly said we were passing the Catholic church. I almost fainted. At first I couldn't believe what he said. Oh, Linda, this is a wonderful day for me."

"Boss, who else knows about this?"

"You, Olga, and me. And, Linda, Matthew doesn't want anyone else to know. He feels he must return to Turkey."

She shook her head and said, "Boss, I can't understand a man like Matthew living in a place like Turkey. Why is he going back there?" I thought, he's going back there because he loves me and doesn't want to disrupt my life.

I said to Linda, "He feels he has more work to do with the villagers. He says he will use his back pay to do a number of things he wants to do there."

"I'm really happy that he got his memory back. I wish I could talk him into coming back here to Lewisburg. Since he won't have a wife maybe there would be a chance for me. What do you think, boss?"

I glanced up at her and said, "No, Linda. I don't think he will come back and if he does ... you're really not his type."

"Yes, you're probably right. I could have played around with him when we were in Mexico if I hadn't found a better offer."

I asked Linda to have J.C. come in to see me. In a few minutes he stuck his head in the door and said, "You want to see me, Chelsea?"

"Yes, J.C. Please come in." J.C. always brought his note pad with him. "J.C., I think I am about ready to do something for Mr. Thorndike's memory."

"What do you have in mind, Chelsea?" I asked if he knew Matthew was returning to Turkey. He indicated he had overheard Linda making the airplane reservations.

"Well, this is my idea of real help to the human race that will have meaning to both Mr. Thorndike and Matthew."

J.C. nodded his head in agreement. "I think that's grand to include Matthew in whatever we do for Mr. Thorndike. So, what project do you have in mind?" I asked how much money we had in the memorial fund. He checked his figures and said, "So far, we have a little over eight million dollars."

"J.C., do you have any idea how much a small well-equipped medical center will cost?"

He reviewed a construction guideline in his note pad and replied, "Well, the southern plant cost us about eighty-two dollars a square foot, constructed with manufacturing flooring."

"How far do you think the eight million will go toward building a small- to medium-size, fully equipped medical facility?"

"I don't know offhand, but I'll get Engineering to work up the figures for you. Where are you thinking of building the facility?"

I looked him straight in the eyes and said, *"In Turkey, J.C.!"* His expression changed considerably.

"Well, I know from the cost reviews of the Turkish contracts that we can probably build over there for about half the cost in the States."

"Get engineering to do a complete set of drawings for the building, operating rooms, recovery rooms, and everything that goes with a medical facility. When you get the plans and the costs bring them in, and get Morgan so we can review them together." J.C. said he would have the project finished about two weeks.

4 Olga and Dad arrived about six. Morgan fixed our drinks and we sat in the den at the fireplace talking about the day's events. Dad said, "Tell me again who this fellow is we treating to dinner tonight?"

"Dad, he worked for Thorndike, was sent to Turkey, and was in an aircraft accident."

Olga added to what I had said, "The main thing Chelsea did not say is that Matthew lost his memory, either from the crash or the operations he had."

Morgan said, "And that is only half the story. The poor guy doesn't remember his life in the States but seems to have made a name for himself in Turkey." Dad wondered how he had survived.

"How was he found?"

Olga responded to him, "Thomas, you remember when Chelsea and I went to Turkey?" He nodded. "Well, we went there because reports coming back to Chelsea and the corporation were that an American who could be Matthew Glyndon was discovered in the Turkish village of Dyerbikier."

Dad still didn't understand. "So, why are you entertaining him at your home?"

Morgan responded before I could answer. "Well, Dad, this guy can't remember his life in the States. He has been treated for the past three weeks in the Mayo Clinic. Apparently the doctors didn't do much for him … "

"Yes," I added, "he was examined by a team of doctors, including Olga, and they couldn't find anything to which they could attribute his loss of memory."

Morgan added, "We are trying to help him by exposing him to our family. He is, or was, I should say, married to a Turkish girl who recently died in a fire."

Dad asked, "Is there anything we shouldn't talk about this evening?"

"Yes, Dad, please help us to keep the conversation light, maybe about the kids and simple things we do. We just want to make him feel comfortable here with us and the children." The doorbell rang, and Chelsea Lyn and I raced for the door. Matthew started to greet me in an intimate fashion when he saw Chelsea Lyn. I introduced them.

"Matthew, this is my daughter, Chelsea Lyn. Chelsea Lyn, this is Mr. Matthew Glyndon. Mr. Glyndon worked for our company several years ago. He is leaving for Turkey tomorrow."

She responded, "What part of Turkey are you going to?" Matthew looked at me and I nodded my approval to answer her.

"Well, young lady, I will be traveling back to my village, a place called Dyerbikier."

Chelsea Lyn pulled out a letter and said, "Is this the town where you live?"

Matthew looked at the letter and said, "Why, yes, that is my home. Do you have a pen pal who lives there?"

"Yes. He's a great pen pal. *He's my real father!*" Oh, heavens, Abel ended up in the same town with Matthew. *What a strange coincidence!*

We escorted Matthew into the den and introduced him to Dad. He greeted Morgan and said he was very grateful to be invited to his home. He said to Dad, "Sir, you have a very beautiful daughter. She and Doctor Olga have been my guides since I arrived here. Ladies, may I thank you both for what you have done for me." *It seemed like a game!* Matthew, Olga, and I knew he had regained his memory. He had to continue his "shy, uninformed" manner this evening to keep our secret. I thought, Chelsea, when Matthew leaves tomorrow he will take our secret with him. His letters, if he writes, will be in general terms even when he asks about Caesar.

I didn't see the boys, so I asked Sylvia if she would bring them into the den. In a few minutes the two of them came crashing into the den and jumped into Morgan's and Dad's laps. I picked up Caesar and said to Matthew, "Mr. Glyndon, this is Caesar. *He is our adopted son!*"

295

Matthew took him into his arms and said, "My, you're quite a big little man, aren't you?" Caesar always took advantage of every opportunity to talk.

"Yes, sir. Do you want to see my muscle?" He pulled up his sleeve and pumped up his little arm for Matthew. Matthew turned away from the group. I suspected his eyes were watering. In a moment he let Caesar down.

He said, "I must be catching a cold." Olga and I were the only ones who knew just what Matthew meant. His little boy had brought tears to his eyes and he had to hide them. Raynor came over to show Matthew his muscles along with Caesar. Matthew took time with both boys. I knew he wanted to hold his son longer, but he shared his time equally with them.

The evening was very draining for Matthew. He had to keep his guard up when questions were asked about the local area. While we drank coffee in the den, Olga directed the conversation as a narrator would. She answered any questions that might have caused Matthew to give away his secret. At the end of the evening, we all escorted him to the door for the taxi back to his motel. I reminded him that Linda would pick him up with his checks and help open a bank account before he departed. He thanked everyone for the evening and asked if he could say good night to the children. I called Caesar first. He lifted Caesar into his arms and hugged him gently and told him to be a good boy. He casually embraced Chelsea Lyn and Raynor. His taxi arrived and he was gone.

As we walked back into the den Morgan commented, "That poor soul. I wonder if he will ever recover his memory."

Dad responded with sympathy, "It is sad. He seems very intelligent. I had a feeling he just didn't want to talk. I thought we should have talked more about Thorndike and his previous job and acquaintances ... "

"No, Thomas!" Olga said. "We have all talked about his past with him and took him around the plant. When he was with us, he only slightly remembered knowing one person."

Morgan responded, "Who did he think recognized?"

"Morgan, I told you. It was Susan Rosco."

He laughed and said, "Yes, but who could forget a dish like Susan?"

Olga interrupted the conversation and said she and Dad had to leave. Her decision was very welcome. We said good night and they departed. Morgan and I climbed the stairs to our bedroom. Morgan seemed to want to talk about Matthew. I asked that we forget the evening since we had done our duty by having Matthew over for dinner.

I said, "I don't know if being here with our family really helped him or not." I knew in my heart he was very sad when he left. He hadn't seen his son in three years. When he held Caesar I could feel his tenderness and love for his son. I had to restrain myself from placing my arms around him and Caesar. He will return to Turkey and I am not sure when he will see his son again. I pray that God goes with him.

5 Linda had coffee made for us when I arrived at the office. She had retrieved the checks from J.C. and was ready to go with Matthew to open his bank account.

"Linda, send Matthew's file with his last tax return to our accounting firm. Tell them to fill out his IRS forms for the past three years. Give them copies of the check stubs and have payroll prepare W-2s for him. They can assume he did not have any other income, property, or anything else that is taxable. And, Linda, tell J.C. to take him off our payroll as of today. I will explain everything to Matthew."

She smiled. "Boss lady, you think of everything, don't you?" I thought, no, Linda, I don't think of everything. If I had thought of everything I would never be in the situation I'm in today. I asked Linda to call me when she and Matthew completed his banking. I want to have lunch with him one more time. I immediately had a guilty conscience.

I called Morgan. "Morgan dear, I'm having lunch with Matthew. Do you want to join us?"

His answer shocked me. "No, babe, you need some time with him before he leaves." I wondered why he said that. I am always questioning whether Morgan really knows about Matthew and me. I need to talk with Matthew privately, anyway. I called Olga and asked if she would meet us for lunch. She gladly accepted. Linda called and I asked her to drop Matthew at the little restaurant near the office. Olga arrived at the same time as I did. We went in and Matthew greeted us.

"Ladies, I was so afraid I would blow our secret last night."

I said, "You did just fine. I don't think you aroused any suspicions about your recovered memory." We had a glass of wine while we waited for our lunch. Olga said she had something to say about Chelsea Lyn's letter.

297

"Chelsea, do you realize that Chelsea Lyn's letter came from Abel in Matthew's village, Dyerbikier? Did you see her letter?" Chelsea Lyn had not discussed the letter with me except to show it to Matthew last evening.

"Only last evening, Olga. She showed the postmark to Matthew and he identified it as coming from Dyerbikier."

"Chelsea, do you know what this means?"

"Oh, yes, Olga. I am well aware of what may happen."

Matthew joined in and responded, "Ladies, what are you talking about?"

I looked at Olga and said, "Olga, we need to tell Matthew about Abel."

Olga said, "Yes, Chelsea, I quite agree. It's your story, so tell him."

I looked at Olga and said, "I don't know quite where to begin."

Matthew became more curious. "What, may I ask, are you trying to tell me, Chelsea?" Why beat around the bush? I went directly to the heart of the secret.

"Oh, heck! Matthew, Pastor Abel Clayborne is on a church assignment in your village."

"So, what's so special about this Abel Clayborne?"

"Matthew, he is Chelsea Lyn's biological father!"

He looked confused again and responded, "So he is Chelsea Lyn's father. She told me last evening and I still don't understand why he is so important."

I looked him in the eyes and said, "Matthew, *I am Chelsea Lyn's biological mother!*"

He hesitated and said, "Chelsea, she is a teenager. So you and this pastor had an affair years ago ... "

"No, it was not an affair!" I very firmly replied.

"Chelsea, why are you telling me about a part of your past?"

"Because you and Abel will probably meet and socialize. Heavens, I don't know how many Americans are in Dyerbikier. I just don't want you and him to suddenly learn that you both have had so much in common with the same woman."

"Oh, I see. You're going to tell me about Abel. May I ask, does Abel already know about me?"

I replied angrily, *"No, of course not!"*

298

He looked at me and said firmly, "Now let me get the facts straight. You and this Abel had a baby, and that baby is now a teenager, Chelsea Lyn, *who lives with you and Morgan.* Am I correct so far?"

"Yes, of course, you know you are."

"Sometime later in your life, *you met me and we had a baby.* Now as I understand the situation, I will know about Abel, but he will not know about me?"

"Oh, Matthew, why do you make things so difficult? If you had not recovered your memory I wouldn't have told you. I just don't want you to be embarrassed."

We ate our meal in almost total silence. Olga had sat quietly during the heated conversation Matthew and I were having. Finally she said, "Matthew, Chelsea is trying to be honest with you and not hurt you more than you have already been hurt. Please accept what she has said as her gesture to protect you."

"Olga, I do appreciate you and Chelsea. And I thank you both from the bottom of my heart that you agreed to keep my secret. I shall write and inquire about Caesar from time to time. I have your office telephone number, and the best hours to call."

"Thank you, Matthew. Can we drop you at your motel? Do you have transportation to the airport tonight?"

He said, "Yes, thank you. Susan Rosco offered to have dinner with me tonight and she will drive me to the airport."

"Good-bye, Matthew. Take care of yourself."

"Good-bye Olga, Chelsea. Thank you for everything." We left him at the restaurant.

I was about to blow my top! Matthew is taking Susan Rosco to dinner, isn't that just grand? Olga knew I was angry.

"What is troubling you Chelsea?"

I almost shouted at her. *"Can you believe that Matthew?* He is going to have dinner with Susan Rosco."

Olga looked rather strangely at me and said, "Chelsea, why are you upset about a thing such as that? Don't you remember, you are married to Morgan. *Morgan is not going out with Susan!* Matthew Glyndon, whom you did not want back in your life, is going out with her. What is your problem?"

I confessed to her, "Oh, I don't know, Olga. I suppose I still have feelings for Matthew even if he doesn't care for me."

299

"Chelsea, you almost have your life straightened out. Please control your emotions. Don't keep getting into the box!" I knew Olga was right. I have to accept my life and marriage to Morgan and not be concerned with past situations. I must accept that my relationships with Abel and Matthew will be only for the children, Chelsea Lyn and Caesar. I cannot keep thinking that a part of either of them belongs to me. Olga reminded me of my marriage to Morgan.

"Chelsea, my dear, you have a wonderful husband in Morgan. He loves you very much and as you said of Mr. Thorndike, Morgan has accepted you with all your faults, totally and unconditionally. I suggest you become involved with Morgan and no one else. Your former lovers have forsaken you. Accept your role and be happy." Olga shoots straight from the hip. She always did speak her mind.

"Yes, Olga, you are absolutely correct. I love Morgan and I will make up my mind. I will not be distracted by anyone else. Thank you, Olga!"

6 Abel and Matthew are gone! They are not completely out of my life, but I can manage any situation that comes up from now on. Our mutual interest will be the *children and nothing more.* I thought, so Matthew and Susan Rosco must have had a week of lovemaking during their stay in Turkey. But that doesn't even bother me any longer. I had this crazy idea that when a man really loves a woman, he will love only her and not play around with anyone else. Morgan and Matthew proved me wrong on that point.

Olga and I drove back to the office. She said she was very happy to see my problems out of the country. She said now maybe I could settle down to more important things. As we left the car on our way to the office Olga took my hand and said, "Chelsea! *I have a big secret to tell you!*" Oh, heavens, not another crisis, I thought.

"What is it, Olga?" She wanted to know if I remembered asking her to tell me first if anything were to happen between her and Dad.

"My dear, *I think I am to become your official stepmother!*"

"*Olga, that is wonderful!* When? Have you and Dad set a date yet?"

She smiled and said, "No, not really. We thought we would break the news to you before we made our plans solid, da?" What a wonderfully shocking surprise. I'd known they would be getting married one day, but this soon after her moving to Lewisburg? Quite a shock to

"My dear, I think I am to become your official stepmother!"

my system. When she and Dad were only dating, she promised not to tell him about my past life. Things may be different after they are married. I am not sure about telling Dad what happened to me. Now that I can trust myself, maybe I will learn to trust my dad with the truth. I must make a special effort to ask God to help me in resolving my fears. Olga said I kept putting myself into a box.

When Olga first came to the States she lived in a small town in central Pennsylvania. She told Dad she would like to be married in the first church she attended after coming to the States. I invited them for dinner so we could discuss their plans. Olga had promised that I would be the one to help plan their wedding. It's always so nice having them visit with the children. Dad wrestles with the boys and Olga sits for long periods talking with Chelsea Lyn.

Morgan and Chelsea Lyn greeted them at the door. "Hi, folks, glad to see you. Come in! Chelsea Lyn, please take their coats."

Olga asked Morgan, "Did Chelsea tell you about our 'secret'?"

Morgan said with a Russian accent, "*Da, that she did!* And have you now planned this happy event?"

"No, Morgan. Chelsea is in charge of the operation. We both want to be married in my first United States church. Chelsea will plan everything for us."

"Where is the church?"

Olga very proudly answered, "My church is in Hop Bottom, in Pennsylvania ... "

Morgan interrupted her. "Did I understand you to say '*Hop Bottom*'? Where on God's green earth is 'Hop Bottom' Pennsylvania?"

Olga was not disturbed. She glared at Morgan and said, "This is a place in the mountains. Morgan, do you remember where my pregnancy center was located?"

He nodded his head and said, "Sure, that was somewhere near the Pocono mountain area in Pennsylvania, wasn't it?"

"That is correct! Well, Hop Bottom is not very far from the pregnancy center's location, which was also in the mountains." I overheard most of the conversation. Morgan never lived in Pennsylvania until he came to work for Thorndike. He doesn't understand about the small towns that were founded by various ethnic groups who came to the States. His amusement at a name such as 'Hop Bottom' was not a surprise to me. I remember visiting Hop Bottom on several occasions. I thought we should get the details set for the wedding.

"Well, have you love birds set the date for the wedding yet?"

Olga said, "We would like spring or early summer, whichever is best for you."

"Are any particular dates special to either of you?" Olga said she came to the States on July 6. She said that would be a good date to get married. Dad agreed and we outlined what we needed to do to have the wedding in Hop Bottom on July sixth. After dinner, Dad and Olga went back to their condos.

I took the details they wanted included and turned the project over to Linda. She was elated to be the point woman on the wedding plan and she said, "Just think! *I will get to visit 'Hop Bottom'* to attend the wedding."

When Chelsea Lyn heard the news she responded, "Mom, do you think Olga will let be one of her bridesmaids?" What a nice idea.

"Oh, Chelsea Lyn, I am sure she would be very happy to have her 'new' granddaughter be one of her bridesmaids. Why don't you ask her?"

She beamed with joy. "*Oh, yes, I will!* When are she and Granddad coming to visit?" My wonderful daughter, she wants to be in everyone's heart.

"They will be coming back to visit soon."

I decided to take a day off. I called Linda from home and relayed Chelsea Lyn's request. "Boss lady, that would be just wonderful! That makes three of us. Olga asked me and her receptionist to join the bridal party. Incidentally, do you know who your dad wants for his best man?" I hadn't even thought of who Dad would want to stand with him. Maybe Morgan could be his best man.

"No, Linda. I'll talk with him and let you know. And, Linda, thanks for everything."

Soon the activity of the house settled into the quietness that I love so much. Sylvia brought fresh coffee to the den. Morgan's design of the den was very flexible. We use the glassed-in area in summer and winter. The den is a large room with a fireplace in its center. At the rear of the room is a circular area that projects onto the patio. The view from this room is simply beautiful. The willow trees wave in the wind as if they are reaching to the sky. The oaks are all bare now. During the day their many branches seem to be lying on the lake waters. The lake freezes at times and the ice glistens in the sunlight.

I sat in the round room this morning and thought about the terrible situations in my past. My father and I are totally reconciled now. When he ordered me out of my home at seventeen I didn't think I would ever speak to him again. *I could never be so harsh with my daughter!* Now that I am older and a mother, I can better understand how he felt then. My time with Abel and Kersi was a very loving part of my life. I think I really learned how to love people when I was with them. If anyone else heard the story of that relationship, they would think I was "brainwashed." But my decision to have their baby was not because of any intensive religious sessions Kersi and I had, but because I loved them both so dearly. Abel and I both felt Kersi would have committed suicide if she could not have a baby to call her own.

When Morgan and I met, we were adversaries. But when I first met him, something in his personality or his friendly ways reached into my inner being. At first, I thought I would never fall in love with a strong-willed, determined, career-seeking individual such as Morgan Gage. But when I thought about Morgan, I could see my personality reflected in him. Maybe we were more alike that either of us would admit. I fell madly in love with him. Our marriage in the Thorndike Convention Center was the wedding of the year, sponsored by Mr. Thomas Thorndike himself.

The night with Matthew in Mexico was a mistake made by a very drunken woman. No love, no attachment. And the one-night event could have been over the next morning. Somehow I became entangled in a web of deceit that hung around my neck like a noose for several years.

Now I can really see the light at the end of the tunnel. My relationships with Abel and Matthew are manageable and must ... *no* ... *not* ... *must* ... *but* ... *will* remain clear of any emotions. It's very strange that I can look over the beautiful scenery from the quietness of the den and think about every emotional crisis that has happened to me and now *take charge of them!*

Chelsea Lyn got a ride with a friend and came home from school early. She went to the kitchen and Sylvia told her I was home. She came running into the den and asked, "Mom, why are you home from work? Are you all right?"

"Yes, dear. I just needed a day off."

"What have you been doing?"

I asked her to look at the scenery. "See that view, dear? I have been drinking it in and thinking about my life."

"Is something bothering you, Mother?"

I smiled at her lovingly and said, "My dear Chelsea Lyn, your mother is the happiest woman in the entire world. She now has complete control of her life."

She looked at me with a questioning expression and said, "Mom, is it because you told me about Abel, my real father?"

"Yes, sweetie, that's part of it. Speaking of Abel! Didn't you receive a letter from him?" She reached into her school bag and handed me the letter.

"I just have not had time to you show Father Abel's letter. You may read my mail. After all, you're my mother!" I felt I had better clear that last point quickly.

"Chelsea Lyn, I have no right to open your mail simply because you're my daughter. You have a right to your privacy, as we all do."

She looked at me and said, "Mother, most of my girlfriends complain about their mothers opening their mail. I thought it was just a mother's right to do it."

I hugged her and said, "Chelsea Lyn, my dear daughter, I would never open your mail regardless of whom it came from. Your mail is your property. Mothers do not have an inherent right to *spy on their daughters!*"

She hugged me very tenderly and said, "Mother, that is one reason I love you so much. You treat me as an my own person! But here is my letter from Father Abel. You may read it."

Abel's letter was very religious and tender. He again asked Chelsea Lyn to forgive us for the act against God. He said he accepted the sin in exchange for his beautiful daughter. He went on to say he was settled into the local missionary church quarters and would be visiting several villages in and around Dyerbikier. Chelsea Lyn interrupted my reading and said, "Mother, isn't that Mr. Glyndon from Dyerbikier where Father Abel is?"

"Yes, dear, that's where Mr. Glyndon lives."

She sat up with a big smile on her face and said, "*Mother, wouldn't it be nice to have them meet each other? To think they were both here in our home and now they are in the same place in Turkey.*" I thought to myself, yes, my daughter, *that is very nice.* Two fathers of my children, by some strange act of destiny, are in the same little town at the end of the earth.

305

"This was my first church in the United States."

I quickly changed the subject. "Chelsea Lyn, dear, Olga wants you, Linda, and her receptionist as bridesmaids for her wedding."

She screamed with joy and said, *"Mother, we must go shopping for a dress!* Did Olga say what color we should have?" How nice to have a daughter who sees so much excitement in being a bridesmaid for her new step-grandmother.

"No, dear, but we have time. Olga selected the date she arrived in the United States as her wedding date … "

She squeezed my hand and responded, "Tell me, Mother, what date? I hope we have time to get my dress and everything!"

I calmed her and responded, "It will be the sixth of July. We have lots of time to shop for a dress and shoes and anything else you may need." Her face glistened with joy. "We will all go shopping together so Olga can pick out our colors and gowns."

7   The quiet time spent away from the office, even thought it was only one day, was a welcome relief from the stresses of being the CEO. This time spent sitting on the patio overlooking the lake was good for my psyche. *My life is no longer a series of crises!* God answered my many prayers and he must be controlling my life.

Going back to the office the next day was easier than usual. Linda greeted me as I entered my office, "Surprise, boss! You don't have any fires to put out today!" I was so happy to hear her words. Not only is my personal life coming together, but Thorndike Industries is also under control.

"Thanks, Linda. That sounds great. So what's on the schedule today?"

"J.C. and David want to brief you on Parnella Verbena and her threat. They are on at 9:30 A.M."

"Do we still have a problem with her?"

Linda looked surprised and said, "I don't know, boss. And your presentation of the Thorndike gift to the city is set for two o'clock today. Nothing else on your docket for the rest of the day." I heard J.C. and David in the outer office and called for them to come in.

J.C. said, "Good morning, Chelsea. David and I want to bring you up to date on the Verbena file."

"Good morning, J.C. Hello, David. So, what do you have?"

David began, "Chelsea, the EEOC people reviewed our actions in the Verbena file and said that we followed every letter of the directives and shouldn't have anything to worry about in an EEOC case."

J.C. added, "Chelsea, Parnella may try and bring suit against you and Morgan for collusion in firing her. This is not part of an EEOC action."

I raised my face to J.C. and said, "Well, J.C., you're the deputy CEO and our top lawyer. Take care of Ms. Verbena. And when she sues and loses, have the provision to collect our fees from her. I can't be concerned with the likes of Parnella Verbena."

"Yes, Chelsea. I will be glad to take this case on personally."

"Thanks for your time, gentlemen. Have a good day!"

Linda asked if I had time to discuss Olga's wedding plans. I asked her to bring coffee and bring her plans in. "Chelsea, if you think I have all bases covered, I will meet with Olga and your dad if you like and brief them."

"That will be great. So what are the wedding plans?"

"I reserved the Grace Lutheran Church for the wedding. The regular pastor is on vacation. A Pastor Charles Gerhold has agreed to perform the ceremony. The nearest place for a reception is the Ramada Inn at Clarks Summit, which is about a twenty-minute drive from the Hop Bottom church. Chelsea Lyn, Olga's receptionist, and I will be the bridesmaids. Photographs and VCR coverage will be provided by a local photography shop. And that's about it. Except I will have cars and drivers to take the wedding party to the church and to the reception. We will all stay overnight at the Ramada Inn."

"Linda, I think you have done it all! Can you come to dinner Friday evening and discuss the schedule with Olga and Dad?"

She smiled and said, "Boss, I was hoping you would invite me to dinner for my efforts."

Morgan and I held a small reception and dinner with Linda as our special guest. She was very pleased. Olga and Dad agreed with her plans and the wedding was set for *July 6th in the Grace Lutheran Church in Hop Bottom, Pennsylvania.*

All my problems have been solved except keeping Dad from learning about my past life. Olga is coming to have lunch with me. I must have an understanding with her. I don't think she will tell Dad, but I've got to be sure.

Linda buzzed and said Olga was here. She rapped on the door and came into the office.

"Hello, Chelsea dear. Thank you for inviting me to lunch with you."

I called to Linda to tell her we would be back in a couple of hours. She wanted a few minutes with Olga when we returned, to talk about the wedding plans. We left the office and drove to Hoffman's Restaurant. Once inside Olga said, "Chelsea, I can see why you and Morgan enjoy this restaurant. It is very cozy." I agreed and we ordered our lunch. Olga will become my stepmother on July 6th. I am about to ask her to keep secrets from my father, her husband-to-be.

I hesitated and then said, "Olga, remember when we talked about Dad not knowing about my past with the Claybornes and Matthew?"

She smiled and said, "Da, I remember. Are we to talk about it again?"

"Olga, I just don't know if Dad will accept what I have done. I'm a little frightened that once you and he are married, you may talk about my past."

"Chelsea, my dear, I do not believe in two people talking about their past when they marry. I have some events in my past that I will not share with your father. I am sure he will not share everything with me either. I just don't think these things are important in our relationship."

"Can I please ask you not to talk with Dad about my past?"

She patted my hand and said, "My dear, your business is your business. If your father learns of your past, *it will be from you and not from me.*"

"Oh, thank you, Olga. I just knew you would keep my secret."

She glanced over the top of her glasses and said, "Chelsea, you worry too much. You have solved your problems with Abel and Matthew. Do not worry about your father, he will not divorce you." Our lunch was served and we continued to talk about our lives.

Linda met with Olga and finalized the wedding plans. The wedding party is to meet in Clark's Summit on the fifth of July for a rehearsal and dinner in the evening. Linda said, "Everything is on GO!"

The date finally came and we all gathered at Clarks Summit. The walk-through went smoothly as Linda directed the processions. At eleven o'clock we all drove to the church. Dad went with Morgan, his best man. Olga, the bridesmaids, and I went in separate cars. Dad didn't want to see Olga in her wedding dress until she walked down the aisle. The crowd gathered and everyone took their places. Olga was to be escorted down the aisle by a doctor friend of hers from their clinic. He was to give her away for her family who are still in Russia.

The music began and the bridesmaids slowly walked down the aisle, one at a time. Chelsea Lyn looked so happy. After the bridesmaids were in place, the organist began the wedding march, "Here comes the bride … ," and Olga marched down the aisle. She wore a light yellow wedding dress with lace along the sleeves and an 18th-century collar. Dad was waiting at the altar in his military dress uniform. My, I thought, aren't my parents beautiful? The ceremony was wonderful!

Olga and Dad selected readings from Corinthians: "Love is patient, love is kind … Love never fails … And now these three remain … faith, hope and love … But the greatest of these is love!"

I thought back to when I'd first heard those verses. Kersi taught them to me, and I could recite them by heart. I silently repeated them as the pastor read from the Bible. Soon the wedding was over and the lines of people greeted Olga and Dad at the church entrance. That evening the guests enjoyed a grand reception and dancing until early in the morning. What a wonderful event in my life!

8

My life took on new meaning in everything I did. I have the most wonderful husband and family of any woman on earth. I shall guard my family with my life. Nothing else will interfere with our happiness. My relationships with Abel and Matthew are clear to me now. They are the fathers of my two children and nothing more. Morgan has accepted part of my past. The only secret I shall keep from him is that Caesar is Matthew's son. If I can ever gather the courage *to tell Morgan about Caesar and have a talk with my dad, my life will be an open book!*

Back at work, my professional life continues to go straight up. I have become a member of several civic boards and an advisor to the State Business Association. The early morning hours are still my quiet time. I enjoy the wonderful view from Mr. Thorndike's office. I look over the entire world when I lean back and let my mind wander. How wonderful it is to be alive! The lake still sends up scents from the boat traffic and I can still imagine the wind and spray in my face as I stand with the windows open, fifteen stories high. I feel like I am a real part of this wonderful world now.

310

"Love is patient, love is kind ... Love never fails ... And now these three remain ... faith, hope and love ... But the greatest of these is love!"

Linda received praises from everyone for her work on Olga's and Dad's wedding. She always comes in with coffee and we chat at the beginning of the day. She is more like a sister than an employee. As she reviews my schedule with me, she has her own style of comments to add. On this day she had scheduled a group of people to see me. The party didn't want to reveal the purpose of their meeting. She laughed and said, "Boss lady, maybe this group is coming to give you an award or something and they don't want anyone to know about it."

"Oh, I don't think so, Linda. This city is full of more deserving people than me."

"Anyway," she said, "I booked them for ten this morning. They said an hour was all they needed." I wondered why this group of people was coming to see me.

Promptly at 9:55 A.M., Linda announced them. The director of the local political party introduced himself and the others. Each person was a representative of a political organization in the state. I asked, "Well, ladies and gentlemen, what can I do for you?"

The apparent leader said, "Ms. Carodine, we represent the core organization of the major political party in this state. We have searched for the past year for someone who could represent the voter and do the job we all believe needs to be done in government. Unfortunately, we have not found anyone with the qualifications we require." He continued, "That is, until now." I looked at him in amazement.

"Sir, may I ask what you mean?"

"We mean, Ms. Carodine, *we are asking you to run for governor of this state as our party's candidate.*" I almost fell from my chair.

"I'm sorry, ladies and gentlemen. I have never considered entering politics. Your offer has caught me by surprise."

The speaker responded, "Ms. Carodine, we did not come here to proposition you with this offer and expect you to accept on this short notice. What we are asking is that you please consider our offer and get back with us, say in about ten days or two weeks, with your decision."

"Well, you certainly did take me by surprise. I take this as a great honor. However, I must think about your offer. The world of politics would be entirely new to me. Thank you, ladies and gentlemen. I shall talk with you again soon."

They thanked me for my time and left the office. As soon as they had gone, Linda came running in and wanted to know what they wanted.

When I told her what they had said I thought she would jump out the window, she was so excited. I calmed her and told her it was something I had to think about and talk about with a number of people. I said, "Linda, anyone who runs for political office has to have a fairly clean slate to be elected. I need to think about mine." She danced out of the office, singing.

When Morgan picked me up at the end of the day I could hardly contain myself.

"Hey, sweetheart, what are you so excited about?"

I squeezed him and said, "Morgan, a group of political party representatives visited me today and asked me to run for governor ... what do you think of that?"

He looked at me with a big grin and said, "Do you need a campaign manager? When do I begin?"

I said, "Morgan, this is serious. I was asked to consider running for governor."

"You're not joking, are you?"

"Of course not. It's true. I was asked to run for the governor of this state in the next election."

He frowned. "Well, if this is a serious offer, we have to do some talking."

"Yes, I know. Morgan, do you think anyone would dig up my past and use it against me if I choose to run for governor?"

He stared at me and said, "Of course, they would. What do you think politics is all about? The more dirt one party can dig up and pin to the other candidate, the better the public likes it. No, darling, nothing in your life would be spared."

"I think you're right, Morgan. I can't have my personal life paraded before the public. *But ... I'm going to give the offer serious consideration before I turn them down!*"

"But until you decide, my lady, are you going to spend more time with your family?"

"Darling, my family is first in my life now. And yes, my family will have me around for a *long, long time ... regardless of my decision!*"